A
BREATH
AFTER
DROWNING

A BREATH AFTER DROWNING

ALICE BLANCHARD

TITAN BOOKS

A Breath After Drowning
Print edition ISBN: 9781785656408
Electronic edition ISBN: 9781785656415

Published by Titan Books
A division of Titan Publishing Group Ltd
144 Southwark Street, London SE1 0UP

First edition: April 2018
2 4 6 8 10 9 7 5 3 1

A CIP catalogue record for this title is available from the British Library.

Printed and bound in the United States.

What did you think of this book?

We love to hear from our readers. Please email us at:
readerfeedback@titanemail.com, or write to us at the above address.

To receive advance information, news, competitions, and exclusive offers online, please sign up for the Titan newsletter on our website:

TITAN BOOKS.COM

For Doug, forever

PART I

1

KATE WOLFE'S 3 PM appointment stood in the doorway wearing a jaw-dropping miniskirt, a light blue tee, plaid knee socks, and chunky platform heels. Fifteen-year-old Nikki McCormack suffered from bipolar disorder. She believed that she was the center of the universe. She lived in a world of her own creation.

"Hello, Nikki," Kate said warmly. "Come on in."

The teenager took three small steps into the spacious office and looked around as if she didn't recognize the place. It was all part of the ritual. Nikki scrutinized the charcoal carpet, the blue-gray walls with their framed degrees, Kate's swivel chair, and her large oak desk, as if something might've changed in her absence. She'd been coming to therapy for seven months now, and the only thing that ever changed was the mood outside the windows—cloudy, sunny, whatever—but Nikki wanted the place to always be the same. Another quirk of her illness.

"Hmm," the girl said, index finger poised between glossy lips.

"*Hmm* good? Or *hmm* bad?"

"Just *hmm*."

Okay, it was going to be one of those days.

The weather forecasters had been predicting snow. They argued over inches. It was deep into winter, February in Boston, but Nikki wasn't dressed for the cold. She was dressed to impress. She wore a flimsy vinyl jacket over her skimpy outfit and a red silk scarf—no gloves, no layers, no leggings. Her pale, slender body was covered in gooseflesh, and her nipples showed through the flimsy tee, but Kate knew better than to suggest more seasonal attire. Nikki might storm out of the office as she had before, and that would be counterproductive to her therapy, so Kate ignored her maternal instinct and kept a steady focus on Nikki's eyes—the azure depth of her sly intelligence. "Have a seat."

Nikki hesitated on the threshold, and Kate could read her emotions morphing across her face like the Times Square news ticker—the girl doubted she was welcome anywhere. She didn't feel loved. She believed people were laughing at her. It saddened Kate to discover that such a smart, healthy, promising young person could have such low self-esteem. It was more than troubling.

"I've been expecting you," Kate said, coaxing her in like a kitten. "Have a seat, Nikki."

The girl entered the office with gawky teenage dignity, sat in the camel-colored leather chair and crossed her waifish legs. Her chunky shoes with their thick wedge heels looked ridiculous on her and were probably dangerous in the snow. Nikki wore enamel rings on every finger and a slender gold chain around her neck. She was heavily made up, with careful strokes of peach lipstick on her skeptical mouth and too much gummy mascara on her eyes. She came across as beguilingly bumbling, and yet there was something disturbingly passive-aggressive about her.

"So," Kate began. "How are you?"

The girl's attention wandered everywhere. She studied the framed art prints on the walls, the overstuffed inbox on Kate's desk, and finally Kate herself. "Yeah, okay. So I've been wondering… how do you deal with your patients and stuff?"

"My patients?" Kate repeated.

"I mean, because we're so messed up? How do you cope? Day after day? How do you sit there and listen to us whine and complain and kvetch—how do you cope?"

Kate smiled. She'd only recently begun her fledgling practice. Her framed degrees barely covered two feet of wall space behind her desk. She had a bachelor's degree in psychiatry and neuroscience from Boston University, and a medical doctorate from Harvard. The birch bookcase held dozens of scientific journals containing articles co-authored by her. On her desktop was the psychiatrist's bible, the DSM-V, the one resource she was constantly reaching for. "How do I cope with what exactly?"

"With the stress? From having to deal with us crazies?"

"Well, first of all, I don't consider my patients 'crazies.' We all deal with stress in different ways. For instance, I like to go running and hiking and rock climbing and work it off that way."

"Seriously?" The girl rolled her eyes. "Because I can't picture you running the Boston Marathon or anything, Doc."

"Did I say marathon? Oh no. Not me." Kate laughed.

11

"But exercise helps with the stress." She was understating it just a bit. She *loved* to go running and hiking and climbing. These activities were her biggest release, next to sleeping with her boyfriend.

"So how did you become a shrink?" Nikki asked, switching subjects.

"It was a long process. I got my BA and did my doctorate, and then there was the internship, the residency and the fellowship. Finally, just this past year, I've started seeing private patients, like you."

"Oh." Nikki smirked. "So I'm a guinea pig?"

"I wouldn't say that."

"No? What would you say?"

Kate smiled, enjoying the way Nikki confronted the world—part adult skepticism, part naïve bravado. "Well, I consider you to be a bright, intuitive, sensitive human being, who just so happens to have bipolar disorder, which you need help managing."

Nikki jiggled her foot impatiently. "How old are you?"

Okay, that was out of left field. "I'll be thirty-two soon."

"How soon?"

Kate's relaxed smile contained a thorn of frustration in it, but she did her best to draw on the fathomless well of patience she'd accrued during her residency at McLean Hospital in Belmont, where she'd dealt with the craziest of crazies. Real hard cases. Human tragedy on an epic scale. Nikki would've been impressed. "Any day now," she answered vaguely.

"Wow. Thirty-two. And you aren't married yet?"

"No."

"Why not?"

"My boyfriend asks me that all the time."

"He does?" Nikki laughed. "James is right. You should marry him."

James. Kate had mentioned him a few times, but she didn't like hearing his name echoed back to her like this, as if Kate and James were characters from some TV sitcom.

"You have a great laugh," she said, redirecting the conversation. "And a terrific smile."

Nikki smirked. "You're one of the privileged few, Doc. I don't smile very often."

"I know. Why not?"

She shrugged. "Maybe because life sucks?"

"Sometimes it does suck. Sometimes it doesn't."

"Wow. You're honest. Most adults won't say 'suck.'"

"Well, I want you to trust me, so I'm honest."

"I do. Pretty much."

"Good."

"So you're going on vacation and leaving me all by my lonesome?" Nikki made a frowny-face. "Please don't go, Doc. Not now. I know. Selfish me."

"Well," Kate said hesitantly, and then smiled. "Everybody deserves a vacation now and then, don't you think?"

"Just kidding. LOL. Sarc."

But they both knew she wasn't.

"Is James going with you? On your vacation?"

This session was veering dangerously off-course, and the

girl's questions were becoming a distraction from her therapy. Kate tried to right the ship, but she wasn't on her game today. They still had a lot of packing to do. "Why all the questions?" she asked. "What is it about me going on vacation that concerns you?"

Nikki scratched her chin with a painted nail and stared at something beyond Kate's shoulder. "What are those? Nuts?" She pointed at the bookcase. "Are you trying to tell me something, Doc? Like maybe I'm nuts?"

Kate was startled to see a jar of Planters Roasted Peanuts on top of her bookcase. Ira must have left them there. Dr. Ira Lippencott was Kate's mentor, a brilliant Harvard-educated psychiatrist with an offbeat sense of humor and a maverick approach to psychotherapy. "No," she said calmly. "That's a coincidence."

"Are you sure? Because, you know, theoretically, I am nuts."

Kate couldn't help smiling. "I assure you it's completely unintentional."

"Ah ha! Nothing's unintentional." Nikki pointed an accusing finger at her and grinned. "You told me that once, remember?"

"Ah ha." Kate tried to appear wise but couldn't help wondering if Ira had left those peanuts in her office on purpose, as a sort of test. And Kate had failed to even notice them. How long had they been sitting there, gathering dust? He was probably wondering what the hell was wrong with his favorite former resident that she didn't even notice the "nuts" on her bookshelf.

"What's that?" Nikki asked, pointing at Kate's desk. "Is that new?"

"Oh. It's a paperweight. A trilobite."

"Wow. And a big one." Nikki McCormack had an interest in paleontology. She knew perfectly well what a trilobite was. "*Coltraenia oufatensis.* Of the order *Phacopida.*" She shifted around in her seat and yanked her creeping miniskirt back down. "Hey, I just thought of something. What if I end up like that?"

"Like what?"

"Like a trilobite? Maybe a thousand years from now? Or maybe just my skull, holding down paperwork so it doesn't blow away? I could end up like that, right?"

"I doubt that very much."

"Why do you doubt it? Why couldn't I end up a fossil on somebody's desk?"

"Is that what you're worried about? Being studied like a fossil?"

Nikki's lips drew together in a long flat line.

Kate picked up the trilobite. "Is that what you think, Nikki? That I'm studying you? That you mean nothing more to me than this trilobite?"

Nikki's troubled eyes glazed over, and she looked away.

"Because nothing could be further from the truth. You're very real to me, and very much alive, and it's my biggest hope that someday soon, you'll learn to love yourself as much as others love you."

Tears squeezed out of Nikki's beautiful eyes and spilled down her cheeks. Eight months ago, Kate had diagnosed her during her crucial four-week stay at Tillmann-Stafford Hospital's Child Psychiatric Unit, and she'd come to the conclusion that the girl suffered from bipolar disease and depression, which made it impossible to predict if she would be alive a few decades from now. Would she live to see thirty-two? Kate certainly hoped so, but the statistics were sobering. Her role was to improve those odds.

"Nikki," she said softly. "We've discussed this before, but I'd like to brush on it again. Since I'll be on vacation next week, Dr. Lippencott would be happy to see you for therapy while I'm gone. Can we set up an appointment?"

"No."

"Are you sure?"

"Trust," the girl said in a shaky voice.

"Trust?"

"I don't *trust* people. I'm supposed to trust them, right? Well, I don't." She grabbed a tissue from the floral-patterned box placed strategically on the blond-wood table next to her chair and blew her nose.

"That's okay. It takes time to trust people. But you can trust Dr. Lippencott. Should I set up an appointment for next Tuesday? Same time?"

Doubt misted her face. "Just because you *say* I should trust him doesn't mean I can or I will."

"No. But what I mean is… I trust him. And you trust me."

"One plus one doesn't always equal two."

"That's true, but—"

"Wait. I almost forgot." The girl lifted her scruffy backpack off the floor, settled it on her lap and rummaged through it. "I got you a few things," she said excitedly.

A red flag went up. "I can't accept gifts from my patients, Nikki. We already discussed this…"

"They aren't gifts *per se*." She took out a handful of weathered items and lined them up on the edge of Kate's desk: a barnacled pair of 1950s eyeglasses; a translucent tortoiseshell comb; and a corroded compass. "You can find the most amazing things at the beach. People throw all this stuff away, and it ends up on some garbage barge in the middle of the ocean, and they dump it overboard, and then it washes ashore. Some of it's very old," she said breathlessly. "And look, I saved the best for last." She reached into a hidden compartment of her backpack and took out a circular piece of metal, which she placed in Kate's hand. "It's made out of lead. Guess what it is, Dr. Wolfe. Go on. Guess."

Kate studied the object in her palm. "A button without the button holes?"

"It's a skirt weight from the twenties. Insane, right? Women used to sew them into the hems of their dresses to keep the wind from blowing them up. Pretty cool, huh?"

Kate smiled. "Very interesting."

"They were so modest back then," Nikki said wistfully.

Kate's fingers curled around the skirt weight. "It was a different time."

"They were all *veddy prop-ah* ladies and gentlemen," Nikki said in a mock-British accent, tugging on the hem of her miniskirt.

Kate tried to hand the gifts back to her, but Nikki shook her head. "You keep them. I'll take them back at our next session. That way you'll have to come back." Her smile was forced. "Where are you guys going for your vacation?"

Kate decided not to press the issue. "Don't worry about it. I'll be back in two weeks."

"Two weeks," Nikki whispered, touching her flushed cheeks. "What if I… need something? I mean, what if something comes up?"

"You can always call Dr. Lippencott, or else you can call me," Kate said. "You have all my numbers, right? Call me any time, Nikki. I mean it. Day or night." She plucked a business card out of the wooden cardholder on her desk and wrote down her personal contact information again. "Everything's going to be okay. That's what I want you to understand."

"Thanks." Nikki took the business card and held it in her lap.

"Promise me you'll call if you need anything. I'm serious. Okay?"

"Okay," she said softly.

Kate gave her an encouraging smile. "You know, my sister and I used to play this game when we were little, where I'd measure her height on the kitchen wall. Always in the same spot, once a week, to see if she'd grown any taller. Savannah was on the short side, and she was an impatient little girl… she couldn't wait to get bigger. And so, just to please her, I'd cheat a little by adding a sliver of height to the chart. She'd get so excited, thinking she'd grown taller during the week. That was our little game." Kate leaned forward. "But I can't do that here, Nikki. I can't add a sliver of height to your chart. I can't fudge the truth. I'm going to be absolutely honest. No cheating. Okay? We've got a long way to go, but I promise, we'll get there together. You aren't alone."

Nikki nodded rigidly. "And you'll be back in two weeks?"

Kate smiled. "Two short weeks."

2

KATE'S BOYFRIEND COULDN'T WAIT for his steaming hot pizza to cool down before he took a bite. "Ow. Ow." Dr. James Hill waved his hand in front of his mouth and gulped down some beer.

James was a psychiatrist in the Adult Locked Unit at the same hospital where Kate worked. His patients were often the toughest to deal with: psychotics and schizophrenics who'd fallen through the cracks; often homeless, often hopeless. James dealt with the pressure by cracking a cynical smile at the broken mental health system that didn't help these people. He shared his stories with Kate and laughed at some of his patients' misadventures. Dark humor was a coping mechanism, and even psychiatrists needed to cope.

"Okay, you can mock me now," he said, wiping his mouth on a paper napkin.

"Me? I never mock you."

"Ha. You mock me every day. As a matter of fact, I'd really miss it if you didn't mock me."

"Okay. Give me a second."

He laughed. "You'll think of something."

"Anyway." She smiled happily. "Thanks for bringing me to my favorite place in the whole world and not insisting we go somewhere fancy." She said the word *fancy* as if it had air quotes around it.

"Fancy schmancy. Who needs fancy? Happy birthday, babe. How's your pizza?"

"I love this fucking pizza."

"It *is* the best pizza on the planet." He gleefully sucked a string of mozzarella into his mouth and wiped the grease off his chin. They were huddled together in their favorite Back Bay dive. It was Tuesday night, and they practically had Duke's all to themselves.

"Anyway, guess what my 3 PM wore today?" She kept her voice low, even though no one else was sitting close enough to overhear their conversation. They'd snagged a secluded booth, their favorite spot, and always broke doctor–patient confidentiality *sotto voce.* Kate and James shared everything with each other, but never outside their private bubble. "She was dressed in the skimpiest outfit. Platform shoes, a miniskirt, and a vinyl jacket. In this weather. No coat, no boots, no gloves. And I had to ask—where's the mother in all this? I'm surprised she didn't get hypothermia."

"Meh. The parents are coping with their own bullshit."

"It breaks my heart all over the place. I should've gone to law school."

He looked her in the eye. "We both know why you got into this field, Kate."

"Yeah, and that's another thing. I mentioned her again today. Savannah."

"So?"

"Nikki's very inquisitive. What if she starts to ask questions?"

He shrugged. "Then you'll deal with it."

Kate shook her head. "It was dumb of me. She's finally beginning to trust me. I told her I'd always be honest with her. But I'm not sure I could handle it if she started asking questions about my sister."

"You'll handle it just fine. Your training will kick in."

"Maybe. Anyway. She wanted to give me some things, and I had to remind her—no gifts."

"What kind of gifts?" he asked.

"Some things she found at the beach. A skirt weight from the twenties. Ever heard of them?"

"Skirt weights? No, but this is intriguing. Why did she give my girlfriend a skirt weight? Does she know something I don't know?"

"Ha. My boyfriend is hilarious. No, apparently flappers used to sew them into their skirts to keep the wind from blowing them up and revealing their legs." She shook her head. "It's so sad. Here's this whip-smart, funny, brave, naïve teenager talking about the olden days, when the women were much more modest. She kept tugging on her miniskirt. It's supposed to be empowering." She shook her head. "I don't think so."

"That's what peer pressure and a lack of parental control will do."

"I'm telling you. It breaks my heart."

He paused with the pizza poised an inch from his mouth and said, "You can't get emotional about your clients, Kate.

It doesn't help them. Not one bit."

"But what if I fail them? What exactly does it prove, after all my years of training, if I can't help them?"

"Some of them you'll fix. Some you won't." James shrugged. "Nobody ever promised you a rose garden."

She cocked an eyebrow. "More snark on my birthday?"

"You're welcome."

Kate leaned back. "You never have a moment of self-doubt, do you?"

"No, but isn't that what you like about me? My blind self-confidence?"

"Yeah, sort of," she admitted with a laugh.

"See?"

"I'm just saying…"

"Hey, guess what? I got you something."

"Sorry, but I can't accept gifts from my patients," she quipped.

"Close your eyes." He dropped his pizza and wiped his hands on a rumpled napkin and waited until she'd obeyed him. Then he took something out of his coat pocket. "Okay. Open." He was holding a ring-sized jewelry box in his hand.

"James, no." She cringed. "Seriously?"

"Relax. It's not what you think."

She covered her face with embarrassment. Today was her thirty-second birthday, and she'd told him repeatedly— no parties, no people, no presents. Just you, me, and Duke's bacon-and-cheese pizza.

"Happy birthday," he said, handing her the little box.

It had a perfect weight to it. Her face softened with delight and dread as she opened it and gazed at the slender silver ring with the dazzling amethyst centerpiece. "Wow," she whispered.

"It's just a ring," James said. "Nothing special."

"It's gorgeous."

"Matches your eyes."

"Ooh. Not exactly."

Kate's eyes were lavender. She blushed easily. She was blushing now. She took the ring out of its velvet box and slipped it on her finger. "Oh, James. I don't know what to say."

"It's just a ring, for God's sake," he said tenderly. "Because I kept passing it in the jewelry store on my way to work, and it reminded me of you every damn day. Same color eyes. Although, yeah, now that you mention it, spoilsport, you're right, it's not the exact color, but close enough. Cut me some slack, slugger."

"It's beautiful."

"Happy birthday." He leaned in for a kiss.

She kissed him gratefully, tenderly, and then paraded her hand. "So, how do you like my non-engagement ring?"

"Yeah," he said with a sarcastic smile. "Your *I'm-not-ever-getting-married* ring."

"My *he's-just-my-boyfriend* ring."

"Christ. You're such a commitment-phobe."

"You can thank my miserable childhood for that."

"Relax. It's an ordinary gift-type ring. Okay? Because I love you."

"I love you, too." She rarely wore rings or necklaces, a fact that she must've mentioned to him a thousand times before. Her sensitive skin couldn't tolerate jewelry. Not even exquisite, expensive jewelry. But James, being a psychiatrist, had assumed it was the thought of marriage, rather than the ring itself, that was causing her to break out in hives. And this was probably a test, or else a "blind trial" if you will, to find out how long she could tolerate the ring before she took it off and put it away in its box. Or maybe he wasn't so much testing her (that would be manipulative) as he was seeking answers. Kate didn't want to get married, and yet she was crazy in love with the guy. Which brought her to the same sore spot in her brain, the gray area she was constantly prodding and poking. *What the hell is wrong with you? Why not marry him? He's fantastic. James is everything you ever wanted. What is your freaking problem?* She figured they were headed in that direction, just waiting for her to make up her mind—put another way, she was waiting to fall in love with the idea of marriage. She'd already fallen in love with James.

In truth, Kate had trust issues. She had abandonment issues. She and her sister, Savannah, had lost their mother early on, and their father had been emotionally remote. Dr. Bram Wolfe, an old-school family physician, possessed the uncanny ability to disappear on you, even when he was sitting right in front of you—emotionally, psychologically, mentally. His eyes would glaze over and his mouth would stitch shut, and he'd zoom a million miles away in seconds. He would stay gone for a very long time—detached, unreachable. It never ceased to amaze Kate, this remarkable disappearing act of his. She called him "the bullet train of fathers," because he could take off like a shot.

And the hits just kept on coming. Six years after her mother passed away, Kate's little sister went missing. It ended badly, and her father vanished for good after that, psychologically speaking. By the time she turned seventeen, Kate's entire family had disappeared on her. Mother—dead. Sister—dead. Father—emotionally unavailable. This trifecta of traumas was at the root of all her deep-seated anxieties and self-doubts, as well as a source of her strength. It was the main reason she'd gone into psychiatry, as opposed to law or medicine.

"Glad you like the ring," James said with grave seriousness now.

"I love it."

Ten minutes later, she was still wearing the ring. They paid the bill at the register and pushed the heavy front door open, laughing at the handwritten sign that said PUSH HARD. Kate made the same joke every time—"Harder, James, harder." And he responded the same way every time—"I'm pushing, I'm pushing."

"God, we are so easily amused," she sighed as they linked arms and tumbled out into the crisp cold night air. Winter in Boston. Dark streets and frosty breath. Soon it would be spring, but not soon enough. They walked the two and a half blocks to James's silver Lexus and got in. She sat shivering inside the new-smelling interior and eyed him suspiciously.

"What?" He activated the seat warmers and started the engine.

"I love my ring. I love Duke's pizza. And I love you."

"In that order?"

"Ha. My boyfriend is…"

"Hilarious, I know." He reached for her hand, turned it over, and kissed the old scars on her wrist. Tenderly. Softly. "I love you, Kate. I'm glad you like the ring."

She could feel the weight of their three-year relationship and luxuriated in the warmth and familiarity of it as they headed towards Harvard Square.

It began to snow, fat white flakes flurrying past their windshield. The sparkling city contained all the magic of a fairytale, and Kate decided to tuck her worries away. Nikki McCormack would be okay. She shouldn't feel guilty about taking a vacation—her first in years. *You're entitled to a life.*

She glanced at the ring on her finger. Perhaps she should marry James. What was her problem? He was handsome and smart and one of the funniest people she'd ever known—he made her laugh from the gut, those genuine belly laughs—and she wanted to spend the rest of her life with him. She just couldn't bring herself to take the next step because… her sister, her mother. The lump of tragedies that sat like a disfiguring scar on her soul.

The Lexus straddled the off-ramp lane, and they took the exit to Harvard Square, which was snowy and all lit up. They drove down Massachusetts Avenue, past the crowded university campus with its centuries-old dormitories, and headed toward Arlington, Cambridge's drab sister city. Before reaching the town line, they took a left onto a quiet residential street—still Cambridge, which mattered to James, that ever-important zip code—and found a parking spot in their brand-new neighborhood.

James propped their freshly minted parking permit on the dashboard, and they got out and inhaled the rejuvenating winter air. Kate's worries receded. Soon they'd be rock-climbing in the Southwest, hiking through the red-clay canyons of Sedona, toasting spectacular sunsets, and tumbling into hotel beds.

But tonight it was snowing, and they were in chilly, intellectual Cambridge, and the moon was just a smudge behind the clouds. Snowflakes dusted their eyelashes. James took her hand and they navigated the icy cobblestones together, half-strolling, half-stumbling past the subdivided Victorians and Gothics, where Harvard grads and post-docs studied in lonely obscurity. The streets were eerily silent except for the whisper of falling snow and the occasional whoosh of tires spinning through slush.

At the end of the block, they turned the corner onto a centuries-old thoroughfare. Around each old-fashioned streetlamp was a halo of falling snow. Their renovated brick condominium was built in 1915, with granite steps and hovering gargoyles on the roof. Several months ago, they'd closed escrow on an incredible two-bedroom in this desirable location and had spent the past five or six weekends painting the walls designer shades of white and installing new light fixtures. A few days ago, they'd rearranged everything just the way they liked it, and now they were ready to enjoy the rest of their lives together. It was a bit overwhelming.

The ring. The condo. The two-week vacation. Might as well be married.

James opened the front door for her, and they stepped into the lobby, where the wood was dark-stained, the lights were elegantly dimmed, and the strange scent of cured animal skins and cracked leather pervaded the warm, stuffy air.

"Is it my imagination," James said, "or are we the only tenants in the building?"

"I know, right?" she agreed. "Where is everybody?"

"How come we never see anyone? Where's the welcome party?"

She glanced at the vaulted ceiling. "I guess we'll meet them eventually."

"*I guesssssss,*" he hissed in her ear, before launching into *The Addams Family* theme song. He grabbed her around the middle, and she caught a whiff of something smoky and elusive about him. He was an athletic man in his mid-thirties, with thick dark hair and warm brown eyes. In the summer, his hair was more golden than brown. He was a typical American male—virile, passionately intense about sports and video games, sometimes loud and opinionated, sometimes vague and introspective, always respectful and well-mannered. When she was with him, she felt indestructible. She supposed it was dangerous to feel that way.

She pressed the call button for the elevator. "Are you ready?" She showed him her ring. "Ready for couple-dom?"

"Readier than you, apparently." He crossed his heart like a Boy Scout. "I will never use first-person-singular again."

Kate laughed. Her phone rang, and she rummaged through her bag, but by the time she picked up, the caller had hung up. She checked the ID. *Unavailable.*

"Hey," he said with mock suspicion. "Was that your other boyfriend?"

"Yeah, he's so annoying."

"I'm jealous. I'm supposed to be the annoying one."

"You are. Hands down."

The elevator creaked to a shuddering halt. It was one of those old-fashioned brass cages you had to operate yourself, prying the stubborn hinged doors open. They stepped into the slightly swaying cage, closed the jittery doors and pushed the button for the eighth floor. As soon as it began to move, they kissed passionately, groping one another like horny teenagers.

The elevator seemed to take forever to climb to the eighth floor. James grew gradually still as the brass cage swayed on its creaky cables—he had a deep-seated fear of elevators that wasn't a secret to her. He'd gotten stuck between floors once as a child, while visiting his grandmother in New York City. He rang the bell and banged on the doors and hollered for help, while the elevator had slowly filled with smoke from a blown motor in the basement—long story, happy ending.

Now his lips tasted cold and ozone-y from the newly fallen snow. Her ring didn't itch. Miracle of miracles. They were on their way up to their very own condo, just a stone's throw from Harvard Square. She was thirty-two years old. She was deeply in love. She wanted this moment to last forever.

The elevator came to a halt, jerking on its rusty cables.

James winced. "I'll have to get used to that."

"Last stop, everybody out."

They pulled the heavy brass doors open.

"Cheaper than a gym membership," he quipped, flinging an arm around her.

They headed down the stuffy corridor toward their unit, their boots leaving crumbs of slush on the mauve carpet. Discreet indirect lighting hid the flaws in the elegant plaster ceiling. They stopped in front of their varnished door with its scratched brass nameplate that said 8D.

"Home at last," Kate sighed.

The landline began to ring inside their condo as James fumbled with his keys.

"Okay," she said. "Tell me again why we gave your mother our number?"

"Meh. Let the machine pick up." James found it much easier to ignore his rich, leisured mom than Kate did. Vanessa Hill was like fingernails on a blackboard—grating. She often called to boast about the Boston charities she was involved with and all the non-profits she was on the board of, but she rarely asked James about his life, which bothered Kate more than it bothered him. He shrugged it off with the kind of resignation he reserved for airports and insurance forms.

He unlocked the door and they tumbled inside, a curl of light sweeping across the hardwood floor. It was dark except for a blue haze coming from the city lights below. James groped at the wall and found the switch, and the place lit up.

The phone stopped ringing.

"Ah," she breathed.

"Nice," he agreed.

They waited for the inevitable voicemail message, but Vanessa must've hung up. It wasn't like her to be so non-verbose.

They peeled off layers of outerwear—unzipping, untying, unbuttoning.

"Yeesh," James complained. "It's like an oven in here."

Despite the stuffiness, Kate was in love with the condo. It was the first place she'd ever owned, and she felt so lucky to have it. The living room was a grand open space with a marble fireplace and an arched doorway leading into an airy dining room. She adored the master bedroom with its muted color scheme and cozy touches. The kitchen and bathroom were lovely in their period simplicity, especially the deep claw-footed tub, where she planned on soaking for hours after a long day at the hospital. The huge kitchen windows were perfect for an herb garden.

"I'm sweating like a pig." James took off his coat and gloves and scarf and dropped everything on the sofa.

"Pigs don't sweat."

"Seriously. Am I the only one who's melting around here?" He struggled with his pullover, peeling it off with a crackle of static, and then eyed the culprit—a hissing radiator in the corner of the living room. He strode over and wrestled with the stuck knob.

"Careful, you'll…"

"Ouch!"

"…burn yourself."

James sucked on his finger and gave her a contrite look, while steam hissed into the room and the copper pipes clanged in the walls.

"Poor baby." Kate walked over to him. "So overheated and everything." She reached for his belt buckle, looped her finger through it and pulled him close. She rubbed her pelvis against his and kissed him passionately.

He scooped her up in his arms, swung her around, and she laughed from deep in her throat as he carried her into their bedroom, nearly scuffing the walls with her winter boots. "Watch it!" she giggled. He dropped her on the bed and removed her boots one at a time. He pinched off her thick socks and unzipped her jeans.

"God, you're gorgeous." He unbuttoned her blouse and bent to kiss the tiny, nearly invisible scars that peppered her skin. Kate had been a cutter once. Razor blades, paperclips, thumbtacks, scissors. What had begun as an extreme response to her sister's death had devolved into a crippling anxiety disorder. She had left little dimple-like scars on her stomach, thighs, and arms, and wore long sleeves to hide them from the world, mostly so her father wouldn't catch on. Cutting herself felt like payback for his neglect. It also relieved some of the pressure she felt as a high school honors student trying to get into a prestigious college. It had lasted for several years, until she got into therapy and learned how to cope. Her mentor, Ira Lippencott, had saved her life. He'd stopped the self-destructive behavior in its tracks and put her on the path to wellness.

The phone rang again.

"Oh God," she groaned. "We need to set some guidelines for your mother. Like no calling before noon or after eight o'clock."

"Just ignore her," James said, sliding his hands under her blouse, an urgency to his breathing. "I always do."

"Oh please." She stopped him. "The last thing I want to hear is Vanessa's voice in the background while we're making love." She could picture his mother tapping her long polished nails on her marble kitchen island, gazing at the clock, and wondering why they weren't picking up. At least she was a good hour's drive away on the other side of the city.

He collapsed on top of her.

"Answer it, James," she pleaded.

The machine picked up. They both turned their heads to listen.

"Kate?" Ira Lippencott's voice came floating through the doorway. "I've got bad news. Nikki McCormack is dead. Call me as soon as you get this."

3

NIKKI MCCORMACK WAS FOUND hanging from the center beam of her parents' living room. A chair had been kicked out from under her. She'd hanged herself with an old clothesline from the garage, although how she'd gotten it up there, nobody knew. Her parents had discovered the body after attending a charity reception at the Isabella Stewart Gardner Museum. Her stepfather grabbed her around the middle, while her mother called 911. Together they lifted the body onto the floor. Ten minutes later, the paramedics pronounced her dead. Nikki was clad in full Goth regalia. Her skin had swelled around her neck and face, and her eyes were black and shiny as olives.

Dealing with the family—their sorrow, their vulnerability—as well as her own shock and grief all night long and into the following morning had given Kate a raging headache no amount of Tylenol could alleviate. The police were polite but thorough. The interview was mercifully short. The rest of the hospital staff was saddened but too busy to talk about it for very long. Nikki had been admitted into Acute Care eight months ago, and some of them remembered her and spoke well of her, and that was about it. Suicides weren't terribly uncommon, but it had never happened to Kate before.

She moved from meeting to meeting all morning until around 10:30 AM, when Ira Lippencott cornered her in the break room. By then Kate was shaking so badly she couldn't keep the coffee pot steady.

"Sheesh. You look like a ghost," he said. "Where's James?"

"Dealing with his own crisis. Agatha's in full meltdown-mode."

He nodded. The reputation of James's most troubled patient was well known in the hospital. "Come with me." He ushered her into his office and made her sit down, while he poured her a cup of coffee from his Breville espresso machine.

Ira's office was full of modular furniture, decorated in a neutral palette. The plants had long outgrown their pots, and now they jammed their leaves against the glass as if they were clamoring to escape.

Ira had been her senior attending and knew all about the tragedies that had shaped her life. As an undergraduate, she'd undergone psychoanalysis with him as her therapist. It was a prerequisite. "You need to know what it's like to sit in the other chair, before you can sit in my chair," he'd explained. This man knew everything about her.

"Here," he said, handing her an espresso. "Now talk."

Kate's shaky hands threatened to spill her coffee all over her lap, so she took a sip and set it aside. "What's there to talk about," she said flatly. "I failed her."

"You did your very best, Kate. You realize that, don't you?"

"I'm her psychiatrist, and I didn't see it coming. And so… I failed her."

"Now's not the time to feel sorry for yourself."

"Sorry for…?" she repeated.

"Self-pity doesn't suit you." Her mentor didn't suffer fools gladly. "Listen to me, Kate. You aren't alone in this. I wake up every day with a few more gray hairs."

"I know, but…"

"But *nothing*."

That did the trick. All morning long she'd managed to hold it together, but now she was flattened by Nikki's suicide. She plucked a tissue out of the floral-patterned box, pressed it to her eyes, and let herself cry.

"I know, I know," Ira said soothingly. "Look, it happens. We've all had patients commit suicide. It's devastating. But believe it or not, you'll learn to live with it."

She nodded. She pulled herself together.

"So. Let's review what you could've done differently," he said. "Tell me, how was Nikki's therapy going?"

"We were making good progress. She was responding well to the new meds."

"And what about the family sessions?"

"Her parents were opening up to the possibility they may have contributed to some of Nikki's issues."

"And her addictive behaviors?"

"She'd stopped drinking and taking drugs, as far as I know. She was slowly pulling her life together."

"Excellent. So? What more could you have done? Canceled

your vacation? These things happen, Kate. It comes with the territory."

"Well, I'm canceling my vacation now." Last night, her dreams had crackled with tension—monsters chasing little girls who snapped in half like twigs. "Elizabeth McCormack wants me to come to the funeral."

"Good. It's advisable to stay in close contact with the family, at least through the funeral, certainly until the autopsy results are available."

Autopsy. That cold word brought it home to her.

"I've been wracking my brains trying to figure out how this could've happened."

"Kate. Please." Ira sighed and pinched the bridge of his nose. "You know better than that. None of this was your fault. Sometimes the darkness takes over."

She gave him a skeptical look. They'd known each other for a very long time. "Seriously? Sometimes the darkness takes over? That's supposed to reassure me?"

"I'm not in the business of reassuring anyone."

"Right, we aren't supposed to comfort and reassure our patients, we're supposed to redirect them toward the path of self-recovery... blah blah blah."

"Exactly."

"I was being sarcastic."

"I know you were."

She felt the old reproach like the hum of an oncoming electrical storm. The events that had shaped her life would never go away, but at least she'd managed to set them aside for a period of time... to place them in a box and mentally tape the lid shut, put the box inside a closet and lock the door. But Nikki McCormack's death had just blown the closet door off its hinges.

"Look, you can handle this, Kate. You've suffered more hardships than most people encounter in a lifetime." He folded his hands on the desktop. "But here's the deal. Nikki's death reflects on me as well. It reflects on the entire department. And I know what you're thinking. So I want you to know: what happened last night had absolutely nothing to do with your sister. Do you accept that?"

"Intellectually, yes."

"Well, I need you to accept it here." Ira tapped his chest. "Completely."

Savannah Wolfe, with her wavy golden hair, her delicate sea-green eyes and excitable laugh had been such a happy, trusting twelve-year-old, that any predator in the neighborhood could have taken advantage of her. She was the kind of enterprising kid who rescued ants from the driveway and raised baby birds with broken wings. Even the smarmiest dog food commercials made her cry. She was willing to help anyone—friends, neighbors, strangers—even a grown man with bloodshot eyes. All he had to do was ask. "Hey, little girl... couldja help me out a second?"

Kate felt a painful throbbing behind her eyes. "Look, I understand these shaky old feelings about my sister don't apply, but..."

"Push aside your emotions." Ira crossed his arms. "I need you to handle this like a professional."

"Of course I can handle it," she said defensively.

"The only thing that counts is that you provided standard care for her symptoms. That's all the hospital wants to know. Did you provide standard care?"

There was a lull before the impact struck. "Standard care?"

"Legally, that's all the hospital requires. Did you use the proper quantifiers to make an accurate diagnosis?"

She nodded with dull recognition.

"The hospital doesn't want to hear what you could've done differently, Kate. You have to quit second-guessing yourself. It doesn't help anyone. You're a brilliant psychiatrist, extremely well qualified, with excellent references. You were treating Nikki for bipolar disorder. You were monitoring her medication and redirecting her behavior in talk therapy. The patient appeared to be stabilized and you were documenting her improvement. Nothing else matters. Now," he said, leaning forward, "can you handle it?"

"Yes," Kate responded, not entirely sure. She'd never lost a patient before. It was brand new territory for her. And Ira wasn't acting like himself. She'd never seen this Ira before. This covering-his-ass Ira.

"When you talk to Risk Management, I want you to give them your clinical observations—period. Don't get emotional. Do you need an attorney?"

"An attorney?" Kate repeated, her heart beginning to race. Getting sued for malpractice was every doctor's worst nightmare.

"The hospital is going to have the hospital's best interests at heart. Just in case a tort action should arise. It's only natural. You need to take care of yourself."

Tort action? Lawsuit?

"Here. I'll give you the name of my attorney. I'd highly recommend him." He opened his desk drawer and handed her a business card. "Tell him I referred you."

"Thanks."

"And don't worry. Everything's going to be fine. We've all been through it before. Now if you'll excuse me, I've had a rough night and I've still got a mountain of paperwork to do. Sorry to kvetch. I'm going to file my progress reports and head home. I'd advise you to do the same."

Kate noticed the shift of light in his eyes. "Ira," she said. "Did you leave those peanuts in my office?"

He gave her a quizzical look. "What peanuts?"

"There's a jar of Planters Peanuts on my bookshelf."

"No. Maybe James?"

"I already asked. He didn't do it."

"Well, I wouldn't give it too much significance. Probably someone's playing a little joke. Anyway, let's talk again in the morning, shall we?"

She stood up and clasped his hand. "Thanks, Ira."

"Don't worry. You'll get through it. Just think of this as a rite of passage."

Kate hurried down the corridor, ducked into her office, grabbed her coat, knotted her scarf and put on her winter gloves. She took the elevator down to the first floor, where she crossed the busy hospital lobby and pushed on the automatic glass doors like they were two giant pillows. She went outside and bummed a cigarette from one of the residents. She breathed nicotine deep into her lungs and recalled her sister's final words to her.

"How long do I have to wait?"

"Just a few minutes. I'll be right back," Kate promised.

"Where are you going?"

"Right over there. See those trees? Don't be scared."

"I'm not scared."

"I know, you're my brave little bud."

"I'm not scared of anything, Katie."

She suppressed a hiccupy sob, and the other smokers turned to stare at her. She coughed a few times, masking her anguish, and they politely looked away. She stood there coughing and smoking and watching her breath fogging the winter air.

4

KATE DIDN'T WANT TO go home, not when there was so much work to be done. She took the elevator back up to Admissions to talk to Yvette Rosales about Nikki McCormack's state of mind eight months ago, since Yvette was the nurse who'd admitted her. The Psych Unit staff was always busy. The phones were constantly ringing. A nurse's job was never done.

Kate walked past the orderlies and RNs in their colorful scrubs on her way to the nurses' station, a sort of bureaucratic port in a brain-chemical storm. Tamara Johnson was a beefy middle-aged woman who knew where all the bodies were buried. Head nurse and chief bottle-washer.

"Morning, Tamara. Have you seen Yvette around?"

Tamara wagged her heavy head. "She's due any minute. Probably wanted her Dunkin's and missed her bus again. I swear she takes that bus as an excuse to be late all the time. How're you holding up, Doc?"

"Not great."

"Yeah, I know. I remember when we admitted Nikki. Scrawny little thing. Bold as could be. She took one look around the place and pronounced everybody *else* insane."

Tamara laughed. "Not her. Just 'every other crazy-assed mofo' in the room."

"That's our Nikki," Kate said with a pained smile.

"Would you like coffee? I just made a pot."

"No, thanks. I'll wait over there."

Kate had brought some paperwork with her and found a seat. The admitting room was an ode to mediocrity—corduroy sofas, imitation-leather chairs, watercolor prints on the exposed brick walls. There were glossy brochures on display at every table.

She opened a manila folder and reviewed her notes. At the time of her admission last June, Nikki was becoming uncontrollable at home. She fought constantly with her parents, took drugs, and drank alcohol. Her stepfather was a strict disciplinarian, and the rebellious teenager missed her dad. The divorce had been especially hard on her.

Somebody shouted, "Get your hands off me, you stinky motherfucker!"

Kate glanced up. Several dozen people were waiting to be evaluated, and she knew most of them from a brief stint of training on the adult ward. She suspected from the way they angled their baseball caps at the security camera that two men she hadn't seen before were drug addicts faking symptoms in order to get a shot of Demerol. There were also a couple of mood disorders; an anorexic; a young mother with postpartum depression; an elderly male who kept cleaning his hands with alcohol wipes; and a pre-teen girl she didn't know sitting prim and apart from the others.

Kate honed in on the central conflict—a cadaverous male schizophrenic who'd veered off his meds was yelling at an elderly female depressive, shouting obscenities at her, and waving his skinny arms. The woman sat twisted in her seat like a wet washcloth, her rheumy eyes full of doubt, as the man loomed over her—if a stick could loom.

An orderly with his keys jangling from his belt loop hurried over and tended to the dispute. Clive Block was famous for his negotiating skills. He got things calmed down and separated the two quickly. Nobody messed with Clive. The nurses didn't even bother calling security. Scuffles were commonplace in the Psych Unit. At all hours of the day or night, you could hear doors slamming and voices raised in anger.

Now Kate turned her attention to the pre-teen in the corner. The girl had a pale blond ponytail, sleepy green eyes, and a calm, relaxed demeanor. For an instant, Kate was reminded of Savannah. The similarity was striking. She wore neatly pressed denim jeans and a pink blouse buttoned all the way up to her throat. Her goose-down parka was folded in half and placed carefully beside her. There was a primness about her, a guarded stiffness. Kate guessed she was around twelve, and she appeared to be alone in the waiting room. Where were her parents?

Kate wasn't able to "spot the crazy," as some of her friends indelicately put it, until she focused on the child's jewelry. Draped around her neck were dozens of silver crosses on slender silver chains, and beaded rosaries were wrapped around both wrists. Kate got an impression of a child who'd been isolated from the world—there was a striking sadness about her. A heart-sinking loneliness. Kate's young patients typically would slouch in their chairs, lean against walls, or curl their shoulders forward in a permanent shrug. But this child sat with practiced poise. She seemed to contain a perfect solitude within her small body. She exhibited an elegant self-discipline that was highly unusual for somebody that age. But again—where were the parents? Perhaps her mother had gone to use the restroom?

Kate was just about to go find out when Yvette Rosales came breezing into the unit, apologizing to everyone within earshot. "Sorry! Sorry! My stupid bus was late again."

Tamara planted her hands on her hips. "Your bus was late? Or *you* were late?"

"I waited and waited and waited."

"Yeah, sure. But you had time to get your Dunkin's, I see."

"Are you kidding me? I can't start my day without coffee and a doughnut."

"We have coffee here."

"That crap? No way." Yvette had dark pink lips and a bad frost job. There was always a pencil or an unlit cigarette stuck in her mouth, and she would rush outside for a smoke during her break. "What are you all of a sudden? My mother?"

"That's right," Tamara said sarcastically. "I'm spying on you."

"Feels like I'm being watched. Like the walls are breathing."

"Did you just say the walls are watching you?"

"Can you prove they aren't?"

Tamara burst out laughing. All was forgiven. "Anyway. Doc's over there waiting for you."

"Who?" Yvette spun around. "Oh hi, Dr. Wolfe. My goodness. Nikki McCormack. Bless her poor soul."

"I'm still in shock," Kate admitted, coming over.

"Such a sad day."

"Can we talk for a minute? I have a few questions about her admission."

"Of course. Let me take off my coat, and I'll be right with you."

Kate leaned against the admitting desk, while Yvette stashed her belongings away. "Who's the girl in the corner?" she asked.

Yvette glanced over. "I don't know. Tamara?"

"Hm? Oh. Her mother brought her in." Tamara shrugged. "She was here a minute ago."

"I've been sitting here for ten minutes, and I haven't seen anyone."

"Maybe one of the other staff knows? I'll go find out." Tamara disappeared into the nurses' coffee room.

The elevator dinged just then and the doors whooshed open, and James strode into Psych Admissions, all business. He took Kate aside. "We're going to see that attorney Ira recommended," he said. "I made an appointment for eleven-thirty. Let's go."

"Wait." Kate balked. "There's no need to overreact."

"I'm not overreacting. I just want to make sure nobody messes with you."

"Nobody's going to mess with me," she said, scowling.

"I'm just looking out for you, sweetie. Let's go. I don't want to be late."

5

ON THE RIDE INTO Boston, Kate tried to suppress the panicky, floppy little breaths that threatened to grow into something worse. The snow-laced city blurred past the windshield like a scratchy black-and-white movie. She'd done her very best to present herself professionally to the world this morning—her greasy hair was pulled into a chignon and her makeup had been carefully applied—but her nerves were raw and ugly. She felt frazzled and exhausted.

They took the GPS-prescribed route to the law firm, situated on the top floor of a monolithic high-rise in the heart of downtown Boston. They pulled into the underground garage and let the valet park their car. Kate couldn't stop shivering as they waited for the elevators.

James squeezed her hand. "You okay?"

"Do I have a choice?"

"I'm going to help you through this, every step of the way," he reassured her.

They took the elevator up to the twenty-fourth floor. The law firm's lobby was a fortress of rose marble. The walls were covered with expensive artwork that echoed the corporate logo.

The receptionist wore Dolce & Gabbana. "Good morning. Can I help you?"

"We're here to see Russell Cooper," Kate said.

"One moment please." The receptionist picked up the phone and punched in a number. "Russ? Your eleven-thirty's here." She placed the receiver down. "Go right in. It's the last door on your left."

Russell Cooper was a middle-aged man with studious gray eyes behind a pair of wire-rim glasses. He wore a conservative suit and a blue silk tie. "Call me Russell. Have a seat." He gestured toward the pair of overstuffed leather chairs facing his desk.

Kate took a moment to admire the panoramic view of downtown. She could see the Prudential from here, glimmering in the distance, brilliant sunshine bouncing off its highly reflective surfaces.

"James gave me the broad strokes over the phone," Russell told Kate. "Why don't you tell me what happened in your own words?"

She cleared her throat and smoothed her skirt across her knees. "Nikki was admitted to Child Psych about eight months ago. She was suicidal. She was on drugs. She was acting out. She met the nine criteria for a major depressive episode. She stayed with us for four weeks, before being discharged and scheduled for outpatient treatment. Since that time, I've been seeing her once a week for behavioral therapy. We also meet with her family periodically. We've adjusted her meds several times, and the latest dosage appeared to be working.

We were making good progress when... when it happened."

"All right. I have a few questions." He glanced down at the checklist on his desk. "Did you explain the potential side effects of her meds to Nikki and her parents?"

"Yes."

"Ignore any pleas for help?"

"No. Well, there is one thing..."

He glanced up. "Yes?"

"I was about to go on vacation for two weeks, which seemed to upset her."

"Did she threaten to kill herself if you left?"

"No."

"Did you provide her with an alternative practitioner?"

"Yes. I encouraged her to see Dr. Lippencott while I was away, but she refused. I also gave her my private contact information and told her to call me any time, day or night."

"Good. Did she call you?"

"Not that I know of." It made Kate wonder about the *Unavailable* caller ID, but Nikki's cell phone number always displayed on caller ID, and Kate would've recognized the Newton area code if Nikki's parents had tried to reach her. Besides, she'd received the call ten minutes before Ira had given her the bad news.

"Was there any mention of suicide in her recent therapy sessions?"

"Not for the past two or three months at least. But we were in the middle of therapy, so it's reasonable to assume that she wasn't entirely out of the woods."

"Was she stable?"

"Relatively stable, in my judgment."

"If that's true, then basically that's all I need to know."

Kate could detect deep lines of cynicism on the man's face. As far as she understood it, Russell Cooper had been Ira's friend since their undergraduate days at Yale, and he'd successfully handled two of Ira's lawsuits.

"We'll argue you met the standard of care," Russell said, "if it comes to that."

"I doubt her family would sue me," Kate muttered.

"You never know. Once the dust settles, after the funeral— that's the danger zone. The family can commence a wrongful-death action against you and the hospital any time they feel like it, right up until the statute runs out. So the question is: did you depart from the accepted 'standard of care' by failing to evaluate Nikki's mental state?"

She shook her head, while James cleared his throat and said, "Kate's one of the best child psychiatrists they have. She won an APF award, which is a big deal in our line of work. She's compassionate and caring and does everything by the book."

"I'm sure she does." Russell smiled and slid his glasses back up the bridge of his nose. "Ira speaks very highly of you, Dr. Wolfe. But the hospital will want to make sure it hasn't breached the standard of care by failing to keep the patient safe from harm. They'll want to make sure she was properly diagnosed, that an adequate history was taken, and that her medication was appropriate."

James leaned forward. "Kate would do *anything* for her patients."

"James," she said reproachfully, blushing.

Russell Cooper smiled. "I'm sure that's true. And the courts have found that a medical provider can't be held liable for mere errors in judgment. But we need to cover all the bases. Unfortunately, malpractice suits are becoming more commonplace, especially when a patient commits suicide."

James glanced at her with concern in his eyes.

"What about the funeral?" Kate asked.

"As far as attending the funeral, that's just fine," he said. "As a matter of fact, I'd encourage as many staffers as possible to attend. It's an excellent way to demonstrate the hospital's concern. However, if you're going to help out with funeral arrangements, Kate, I'd advise you to keep the meetings short. You can be open to people's grief, but if they ask about Nikki's treatment, you need to remind them it's confidential."

"Of course."

"The family may not even think about suing you, but there are plenty of attorneys out there who are on a mission to hold psychiatrists accountable. So by all means, set up a meeting with the family to discuss eulogies, donations, cards, whatever you like. Honor their requests, but don't volunteer. Let them call the shots. Basically, you want to be supportive without opening yourself up to a lawsuit," he said. "Any questions?"

Kate frowned. "What happens next?"

"First, the hospital will carry out an internal investigation, sometimes called a psychological autopsy. It will be thorough, but quick. They don't want to open a can of worms for discovery by the plaintiff's attorney. However, Risk Management is going to have the hospital's best interests at heart, Kate. Not yours. So my advice to you would be to cooperate fully, but be cautious. Choose your words carefully. I'd like to be there for the interview. Just a precaution."

"When will this happen?" James asked.

The attorney shrugged. "Usually right away."

Kate brushed away a distracting strand of hair and said, "I've been trying to figure out how I might've handled things differently…"

"Please don't do that." Russell shook his head. "Keep those thoughts to yourself. I have one thing I tell every doctor who comes through my door: the family is saddled with the burden of guilt. Nobody needs a psychiatrist who's saddled with it too." He checked his watch and tucked in his chin. "Any other questions?"

"I don't think so." Kate glanced over at James, who shook his head.

"Good." His smile was more of a wince. "Let me know when Risk Management gets in touch, and we'll set up a meeting."

They all stood up at once.

"Appreciate your help." James gave him a hearty handshake.

"Nice to meet you both," Russell said warmly, shaking Kate's hand.

She smiled gratefully at him. "I feel much better now."

"No worries. I got your back."

6

THE ELEVATOR RIDE DOWN to the garage seemed to take forever. They waited an eternity for the valet to get their car.

"Where do you want to eat?" James asked.

"There's stuff in the fridge," Kate said, putting on her gloves.

"Okay, listen. After lunch, I'd like to do some role-playing for the Risk Management interview."

"Seriously? Role-playing?"

"You can't just wing it. Remember what Russell said. You have to choose your words carefully."

She shrugged indifferently. "I'd rather go back to work."

"There's no more work today. You're exhausted. I'm exhausted. We were supposed to be in Sedona right now, remember? We're going home."

"I'm just saying… it would be nice to keep busy," Kate objected weakly.

"Nobody's putting any pressure on you to go back to work but you."

"Okay, but don't expect me to be happy about it."

"I get that. But I'm in charge today. For your own good."

The car's heater blew hot air around their ankles as they

headed back into Cambridge. It was snowing again. The windshield wipers swept away fat white flakes that landed with stunning clarity on the glass. They drove past the frozen river, while flurries blurred the road ahead. She shivered, cold as marble beneath her winter coat.

All of a sudden, a dark blue sedan in the passing lane veered in front of them and decelerated rapidly. James hit the brakes in order to avoid a collision, and the Lexus skidded across the road, sliding toward the guardrail before coming to an abrupt halt in the emergency lane. "Fuck!" he cried, as their heads jerked forward and their seatbelts took the strain. Kate bit her tongue and could taste warm blood in her mouth.

"Did you see that asshole?" James said through gritted teeth, flashing his emergency blinkers. The blue sedan took the next exit and disappeared into the flurries ahead. "That idiot cut me off. He could've killed us! I'm amazed the airbags didn't deploy." He looked at her and blinked, climbing down from the dizzying heights of his outrage. "Kate? Your lip is bleeding. Kate?"

She heard a flapping sound and realized it was her wildly beating heart. She saw something strange move toward them through the snow, something odd and whimsical, like a seahorse bobbing around inside an aquarium. It was a little girl. This shocked her so much, she unfastened her seatbelt and got out of the car.

"Where are you going?" James cried out. "Get back in the car!"

Kate stood by the side of the road, staring into the

snowstorm, clumpy flakes sticking to her face and hair. She gazed at the falling snow and whispered, "Savannah?" Snow swirled in the wind, creating new shapes, and Kate had the sensation that she was being warned. *Danger ahead.*

"Kate?" James shouted.

Her head was spinning. Her skull throbbed. Was she having a stroke? In the blink of an eye, the illusion was gone.

He got out of the Lexus and strode through the driving snow. "This is dangerous. What are you doing?"

"I just saw something."

"What?"

She balked. She could tell by the set of his jaw that he was beginning to lose confidence in her. That he was becoming afraid for her.

"What did you see?" He gestured wildly into the snowstorm. "There's nothing out there."

"My head is pounding."

"We've both had an incredibly stressful day. Let's go home." He tried to take her by the elbow, but she brushed him away. "Kate… please."

Back in the Lexus, he watched for oncoming traffic as he pulled out onto the road, while Kate stared at the frozen river, little vortices of snow curling off its surface. She rubbed her temples.

He shot her a concerned look. "Are you getting a migraine?"

"I think so."

She got them about twice a year. Sometimes the pain was so bad she had to lie down for twenty-four hours. Her stomach was doing somersaults. "Today totally sucked."

He nodded solemnly but couldn't help himself. In typical James fashion, he burst out laughing. Soon they were both laughing. It was the kind of sick humor that grabbed you and shook you and wouldn't let go. She laughed so hard, her stomach hurt. Her temples were throbbing.

"Everything's going to be okay," he said with tears in his eyes.

"Just get us home in one piece, you jerk."

7

THE GARGOYLES LOOKED OMINOUS in the snowstorm. They crouched in the corners of the building, as if ready to pounce on unsuspecting passersby. The lobby seemed much less elegant than it had last night. Kate and James weren't laughing anymore. And they didn't feel like fooling around.

Their front door stuck a little as James pushed it open. Kate entered the high-ceilinged living room and collapsed on the sofa.

"Coffee?" he asked from the kitchen.

"Is there any wine left?"

"Just Heineken. Want me to go get some?"

"No, babe. Stay with me," she pleaded.

He came into the living room and handed her two Aleves with a bottled water. "Here, take this," he said gently. He sat down beside her, ready to comfort her, but suddenly she couldn't stand his sympathy anymore and got up and padded around the living room in her stockinged feet, feeling claustrophobic. She wanted to hit something.

It had stopped snowing outside. According to the weather report, the cloud cover would burn off by mid-afternoon, but Kate didn't want the sun to come out. She preferred the blanketing gloom of winter. She wanted to curl into a hibernating ball without having to explain herself.

She stood in front of the bay windows overlooking Massachusetts Avenue and watched the traffic as it whooshed past in slow motion. Another effect of the migraine. She crawled into James's lap and closed her eyes.

"Today was bad, but I'll get past it… and I'll be stronger because of it."

"That's my girl." He kissed her forehead and stroked her hair, and her greasy chignon fell apart beneath his fingers.

She took a deep breath and sighed. "I'm afraid to tell you what I saw."

"I'm not going to judge you, babe."

"I saw my sister, coming toward me through the snow… trying to warn me."

"A visual hallucination from the migraine."

"That's what I figured."

"Combined with snow flurries playing tricks on the eyes. Combined with a near-collision on the road. Combined with a sleepless night…"

"Gotcha."

"You haven't had nightmares about Savannah in a long time. You're under a lot of stress right now and Nikki's death came as a terrible shock. It's pretty obvious that stirred everything up."

"So I'm not crazy?"

"No, and I should know. I've got an MD after my name and everything."

She smiled through the pain.

"Hey, I have an idea. After the funeral, let's take a few days off and head down to the Cape."

She rolled her eyes. "I can't go anywhere yet. There's the Risk Management interview."

"Okay."

"And what if Nikki's parents file a lawsuit?"

"Let the hospital handle that."

"Anyway, I won't be able to relax until everything's settled down. I'm sorry we lost our deposit, James. But I'm going back to work. I can't leave right now."

He frowned. "Listen, sweetie, you're a dedicated doctor, and I love that about you. But even superheroes have their limits, right? You've been up all night. You're under an enormous amount of strain. It's no surprise you're seeing things, because at some point the dam is going to burst and—"

"Hey," she interrupted. "No lectures."

He sighed. "I'm just saying, it's been more than a year since we've taken a vacation, and you can't keep going like this. Besides, I think your workaholism is a manifestation of a much deeper issue…"

"Shh." She put a finger to his lips. "We're going to be okay."

"But…"

"I promise. Everything's going to be fine. Once the funeral's over we'll book another two-week vacation for the end of April. Cross my heart."

"End of April?"

"Best I can do."

"Deal." He kissed her. "Forget Sedona, we weren't thinking big enough… Let's go to Cancun… or maybe the Cayman Islands."

She curled up beside him and listened to him plan their trip. It was so warm and cozy with just the two of them, she never wanted to move.

James finally stopped talking. "What are you thinking?"

She nestled into him. "I was thinking about the time… they wouldn't let me into the morgue, because I was too young. So Dad went in by himself, but he left the door open a crack, and I could see her lying on a table covered with a sheet, and I remember staring at the bottoms of her feet. It's funny, because you don't usually notice people's feet. Savannah's were so small and blue, and I remember thinking that was odd—they were dusk-blue. And there was this man, the medical examiner, and he saw me watching, and he got very angry. My father had to take me home. We didn't speak in the car. We never talked about it again."

Savannah had been abducted by a man with a history of DUIs and domestic abuse arrests, a monster who'd buried her alive in his backyard. Alive. Kate could barely fathom it. Even now, after all these years, she could still hardly process it. *Buried alive.*

Savannah's killer was on death row. His name was Henry Blackwood. It sounded like a serial killer's name. It suited him. Kate hated thinking about him or even acknowledging his existence; she wished she could blot him out of her mind completely. There had been appeal after appeal, and she'd spent years wishing it would be over with. And soon it would be—the execution was scheduled for next week. But there were some misguided people—a bunch of blustery do-gooders and anti-death-penalty advocates—who blindly believed in his innocence. They somehow kept finding Kate's email address, which she kept having to change, and appealed to her to step forward and save his life. Her sister's killer! How absurd was that? How *sick*. Sometimes she wished they were all dead. But she kept these thoughts to herself, on a shelf next to Savannah's cold blue feet.

A few hours later, James was busy working in their shared office space, while Kate sat staring in exhausted silence at a PDF of the funeral announcement she'd received from Nikki's mom. Anxiety nibbled around the edges of this new dilemma. In her accompanying email, Elizabeth McCormack had asked Kate to say a few words at the funeral, and Kate had no idea where to begin. What could she say without entering forbidden territory? Everything was protected by doctor–client privilege. Nikki would've died of shame if her parents ever found out half the things she'd said about them.

The doorbell rang. "I'll get it," Kate called out, hurrying down the hall. She swung the door open.

An elderly woman stood on the threshold—petite and platinum-haired, wearing a navy blue skirt and an Ann Taylor blouse. Her smile was apologetic. "Hi, I'm Phyllis Wheaton, your downstairs neighbor from 7D. Sorry to bother you, but my bathroom ceiling is leaking, and I'm pretty sure it's coming from your unit."

"Oh no. Please come in. My name's Kate." They shook hands. "Nice to meet you. Wait here a second. I'll go take a look."

Kate bolted for the bathroom, where a pool of water had accumulated around the toilet pedestal on the tiled floor. The toilet was making a gurgling sound. "James?" she hollered. "Our toilet is leaking."

James came bustling out of the office to inspect the toilet while Kate hurried back to Phyllis Wheaton. They could both hear James jiggling the toilet handle and removing the tank lid.

"Sorry about that," Kate said. "We'll call a plumber immediately."

"Do you have someone in mind?"

"Not really," Kate confessed. "This ownership thing is new to us. We're used to calling the landlord over every little hiccup."

Phyllis smiled and handed her a slip of paper. "I took the liberty of writing down my plumber's number, just in case. I hope you don't mind. He's very good."

"Great."

"In the meantime, do you know how to turn off the main water supply?"

Kate shook her head. "James?" she called out. "Do you know how to turn off the main water supply?"

"No," he shouted back.

She smiled apologetically. "How helpless can you get?"

"Let me show you. It's the stopcock under the kitchen sink."

Kate followed her into the kitchen and watched as she knelt down in her navy blue skirt and explained what she was doing as she turned off the stopcock.

"There," Phyllis said. "All set. The toilet should stop leaking in a few minutes. Was there much damage?"

"Not too much. I'm sorry about this. We didn't even notice."

"No problem." Phyllis wiped her hands. "Call me if you need anything. I jotted down my number, too."

Kate glanced at the slip of paper. "Thanks." She walked Phyllis to the door and waved goodbye, then called the plumber, who said he'd be there in an hour. "What else can go wrong?" she muttered.

She looked in on James, who was hunched over his laptop, typing furiously. "I called the plumber," she said.

He glanced up. "We have a plumber?"

"Well, technically it's Phyllis's plumber. Now he's ours."

"Is that a good thing?"

"I totally trust her. She knows how to handle a stopcock."

Against all expectation, he didn't crack a joke in response.

"Oh come on. Stopcock? I handed you that one."

"Sorry, hon. I'm in the middle of Agatha hell."

"What happened now?"

"She attacked Larry Milroy, one of the nicest guys you'd ever meet, a total milquetoast. She was holding him hostage."

"So you're going back to work?"

He nodded distractedly. "In a bit. They want my notes on our last group session together, and I have to attend a team meeting later on. But I'll wait for our new plumber to make an appearance first, see if I can learn anything. And you're going to get some rest."

"Twist my arm."

"Good." He continued typing furiously.

She decided to get out her sister's old backpack, even though James hated it when she did that. He said that it only encouraged the re-emergence of all the negative emotions she'd managed to bottle up inside her adult brain. But Kate figured it was therapeutic, so she went into their bedroom, slid the cardboard storage box out of the closet, and popped the lid. The box was full of Kate's childhood belongings— birthday cards from her mother, old-fashioned dolls, stuffed animals with careworn ears. Savannah's backpack was at the bottom. It was made of pink canvas fabric and had sweat-stained leather handles the color of beef jerky.

She listened to make sure James wasn't coming before she lifted it out of the box and settled it in her lap. She sorted through the junk inside—all the things her sister had once considered essential. A large purple comb, a stale pack of chewing gum, a Hello Kitty mirror, a *Nightmare Before Christmas* notepad, and a near-empty bottle of citrus perfume. Kate uncorked the bottle and inhaled deeply—it smelled just like Savannah. She could picture her elfin face, her rascally eyes and her self-effacing smirk. *What a dork I am, I burped in front of this boy I like.*

Now Kate examined each item as if it would tell her something different this time. She slipped Savannah's

Moleskine diary out of its canvas compartment and flipped through the pages. She'd read her sister's diary many times over the years. She selected a passage at random and studied the tiny, fuzzy handwriting.

What if you were walking thru the woods and you picked up a
rock and it turned out to be the most valuable rock in the world?
Maybe it looked like a regular rock but what if it wasn't? What
if it was a Magic Rock that could grant you three wishes?
OR considder this… what if you ignored it and kept walking?
Hey dumbo! You just missed something incredible and possibly
amazing. Imagin what your life would've been like if you'd
picked up that rock??? Three wishes! What would you wish for?
I'd wish for—my mother back, a pony, my dad to be happy. My
friends keep asking me why I collect stuff like peblles, feathers,
leaves, seashells, potatoe chips, and rocks. And I tell them…
YOU SHOULD TOO. Because it could change your life forever.
You never know.

Kate smiled. She would have to be fearless. She would have to pick up these ordinary rocks, because you never knew.

Her phone rang, and she scooped it up. "Hello?"

It was Tamara. "Sorry to bother you, Doc, but we have a problem."

8

KATE HEADED DIRECTLY FOR the nurses' station, where Tamara stood with her hands on her wide hips. "I know you need this like a hole in the head, but she asked for you." She glanced over at the girl in the corner of the waiting room. "She said she needs to talk to Dr. Wolfe. She saw your nametag, I guess."

"No problem. What's the story?"

"Her name is Maddie Ward. Her mother dropped her off this morning, but we can't find her anywhere. She didn't talk to the staff or fill out the required forms. Nothing."

Kate nodded. "Okay, I'll go check it out."

The crucifixes were still draped around the girl's neck, the rosaries wrapped around her wrists. As Kate approached, she noticed something she hadn't spotted before—Band-Aids on the girl's neck and hands.

"Hi, I'm Dr. Wolfe. Mind if I sit down?"

"Okay," the girl said softly.

Kate took a seat. "Can I call you Maddie? Do you mind?"

Maddie nodded shyly, and Kate was struck once again by the resemblance to Savannah—same sea-green eyes, golden hair, and lightly freckled face. There was even a widow's peak hidden under her blond bangs.

"Where are your parents?" Kate asked.

"Mommy left."

"Oh. Where did she go?"

"Home."

"Is she coming back?"

"I don't know." Maddie shrugged and played with her rosary beads.

"What's the jewelry for?"

"Mommy says it's for protection."

"Really?" Kate frowned. "Protection from what?"

"I don't know," Maddie admitted.

"Wow. She must really want to keep you safe."

Maddie's mood seemed to darken. "I don't like them," she said, suddenly frantic, removing the rosaries and crosses, as if she'd been dying to get rid of them.

She handed everything over to Kate, who said, "Okay. I'll ask the nurses to hold onto these for you. Be right back." She took the jewelry over to the nurses' station and asked for an envelope. She put everything inside, wrote Maddie's name on the front, sealed the envelope, and asked Tamara to stick it in the locker along with the other patients' confiscated belongings. Her immediate thought was: *Okay, this girl's mother is a religious fanatic, and her reaction is perfectly normal.*

Maddie smiled as Kate took her seat again.

"Whenever you want them back, let me know."

"I don't want them back. Ever."

"So your mom dropped you off here this morning and then went home?"

She nodded.

"She can't do that, Maddie. We have a policy. She can't just leave you here. I'd like to talk to her. What's your home number?"

Maddie rattled it off, and Kate recognized the familiar area code. "Do you live in Blunt River, New Hampshire?"

"Wilamette."

"Wow. Right across the river. You're a long way from home."

Maddie shrugged.

Wilamette shared a border with Kate's hometown, but the two municipalities were miles apart in terms of social and economic disparity. Wilamette was basically Blunt River's ugly stepsister.

"We're practically neighbors," she told the girl. "I grew up in Blunt River."

Maddie smiled.

"Wait here. I'll be right back." Kate left Admissions to go stand in the corridor, where the cell reception was better. She dialed Maddie's home phone number, and a woman with a soft, crinkly voice answered.

"Hello?"

"Ms. Ward? My name is Dr. Wolfe. I'm calling from Tillmann-Stafford Hospital. You left your daughter in our care this morning, and I wanted to..."

Click.

She stared at her phone. She hit redial.

"Hello?" said the wrinkly voice.

"Sorry, we got cut off. Or did you just hang up on me?"

"What do you want?" the woman snapped.

Kate was taken aback, but it wouldn't be the first time she'd had to deal with an uncooperative parent. "Your daughter has been sitting in our admitting room all day. Did you drop her off here this morning?"

"She's sick. She needs help."

"This is a psychiatric unit. Does she need to be admitted to the ER?"

"No. She's sick in the head."

"I'm sorry, Ms. Ward, but—"

"Please. It's *Mrs.* Ward. I'm not a Ms. Okay?" She had the dry voice of a longtime smoker.

"Why didn't you admit your daughter, Mrs. Ward? What's going on?"

"I don't know what to say."

Kate had a mental picture of Mrs. Ward, similar to the women from her hometown who hadn't been so lucky in life; who'd married badly or dropped out of school after getting pregnant, who would starve themselves just to afford another carton of smokes, but never deprive their kids. They loved their children to pieces but didn't know how to be good mothers, hitting them in the grocery store when they wouldn't stop screaming or whining, then daring the other shoppers to judge them. *Let he who is without sin cast the first stone.* Their lives were mostly out of control, because they were so rooted in their troubled pasts.

"You can't just drop her off and go home. There are procedures to be followed. Forms to fill out. You and your husband need to come down here so that we can discuss Maddie's situation, otherwise you'll have to take her home. I don't want to have to call social services, but—"

"Okay," she interrupted. "I'll come."

"And your husband as well?" Kate was concerned that this woman might not be stable, and she wanted to meet them both.

"Yeah, okay."

"Good. When are you available?"

"I can be there at four."

"Okay. I'll see you at four o'clock this afternoon. In the meantime, I'll make sure Maddie has something to eat and…"

Click.

"What the hell…?" Kate stared at her phone. "What is wrong with you, lady?"

It took a moment for her to compose herself and coax the professional Kate back into broad daylight. Sometimes the parents turned out to be more psychologically damaged than Kate's troubled patients.

Once she got back to Admissions, she found Maddie in the same position on the sofa, except now she was jabbing herself with a pencil. Gently. Absently. Stabbing the sharp end of the pencil into her thigh through her neatly pressed jeans.

Kate tried not to alarm her. "Maddie? I'll take that now."

The girl paused. "They aren't coming, are they?"

Kate nodded. "They'll be here at four."

"No, they won't." She jabbed the pencil a little harder

into her left thigh. There were spots of blood on her jeans.

"Maddie, please." Kate held out her hand. "Give it to me. Now."

The girl froze and looked at the pencil as if she didn't know how it had gotten into her hand.

"I'll take that."

After a moment, she handed it over. There was blood on the tip.

Kate called Yvette over. Although the nurses seemed like formidable characters, they were great with the kids. Yvette strolled over. "What's up, Doc?"

"We need to admit her. She's cutting herself." Kate held up the bloody pencil.

Yvette put on a pair of gloves and called out, "Tamara?"

A collective sigh went through the nurses nearby, though no patient would have detected it. *Ah,* they seemed to acknowledge in unison—*we have a cutter.*

Yvette leaned down, the loose flesh of her jowls moving. "You hurt yourself, sweetheart. You're bleeding. This is a hospital. We can help."

The child played nervously with her bangs and her long blond ponytail. She cast a deeply skeptical glance Kate's way. She gave off a small heat, like a flushing rose.

"We need to put a Band-Aid on that and make sure it doesn't get infected," Yvette explained. "Okay?"

"Are they really coming?" Maddie asked Kate.

"Your mother said she'd be here at four."

"Don't hold your breath."

Kate balked. It was such an adult thing to say.

Yvette held out her hand. "Will you come with me, young lady?"

Maddie scooped up her jacket and climbed down off the sofa like a condemned prisoner.

9

THERE WAS SOMETHING DISTURBINGLY truthful about the mentally ill. They had the kind of clarity that most people lacked, an ability to cut through the bullshit and say exactly what was on their mind, no matter how warped or confused. Even their delusions were layered with meaning and truth.

Exam room 4 was an amalgam of sterile disinfected surfaces and well-stocked medical supplies—tongue depressors, Q-tips, gauze bandages, surgical tape. Maddie sat on the padded table kicking her bare legs back and forth, hands placed primly over her knees to keep the paper johnny from inching up. She seemed more curious than afraid.

The harsh fluorescent lights illuminated a multitude of scars and scabs on the girl's undernourished body. Kate counted at least fifty old injuries, along with some newer abrasions—mostly scrapes and small puncture wounds. Whether these were self-inflicted or evidence of abuse had yet to be determined.

Yvette rolled her eyes in disgust as she finished bandaging the fresh wounds. "I gave her a Children's Tylenol for the pain. I'll put her on one-to-one until she's admitted."

"*If* she's admitted," Kate corrected.

"If that child isn't admitted by the end of the day, I'll call social services myself." She left in a huff.

Once they were alone, Maddie asked, "What kind of doctor are you?"

"A psychiatrist."

"Oh." The girl scrunched her nose.

"Why? What's wrong?"

"I don't like psychiatrists."

Kate smiled. "Why not?"

Maddie shrugged. "Just don't."

"How many psychiatrists have you been to, Maddie?"

"Three."

"Back in Wilamette?"

"Blunt River. At the hospital there."

"And you didn't like any of them?"

"The worst was Dr. Quillin. He smelled funny."

Kate couldn't help laughing. "Well, the truth is, us doctors are only human. Despite our white coats and fancy degrees, we all have failings. For instance, my stomach growls when I'm hungry. And I mean... it can get really loud."

"Mine too." Maddie giggled.

"It's embarrassing."

"Mine sounds like a lion."

"Mine's more of a ticked-off badger."

They had a good laugh over that.

"So tell me about Dr. Quillin. Besides the funny smell."

Maddie wrinkled her nose. "He used to call himself a 'professional listener.' I was supposed to do all the talking, but

Mommy said, 'I'm not paying you to listen! I'm paying you to fix her!' So she took me to see Dr. Hoang. But he couldn't fix me either. And neither could Dr. Madison."

"Actually," Kate told her, "psychiatrists aren't supposed to fix people."

Maddie seemed surprised. "They're not?"

"No. We don't have that kind of power. See?" She held up her hands. "No magic wands. No fairy dust. I can't cast any spells. I can't fix you all by myself, Maddie. But I can help you fix yourself. And I know for a fact that it works, because I've seen it with my own eyes."

The girl smiled hopefully.

"Can I ask you something?" Kate said. "Do you ever see things other people don't? Any visions? Angels? Perhaps something scary?"

Maddie shook her head.

"What about voices? Do you hear voices in your head?"

"Only one," she admitted.

"One voice? What does it say?" Kate asked.

"Bad stuff."

"Like what?"

"It tells me I'm stupid and dumb and smelly. Stuff like that."

"Ah." Kate nodded. "And what does it sound like?"

"Like... um..."

"Is it masculine? Feminine?"

Maddie shrugged.

"Boy? Girl? Soft? Childlike?"

She shook her head mutely.

"More like a grown-up?"

Maddie nodded.

"Grown-up? Okay. But you don't know if it's male or female?"

No response.

"Does it sound like a character on TV?" Kate persisted. "Or maybe a person you know in real life? A teacher or relative? Your dad perhaps?"

Maddie said nothing. There were goosebumps on her legs.

Kate sensed the child knew exactly who the voice sounded like, but wasn't ready to reveal it just yet. "Does the voice ever tell you to hurt yourself?"

"I'm cold."

"Maddie…?"

"It's cold in here."

Kate decided not to press it. Sometimes you had to pick your battles. New patients had a tendency to scare easily, and if you pushed them too hard in the beginning, you risked losing them forever.

She draped a hospital blanket over Maddie's legs. "We'll talk about this some other time. You can get dressed now. The nurses' aide will be right in. Are you hungry?"

Maddie perked up. "My stomach's been growling," she said excitedly, putting her hands over her belly. "Did you hear it?"

Kate picked up the patient chart and walked to the door. "The nurses' aide will take you to the cafeteria. They have pizza and everything." She turned and left, scribbling notes, but once she got outside the exam room, she realized her mistake. She'd let her patient down. Their one connection— their growling stomachs—hadn't merited any reaction from her. By not sharing Maddie's inside joke, Kate had responded like a typical doctor. Worse, she'd responded like her father. And that cut to the bone.

At the same time, you couldn't get too close to your patients, or they might become confused. Roles merged. Lines blurred. How close was too close? It was up to Kate to maintain a healthy doctor–patient relationship and define the boundaries. But she could just hear the gears in Maddie's busy brain ticking away. *Why didn't you take me to the cafeteria, Dr. Wolfe? Why are you abandoning me just when I was starting to like you?* Kate was supposed to draw the most deeply personal information out of this child, and yet she wasn't supposed to get too personal. It was a balancing act.

The on-duty aide, Claire, was busy texting her boyfriend in the break room. Kate filled her in on Maddie's condition and asked her to escort their new patient down to the cafeteria. Then she went upstairs to her third-floor office and called James.

"Guess what? I've got a new patient," she told him. "A cutter. She hears voices. Well, one voice at least. An adult-sounding voice of indeterminate gender. Her mother dropped her off this morning and left her here to fend for herself…"

"So… right back on the horse, eh?" he said thickly.

She could tell he wasn't happy about it. "She asked for me," Kate explained. "We met earlier this morning. Turns out she doesn't like male psychiatrists. They smell funny, among other things. But hey, it's a good thing, right? It'll keep me out of trouble."

"I guess," he muttered.

She grew defensive. "I can't just sit around twiddling my thumbs."

"No one's suggesting any thumb-twiddling."

"Besides, she needs me."

"They all need us, Kate. Don't get sucked into that trap. Anyway, I've got my hands full right now—the plumber's here."

"Does he look like he knows what he's doing?"

"More than me. He's almost done. Then I'm coming to the hospital."

"For the team meeting?"

"Yeah. More Agatha drama. We'll talk about it later. Do me a favor, though. Come home as soon as you get this new patient oriented. Okay? Promise me."

"I promise."

"Love you."

"Later, 'gator."

Kate passed the time waiting for Mrs. Ward by catching up on her paperwork and taking back her regular appointments—they'd been distributed among the other child psychiatrists in the unit, but now that her vacation had been postponed, Kate decided to resume her regular duties. Her overworked colleagues were more than happy to oblige.

Around three in the afternoon, her phone rang. It was Mrs. Ward.

"I'm in the parking lot," she said in her dry voice.

Kate glanced at her watch. "I thought we said four?"

"Well, I'm here, aren't I?" Mrs. Ward snapped.

Kate sighed inwardly. "My office is on the third floor. Just follow the signs to a pedestrian passageway and—"

"No. You don't understand. I'm not coming in."

"Excuse me?"

"I'm not coming into the hospital."

Kate stood up from her desk and walked over to her window. Across the well-maintained courtyard was the hospital's multi-story parking garage. Six glass-walled pedestrian walkways provided safe passage into the west wing from all levels of the garage. "Mrs. Ward, please. We need to discuss Maddie's case…"

The voice rose a pitch. "I'm not coming in!"

Okay. Nosocomephobia—fear of hospitals. Religious obsession. Yikes. Deep breath. "Where are you now?" Kate asked.

"Second level. North side. Next to a stairwell."

"I'm on my way."

She found Maddie's mother sitting behind the wheel of an idling blue Toyota Camry plastered with Six Flags bumper stickers. The car faced out of the parking space and the motor was running, as if she were primed for a quick getaway. Mrs. Ward wore pink Gap sweats and a confused look. She sat gripping the steering wheel and she seemed oddly familiar to Kate.

"Hello?" Kate tapped on the glass. "Mrs. Ward?"

The window ferried down. The thirty-something woman with short dark hair wore large sunglasses that hid her eyes. She had a gaunt face with a nose that looked as if it had been broken at some point in the past. Kate noticed a few small green bruises on her neck. There was a dryness about her—dry skin, dry hair—that complimented the unusual scratchiness of her voice. She had the crouched, tenuous demeanor of a battered woman, as if she'd taken a pounding all her life.

"Where's your husband?" Kate asked.

"He works long-haul. He just got back from a three-week stint. He's out cold on the sofa. I didn't want to wake him."

"Not for something as important as this?"

"Not for anything."

"Why? Would he get angry?"

The woman stared at her. "Look. I came here like you said. It's just me. End of story."

"Okay, fine. We can talk in my office," Kate said firmly. "Follow me, please."

"No," Mrs. Ward said, just as firmly. She handed Kate a heavy, rumpled shopping bag through the rolled-down window. "Here. Take this."

Kate hesitated. "What is it?"

"Clothes. For Maddie. Please." When Kate didn't take the bag, Mrs. Ward let it drop to the ground; it landed in a grease puddle.

Kate scooped it up. "You can't just leave your daughter here, Mrs. Ward. We need to discuss her situation and make an evaluation. And then if we decide to admit her, you'll need to fill out some paperwork—"

"Show me the paperwork. I'll do it right here."

Kate took a frustrated step backward, sorely tempted to walk away, but this could be her only chance to get a signature on paper. She took out her phone, called the nurses' station, and asked Yvette to grab the paperwork and bring it out. Then she leaned into the car and said, "What's going on, Mrs. Ward?"

"Nelly."

"Are you all right, Nelly? Is everything okay at home?"

"I'm here about my daughter."

"What's the problem with Maddie? We found her cutting herself in Admissions. Jabbing a pencil into her thigh. We found dozens of old scars on her body."

"She does that to herself," Nelly sputtered. "Like I said, she's sick in the head. Possessed or something."

"She may be suffering from a mental disorder and the self-harm could be a sign of an early break," Kate said.

Nelly stepped on the gas, and the car jerked forward, giving Kate a start and forcing her to jump backwards. She almost tripped over the cement divider. Nelly hit the brakes and shrieked, "Do you think this is easy for me? Do you?"

Deeply shaken, Kate struggled to regain her composure. The woman had almost run her over. She took a deep breath and reminded herself this wasn't about her or Mrs. Ward. It was about Maddie. "No, I don't think it's easy for you," she asserted. "Please don't go. Someone is bringing out the paperwork now."

Nelly sat trembling behind the wheel. "Are you going to be her doctor?"

"Not if you don't want me to."

"Just the opposite." She stared straight ahead. "Maybe you can help her."

"Can you elaborate? We need more information about Maddie's illness, her symptoms. When did they start? Why do you think your daughter's possessed?"

"She won't listen to reason. She locks herself in her room and refuses to come out. She hates her dad and me. She hoards stuff like a little pack rat. She bites and cuts herself. She refuses to go to school. She hears things that I don't hear, and it scares the living daylights out of me. I'm at my wit's end. So I brought her here, because I know you'll take good care of her."

Yvette came jogging into the garage, her nametag on its lanyard bouncing all over the place, puffing and gasping for breath. She thundered to a halt and thrust the paperwork into Kate's hands. "Is that everything you need?" she wheezed.

"Perfect. Thanks, Yvette."

"Good, because I'm not doing that again." Yvette nodded at Nelly and headed back to the hospital with the commanding, take-no-prisoners stride of the psychiatric nurse.

"Okay," Kate said, thumbing through the standard admission forms. "We'll need to admit Maddie for observation. She's clearly a danger to herself. Please write down your home address and an alternate number where you can be reached in case of an emergency. And reconsider coming inside so that we can discuss Maddie's treatment. It would be extremely helpful if—"

"Pen," Nelly barked. She stuck a scrawny, bruised arm out the window and waved her hand with exaggerated impatience. "We just have the one phone. We can't afford cell phones or what have you."

"Here." Kate handed her the pen and the paperwork, and watched as she signed on the dotted line.

"Is that all?"

"Plus today's date," Kate said. "And I'm going to need your insurance card number. And you need to sign there. And there." She pointed through the rolled-down window. "And if you could fill in her medical history, any health problems…"

"She was a healthy child. Where else? Is that all?"

"There." Kate pointed. "And the HIPAA. Last page. Two places. That's right."

Nelly finished signing the forms and handed everything back. "We all done here? We good?"

"Yes."

Kate tried one more time—not because she thought it would work, but so she'd be able to say that she had given Maddie the proper standard of care. "Won't you please come inside? Just for a short while? The more information the better."

The woman sighed and adjusted her hands on the wheel. "She was a good girl. Cute as a button. Now it's hard work. I miss my daughter. I want my little girl back."

"All right. We can keep her for up to a week for observation…"

"She's healthy. She's had all her vaccines. I was good about that."

"This paperwork will allow us to admit her for observation for seven days, ten days tops, but I'll need you and your husband to come in tomorrow for a meeting…"

"Can I go now?"

Kate took a breath. "How's tomorrow afternoon?"

Nelly removed her sunglasses and rubbed her eyes, revealing her whole face for the first time. Kate suddenly felt numb with shock. Nelly didn't seem to notice, and said, "Please. Just take care of my little girl. Make her better. Because I sure can't." She released the hand brake and took off in a scarf of dust.

"Wait!"

The car disappeared around the corner, and Kate could hear the Camry's tires squealing through the twists and turns of the vast parking garage. She looked down at the woman's scratchy signature and felt a swirling nausea. *Nelly Ward.* Except that wasn't the name she'd gone by when Kate had last seen her. In high school she'd been Penelope Blackwood, niece of Henry Blackwood, Savannah's killer.

Feeling lightheaded, Kate took off after the Toyota. She hurried down the cement steps until she got to the ground level and took off running across the brick courtyard. But by the time she reached the entrance gates, Nelly Ward was gone.

10

KATE FOUND JAMES IN the Adult Psych Unit, where the more violent patients were cared for. He stood in front of the door to the time-out room, looking through a nine-by-twelve-inch window. The time-out room was where patients could scream and throw tantrums without injuring themselves—basically a padded cell.

"Hey," she said.

He turned with a distracted look. "Kate? Is everything okay?"

"Yeah. Can we talk?"

"Hold on a second." He spoke to a clipboard-carrying resident about the patient in the time-out room—a middle-aged man who never smiled and rarely moved, but who was now railing against the entire world. James escorted her into the day room, where sunlight spilled through the wire-mesh windows.

Most of the patients milling around in the shabby communal area were heavily medicated. The furniture was bolted to the floor and the paintings were glued to the walls.

"What's up?" he asked with a concerned look.

"My new patient—the one I told you about? Her mother

just signed the admission forms. There's her signature, Nelly Ward. At first I didn't recognize her. But then she took off her sunglasses, and I realized I'd gone to school with her. She's aged badly and dyed her hair dark brown, but it's definitely her. Her name used to be Penelope Blackwood. Penny for short. She's Henry Blackwood's niece."

"Are you sure?" James said.

"They live in Wilamette, which is right across the river from where I grew up. And there were only a few Blackwoods in Blunt River County that I know of. Henry Blackwood and his brother's family."

James rubbed his chin. "Did you ask her about it?"

"No. She was gone by the time I realized who she was. But here's the thing. On the night Savannah went missing, Blackwood was supposed to be with his niece Penny the whole time. She was his alibi. But during the trial, Penny testified under oath that her uncle had disappeared for six hours that night. She must've changed her name from Penny to Nelly." Kate shook her head. "I don't understand. Why would she drive all the way down here just to drop off her daughter at my hospital? She knows who I am, right? I didn't change my name. I'm not trying to hide my identity. Besides, there's an excellent psych unit right across the river, with plenty of good female psychiatrists… so why pick me? It doesn't make sense."

"Deep breaths."

Kate drew back. "Deep breaths?"

"You sound upset."

"I am upset."

Some of the patients turned to stare.

"Come over here," he whispered, escorting her into the farthest corner of the room. "Sorry, but you need to calm down. You're under a lot of pressure right now, and this isn't helping."

"I'm having a perfectly normal reaction to a very creepy encounter."

He studied her with sympathy. "The world is full of whackos, Kate. We both know that. Maybe it wasn't intentionally creepy? Maybe it's more innocent than creepy? I mean, your reputation precedes you. It's not every day one of us gets an APA award. Penny... Nelly... whatever her name is... she probably read the *Globe* article about you and remembered who you were from school. And now she's got a very sick kid of her own who needs a good female psychiatrist and she's desperate... and she thinks, okay, I'm going to take my child to see this person. Is that so far-fetched? So she drops off her mentally ill daughter at the hospital where you work because she read an article that said you get great results."

"If that's true, then why all the secrecy? Why not tell me?"

"Maybe she was afraid you wouldn't treat her daughter if you knew the truth?"

Kate frowned. "I probably wouldn't."

"There. See? That's why she didn't say anything."

Kate fell silent.

He took her hand. "You're still wearing my ring, I see."

"I haven't had time to think about whether it itches or not."

He smirked. "Maybe if we called it an engagement ring."

"Are you trying to piss me off?"

"No, I've fulfilled my quota today." There it was again—that crooked-ass grin of his, the one thing that never failed to lift her spirits. "Life has a funny way of fucking with us, Kate."

"So I'm fucked? Is that what you're saying?"

"No, silly. We're both fucked."

She cracked a smile. "Shut up."

"Inject some irony into your veins, quick."

"Shut up, you dork."

"You can abuse me all you want. Go ahead. I can take it."

"Asshole."

"There. Better now?"

"Yes. Actually."

"You're welcome. Just take it in stride, okay?" He caressed her cheek. "Be my hero, Kate. I need you to be strong for me."

"Yeah, I'm fucking Lara Croft."

"You are Lara Croft. Which means that *I'm* fucking Lara Croft."

"Ha. My boyfriend is hilarious."

"See you tonight, babe." He gave her a fist bump.

She paused. "I've got to get Maddie admitted, so I may be a little late."

He smiled cynically at her. "A little, huh? I've heard that song before."

"Okay. Maybe a lot late." When he didn't respond, she said, "Hey, this is what we both signed up for, isn't it?"

He nodded. "Not to worry. Just take care of yourself, Kate."

"I'll call you later, babe."

11

KATE SPENT THE REST of that afternoon and evening with Maddie Ward, who turned out to be fourteen, and not twelve, as Kate had assumed. Maddie came across as very childlike for a fourteen-year-old, which alarmed Kate and sent up a red flag. Delayed puberty was fairly common, with plenty of causes: genetic, hormonal, environmental. Sometimes a child's growth spurts occurred on the outer edges of her teenage years, but Maddie was small for her age, without any of the precociousness of a typical teenager; she hadn't even begun menstruating, and her immaturity could be a symptom of serious abuse.

They'd taken away Maddie's pink blouse and jeans, her backpack and goose down jacket, and now she wore the pajamas her mother had dropped off in the rumpled grocery bag, along with a pair of grippy hospital socks from her "welcome" bag. The nurses let her choose the color, and Maddie had picked bubblegum pink.

She sat in an adult-sized wheelchair, looking orphaned, while various hospital personnel came and went, wheeling her from one department to another, monitoring her vitals, scanning her insides and running a bunch of tests to see if there was anything physically wrong with her.

Once in a while, Kate would step out into the hallway and try reaching the Wards on their landline, but they weren't picking up. They must've unplugged their answering machine, too, because she couldn't even leave a message.

The hospital's forensic psychiatrist photographed all the scars and scabs on Maddie's body and went away to make a professional assessment, while Kate called up the electronic medical records on her laptop and read through the doctors' notes and diagnoses in order to piece together a medical history—childhood illnesses, physical injuries, drug interactions. She was looking for a pattern of abuse and neglect.

She didn't find much. There was a broken finger at age five, when Maddie "accidentally" caught her hand in a car door. There were two fractured ribs and a concussion at age eight, when she "fell out of a tree" in her backyard. There were minor sprains and injuries at school, but no history of cigarette burns or choke marks, no signs of malnutrition. The most troubling aspect for Kate was the lack of regular doctor's visits, just a handful of emergency room visits and a string of psychiatric consultations. This wouldn't have been unusual if the parents didn't have health insurance, but the Wards were adequately covered. Most parents rushed their kids to the doctor at the first signs of a sniffle. Not the Wards. That alone was highly suspicious. Maddie was generally healthy, but she was definitely not okay.

After a hearty meal in the cafeteria, Kate's patient was

looking better. Her eyes were clear. Her cheeks were rosy. She'd perked up a little. Kate wheeled her over to Radiology to have X-rays taken of her bones, since any fractures, fresh or healed over, could provide evidence of abuse in the home. Abused children had a tendency to protect their parents—sometimes out of love, sometimes out of fear.

In between each intrusive medical procedure, Kate plied her patient with questions in order to get past her built-in apprehension. While they waited for the X-ray tech to arrive, Kate said, "I had a favorite tree I used to climb in our backyard. This huge old oak. I'd always climb as high as I could, because… from way up there, life didn't seem as daunting."

Maddie smiled. "I fell out of a tree once. It really hurt."

Kate nodded. *Such a childlike way of speaking.*

"I had to go to the emergency room."

"When was this?"

"I was eight. I hit a branch on the way down and broke my ribs."

Kate winced. "Ouch."

"I had to stay in the hospital overnight."

"Do you know why you're in the hospital now?"

Maddie shrugged. "Because I'm sick in the head?"

"We're trying to figure out what's going on." Kate reached for the girl's forehead to brush away a few stray hairs, and Maddie flinched. That flinch told her a lot. "Sorry. I didn't mean to startle you."

"You didn't," she said defensively, playing with her ponytail.

"What does your father do, Maddie?"

"He drives a truck. He's gone a lot."

Maddie's demeanor was that of a ten-year-old, both emotionally and mentally, and Kate was deeply concerned. "But he's home now, right?" she asked.

"Not for a few more days."

"Oh. Really?" Nelly had told her that Mr. Ward was resting at home. "Are you sure about that?"

Maddie nodded.

Kate decided to drop it for now. "So it's just you and your mom and dad at home? Any brothers or sisters?"

"Nope. Just me."

"Do you have any pets? A dog maybe?"

She shook her head. "We had a hamster at school once."

"Yeah?" Kate smiled. "I had a hamster. I called him Felipe."

Maddie giggled. "Ours was called Snark."

"Snark the Snarky School Hamster?"

Maddie had a ticklish laugh.

"Did you ever wish you had any brothers or sisters?"

"Uh huh. But Mommy says I'm a handful."

"I see."

Mommy? Most fourteen-year-olds called their parents Mom and Dad.

"My best friend has two brothers and three sisters."

"Wow, that's a full house. Who's your best friend?"

"Melissa."

"What's the one thing you like most about Melissa?"

Maddie thought for a moment. "Her family."

"What about them?"

"They're nice."

"Nice as in… what exactly?"

Maddie bit her lip before elaborating. "They don't fight. They laugh a lot. They play practical jokes all the time, and it's funny. And they have fried chicken for dinner and chocolate ice cream for dessert."

"Wow, that's cool."

Maddie giggled. "It's *really* cool."

Kate seized the opportunity to wade into forbidden territory. "Do your parents fight a lot?"

"Sort of."

"Does it make you uncomfortable when they fight?"

Maddie nodded, eyes downcast.

"Do they scream? Shout? What?"

"There's lots of shouting."

"Anything else?"

Maddie didn't answer.

"Pushing and shoving?"

"Sometimes." She peered at Kate through her long eyelashes. "Daddy pushes Mommy sometimes. Especially when she calls him a loser."

"Does he ever hurt her?"

"No." Denial.

"Are you sure?"

"I don't know." Hesitation.

"Does he ever shove you? Shout at you?"

"Maybe." Semi-confession.

Next came the big question. It was like crossing a psychological landmine. "Does your father ever hit you, Maddie?"

She paused for a few seconds. "I have to go to the bathroom," she said finally.

"Okay. I'll get the nurses' aide."

Susie Potts was on duty tonight, a twenty-five-year-old so perky and sweet her personality oozed out of her like raspberry pie filling. She reached for Maddie's hand and said, "Hey, bunny. Escort time. Gotta pee? Let's go."

Maddie wasn't allowed to use the restroom without a chaperone, since she was on suicide watch. Susie, although often distracted, was a natural, entertaining the children with shadow-puppets and telling funny stories. Whereas Kate had the burden of getting to the truth.

When Maddie returned from the restroom, she was much less responsive to Kate's questions. It must've been the last one that shut her down. *Does he hit you?* Perhaps a bridge too far.

Maddie squirmed and complained about the hospital wheelchair being uncomfortable. Kate cancelled the final test, sent Susie back to the break room and wheeled Maddie past the nurses' station, where the night staff sat gossiping, their whispered conversations sprinkled with juicy exclamation points.

Maddie's assigned room was at the end of the corridor, where another young patient was sound asleep. It was eleven o'clock, and after such a long day of being poked and probed, Maddie finally lost it and became inconsolable. "I want to go home," she sobbed. "Where's Mommy? I want to go home!"

Kate tried to comfort her as best she could, but the girl had reached her breaking point. Maddie's roommate woke up and complained about the noise. Kate authorized a sedative, and one of the night nurses came into the room with a loaded needle and plunged the syringe into Maddie's backside. Meanwhile, Kate gave Maddie a running commentary, explaining what was going on every step of the way: why she'd decided to give Maddie a sedative; what her mother had said about Maddie needing help; why Kate was so concerned about her self-inflicted injuries; and what they were attempting to do, the entire hospital staff—trying to help her.

Maddie grew lethargic as the meds took effect. She could barely speak or move. At least she was no longer upset—the poor kid didn't have any energy left for that. Her pupils were the size of pinpricks. It bothered Kate a great deal, but after years of experience, she knew that it was for the best. Finally, Maddie closed her eyes and drifted off to sleep.

Out in the hallway, Kate tried to reach Nelly again, but the phone rang and rang into a non-compliant void.

She monitored Maddie for the rest of the night and consulted with various specialists on her test results. There were some old callus-formation fractures on Maddie's ribs that corresponded with the report that she'd fallen out of a tree—however, it didn't rule out physical abuse. The bite marks on the child's forearms were determined to be her own, when measured against the dental imprints of her teeth. The scabs and scars on her arms, thighs and calves were superficial and probably self-inflicted, since there were no injuries anywhere on her body that the patient couldn't reach on her own. That didn't preclude abuse, but it went a long way towards discounting it. Most significant of all, there was no evidence of vaginal trauma or sexual abuse. *Thank God for that*, Kate thought.

Exhausted but satisfied she'd gotten Maddie safely admitted, Kate put Susie in charge of keeping an eye on the girl and went upstairs to her office to type up her notes. As dawn approached, she went back downstairs, dismissed the tired-looking aide, and watched the horizon turn from pink to ruby red in a few spectacular minutes.

She returned to Maddie's room to check on her patient. Kate studied the swollen veins on the girl's forehead and wondered what could have driven the child to cut and bite herself. Given Penny Ward's troubled history, perhaps it wasn't such a leap. Besides hearing a single voice inside her head, there were no overt signs of schizophrenia—no visual hallucinations, no flat affect, no odd or eccentric behavior, no grooming issues. But schizophrenia wasn't the only option. A self-harmer could be diagnosed with personality disorder, bipolar disorder, anxiety disorder, or any other number of syndromes. Kate would have to search for a deeper meaning other than disease or chemical imbalance. She wanted to know why Maddie Ward was here and what her parents might've done to her.

Around 6 AM, Maddie woke up.

"How are you feeling?" Kate asked. She'd been answering her emails on her iPhone, and her head was buzzing from overwork and lack of sleep.

The girl snuggled deeper into her blankets. "Semi-weird."

"Hm. That's a good one." Kate smiled. "I'm feeling semi-weird myself. Any numbness? Tingling?"

"No."

"Sorry about the tests. And the shot."

Maddie scrunched her nose. "You say you're sorry a lot."

"I do?" Kate made a face. "Gee, I'm sorry about that."

Maddie giggled. "So sorry for being so sorry all the time."

"Awfully sorry for all my sorries."

They both laughed.

Then Maddie asked, "What's wrong with me?"

"That's what we're trying to figure out."

"Will I be okay?"

"I believe so, yes," Kate said confidently.

The girl closed her eyes and was asleep within minutes.

Soon the morning aide, Claire, was back, looking fresh as a daisy, and Kate had a craving for nicotine that she wisely ignored. She decided to get a cup of coffee instead and bumped into Ira in the break room.

"Jeez Louise," he exclaimed. "You look terrible."

"Thanks a lot."

"Come into my office for a second."

A wash of morning light poured in through the hermetically sealed windows. Ira took a seat behind his desk, while outside a snowplow dragged its blade across the courtyard with a scraping sound.

"What's going on? I thought you were taking a few days off?"

"I've been up all night with a new patient, Maddie Ward. Her mother dropped her off yesterday and abandoned her, literally draping her in crucifixes and rosaries. She's fourteen years old, but she acts much younger, more like a ten-year-old. She's been having aural hallucinations, and her mother thinks she's possessed."

"No kidding?" His eyes widened with interest. "Are they religious fanatics?"

"I don't know. Possibly. Anyway, her mother refused to come into the hospital. She signed the paperwork in the parking garage yesterday and drove away." Kate decided not to mention her personal connection to Nelly, not just yet. It would only complicate things, and besides, she wanted to do a little more digging into the matter on her own.

"I've got news for you, Kate," Ira said. "You can't be a doctor twenty-four-seven. You just lost a good night's sleep, right when you needed it the most. So what gives?"

"I couldn't bear the thought of her spending last night in the hospital alone," Kate confessed. "I suspect there's abuse in the home. Maddie's father. No conclusive proof yet. Just a gut feeling."

"Since when are you a mother substitute? You can't blur the lines, Kate. This isn't about you. It's not about appeasing your guilt for something you may or may not have done sixteen years ago."

Kate lowered her gaze and stared at her hands. "Wow, Ira. Don't hold back."

"You know me, Kate. I tell it like it is."

Her cheeks flushed. She looked at him. "This has nothing to do with sixteen years ago. Okay? And you're right, I am a poor mother substitute. But at least I was there for Maddie when she woke up this morning. If she trusts me, maybe she'll open up and tell me what the hell is going on."

He grinned. "I like it when you defend yourself."

"Was that a test?"

"Maybe."

Kate scowled. "I'm not in the mood to be your guinea pig, Ira."

He shrugged.

"Anyway, so far, it looks as if most of her wounds are self-inflicted, including the bite marks on her arms—they match her dental impressions."

"So she's a self-harmer?"

Kate nodded. "But Mrs. Ward thinks she's possessed."

"Interesting. Does the child believe she's possessed, too?"

"Hard to say. She relinquished the crosses and rosaries pretty quick, which could imply she's a believer, since the devil is supposed to reject all religious symbols. It could be a case of 'possession syndrome.'"

"Okay," Ira said. "Let's go with that for now. Don't challenge her belief system. Let's accept the delusion as a baseline and deal with it through the patient's eyes."

"Right," Kate agreed. "If she's having an acute episode, then she's confused and gullible, and her mother is providing her with the answer."

"A crazy answer, sure… but let's go ahead and talk about the demons, if that's what she wants to do," Ira said.

Kate nodded. "Use the patient's own belief system to treat her."

"Exactly. What's their religious affiliation? How was she raised? Let's delve into the family background. Find out more about her parents. I'd like to consult on the case, if that's okay with you."

"Great. I'd welcome it."

His phone rang. "Hold on." He spoke to the department chair for a moment, then hung up. "How's everything else, Kate? How are you handling Nikki's suicide?"

"Okay, I guess." She shrugged. "To be honest, it's nice to have a distraction."

He nodded. He waited.

Kate blurted out, "I mean, I'm dealing with it, you know? But it makes me question everything I've been doing for the past couple of years. How many other mistakes have I made? Are any of my other patients going to kill themselves? Am I missing all the signs? I have to admit, it's taken a wrecking ball to my self-confidence."

"I'll tell you a story," Ira said. "Ten years ago, this very successful man took an overdose of sleeping pills. He had everything going for him—money, family, career... but he was deeply depressed. I took him on as my patient, and after a few years of therapy, he got better. He was no longer suicidal. He resumed his career as a high-profile attorney. He got back with his estranged wife. I was over the moon about it. But then one day, guess what happened next?"

"He committed suicide?"

"Nope. Cardiac arrest. Ironic, huh? Here I'd managed to save this man's life against all odds, but he died anyway. Why?

Because we're only human, Kate. We aren't God. Far from it."

She frowned. "I guess you handle life's ironies better than I do."

"Well, you can't fight reality. Just because we're psychiatrists, doesn't mean we control our patients' destinies, anymore than we can control our own. All we can do is help them find their way through the darkness. If we're lucky."

"So basically we're flashlights?"

He laughed. "Yes, we're flashlights."

The echo of Savannah's bright laughter rippled through her. One hot summer night sixteen years ago, Kate had given her little sister a flashlight, but instead of . finding her way home, Savannah was lost forever.

Before he buried her alive in his backyard, Henry Blackwood had shaved Savannah's entire head, even her eyebrows. The police never found the clippings. Among the questions still haunting Kate, that was the biggest one of all—where was Savannah's long blond hair?

12

KATE WENT HOME TO prep for the Risk Management interview and get some well-deserved sleep. James was at work. She found his note on the kitchen island. *I like you, do you like me? Check box—yes or no.*

She smiled and checked yes. She kicked off her shoes, poured herself a glass of wine, and curled up on the sofa, where she wrote down her responses to imaginary questions in longhand on a notepad. After a while, she couldn't follow the hieroglyphics of her own handwriting anymore and nodded off.

"Am I a bad person?"

"No, Savannah. You're good through and through."

"But I think bad thoughts sometimes."

"We all do. It's called being human."

The day after Savannah went missing, dozens of reporters descended on the town. During the first forty-eight hours, missing-child posters popped up all over the county. Volunteers scoured the woods and fields. Four days later, cadaver dogs found her body buried behind Henry Blackwood's house, less than thirty feet from his back door. Her sister's tragedy led the nightly news for weeks.

Blackwood lived in a suburban home with a pickup truck parked out front. He and his wife had divorced years ago. They didn't have any kids. The Wolfe girls rarely spoke to Mr. Blackwood, even though they walked past his house every day on their way to school. He had blond hair, freckled skin, sea-green eyes, and a widow's peak. He was the unfriendly neighbor who kept his property spotlessly clean, picking up litter by the side of the road and tying the lids of the garbage cans shut with a length of rope in order to keep the raccoons out. Later on, that same rope was used on her sister.

Throughout the years, Kate periodically had the same dream. She would find herself back inside the cabin in the woods, only Savannah wasn't there—just her size six jogging shoes with the big Ns on the sides. In Kate's dream, something reached out of the darkness and grabbed her by the ankles and dragged her relentlessly backward. She would scrape her nails across the splintery boards screaming, "Savannah!"—thinking her sister must be hiding in the shadows. She always struggled but couldn't escape the relentless pull, and when she woke up, her mouth tasted like dirt.

Now she sat up gasping for air, furious that it was happening all over again. The nightmares, the anxiety attacks, the self-doubt. Kate thought she'd managed to move on, but some things never left you.

She fetched her wallet and pulled Savannah's careworn picture out of its hidden compartment behind her credit cards. She poured herself another glass of wine and gazed at the old snapshot. Her little sister was like a sugar-icing rose—so sweet and delicate, you couldn't imagine that anything bad would ever happen to her. Their mother used to say she was made out of caramels and moonbeams. Kate had only wanted to protect her. She hadn't meant to hurt her.

At the funeral, she was compelled to say goodbye to her dead sister in her child-sized casket. Savannah's skin was a bloodless color, like rancid milk, and she wore a wig because her hair was all gone. The mortician's assistant had even penciled in eyebrows, and Savannah would've loved that. A grown-up wig and grown-up eyebrows! Cool!

In a near panic, Kate tucked the picture away and tried to think about something else. Anything. She sat on the sofa surveying the beautiful condo. How lucky they were. She was tempted to call James just to hear his voice, but the locked unit was always so busy, and she didn't want to disturb him. Besides, he couldn't be her rock every single second of every day. She had to handle some of this on her own.

She remembered the nightmares piling up after Savannah's murder. She remembered waking up screaming, "Mommy!" But their mother was gone. She never screamed, "Daddy!" When the nightmares got really bad, she would get up in the middle of the night and wander around the house, searching for her father. More often than not, he wouldn't be there. His car would be gone from the driveway, and she'd have to face the horror of her sister's murder alone. Kate used to whisper to the empty house, "I'm sorry, Savannah, do you forgive me?" And when she fell asleep, she would have the terrible cabin dream all over again.

It took her years to overcome her fears and eventually stop tormenting herself. One night, in a radically different dream, her sister appeared out of mist, and Kate could feel Savannah's thin, graceful fingers lacing through her hair. In this rare peaceful dream, Savannah sat next to her and carefully braided Kate's long auburn hair. "Perfect," she said when she was done. Kate woke up sobbing.

Ira interpreted the dream as a crystallization of her own self-forgiveness. He said it had nothing to do with spirits or ghosts, except as a metaphor for healing. But Kate couldn't help feeling that her sister had actually visited her that night in some form or another. An irrational belief—but one she clung to. Because Savannah's forgiveness meant everything in the world to her.

Kate poured herself another glass of wine. Then another. Soon she'd polished off the bottle, and the world became soft-focus—a rubbery, cushiony world. Nice and bouncy. She got off the sofa and stood in front of the panoramic windows, swaying slightly with each intake of breath.

Late that evening, James came home thoroughly drained. Kate had never seen him so burnt out before. He collapsed on their queen-sized bed without bothering to get undressed. "Hey, you," he muttered into his pillow, already half asleep. "Whazzup?"

"Hey, beautiful." She tugged off his boots and climbed into bed with him.

He gathered her in his arms. "How ya doing, sweetness?"

"Fine. I was shitty before. Many, many glasses of wine ago."

"Hey. Whatever does the job."

"Are you encouraging me to become an alcoholic?"

"No. I'm encouraging you not to care so much."

"Ha, that'll be the day."

"Look at me. I had a shitty day, ten-hour shift, I haven't had an ounce of alcohol, and I don't care. See?"

"I guess you're just more tougher than me."

"More tougher? I am?"

"Mm." She kissed him.

A few minutes later he found his second wind, got out of bed, and retrieved his messenger bag. "Hey, I picked these up on the way home." He rummaged through the inner pockets and produced a handful of glossy travel brochures. He dropped them on the bed and sat down beside her. "What d'you think? Cancun or the Caymans? Or maybe Hawaii? I dunno. I was leaning toward Cancun."

"Wow," Kate said, picking up a brochure. "We don't have to decide right this second, do we?"

"April's not that far away, dude. Look at this. Pristine beaches, kayaking, margaritas, the Mayan ruins in Coba. Snorkeling, sunsets… did I mention margaritas? Just what the doctor ordered."

Kate frowned. "Yeah…"

"What?"

"Sorry, I can't think straight. I wasn't prepared to plan our whole future tonight."

"Our whole future? It's just a vacation."

She dropped the brochure on the bed. "I've got a lot on my mind lately."

"Okay. But look at this…"

"Not until after the funeral and the Risk Management interview, we said. Right?"

"I know. But there's always going to be another crisis, Kate. There's always going to be another patient. Come on, we deserve this. Sunny skies, blue ocean…?"

"Do I have to decide right this second?" she asked defensively.

His face fell. He scooped up the brochures and shoved them back in his bag. "I understand you're under a lot of stress right now. I didn't mean to come across as an asshole, Kate. But I'm worried about you. I don't like what this is doing to you… how it's affecting you."

She drew back. "Are you talking about the hallucination?"

"Sort of," he admitted. "That was pretty upsetting."

"But I thought we agreed it was a symptom of the migraine?"

"It could be a symptom of a lot of things."

She stared at him.

"Listen, I love you. I'm not the enemy here. What about my idea of driving down to the Cape next week? Just for a couple of days."

Her finger began to itch. She glanced at her ring. "Maddie needs me," she said. "She'll only be under my supervision for seven days…"

He heaved a frustrated sigh. "You're right. Sorry, babe. I understand how hard this must be for you, because I've been through it myself… Remember Desiree? She swallowed drain cleaner, for chrissakes. What a horrible way to go. But you've got to believe me when I say I want to help. I want to protect you from your awful childhood, Kate. Do you realize how scary this is for me? I mean, the execution is *next week*. We weren't supposed to be here when it happened, remember? We were supposed to be in a hot tub in Sedona, drinking margaritas, no TV, no Internet… just you, me, and the stars."

"I know," she said sadly. "But it's unavoidable now."

He wrapped his arms around her and drew her close. She rested her head against his chest and listened to his heartbeat, which was slower than hers. He took her hands and turned them over. He traced the old scars with his fingers. She had tried to kill herself on her eighteenth birthday, but she'd done it all wrong and missed the vein.

"Look," he said, "I can't imagine what kind of hell you've been through… how difficult your life must've been… and now, to have to relive it all over again. But my instinct is to protect you. I'm a guy. It's a guy thing. You get that, right?"

She nodded solemnly. "Maybe we shouldn't have moved in together?"

He drew back. "What?"

"Maybe it's too soon for this?"

"Is that your takeaway from our conversation? That we should call it quits?"

She shrugged, tears welling. "It's never too late."

Instead of getting angry or offended, he laughed. "Those are bad, bad words." He folded her in his arms. "I'm sorry, but it's way too late. You're stuck with me."

She sighed, deeply relieved.

13

ON FRIDAY MORNING AT 8:50 AM, Kate parked in the six-story hospital garage and went over her prepared statement in her mind, reluctant to leave the warmth of her car for the interview with Risk Management at nine o'clock. After all, the risk was mostly hers.

She loosened her grip on the wheel, switched off the ignition, and stepped out of the car, then stood for a moment inside the vast cave-like structure. It was a cold and echoey kind of place. A nowhere kind of place. You could hear the steady whoosh of cars circling the levels, a high-tide sound. A person could drown in those circlings.

On an impulse, instead of taking the pedestrian walkway directly into the west wing, she headed down the stairwell and crossed the courtyard, past the frozen fountain and weathered benches. It had been a long time since she'd entered the hospital through the main doors.

The beautiful old building had an aura of sleepy dignity about it. The walls were composed of thick granite blocks, and the arched windows reminded her of heavily lidded eyes, as if the hospital was always on the verge of nodding off. In front of the main entranceway, a little boy stepped on the automated rubber mat over and over, making the glass doors slide open and shut, enthralled by his newfound superpower. She watched with genuine amusement, her winter coat flapping around her knees, until his mother came along and whisked him away.

If only I could control my life like that, she thought, stepping on the welcome mat and watching the doors glide open. Simple.

Inside, she greeted the security guard, Bruce, a friendly guy with a clean-shaven face and a hangdog expression, who ushered people through the metal detectors with all the grace of Fred Astaire. He waved his magic wand and said, "Have a blessed day, Doc."

"You too, Bruce."

Kate caught a crowded elevator to the psych department on the second floor, and used her pass key to open the double doors of the Children's Psych Unit. Across the hallway, through another set of locked doors, was the Substance-Abuse Treatment Center. Upstairs on the third floor was the Adult Psychiatric Intensive Care Unit, accessible by private elevator or locked stairwell—for hospital personnel only. Admission to all three programs was voluntary, but the exit doors were locked so the hospital wouldn't be held liable if a patient escaped the premises without being properly released.

The smaller of two conference rooms had been reserved for today's interview. Kate's attorney was already there, along with the Risk Management representative, a stout woman in a cashmere pantsuit who sat with her fingers laced together.

Russell Cooper was an intimidating presence in his Armani

suit, Bulgari watch, and gold cufflinks. "Kate, this is Felicia Hamilton from Risk Management. Felicia... Dr. Kate Wolfe."

"Nice to meet you."

"Same here."

They shook hands.

Kate settled into a vinyl-padded chair next to Russell and studied Felicia Hamilton. She appeared to be in her mid-forties, with intelligent gray eyes and short sleek hair. A professional with a permanent poker face. Felicia opened her briefcase on the table and took out a digital recorder, a fountain pen and a clipboard. She placed the recorder on the table and said, "Do I have your permission to record this interview?"

"Yes." Kate glanced at her attorney for approval. Russell nodded. Her heart wouldn't stop racing. There were several bottled waters on the table, and Russell slid one over to her.

"Thanks." She twisted off the cap and drank. Then came the questions. She reminded herself to keep it brief and truthful.

"On June 2nd of last year, Nicole McCormack came to the hospital for emergency psychiatric treatment and was admitted for observation," Felicia said in the blandest of tones. "Why did you release her four weeks later?"

"Traditionally, lower-risk patients are treated on an outpatient basis."

"So she was no longer suicidal?"

"She was working on healthier ways to express her negative feelings. I decided that her risk of suicide wasn't high at that point."

"When you say 'wasn't high,' what do you mean?"

"Nikki came to regret what she'd done. Her psychological state had improved significantly, and her depression had lifted. After four weeks of treatment, I concluded she was no longer at risk of self-harm."

"And what was the outpatient treatment plan?"

"She was to continue medicating and see me once a week for talk therapy."

"And how was that going?"

"Very well. She was fully engaged in working through her emotional issues."

"What was her mental state before her death?"

"She was doing very well, like I said. She wasn't acting out or skipping school. She hadn't reported any suicidal urges for months. She wasn't giving away any of her personal possessions, except... well, that's not important." Kate caught Russell's wince in her peripheral vision. *Don't volunteer unnecessary information.*

"Let me be the judge of that," Felicia said.

"She gave me a few things she'd found at the beach," Kate explained. "I had to remind her, we can't accept gifts from our patients. Hospital policy."

"I see. What sort of things?"

"Just a..." How did you explain a skirt weight? "A few seashells," Kate lied.

"And how was her family situation?"

"She and her mother were still arguing quite a bit," Kate said. "Nikki thought her stepfather was too controlling. However, she was learning to communicate her needs and concerns to them."

"Were there any other suicide attempts in her past?"

"Just the one that brought her to us to begin with."

"I see. And what was the method?"

"She overdosed on aspirin."

"And more recently, was she drinking alcohol or taking drugs?"

"I'm confident she was no longer doing drugs. However, it's possible she wasn't entirely forthcoming about her alcohol intake."

"Okay. But did she display any of the symptoms of addiction?"

"None whatsoever."

"Any history of mental illness in the family?"

"Not according to her mother."

"Did she have any phobias?"

"Just that she was afraid of people's tongues."

"People's tongues?"

Kate nodded. "The tips of people's tongues bothered her. Also, she was afraid of the plumbing... old pipes in the house, the noises they made at night."

"In your opinion, did this constitute cause for concern?"

"No. A lot of people have strange phobias. Those were separate issues from her main illness, which was bipolar disorder."

They talked about medication and discussed Nikki's state of mind during her last session with Kate. Felicia spoke in a monotone, conferring little emotion one way or another. Finally, she concluded the interview by saying, "Is there anything else you'd like to add?"

"Only that I consulted with my supervisor on the case. Dr. Ira Lippencott."

Felicia nodded politely. "Thanks for your cooperation, Dr. Wolfe." She packed up her briefcase and stood up. "You'll be hearing from us in a few weeks. In the meantime, here's my card."

"We'll call you if we have any questions, Miss Hamilton," Russell said. As soon as the door closed behind her, he turned to Kate. "You handled that very well."

She excused herself and rushed to the bathroom. She fought off a wave of disorientation as she studied her face in the mirror. She could feel the strain accumulating behind her eyes. She splashed cold water on her face and grabbed a paper towel. She hated her own vulnerability.

In psychiatry, a person's core vulnerability was the emotional state that was most terrifying for them—fear of harm, fear of shame, fear of isolation. Kate's was her sense of failure at not being able to help her sister, and by proxy, her young patients. It kept her working long hours. It made her struggle to become a better doctor. She had failed to protect Nikki. She would not fail again.

14

KATE FOUND MADDIE WARD alone in her room.

"Good morning," she said. "How are you feeling?"

The girl rubbed her tired eyes. "Okay, I guess."

"Your tests all came back negative. Which is a good thing."

"Why is negative good?"

"It means we can rule out brain injury or other neurological causes." She didn't add that they still had to find out where the aural hallucinations were coming from, why Maddie was cutting and biting herself, and what combination of family dysfunction, psychological factors and chemical imbalance was causing her depression. "How do you feel in general?"

Maddie shrugged listlessly. "I don't know."

"Been a rough couple of days, huh?"

This morning, she looked different—older. More like a fourteen-year-old, and less like a twelve-year-old. The nurses had confiscated her gold stud earrings, leaving little holes in her earlobes. Her long blond hair was out of its ponytail and fell across her shoulders in swirly loops. She sat cross-legged on the hospital bed and gazed forlornly out the window. Her eyes had grown-up sorrows in them. Usually, when you walked through a psych ward during visiting hours, the rooms would be packed with family members bearing gifts. But Maddie Ward had been alone for forty-eight hours. No cards. No flowers. No phone calls. No visitors. That in itself constituted neglect, in Kate's mind.

"Have you been getting along with your roommate?"

"Yeah."

The roommate's bed was made. She was probably in the day room. A sixteen-year-old anorexic—one of their frequent fliers.

"Is everything else okay?" Kate asked, nudging her into the conversation.

Maddie's eyes grew soft and fragile, and suddenly the little girl re-emerged. "Is she a suicide risk like me?"

"Who? Your roommate?"

"Is that why they keep checking on us?"

"The nurses just want to make sure you're safe."

Maddie's mood shifted. "They don't know what they're dealing with," she said darkly.

Red flags popped up all over the place. It was such an adult thing to say. "What do you mean? What are they dealing with?"

"They're having a fight over my soul," Maddie whispered conspiratorially.

"Who?"

"My parents."

"Are you talking about the Devil? Possession?"

Maddie gazed out the window and didn't answer.

Kate pulled up a chair and took a seat. "Maddie, does

your father have a work number where he can be reached?"

A head shake. "We're not supposed to call him at work."

"I see. Then how do you contact him in case of an emergency?"

Maddie shrugged. "I don't know."

Taking a different tack, Kate took a pack of chewing gum out of her pocket. "Would you like a piece? It's spearmint."

Maddie grinned. "Thanks."

Kate handed her a stick of gum and watched as she unwrapped it and folded it into her mouth. Maddie drew her knees toward her chest and chewed contentedly, the smell of spearmint wafting Kate's way.

She tried again. "If there was an emergency at school, and your mother wasn't available, who would the principal call? Do you have any relatives nearby? Any aunts or uncles? Cousins or grandparents?"

"Nope."

"Nobody?"

She shook her head.

"What if the school had to reach your dad in case of an emergency?"

"Calling him wouldn't stop me," Maddie said harshly.

Kate paused. "What do you mean?"

"When I say I want to kill myself, I mean it."

Most fourteen-year-olds couldn't articulate their alienation like this, let alone admit to suicidal tendencies. "Why would you want to kill yourself?"

"I don't know."

"Does the voice inside your head tell you to kill yourself?"

Maddie stopped chewing.

"When your father gets angry, does he ever hurt you or your mom?"

"Why do you keep asking me that?"

"Because you haven't answered the question yet."

The girl's face reddened. She studied Kate as if she were the enemy—and perhaps she was. "Once, when I wouldn't stop bugging him, he pushed me."

"What were you bugging him about?" Kate asked.

"Stuff."

"What kind of stuff?"

Maddie shrugged noncommittally. "Sometimes I feel like bugging him."

"And he shoves you away?"

"Only because I annoy him. Like this." She nudged Kate gently.

"No harder than that?"

"No."

"More than once?"

"I told you!" Maddie's face darkened. Her eyes watered.

"Are you sure?"

"Why do you keep asking me that?" Bright tears spilled down her cheeks.

"Sorry," Kate backtracked. "I didn't mean to upset you."

Maddie wiped her wet face.

"Is he religious?" Kate pressed.

The girl sighed. "I dunno."

"Is your mother religious?"

She sniffled, and Kate handed her a box of Kleenex. "She's Catholic. She believes in God. She believes in Jesus and the Holy Ghost and the Devil and hell and curses. Daddy doesn't."

"What do you believe in, Maddie? Do you believe in the Devil?"

Maddie's eyes widened. She stared at Kate with growing anguish. "Mommy says she went to school with you, a long time ago, and one day your sister disappeared, and the whole town went looking for her, but then when they finally found her, she was dead. Buried alive."

Kate's heart skipped a beat.

"Mommy says that's what happens to bad little girls. They get killed."

Kate sat in troubled silence, leaping back in time. She had been sixteen when Savannah disappeared, and Penny had been eighteen, a senior in high school. Kate barely remembered the shy, awkward, blond-haired girl who kept mostly to herself. A shrinking violet nobody thought much about, truth be told, until her uncle's trial, when she was suddenly everywhere—on TV, on the Internet, in the newspapers. Penny was the state's star witness and had put Blackwood in prison, but you could tell she hated the limelight. When the cameras were on her, Penny would duck her head and raise her hands in front of her face.

"What else did your mother tell you?" Kate asked.

Maddie frowned. "She says you can fix me."

"Is that all?"

A shrug.

"You just said you didn't have any relatives. Did you forget about your mother's uncle? Henry Blackwood?"

Maddie flinched. "He's in prison."

"Do you know why?"

"No."

"Are you sure?"

The girl was becoming evasive—probably trying to protect her mother from Kate's scrutiny.

"What else did she say about me?" Kate persisted. "Besides the fact that my sister was killed, and we went to the same school together?"

Maddie gave her a worried look. "Are you mad at me?"

"No."

"But your face is red."

Kate drew a breath. "I'm just surprised, that's all. I was heartbroken when I lost my sister, and it's still very painful for me."

Maddie nodded solemnly. An empathetic warmth suffused her cheeks.

Kate experienced a creeping paranoia, but she would have to check her anger and confusion at the door and deal with it later. "Okay," she said. "Let's back up a minute. I have a few more questions about the voice. When did you start hearing it?"

Maddie sighed. "I don't remember. A long time ago."

"What's the worst thing it ever said to you?"

"Jump out a window."

"It told you to jump out a window?"

"I was upstairs in the attic, and it said, *Do it*. And I knew what it meant, because I jumped out the window."

Bad news. This was a clear sign of psychosis, a voice demanding that its host do something terrible and the host complying. "When was this?"

"I was eight years old."

Kate cocked her head. "But weren't you eight when you fell out of a tree?"

"No. I jumped out a window and hit the tree on the way down."

"So you didn't really fall out of a tree?"

"No."

"Did anybody push you out of that window?"

Maddie made a face. "The voice said do it. So I did it."

"Can you hear the voice now?"

She paused for a moment, then shook her head.

"How would you describe your relationship with your mother and father?"

The girl eyed her suspiciously.

"Just say whatever pops into your head."

"They're afraid of me."

"Why?"

"They don't understand me."

"And how does that fear manifest itself? What do they do?" *Besides*—Kate thought sarcastically—*drape you in rosaries and drop you off at some faraway hospital, and then scurry home.*

"Mommy prays all the time."

"What does she pray for?"

"For me to get better."

"Does she believe in possession?"

"That's sort of an understatement."

Another oddly adult response from a child-like teenager.

"Does she think you're possessed?" Kate asked.

"She doesn't talk about it much."

"Why not?"

"My dad told her not to."

"So your father doesn't want her saying you're possessed?"

"Once, she said there was a demon inside me, and he hit her."

At last. "He did?"

"He slapped her across the face."

"Just once? Or more than once?"

"Like this." She demonstrated by slapping the air.

"And what about you, Maddie? Has your father ever slapped you?"

"No." Defensive posture.

"Are you sure?"

"I probably deserved it," she blurted out.

"But you just said he didn't hit you."

"Sometimes I make stuff up," Maddie admitted.

Uh-oh. That put a new wrinkle into the mix. But psychosis and lying weren't mutually exclusive. Abused children sometimes lied to cover up their parents' sins, making it difficult to untangle the truth from delusion and flat-out falsehoods.

"He hit you? Why? What happened? What were the circumstances?"

"I told him something he didn't want to hear."

"What was that?"

"I can't remember."

"Try."

"Stop asking! They love me."

"I'm sure they do," Kate acceded.

"They're just messed up." The girl's voice grew high and tight. "They love me."

"Does your father—"

"My *stepfather*," Maddie snapped.

"Oh. He's your stepfather?"

Maddie nodded, her gaze fixed on the view beyond the window.

"I didn't realize…"

"My real father's dead."

"Sorry."

"Don't be."

Kate frowned. "I'm going to ask your parents to come visit you today."

"Good luck with that."

Another strange response.

"Why do you say that?" When Maddie didn't answer, Kate said, "I haven't been able to reach them at home. Is there another number where they can be contacted?"

Maddie shook her head wildly. "Mommy doesn't like cell phones. She says the government could be listening in."

"Listening in?"

"I'm tired of talking."

"Okay. Well, hopefully they'll come visit you today."

Kate knew that her questions were becoming increasingly intrusive, and it was obvious that Maddie needed some space. She walked out of the room and stood in the hallway, while keeping one eye on her troubled patient through the open doorway. She called the Wards at home again. This time their machine picked up and Kate left a brief message.

She had only looked away for a second, but when she glanced back into the room, Maddie was banging her fists on the window, attempting to break the glass.

Kate hurried back in and grasped Maddie by the arms. "Shh, it's okay." This was a setback. Clearly Maddie could no longer be left alone. Not even for an instant.

15

KATE WENT UPSTAIRS TO the Adult Psychiatric Intensive Care Unit to talk to James. He was finishing off a group therapy session, sitting in a circle with twelve patients in the day room. James's most difficult charge, Agatha, stood in the center of the group, making the thin, depleted wail of a cat in heat. Her arms shimmied in a sort of dance. She tried to explain herself, but only seemed capable of producing streaky, mascara-laced tears.

Kate hung back and waited. Rumpled, out-of-date magazines were strewn around the lounge. Every inch of upholstery was coffee-stained, and the ugly wallpaper looked like a Rorschach test.

A few minutes later, group was over, the participants gazing at one another with cloudy, abnormal eyes before shuffling away. James came over to Kate and said, "I have a mega-headache. Let's go."

They went downstairs to the cafeteria, which smelled of fried onion rings and warmed-over meatloaf. Attending physicians, residents, visiting scholars and other hospital staff rotated through, loading up their trays with additive-laden pre-packaged food, while smokers got their fix out on the terrace.

James popped a couple of Excedrins and swiped two trays for them. He handed Kate one and ordered a cheeseburger, fries and an iced tea. She got a cup of coffee and a sorry-looking slice of apple pie, and they found a table in back next to the recycling bins. A pungent smell wafted toward them, turning her stomach. She watched James bite into his cheeseburger and sop up the grease with a bunch of napkins, undeterred by the funky odor.

"How's it going with your new patient?" James asked.

"I'm very concerned about her environment. Maddie gave me conflicting stories, but I'm leaning toward a potentially abusive stepfather, which would explain her mother's demeanor the other day. I've been trying to reach her—Nelly, I mean—but she's not returning my phone calls. She doesn't have a cell phone, apparently, so I'm thinking of driving up there this afternoon. Get to the bottom of things."

"Right, like why she picked you, of all people, to treat her child."

"And why she didn't mention the fact we went to school together. Or who her damn uncle is."

"You know, I've been thinking," James said. "She might be angling to get your support for a petition to the governor to delay the execution next week."

"I was thinking the same thing."

"The timing is suspicious."

Kate nodded resignedly. "Want my pie? I'm not hungry."

James shook his head but took it anyway. He picked up his fork and took a bite. "Don't let her pressure you, okay? She might try to suck you into the whole anti-death-penalty fracas. If she brings it up, just remember, you don't have to sit there and take it. You can walk away with a clean conscience. Don't let her guilt-trip you."

"I won't."

"That's my baby." His arduous morning was etched into his face. "Want me to go with you?" he offered.

"Nah. Then she'd really clam up."

"You sure?"

"She's a little high-strung. I'd better go by myself." Kate reached across the table and squeezed his hand. "How's your headache? Are you okay?"

"If by 'okay' you mean beaten to a pulp by my so-called profession, then sure."

She rested her hand on his forehead. His skin was clammy and cool, belying the feverish spots on his cheeks. "Deep breaths. In and out."

He laughed. "Shut up."

"Oh come on. Where's the confident psychiatrist I used to know?"

He waved his hand unenthusiastically. "Yo. Right here."

"Yeah, I haven't seen him around lately."

"He's underneath all this collaborative intensive short-term dynamic therapy."

They gazed at one another.

"Seriously. Are you okay?"

He cracked a defiant smile. "Oh, I have fleeting moments of lucidity."

"Agatha?"

"Feels like I'm living inside that movie, *Whatever Happened to Baby Jane?* She's definitely plotting my destruction. Maybe I should just inject myself with Haldol and call it a day."

"Want me to beat her up for you?"

"Nah." He sipped his iced tea. "I think that's illegal."

She touched his arm.

"What gets me is she's really smart and observant," he said. "It's such a tragedy. She could've been a valuable member of society, if it weren't for her borderline personality disorder… I hate to admit it, but most of these people who come to us for help, Kate… they're lifers. You release them and hope for the best, but you know they'll be back."

"End of April," she promised. "Cancun. Or the Caymans."

His eyes lit up. "Yeah?"

"Unless you'd rather go to Disneyland?"

"No, I'm good." He beamed and dug into his apple pie.

At that moment, Jerry Meinhard walked over to their table and said, "Hello, ladies and germs. What's up?"

Kate groaned internally. Jerry was the psychiatry department clown, and certainly not a doctor she would have trusted with her mental health.

"Jerry," James said drearily.

"Nothing much," Kate muttered.

"I got a new one for you. Psychotics build sandcastles, and their shrinks collect the mortgage." Jerry looked at them expectantly. "Huh? Get it?" He laughed out loud. "I thought it was funny."

Kate gave him a dour look.

"Ouch, J-Man. Your girlfriend doesn't like me."

"Leave us alone, Jerry. We're having an adult conversation here."

"Ooh, so sensitive. Okay, I'll abscond to the kiddie table," he said and left.

"Hey," James whispered. "Maybe he put those peanuts in your office?"

"Sheesh," Kate said. "Of course. Jerry the Joker."

"Want me to beat him up for you?"

"Nah. I have a feeling it would only encourage him."

"True. Best to ignore the putz."

She leaned forward and cocked an eyebrow. "I'll get him back."

"How?"

"I don't know. But he'll never see it coming."

There was that beautiful crooked-ass grin of his. "I like the way you think, Dr. Wolfe."

16

AFTER HER SHIFT WAS over, Kate took the 95 north out of Boston and drove past mini-malls, industrial parks, forests, and lakes on a steady trajectory toward Blunt River, New Hampshire. It was mid-afternoon and the traffic wasn't bad for a Friday.

Sixteen years ago, Penny Blackwood had sealed her uncle's fate inside a Manchester courtroom after his defense team claimed he was with her on that fateful night. But Penny contradicted his sworn statement, testifying that her uncle had left the house for six hours that evening, returning in a disheveled state. The jury believed her, not him. The state's evidence alone had probably been strong enough to convict Blackwood, but Penny had made certain that the monster was put away. Kate recalled her vaguely, with pity—a shy dishwater blond drifting through the high-school hallways like a ghost, never calling attention to herself. An invisible kid, like so many of Kate's troubled patients.

Although she wasn't allowed inside the courtroom while Penny was testifying, Kate had seen plenty of video footage of the state's star witness leaving the courthouse on the six o'clock news, deluged by reporters and camera crews clamoring up the steps and shouting questions at her. She would drape a sweater over her head in order to hide her face. On TV, Henry Blackwood always looked the same. He frowned a lot. He had a nasty shadow across his face. Kate couldn't think of him now without those grainy media images playing inside her head, as if he didn't exist except in some staticky, cathode-ray memory.

She'd been driving for over an hour now through patches of snow and patches of sunshine, and she'd fallen into a kind of waking slumber. She turned off the radio and drove in silence along the eastern branch of the river. She was in southwestern New Hampshire with its hazy mountains and wintery landscape—a palette of gold, platinum, and silver. Some of the houses were stately, whereas others had junk stacked in the yards.

The town of Blunt River had once been a manufacturing hub for shoes, and its Ivy League university was nearly as old as Yale. The town's greatest shame was its crumbling lunatic asylum, closed in 1996, now just a cluster of deteriorating edifices nestled in conservancy lands not far away from the modern, university-affiliated Blunt River Hospital with its updated, compassionate psych ward.

Kate's mother had been committed to the old asylum when Kate was ten years old and Savannah was six, both of them too young to appreciate what was going on. At the beginning of her illness, Julia Wolfe heard voices. She saw things no one else did—faces in the window, strange lights coiling through the air. She was convinced somebody was following her all over town. At the asylum, Julia was treated for bipolar disorder and a major depressive episode. Bipolar disorder, or manic depression, was a brain chemistry disorder, a chronic illness with mood swings that ranged from depression to mania. In some cases, bipolar disorder was accompanied by visual or auditory hallucinations. These psychotic symptoms were more commonly linked to schizophrenia, however, and as a result, patients with severe mood swings who also hallucinated were often incorrectly diagnosed. The doctors insisted that Julia's bipolar disorder had manifested itself in hallucinations, but her delusions were so severe, Kate often wondered if her mother had been misdiagnosed. Bipolar schizoaffective disorder might've been more accurate.

The doctors released her six months later. A few weeks after that, she filled her pockets with rocks and drowned herself in the river like Virginia Woolf, her favorite writer.

Kate took the exit ramp off the interstate and followed the familiar, arcing road toward Blunt River. She hadn't been home in three years—not that her father ever complained. She rarely heard from him, except for the obligatory Christmas card or birthday gift—always a book. She made an attempt to call him a couple of times a year and usually got his machine. *You have reached Dr. Wolfe. Leave a message after the tone.* Eventually, she'd stopped leaving messages, because there was so little to say.

Now a wave of dread washed over her, along with a splash of nostalgia. Her curiosity was piqued. Nothing had changed—Blunt River was the same quaint New England town it had always been, charming and slow-paced, with a prestigious university nestled in its bosom. Her hometown. She passed by cottages and Gothics and Victorians where some of her childhood friends used to live, people she'd lost contact with years ago: she used to play doctor with Ashley Walsh's brother in that green house; in that split-level she'd once barfed in Dara Bogdanova's bathtub; in that Tudor-style home, she'd been the most unpopular sleepover guest ever when she couldn't stop trashing Alanis Morissette.

She slowed down for the blinking yellow light and took a left onto Three Hills Road. She felt a slight apprehension as she dipped and rolled over the three hills—up and down, up and down, like riding a galloping dragon.

Almost home.

Well, not exactly. She hadn't told her father about today's little excursion and didn't plan on dropping by unexpectedly. Instead, she would cut through her old neighborhood on her way to Wilamette. Hi Dad, bye Dad. Sorry, Dad.

The GPS system spouted directions, and Kate mindlessly obeyed, turning left, driving one-point-five miles, taking a right, et cetera. The town the Wards lived in, Wilamette, was an ugly carbuncle of a place on the other side of the river. She crossed the rib of steel spanning the cold blue river and passed a sign that said WELCOME TO WILAMETTE—LUMBER CAPITAL OF THE WORLD. Lies, all lies.

Here the landscape changed dramatically. The roads were in terrible shape. Half the shops on Main Street were boarded up and the hardware store had a 60% OFF sign in the window. Daffy's was The Four-Leaf Clover now, and Barney's

Bar & Grill was a fast-food joint. The movie theater had been permanently shuttered. After a mile or so, Wilamette's depressing commercial drag head-butted into a demoralized dead-end, and Kate had to turn left at the railroad tracks in order to keep on going.

What had once been a booming logging town was now struggling to rebrand itself into a woodsy, idyllic tourist destination. Good luck with that. Wilamette boasted bike paths and hiking trails, but the infrastructure was pretty torn up, the roads pitted with potholes. There were too many disintegrating trailer parks and bungalows painted "fun" colors that'd been passed from one generation to another. A few candy stores and souvenir shops had sprouted up here and there, but the poverty was spreading. The people were struggling, the mayor was corrupt, and it had been like this forever.

She took a right at the intersection and meandered for miles into the hills, past illicit farmsteads—puppy mills, mink farms, pot farms. The good people of Wilamette enjoyed collecting car parts and rusty wheelbarrows. Some of her friends from Wilamette used to laugh at their parents' oddball behavior, and she wondered if those same bright, ironic, promising Gen-Yers were still trapped here. Or had they escaped "Whack-o-mette" for more sophisticated destinations? Hopefully some were on a mission to drag their hometown kicking and screaming into the twenty-first century.

It was late in the afternoon by the time she'd reached Nelly Ward's drab-looking mid-century modern. The navy blue Toyota Camry was parked in the driveway. The residence was at least sixty years old and poorly constructed, as if it were being pulled apart by an angry seamstress—cracks in the siding betrayed the subsiding foundations.

Kate parked on the street and got out. Rows of icicles hung like tinsel from the roof. She trudged up the walkway with a sense of purpose and rang the doorbell.

When Nelly answered she gasped, "What're you doing here?"

"We need to talk."

"You could've warned me you were coming."

"I tried to. Did you get my messages?"

After a beat, Nelly relented.

The instant Kate stepped inside the house, she was hit with a blizzard of smells: mildew, garbage, cigarettes. She expected to see crosses and other Christian symbols hanging on the walls, but instead there was a mixed bag of good-luck charms: Native American totems, New Age amulets, four-leaf clovers, and primitive talismans. There were a couple of medieval-looking crucifixes, but they were far outnumbered by the New Age objects.

Nelly followed her gaze, then held out her scrawny arms for inspection, dozens of silver-and-turquoise bracelets jangling from her wrists. "The Aztecs and Mayans used to believe that turquoise and silver kept the evil spirits away. So I figured, what the heck? The more the merrier. Not that it works," she muttered. "I have the worst damn luck."

Kate wondered what it was like for Maddie, growing up in this cramped house where the walls seemed to close in on you.

Somebody had struggled to make the place cheery and bright, but the venetian blinds were snapped shut, allowing no sunlight in. Kate spotted a framed photograph on the mantelpiece—the happy couple on their wedding day. Nelly's husband was a big guy in a tux, with broad shoulders and collar-length dark hair. The bride beamed with joy, but the groom wore a slight scowl that gave the picture an aura of unhappier things to come.

"Mind if I sit down?"

"Anywhere," Nelly said with a shrug.

Kate sat on the edge of a large plaid sofa that smelled faintly of dog. She decided to come out with it. "You're Penny Blackwood, aren't you? Henry's niece?"

"I am," Nelly admitted drily. "I changed my name for obvious reasons."

"Why didn't you tell me that the other day?"

"I don't know." There were dark circles under her eyes. It was hard to believe they were only two years apart—Nelly seemed so much older. She wore a pink turtleneck sweater, slender brown slacks, and a pair of terrycloth slippers, the open-heeled kind you could shuffle around in like two comfy shoeboxes.

"I don't get it," Kate said. "Why drive your daughter all the way down to Boston when there's an excellent psych ward right across the river? Why go so far out of your way?"

Nelly plopped down in a vinyl armchair. "I don't know."

"Look," Kate said, softening a little, "there are plenty of excellent female psychiatrists in Blunt River. Why pick me?"

"Well, for one thing, I read about you in the *Globe*. That award. And I've had it up to here with these so-called experts,"

Nelly snarled. "They don't know shit, in my opinion."

"Dr. Quillin and the others? Maddie mentioned them to me."

"Dr. Quillin, Dr. Madison, Dr. Hoang. Overpaid hacks, the lot of them. You get conflicting advice all the time. She's bipolar—no, she's schizophrenic. And the drugs they prescribe only seem to make things worse. And nobody can give me a straight answer. In the meantime, she keeps getting worse."

"So you chose me?" Kate asked, trying to keep her voice level. "Out of all the doctors at Tillmann-Stafford? Because you got frustrated with the ones in Blunt River and you read about me in the *Globe*?"

"What do you want me to say?" Nelly stood up anxiously.

"The truth would be nice."

"The *truth*?" Nelly was shaking slightly, like a dog backing up on its hind legs. "My uncle didn't kill your sister," she blurted out, as if she'd been dying to say it all along. "How's that for the truth?"

Kate's stomach dropped.

"And now he's going to die for something he didn't do."

"But it was your testimony that convicted him," Kate said through clenched teeth.

"Doesn't matter. I know for a fact he didn't do it."

"Really? That's odd, because my sister was *buried in his backyard*. How do you explain that? And why did you testify against him?"

"All I know is an innocent man is going to die," Nelly said stubbornly.

Kate scowled. It made sense to her now. *That's why you brought Maddie to see me. This is all about your guilty feelings. You ratted your uncle out at the trial, and now that he's about to be executed, you've decided to change your story, and you thought you could drag me into it. Well, tough luck.*

Kate stood up. "There are plenty of other qualified psychiatrists in the Boston area. In the meantime, I'll ask my colleague, Ira Lippencott, to take over Maddie's treatment for now. He's a renowned child psychiatrist, one of the best—"

"No!" Nelly stood trembling in front of Kate, a skinny woman with saucer-sized eyes. "Please… I'm sorry. I didn't mean to upset you. I remember you from school. Do you remember me?"

Kate nodded. "Vaguely," she admitted.

"You and your sister used to walk past my uncle's house on your way to school every day. I'd wave at you sometimes from the upstairs windows—do you remember me now? You're both so vivid in my mind, the pretty redhead and her little blond shadow."

It shocked Kate to realize that Penny had been aware of them, because she couldn't remember anyone waving at them from Blackwood's house. More importantly, she didn't want to discuss her dead sister with this woman, because even though Nelly Ward was innocent, she'd been tainted with her uncle's monstrousness.

On some level, Kate wanted to punish her. "How come you haven't been to the hospital yet? Maddie needs you more than ever."

"I don't know." Nelly cupped her hands over her face.

"What's going on? Are there problems at home? Is it your husband?"

"No. Jesus."

"Okay, look. I can recommend some excellent female psychiatrists…"

"No!" Nelly shouted, eyes tearing up.

"You want *me* to treat her? Why?"

Nelly shook her head. "Look, I've been keeping track of you over the years… I'm no stalker, it's just that I felt so bad about your sister… such a horrible thing… and my uncle didn't do it, you see. I know for a fact he's innocent. And so I figured… well, maybe I wasn't thinking? Maybe I'm just *stupid*?" she said with unexpected ferocity.

Now Kate understood where the voice in Maddie's head was coming from. "Listen," she said softly. "You aren't stupid. You're just as confused as the rest of us."

"Confused? Absolutely. Unlucky? Definitely. We don't all have perfect lives," Nelly said bitterly.

It felt like a kick in the gut. "Are you calling my life perfect?" Kate said, trying not to let her anger into her tone.

"No, no," Nelly backtracked. "Not perfect. But certainly privileged."

"Privileged? My mother committed suicide. My little sister was abducted and murdered in a disgusting way—"

"I know, I know. I'm sorry! I didn't mean it." Nelly waved her skinny arms, as if trying to push the force of Kate's righteous indignation away. "Listen… I'm begging you…

my uncle didn't do it. I swear to God, he didn't do it."

"Stop saying that."

"He didn't leave the house that night. He was with me the whole time."

"So you lied on the witness stand?"

"I was a basket case back then. I didn't know any better."

"But you told the judge that your uncle left the house for six hours. Why would you lie about such a thing?"

"Because I was ashamed."

"Of what?"

Nelly wrung her hands. "Something."

"What?"

"Do I have to spell it out for you?" Her voice was anguished.

"Apparently so."

Nelly plucked a pack of Marlboros off the mantelpiece, fumbled with a box of matches, lit a cigarette, and exhaled a thread of smoke. "My uncle was abusing me."

Kate froze, though she didn't know why it surprised her.

"For years." Nelly winced. "Please."

For the first time, Nelly was making sense. Because if it was true, then the victim would carry the guilt and shame around with her forever. "So there was no six-hour gap? Is that what you're saying?" Kate said.

Nelly sighed heavily. "We were alone at my folks' house. They were out of town. They did that sometimes, asked Uncle Henry to watch over me. Ha. He watched over me, all right. He'd been babysitting me for years. He loved that. My father was such a worrywart. He thought, we can't leave Penny alone in the house, she'll have boys over, she'll get in trouble… Me? The biggest wallflower in Roosevelt High? But they trusted Uncle Henry…

"He'd do stuff to me, and we'd eat a meal and watch TV, and then he'd talk about himself. Like I cared. And then he'd do stuff to me again, and we'd watch TV again. It was endless. In his twisted mind, we were star-crossed lovers. I was like a secret girlfriend. But I was scared stiff." Nelly's eyes swam with tears. "The police pressured me into lying. They kept me at the station house for hours, asking the same questions over and over again. *What was he doing the whole time he was in the house with you? What do you mean you watched TV? Is that all? He didn't go out for a beer? Did he leave the house at any point? Why are you lying to us? We don't believe you. You'll be arrested for perjury. He must've left the house at some point.*" She wiped her nose with the back of her hand. "They didn't want the truth. They kept me locked inside this tiny room with nothing to drink, no pee break, no lawyer. I felt like a criminal. I was scared to death. It wore me down. I just wanted to go home. *What do you mean, he was with you the whole time? He must've gone out at some point. He went out, right?*" They were so convinced of his guilt, I figured… maybe if I told them what they wanted to hear, they'd lock him up and throw away the key, and I wouldn't have to deal with it anymore. You know? I thought about that real hard."

"Okay," Kate said softly. "But if he didn't do it, then who killed my sister? Who buried her in his backyard?"

"I don't know. He had plenty of enemies. He owed money all over town." Nelly shook her head. "But I'm telling you…

143

he never let me out of his sight. Always pawing at me. He wouldn't leave me alone."

"But the evidence against him was overwhelming," Kate argued. "His prints were on the shovel. His hair was tangled up in the rope." She paused a moment, thinking how best to explain. "Listen, I understand. Our memories can be tricky. How do you know you aren't confusing events, dates, places? There's something called false memory syndrome. Maybe deep down, you don't want to be held responsible for your uncle's execution?"

Nelly's mouth was pressed shut. She glared at Kate. At some point in therapy, all of Kate's patients glared at her like that. "Look, Dr. Wolfe. I'm not lying. My uncle was a brutal man. I hate him for what he did to me. But he didn't kill your sister. And I don't know who did. But whoever it is… he's still out there."

17

FIVE HOURS LATER, KATE was sitting cross-legged on their bedroom floor, about to lose her lunch. She tried calling James again, but it was going straight to voicemail.

There was an empty wine bottle and a plate of cigarette butts on the rug in front of her. There was a scrapbook full of pictures she'd been pawing through, faded color snapshots of her family on birthdays and holidays. Tension had built up behind Kate's eyes. It hurt to swallow. The grief was right there. So close. Her emotions were at a tipping point. But she refused to cry. She needed to handle this professionally. She had to hold it together.

The front door bumped open and shut. "Babe?" James called from the foyer.

"Oh my God. James? Where've you been? Why was your phone off? I've been trying to reach you for hours!"

He came to the doorway holding a paper bag from Safeway. "Sorry, sweetie. I forgot my charger. What's wrong? Are you okay?"

"Nelly Ward told me that Henry Blackwood didn't kill my sister… that whoever did it is still out there. She claims the police pressured her into lying, that she lied on the witness stand, and that he didn't leave her for six hours. She says he never left her alone for a second."

"Whoa, slow down." James came into the room, dropped the grocery bag on the bed, and sat down on the floor next to her. "Okay, first…" He cupped her face in his hands and lovingly kissed her.

She pulled away. "What if it's true? What if he didn't do it? What if they're about to execute an innocent man?"

He gave her a skeptical look. "Do you honestly believe that?"

Kate shook her head. "I don't know what to think anymore. I'm pretty convinced Nelly was telling the truth. She said her uncle was abusing her for years. That much rings true. But if he never left her side that day, then that means…"

"Hold on. This is classic guilt-driven behavior. She's probably having second thoughts about the execution. He was abusing her? Okay. But the jury saw all the evidence, Kate. It was a solid case. With or without her testimony."

"But she was so convincing…"

"She might believe it. Doesn't make it true."

"Right." She nodded reluctantly. "False memory syndrome. I did think of that."

"And besides, why hasn't she gone to the defense team with this information? That's the proper way to handle it. Why tell you and nobody else?"

"She's embarrassed…"

"Kate."

"You're right," she said with a heavy sigh. She squinted at him. "I couldn't reach you. Where were you? They said you left the hospital hours ago."

"I traded shifts with Peter and took some time off."

"You left work early?"

"I needed to clear my head. I had a few drinks. Hung out at Best Buy. You know. Guy stuff." He picked up the empty wine bottle. "Wow, too bad. We could've gotten wasted together."

"What's in the Safeway bag?"

He helped her to her feet, and they sat on the edge of the bed together. He overturned the bag, and a family-sized bag of Stay Puft marshmallows spilled out.

"Marshmallows?" Kate said. "Seriously?"

"I was drunk-shopping."

"I nearly lost my shit when I couldn't reach you."

"Sorry, babe. It won't happen again. I promise." He ripped the bag open. "Want one? They're like medicine."

"No, thanks."

"Come on. Can't I tempt you?" He popped one into his mouth. "Yum."

"So you went to a bar? You had a few drinks?"

"Listen, I've been thinking a lot about us lately. About our future. I can't imagine what you've been through, Kate… this whole ordeal with Nikki and the execution… so I have a suggestion."

"What?"

"Don't get mad at me, okay?"

"Just tell me."

147

"Maybe you aren't the right person to be treating Maddie Ward?"

"James…"

"Let's try to be objective about this. Look at how complicated it's getting."

"You're right. It is complicated. I've been sitting here thinking the very same thing. But then, I came to the conclusion that I shouldn't be making decisions based on Nelly's behavior. Maddie's just beginning to trust me. We've bonded. I know I can help her."

"If you think you're going to have one of those 'eureka' moments, I guarantee you, it'll break your heart. You know as well as I do we're just a part of the process when it comes to our patients. Most of them will be in and out of mental health facilities for the rest of their lives. We can't fix them all by ourselves. None of us is a miracle worker."

"She's only got five days left. Eight tops. We can't afford to change horses midstream."

"Kate…"

"I'm not going to let anything cloud my professional judgment, okay?" She could tell he'd given up arguing, because his shoulders slumped forward—that was his tell. She glanced at the marshmallows on the bed. "Is that your dinner?"

He kicked off his shoes. "Lie down next to me."

"James…"

"Lie down." He patted the mattress.

She heaved a sigh and settled in next to him. He wrapped his arms around her, and they breathed softly against one another.

"Let's not fight anymore," she said.

"Sorry, were we fighting?"

"Sort of."

"Ah. Then I have the solution." He reached for the bag of marshmallows. "We can't argue when our mouths are full of marshmallows. Come on. Join me in delicious goodness."

She giggled.

"You have the most incredible laugh."

She reached into the bag, and they ate marshmallows and watched the day's light dissolve into darkness.

The hurt was always there, like a round pebble she couldn't un-swallow. When Kate was a little girl, the world felt safe and welcoming, because it was limited to her house and her dolls and her parents and her pesky kid sister. It was popcorn and play dates and her dad singing "Whip It" by Devo in a goofy voice. But Kate had been forced to accept that life wasn't warm and fuzzy. At the tender age of sixteen, everything had turned darkly sinister. She stopped trusting people. She stopped believing in her father's infallibility. She no longer moved fluidly into her bright future without expecting to get hurt. Sometimes, it hurt badly.

On the day of her mother's funeral, twenty-two years ago, it rained heavily. Kate was a skinny ten-year-old, and the church doors wouldn't open. She shoved hard on the right-hand door, but it wouldn't budge. Was the church locked? She and Savannah pushed hard on the left-hand door, but it wouldn't open either. The girls panicked and shook both doors. "Let us in! Let us in!" Then their father demonstrated how to open it. *Pull, don't push.* Maybe that was a metaphor for life?

Inside the packed church, they sat next to each other in the front pew. Their father was so stripped of life, he could've been a corpse. Kate remembered thinking that her mother was more alive in death than their father was just then. And afterwards at the cemetery, when they lowered Julia's casket into the ground, Savannah had collapsed into Kate's arms. But years later, at Savannah's funeral, Kate had nobody's arms to fall into.

Now she had James.

She snuggled deeper into his embrace and closed her eyes.

18

ON SATURDAY MORNING, KATE woke up and squinted at the alarm clock. "Oh my God. I overslept!"

James was standing in front of the mirror, freshly shaved, showered, and ready for work. "Relax. You've got time."

"But the funeral's at ten!"

"I thought you said noon?"

"Oh shit. I was going to write something over coffee this morning." She leapt out of bed. "Nikki's mother asked me to say a few words."

"Okay, so? Plan B."

"That *was* Plan B."

He put on his tie, expertly shimmying the knot up to his neck. "How can I help?"

"I don't know. I've got writer's block. My head keeps filling up with clichés."

"Just express how you feel. Clichéd or not. Write what's in your heart."

She focused on his face. "Oh wow. I never thought of that."

He grinned. "Shut up."

"Can I quote you? 'Let yourself feel. Express what's in your heart.'"

"Yeah, I get it. I'm a pompous ass."

"Well, you got your PA from Harvard, didn't you?"

"Pompous Ass? Don't be absurd. Yale." He kissed her goodbye. "Relax. You'll do great, like always."

After he was gone, Kate ran around getting ready and wasted precious time debating with herself—gray, black or navy blue? What did people wear to funerals nowadays? She accidentally ripped her pantyhose and spent the next five minutes looking for a pair that didn't have any runs in it. She settled on a dove-gray suit. She didn't have time to make a cup of coffee.

As Kate drove out of the city she tried to shape a speech inside her head, but yesterday's conversation with Nelly kept crowding everything else out. She felt a stark churning in her stomach. What if James was wrong? What if Nelly was telling the truth? She'd let James reassure her, because he was her rock and she wanted to believe him. She didn't want to think Savannah's killer was still out there, abducting little girls. There had been a couple of slightly similar cases in Blunt River County over the past decade or so, and they'd both happened while Henry Blackwood was on death row. Still, that didn't mean much; teenage girls were often the target of predators.

She tapped the steering wheel, trying to remember the cases. Ten years ago, a hiker stumbled across the remains of a murdered teenager in The Balsams, a densely wooded area west of town. Fourteen-year-old Hannah Lloyd had been found strangled to death. The sensational murder trial dominated the news at the time. The defendant, a convicted pedophile and Hannah's next-door neighbor, had ultimately gone free when the trial ended in a hung jury. Before the DA could mount a second trial, the suspect shot himself in the head.

Then, about a year ago, fifteen-year-old Makayla Brayden went missing, and she had never been found. A $15,000 reward had been posted for information leading to an arrest. There was no reason to connect the two cases—Hannah Lloyd's killer was known, and according to the papers, Makayla Brayden took drugs and ran away from home, putting her at high risk for predation.

This line of thought wasn't getting her anywhere. Kate spotted a Dunkin' Donuts and pulled over. She hurried inside and bought a donut and a large coffee. Back inside the car, she opened her spiral notebook, dug a pen out of her bag, and stared at the blank page. *Write from the heart.*

Loss. Grief. Kate understood what it was like to lose a loved one. You shut down, you broke down, sometimes you screamed. You got angry with yourself and you got angry with God. You threatened to stop believing in Him, even though you were on the fence. You cursed Him out, you pleaded, you seriously lost your shit. You lost your appetite. You felt sorry for yourself. You felt sorry for the world. Why—this word rang out inside your head like a cathedral bell. *Why why why?* Why was this beautiful person gone? Why did the universe allow it? You hated this hollow feeling. You hated the sun for rising. Sunsets made you cry. Nights were hard. Weeks passed and the hurt didn't get any better.

She checked her dashboard clock. Time to go. She'd written two barely legible pages, which she jammed into her bag. She hadn't touched the donut. She capped her coffee and took off.

Ten minutes later, she heard church bells ringing in the pricey Boston suburb where the McCormacks lived. It was a gorgeous February morning, sunny and breezy. Gas-guzzlers competed for space with hybrids in the church parking lot. A large crowd had gathered in front of the church—Nikki's family and friends, her neighbors and classmates, many holding one another for comfort. Kate found a parking space and joined the crowd, worried what they would think of her once she'd introduced herself. *Oh, you're the shrink who couldn't save Nikki.*

Savannah's funeral had been crammed with strangers—reporters and camera crews straining at the barricades, volunteers and well-wishers from all over. The Blunt River Police had done their very best to protect Kate and her father from media scrutiny, but a good story was hard to ignore. Their dumbstruck faces were plastered all over the nightly news, shots taken as they scurried up the church steps or led the funeral procession. In those grainy images, Kate looked like a child experiencing adult pain for the very first time.

Now her nerves were frayed. The notes she'd made for her speech were crumpled up in the bottom of her bag. Nikki's biological father stepped out of the crowd and greeted her warmly.

"Dr. Wolfe, thanks for coming." He gave her a hug. "Nikki adored you. She learned so much about herself in her sessions with you." He had short red hair and hazel eyes that were shot

154

through with broken blood vessels. He was a couple of years older than Kate, but so deferential and full of goodwill that he made her feel ancient.

Other introductions were made, more kind words were exchanged, and then Kate followed the other mourners into the church. A rose-draped cherry-wood coffin was propped in front of the altar, in between an arrangement of balloons and a large glossy photo of Nikki—her high school picture. Kate happened to know that Nikki hated this picture, which she claimed made her look like an artificial person.

Kate found a seat next to some of Nikki's cousins, while the minister took his place behind the carved mahogany pulpit and said, "We're gathered here today to celebrate a precious life, one that was taken too soon from this world…"

He spoke for twenty comforting minutes, before introducing Nikki's creative writing teacher, a middle-aged woman who spoke about Nikki's great gifts as a writer. Next came Nikki's best friend from high school, a pink-haired girl with kohl-rimmed eyes who told stories about her BFF's sneaky sense of mischief. More friends and relatives spoke, and then it was Kate's turn.

On her way to the podium, she thought about Nikki's fondness for licorice whips and *Minecraft*. She liked to say "fuck-a-duck." She liked to dress all in white with blood-drop earrings, like Dracula's bride. Kate knew a few things about Nikki that she couldn't share with this audience: she'd taken ecstasy more than once; she'd called her mother a cold, uncaring bitch; she blamed her stepfather for drinking too much. She loved them both, but they wouldn't let her be herself. She felt like a loser half the time. The other half, she felt like Miss Universe. She had self-destructive mood swings. One week she'd post a hundred selfies on Instagram but the next week she'd cancel her account.

Kate couldn't publicly reveal what had caused Nikki's initial break with reality eight months ago. Last year, she'd developed a crush on a boy at school who didn't love her back. For months, Kate had been piecing together the girl's shattered psyche while explaining that sometimes our love wasn't reciprocated.

Now her mind went blank as she took her place behind the podium and looked at the congregation. The pressure was intense. Two-hundred-plus people waited for her to cough up an explanation. *Finally, here's an expert who can tell us what went wrong. Finally, someone with all the answers.*

But honestly, what could Kate say? She had no idea why Nikki had chosen to end her life at such a time, in such a way.

She took a deep breath. "The worst thing I can say about Nikki is that her illness finally won. The best thing I can say about her is… well, there are so many best things. Her smile lit up half the planet. She radiated a wonderful self-possessed energy. I'll never forget the day she came into my office, soaking wet. It was early September, one of those warm Indian summers, and she'd forgotten her umbrella. I offered her my sweater but she refused. She told me that she loved the feeling of being so close to nature that you were immersed in it. That day we talked about her future… she was so excited about the countless possibilities ahead of her.

We made a lot of plans. She dazzled me with her enthusiasm.

"Part of what made Nikki so special is the same thing that took her down—her illness. She had visions, good and bad. She had up-days and down-days. The down-days were rough. But the up-days were remarkable. Not too long ago, she came into my office holding an imaginary kitten. And by the end of the session, I was holding that kitten in my lap." Kate smiled. "Of course, I gave it back. Reluctantly."

Smiles rippled through the congregation. Standing at the back of the church was an older man who nodded as she glanced his way. He seemed awfully familiar, but she couldn't seem to place him.

"One day, Nikki came to me with a school assignment. The students in class were supposed to come up with their own epitaphs. She already had hers. 'Here lies Nikki McCormack— there was nobody braver.' And she was. Brave. Funny. Fearless. Bold. Smart. Sensitive. Inquisitive. Courageous. And maybe we can all honor her memory today by being just as brave as she was. At least, I'm going to try."

Kate felt emotionally raw as she picked up the rumpled pieces of paper and made her way back to her seat. A group of Nikki's classmates got up to sing "Angel" by Sarah McLachlan. When it was over, there wasn't a dry eye in the house.

The minister thanked everyone for coming. The ceremony was over. The heart-shaped balloons were taken outside and released. Kate had done her very best. She only hoped it was enough.

19

OUTSIDE, THE CROWD DISPERSED as people got in their cars and drove across town toward the cemetery. A winter storm was moving in swiftly. Clouds rolled like a herd of buffalo along the horizon.

The burial was deeply moving. People sang and recited poetry. Soon it began to snow—the angels were weeping, Nikki's cousins all agreed. At the end, Nikki's mother broke down, weeping uncontrollably and sitting cross-legged in the snow. Nikki's father and stepfather escorted her back to the embrace of her family, where she was engulfed and smothered into silence.

A catered luncheon was served at the McCormacks' postmodern home in their exclusive Newton neighborhood. Kate couldn't help but notice the sturdy cedar beam that ran across the living room ceiling where Nikki had hanged herself. How were they ever going to live underneath that beam?

She wandered around the house, finding all the proof she needed that Nikki's parents had doted on her—expensively framed childhood drawings, family photos trapped in Plexiglas cubes, bookshelves dedicated to Nikki's honors and awards, ribbons for perfect attendance and certificates of achievement, trophies for soccer and track-and-field. Hanging on a peg in the mudroom was Nikki's red vinyl jacket, and underneath the Shaker-style bench were her battered Converses, knotted together at the laces like an old married couple.

Nikki's stepfather, George, was a tax attorney who had spared no expense for his only stepchild. It was painfully obvious that her parents—all three of these hurting people—cared deeply about Nikki, despite the ugliness of the divorce.

Outside, the snow flew about as if in celebration. Inside, people gathered together in small groups, talking softly. Kate found herself involved in a revolving conversation about loss and grief. She followed her attorney's advice and let the McCormacks take the lead.

She eventually found herself in the family room, which a handful of teenagers had taken over, texting and playing video games. One of the boys picked up a red rubber ball so cracked with age it looked like a huge blood-soaked eyeball, and tossed it to one of the girls. They all ignored Kate, so she left and wandered down another hallway lined with pictures of Nikki at various stages of development—pudgy toddler, skinny tomboy, gawky tween, beautiful swan. Kate took out her phone and texted James. *Very sad. Lovely people. Great eulogies. Did my best. Spoke from heart.*

Lunch was served. People stood around eating quarter-sandwiches and arugula salad off of paper plates, awkwardly balancing their wine glasses and plastic utensils.

James texted her back: *Bedlam here. Miss you.*

Once it stopped snowing, the young people went outside.

Kate watched from the French doors as Nikki's friends remembered her in their own special way, laughing and sobbing, dueling breath clouds painting the air. They threw snowballs and traded war stories, and Kate found their raucous grief to be much more honest than the long faces indoors.

After a moment, she sensed a presence watching her and turned to find the older man she'd seen at church standing six feet away. He was in his mid-sixties and seemed very comfortable in his own weather-beaten skin. He was tall, like her father, but more muscular, formidable and square-jawed. He had a leathery, old-school style that reminded her of a character actor from a black-and-white western. Strong, proud, confident. Not ashamed to be different. He wore a fringed calfskin jacket and a bolo tie. He was idiosyncratic, and yet he radiated a temperate kind of professionalism.

"Hello, Dr. Wolfe," he said.

"Sorry, have we met?"

"Palmer Dyson." He reached out to shake her hand. His grip was firm. "I was one of the detectives on your sister's case."

Kate felt the surprise in her gut. She'd met him sixteen years ago, only he'd been much younger then, and thinner, with short dark hair and long ugly sideburns. He had worn sharkskin suits—none of these cowboy trappings.

Detective Palmer Dyson had been one of dozens of investigators working on her sister's case—a polite, respectful, observant man who stayed mostly in the background. In contrast, she vividly recalled the lead detective, Ray Matthews, a scary-looking older guy with ginger hair and acne scars, who'd passed away a few years ago. And then there was the rookie detective, Cody Dunmeyer, now the chief of police, a handsome young man who'd managed to soothe Kate's frazzled nerves while asking her some very probing questions. And last but not least was the medical examiner, Quade Pickler, with his outdated mullet hairdo and his cynical, mistrustful eyes—he was the one who'd gotten so upset when she peeked through the cracked-open morgue door.

So many professionals had been involved it was hard to keep track of them all. The FBI initially, because of the kidnapping angle, and the Blunt River PD, but also state troopers, social workers, members of the medical examiner's office, volunteers from various missing-persons organizations, attorneys from the prosecutor's office, private detectives, and the media. Kate had forgotten most of them in the blur of activity surrounding Savannah's death.

She would probably have forgotten Dyson, except that he hadn't allowed her to. Over the years, she'd received dozens of letters from him requesting a meeting to discuss an important matter involving her sister's case. He signed his name with a flourish—*Palmer.* She'd thrown all his letters away, along with hundreds of other requests from people wanting to "discuss" the case with her: reporters on deadlines, authors with book proposals, psychics with visions, anti-death-penalty advocates with an agenda, true-crime bloggers, serial-killer fanatics, and various assorted freaks too scary to mention. She didn't want to talk to any of them. She didn't want to talk to Detective Dyson now.

"Sorry," she said. "I didn't recognize you."

"Been a long time."

"You used to have sideburns."

"Oh yeah, the sideburns." He laughed. "A holdover from the seventies. I have a tendency to hang onto things beyond their expiration date."

She smiled nervously. "What are you doing here?"

"Nikki's uncle." He pointed out a gray-haired man across the room. "He used to work for the district attorney's office in Concord."

"Oh."

"Nelly Ward tells me you're Maddie's psychiatrist now?"

Kate was taken aback. "She told you that?"

"It's a small world in our little corner of New Hampshire. Probably one of the reasons you left, I'm guessing. Everybody knows everyone else's business. Claustrophobic for some. Paradise for others." He smiled. "Like I said, I have a tendency to hang onto things. For instance, your sister's case."

Kate stared at him. Maybe this was how police detectives operated, especially detectives who held onto sixteen-year-old closed murder cases. They poked their nose into your business and wrote you letters, inviting you to meetings you'd never attend. They asked you to revisit what was dead and buried in your head, if not your heart. They had ulterior motives.

"Look, Dr. Wolfe, I'm sorry to bother you." He placed his hand on her arm, and it was like being courted by a civilized bear. "I don't know if you've read any of my letters, but I've been investigating some unsolved cases involving local girls gone missing. You may have heard of some of them. Makayla Brayden, for instance, who was from Blunt River. But there have been others, lesser known, from nearby towns... Anyway, I believe I see a pattern."

"I have to go," Kate said, feeling panicky and hemmed in. It was strange to hear Makayla's name so soon after thinking about the case herself. She looked around for an exit.

"That's okay. I get it."

"Excuse me?"

"You don't want to deal with it."

"I don't know how to respond to that," she said angrily. "As for your letters, I threw them all away. I'm trying to move on with my life."

"Fair enough."

"Now if you'll excuse me..."

"I didn't mean to insult you." Again, he rested his hand on her arm. "Indulge me for a moment. It's just that Nelly has confided in me a good deal these past few years. And just recently she told me that she lied on the witness stand sixteen years ago. She insists they locked up the wrong guy."

Kate's heart was thundering. "How can you even say that!"

A few people turned to stare. She stormed off in search of her coat, but the detective followed her to the sunroom, where outerwear was piled high on a beige loveseat.

"Please, let me explain," he said as she rummaged through the pile, pulling at parkas and wool jackets in search of her camel-hair Hugo Boss, the one that had cost her a mint. "I don't mean to impose on you," he said softly. "But if I could just have a minute of your time…"

"You've taken all the minutes I can spare." She found her coat.

"Here. Let me help you with that." He tried to take it away from her.

"No thanks, I've got it." She snatched the coat away and put it on. "Excuse me," she said and made her way to the front door and out of the suffocating house.

The detective caught up with Kate at the bottom of the driveway. "Dr. Wolfe? One last thing. I'd like to explain how your sister changed my life."

Kate froze—it was such a hurtful thing to say. "Did you put her up to this?"

"Sorry—what?"

"Nelly Ward? Did you convince her to bring her daughter to Boston for treatment?"

"No." He drew back, seemingly deeply offended. "Not at all. I bumped into Nelly yesterday, and she told me what was going on. I'm a detective. I'm nosy. It's either a blessing or a curse, depending on your perspective. Look. Can we discuss this over coffee?"

"I really have to go," she said stiffly.

"Just to be clear, I had nothing to do with Nelly's decision to drive down to Boston," he said emphatically. "It's none of my damn business. Maddie's a sweet kid who for some reason keeps hurting herself. That's all I know. I didn't mean to upset you. It certainly wasn't my intent. I'm not good with people, I guess."

She got in her car, slammed the door and buckled up. He tapped on her window, and she rolled it down.

"Look, here's my card."

She accepted it wordlessly, hoping to get rid of him.

"I understand evil, Dr. Wolfe. I have lived with it. I have hunted it down. And believe me… there's a killer out there. Unknown, unsuspected, uncaught. Call me if you change your mind."

20

IT WAS PSYCH 101. When faced with an unpleasant truth they weren't equipped to handle, most people ran away. Kate found herself running home to Blunt River, New Hampshire. She had a powerful urge to visit her father, since he was the only person who understood her losses as deeply as she did.

Downtown Blunt River was a bustling commercial district full of restaurants, cafés and boutiques, with lots of pedestrians milling about—mostly college students and office workers. The streets unfolded in a grid pattern, neat as a Monopoly board. Many of the historic shoe factories had been repurposed into high-end condos and office parks, but despite the modernized sheen, nothing of significance had changed over the past couple of decades. The Stoned Café was as popular as ever. The retro movie theater was showing a Fellini retrospective. The Thyme-to-Eat Diner was open for business, a decadent high-fat eatery where the waitresses called you "dollface."

Kate turned off the main drag and drove past the mom-and-pop stores where she and her friends used to hang out after school: the vintage clothing boutique, the indie record store, the cozy feminist bookshop where she and her BFF Heather drank organic coffee, thinking it made them look sophisticated and grown-up.

She left downtown behind and took a meandering three-mile route back to her old neighborhood. She spotted the yellow-brick funeral home where they'd picked up Julia's ashes, and a dull ache settled in her stomach. On the drive home, Savannah had insisted on holding the cardboard box in her lap. She kept shaking it to confirm that it contained their mother's ashes, with maybe a few bits of bone. See, Kate? Do you hear that? Shake-shake-shake. And Kate had been mortified but fascinated, which explained her half-hearted attempts to stop her sister. Their father hadn't said a word. Savannah kept shaking the box, trying to provoke a reaction out of him. It didn't work. Anything—even a bark of anger—would've been preferable to that stony silence.

She drove past snowy fields and dense woods, sycamores and hemlocks swaying in the wind, skeins of snow blowing off their branches like the Dance of the Seven Veils. Almost home. Her stomach sparked with every passing landmark.

Her apprehension ticked up a notch as she rode the three hills up and down. Her father's house was a renovated gem of salvaged lumber painted deep forest green with stone-gray trim, a combination of colors that pulled the harmony out of the wood and created the illusion of coziness and warmth. The house could've been torn from the pages of *Country Living* magazine, but it was all smoke and mirrors. Her father lived here alone. His family had fled.

She pulled into the slushy driveway and parked behind

his Ford Ranger. She took a sharp breath and got out. The cold winter air smelled crisp and delicious. Emerald rows of evergreens defined the white hillsides.

Bram Wolfe came to the door with a plastered-on smile, which surprised her. She never knew what kind of mood he'd be in. Today, he seemed happy to see her. Maybe this time would be different? After her last visit, she'd been depressed for days. Her relationship with James had been pretty new back then; she could remember complaining to him, "I keep expecting my relationship with my father to improve, but it never does."

"Doing the same thing over and over, and expecting different results, is the very definition of insanity," James had joked. He hadn't meant her to take it seriously, but she hadn't been back in three years.

Her father wore a woolly sweater, tweed slacks and polished loafers. He had a perspiring face and a prominent aristocratic nose. His shoulder-length hair had gone completely white, and he tucked it behind his rather large ears. He was tall, and like most tall men, he had a tendency to slouch. Kate had never been able to find herself in him—she took after Julia, thank God. Both she and Savannah shared their mother's heart-shaped face, her slender frame, her ballerina-like grace and excitable laugh.

"Hey, Dad," she said with a wave. "How are you?"

"Fine. You?"

"Good."

"How was the drive?"

"Can't complain."

His self-consciousness was contagious. He crossed his arms, and then uncrossed them, while she wobbled the last few yards across the snow and tripped up the porch steps, where she planned on greeting him with a hug. But he beat her to it, gripping her by the elbow and reeling her in, pulling her towards him and giving her a chaste peck on the cheek—except they both moved their heads at the same time and accidentally locked lips.

"Oh sheesh," she muttered. "Let's pretend *that* never happened." She laughed and wiped her mouth. *Oh God, I'm home.* His lips were papery dry. "James wanted to come," she lied, "but there was a crisis at the hospital."

"Oh. Well, I hope everything's okay."

She shrugged. "The locked unit is a cornucopia of alternate realities."

He either missed the irony or ignored it. "I don't see a ring yet."

She'd taken off her birthday ring, hoping to avoid this very question. "Nope," she said with a shrug. "I'd tell you if I was getting married, Dad."

He nodded slowly. "I see."

What did he see? What did he understand about her? What had he ever understood about her?

"Maybe next time you can bring James," Bram said.

"Oh. Absolutely. He wants to meet you."

"I'd like to meet him, as well."

Her stomach tensed—well, was that it? Had they already run out of things to say?

"Come inside," he said.

The front hallway was clean and tidy. Her father's winter coat hung from the iron coat rack, and his well-insulated boots were tucked underneath the pine bench like battle-hardened soldiers awaiting orders. The woven Navaho basket held today's mail. The ceramic Chinese bowl cradled his car keys and spare change.

Kate stomped the snow off her boots, shrugged out of her coat and placed everything next to her father's. Then she followed him into the living room, where the gauzy curtains hung like ghosts, catching the silvery winter light. The house was large and airy, with lots of dark colonial furniture and ever-growing piles of books and magazines.

"You're looking well, Kate."

"You too, Dad."

Okay. How many more bland pleasantries were they going to exchange? She had to break through this wall of avoidance if it killed her. "Well, Dad, I figured it's been a couple of years since we last saw each other."

"Three."

"Right. Three years. That's a long time."

"Glass of wine?" he offered politely.

"Sure." She collapsed in the wingback chair, her favorite piece in the room. Savannah had preferred to snuggle up on the velvet sofa next to the French doors, where she'd do her homework by the dying light of day.

"Be right back." He disappeared into the kitchen, and she could hear him uncork a bottle of wine and fetch the long-stemmed glasses from the china cabinet. "How was your trip?" he asked her—again—through the open doorway.

"Uneventful," she responded.

"That's good."

Next they'd be talking about the weather.

The house was so quiet. No music, no pets. Just her dad and his beloved solitude. She got up and studied the family portrait above the mantelpiece. There was ten-year-old Kate before her mother had killed herself. What a happy-go-lucky kid. No suicide cuts. No evidence of self-harm. In the painting, her parents were smiling, and Kate's arm was draped protectively around Savannah's shoulders. It made her want to scream, "Take better care of her! She's fragile!"

"Lunch is served," Bram announced.

Kate joined him in the dining room, where the table was set with the good china. Lunch was cold salmon and artichoke salad. "Wow. I wasn't expecting this," she said, pleased he'd made an effort. Usually they shared leftovers from the fridge. "Thanks, Dad."

"Well, today is a special occasion." He handed her a glass of wine.

"Special?"

"As you say, we haven't seen each other in quite some time. Cheers."

They clinked glasses and chatted about mindless things. Catching-up things. Whatever-happened-to sort of things. He watched her keenly as the conversation meandered over familiar territory—friends, relatives, local businesses changing hands, obituaries. Finally, they ran out of topics.

Kate tensed, not knowing where to begin. How to broach the subject. So she ran headlong into it and said, "Henry Blackwood's going to be executed soon."

Bram nodded solemnly. "Next week."

"Did you get an invitation from the Department of Corrections?"

"I threw it away."

"Me too."

"I'd be satisfied just to hear about it on the news."

"Dad?" she hedged. "Do you think it's possible he didn't do it?"

He stared at her. He put down his fork. An oppressive weariness came over him. "Who've you been talking to? Is it those anti-death-penalty people? They're relentless. That's why I screen my calls."

"No," she muttered. "It's just that over the years, a few other girls from the area have gone missing… or turned up dead… Hannah Lloyd and Makayla Brayden… and I was wondering if you thought it was possible—"

"No," he said stiffly. "Not possible."

"But, Dad…"

"I don't want to talk about this, Kate."

She felt his anger like a splash of cold water.

"Is that why you came home? Because you're wasting your time."

"Wasting my time?" she repeated. James was right. Nothing ever changed.

They ate the rest of their meal in sullen silence. In between bites, her father gazed out the window. As the silence solidified between them, he began to relax. His shoulders lost their tension. His face released its tight lines. He seemed to take comfort in the growing distance between them.

A sourness settled into her stomach. Back in Boston, Kate was a doctor. Here, she was a doctor's daughter. Back in Boston, she cured sick children. Here, her sick mother could never be cured. Here she was an object of pity. A nobody. A nothing.

After lunch, she went upstairs to wash up. The floorboards creaked in all the familiar places as she approached Savannah's bedroom at the end of the hallway. She paused on the threshold and recalled the night she'd lost her little shadow.

Where are we going, Kate? What's the big deal?

Shh. Promise you won't tell.

I won't! I promise.

We'll get into trouble if Dad finds out.

I won't tell a soul! Where are we going?

Savannah had been bursting with excitement at the prospect of a nighttime car ride. *Yay! Cool!* She was up for anything. Their father was working late, as usual, and Kate had just gotten her driver's license.

Can you keep a secret?

Yes!

It's totally confidential.

My lips are sealed. See? I'm throwing away the key.

Now Kate went over to the bureau where Savannah's old Magic Eight Ball sat gathering dust. She picked it up and turned it over. *Reply hazy, try again.* Savannah's beat-up skateboard stood on its leading edge in a corner of the room. Her old-fashioned canopy bed held a jumble of Barbies and Cabbage Patch dolls. On the nightstand was her cherished Hello Kitty backpack, its yellow Nickelodeon button still pinned to the strap. The room hadn't changed in sixteen years. Savannah would've been twenty-eight years old today. A beautiful swan.

Kate put the Magic Eight Ball down and opened the dusty cigar box full of things her sister used to collect—marbles, feathers, insect casings, a headless doll. The china doll used to be hers, except one day it disappeared. Kate only found out where it went after Savannah's death. The doll minus its head belonged to Savannah now.

She went to stand in front of the drafty old-fashioned windows overlooking the backyard. Through hairline cracks in the glass, she spotted her favorite tree—a muscular oak with fort-like branches. And there was the old shed where they stashed their bikes and roller-skates. Nothing had changed, and yet her sister's absence was deafening.

She felt a chill creep over her as she hurried downstairs. "Dad?"

"In the living room." He'd settled into his favorite armchair, a cracked-leather monstrosity. His polished loafers were parked on the threadbare rug and his feet were crossed on the matching ottoman. His socks were brown. He rested heavy sections of *The New York Times* in his lap and peered at her over his reading glasses. He wore a look of polite resistance—she was interfering with his routine.

"Can we talk?" she asked. "I mean *really* talk?"

He shook his head. "Not about that."

"No, Dad," she agreed. "Not about that."

"Because I refuse to pick at old scabs."

"Okay. No picking. I promise."

"All right." He put the newspaper down. "I'm all ears." He had aged quite a bit in her absence. His hairline had receded, his paunch was a little rounder, and his jowls sagged. Gravity was winning.

She plopped down in the wingback chair and confessed, "It's been hard for me to come home after having lost so much at such a young age… It's not easy to overcome."

"No," he said soberly. "I don't expect it would be."

"But I have a few questions about those early years. Do you mind?"

He shrugged. "I'm not sure I have any answers, but go ahead."

"I remember feeling an undercurrent of tension between you and Mom."

"I loved your mother."

"I know. But she wasn't always happy, was she?"

He shrugged. "Nobody's happy all the time."

"True. But I sensed she wasn't happy in her marriage."

He rested one mottled hand over the other. "I can be a difficult guy," he admitted.

"I realize her illness must've been hard on you…"

"I think that's why you became a psychiatrist, Kate. To find out what went wrong."

"Maybe," she hedged. "But I also wanted to be a doctor like you."

"Ah." He nodded, as if he hadn't thought of it before. Despite the fact that she'd asked for a stethoscope for her fifth birthday. The year after that, it was a microscope, so she could start preparing for her medical degree.

"What else would you like to talk about? You have my undivided attention."

She gave him a skeptical look. "Undivided?"

"Why? Don't you think I'm listening?"

"Half of you is listening. The other half is dying to get back to the book review."

He clasped his hands over the newspaper as if to prove that he didn't care, but they both knew it wasn't true. "I'm listening, Kate," he said with a rubbery edge to his voice.

She heaved a frustrated sigh. "You may be listening, Dad, but we aren't exactly connecting, are we?"

He squinted at her. "Is that my fault?"

"You have to admit, you were never the easiest person to get along with."

"True."

"And this is probably the longest conversation we've had in… I don't know how many years."

He shrugged. "I'm a busy guy. You're a busy gal."

Kate leaned back in her chair. "You never remarried," she said. "Why not?"

"I never felt the urge, I guess. I loved your mother. That was enough."

"I remember the two of you fighting a lot."

"We didn't fight."

"Bickering. Arguing. Having a lot of disagreements."

"'A lot' is a relative term," he said. "To a child, it might seem like a lot. It was probably average."

"That's true."

"Thanks, Kate. I'm glad that I could be right about something."

"Sorry, was I being critical?"

"No. Just exacting. Like me." He smiled.

"What precipitated Mom's breakdown?"

"Don't you remember? She became depressed to the point where she started hearing voices telling her to leave me. To leave us." He squirmed. "Feels like I'm on the hot seat."

"You said we could talk—"

"Relax. I was joking."

"How am I supposed to know when you're joking?"

"You don't know?" he asked with disappointed eyes.

"No. You're always so serious."

His shoulders slouched. "I thought you knew me better than that."

"I never know when you're joking," she admitted.

"Never? That's pretty definitive."

She felt defeated. "Well, anyway. Thanks, Dad. I really appreciate it. You look tired. Maybe we should call it quits?"

"Are you sure?"

"Yeah."

"Wait here. I've got something for you." He put down the

paper and stood up. His tallness always startled her, like a human jack-in-the-box. He moved with awkward strides through the arched doorway that separated the living room from the dining room, and headed toward the back of the house.

About ten years ago, Bram had converted the old-fashioned parlor into a bedroom, moving all his belongings downstairs so he wouldn't have to leave the first floor again. His excuse was that it saved on the heating bills, but it was one of those eccentricities that had taken her by surprise. No matter how much Kate thought she knew her father, he always managed to confound her. The downstairs "bedroom" had no door and was quite messy, which she considered proof of his aloofness and isolation. Proof that he never had visitors over. Someone as private as her father would never set up a bedroom on the first floor and leave it doorless if he planned on having guests for dinner.

She could hear him rummaging around inside his makeshift bedroom. Dresser drawers scraped open. A wooden chair was dragged across the floor. Something dropped and ping-ponged across the rug.

A few grunts and another couple of bumps later, and he was back with his right arm extended. "Here. Take this," he said. "It was your mother's. I'm sure she'd want you to have it, Kate."

She held out her hand, and he dropped something into it— her mother's wedding ring. A modest diamond set in a simple gold band. "Oh, Dad," she gasped.

"Happy birthday."

She studied the ring in the palm of her hand and

remembered how badly her mother's fingers used to itch. It got so bad sometimes that Julia would tuck the ring away in her jewelry box and whisper, "Shh. Don't tell Daddy."

She wanted to show him how moved she was by this gesture; he rarely gave her anything personal. But she reacted initially with deep-seated cynicism—he had to be kidding. Seriously, a wedding ring? *Here ya go, you and James can get hitched now.* Hint hint. Then her cynicism transformed into smoldering resentment. Bram Wolfe was not a subtle man. It was obvious he disapproved of Kate and James living together without a marriage license. Her feelings morphed again uncomfortably. As a psychiatrist, she couldn't help but notice the subconscious incestuous underpinnings of such an act. Metaphorically speaking. Father gives daughter a wedding ring.

But no, that was ridiculous. Finally she allowed herself to be moved by this rare show of emotional vulnerability. *Here's something I can give you that I think you might like—it belonged to your mother.*

"Let me tell you a story," he said, taking his seat. "When I first met your mother I was just starting out. My mentor, one of the town's few family physicians at the time, had just asked me to take over his practice. He was retiring, so I moved down here from Maine. It wasn't easy. I had to take out a large loan, and I could barely afford to hire a secretary, but somehow I managed. Anyway, this beautiful young woman came to me one day, complaining of a bad cold. I prescribed a bottle of cough syrup and promptly told her I wouldn't be treating her anymore. She took offense and asked why. I told her—'Because

I'd like to ask you out on a date.'" Kate smiled, even though she'd heard it a million times. "Six months later, I bought your mother that ring."

Kate gazed at the tarnished wedding ring.

"So when you ask why haven't I gotten married again? Perhaps it's because that kind of love is very rare."

There was a long pause, while the tick-tock of the grandfather clock stretched, and everything inside her head crackled like frost. Her father did have a heart, after all. Why did she need to be reminded of that?

"It's so quiet in here," she whispered after a moment.

"I enjoy the silence. I'm used to it."

"Don't you ever get lonely?"

He shrugged. "I don't think about it."

"There's a big world out there, Dad."

He squinted at her as if she'd gone out of focus. "Kate, I have a passport. I've been to Rome, Paris, and the Virgin Islands. I watch HBO and Showtime. Just because I never moved out of Blunt River doesn't make me a rube."

"No, I didn't mean that…"

"I have a full and busy life," he said defensively.

"What I meant was… I'm sorry we've been out of touch."

"Me too." He made a big show of picking up his newspaper and snapping it open. "I imagine you'll be getting back to Boston soon?"

"Yes." She understood something just then. For years she'd desperately wanted her father to love and accept her, but the truth was she didn't fully accept and love him. She used to, before her mother had committed suicide. But then, as her father gradually pulled away from her, so Kate had pulled away from him.

With great reluctance, she got up to leave. He followed her into the foyer and watched as she put on her coat and boots. She found her car keys in her pocket and said, "Call me once in a while, okay?"

"You never pick up."

"Leave a message. I'll call you back."

"Maybe the lines of communication aren't so much broken," he said, "as they are clogged. Like bad arteries."

"Well, you're a physician." She smirked. "Isn't there a pill for that?"

"I wish there was." He gave her a genuinely relaxed smile. "See you later, sweetheart."

"Later, Dad." She kissed his cheek. "I love you."

"Love you, too."

The rarity of the exchange dragged through her like a bullet.

21

KATE SAT IN HER car with the engine running, not ready to leave Blunt River just yet. It had all happened for her here—first crush, first kiss, first prom. Half of her childhood friends were still listed in the Blunt River phone book. Her kindergarten buddy Marigold Hotchkiss lived in that peeling Gothic with the plastic Santa propped in the front yard. Her best friend from high school, Heather, was a hugely successful real estate agent who hadn't let Kate's tragedy prevent her from earning a juicy commission on Henry Blackwood's "house of death." Kate's arch rival from the fifth grade, Jewel Curtis, taught self-defense for girls and used Savannah's story as part of her marketing strategy. The first boy Kate had ever kissed—whose kisses she'd once treasured—was now the town treasurer. Funny how life rambled on.

She backed out of the driveway and honked goodbye. On an impulse, she took a left instead of a right at the blinking yellow light and headed for the thickly wooded area west of town called The Balsams, a wilderness preserve boasting 8,000 acres of mature hardwoods, trout streams, and recreational trails.

Fifteen minutes later, she located the old logging road and

drove for a mile or so along a bumpy gravel road, tires popping over icy patches until she finally rolled to a stop. She sat shivering inside her car as the engine ticked down and couldn't believe she was here. The cabin in the woods. Why had she come?

She hadn't been back since *that* night. She got out of her car and headed north through the woods, where the snowdrifts were over a foot deep in places. People rarely came out this way in the winter, but the warmer months were another matter. The old logging road used to be a lovers' lane, and the cabin had once been popular among high school students looking for a place to party after the big game. Now it was a favorite Halloween haunt. Local kids held séances in the old cabin, hoping to conjure up the dead. Savannah Wolfe had become something of a legend around here—an amusement for some, a campfire story for others. The cabin in the woods was almost as good as Haunted Acres out on Route 27. Her little sister had been turned into fear porn. The thought of it was crushing.

Kate hiked another twenty yards or so through the prison-bar tree trunks on an exhausting trek through the knee-deep snow. She was perspiring heavily under her winter clothes by the time she reached the cabin. She stepped onto the dilapidated porch and waited for her heart rate to slow down. The battered door was wide open, as if the cabin had been expecting her.

She shivered as she crossed the threshold, and one of the floorboards made an audible *crack* like a gunshot. The walls were covered with graffiti. The floor was carpeted with crushed beer cans and fossilized condoms. The roof had been leaking for decades and was pocked with holes large enough to invite in hanging vines; rusty clumps of dead foliage that swayed from the ceiling like broken chandeliers. More vines grew in through the shattered windows and crawled across the floor, where they clutched cigarette packs and empty beer cans like obstinate drunks, refusing to leave after last call.

It was so gloomy inside the cabin that she dug the keys out of her coat pocket, turned on the halogen penlight attached to her keychain, and directed the small beam over the graffiti on the walls. Names. Dates. Insults. She could make out peace signs and penises, four-leaf clovers and middle fingers, words of both love and hate. Icy water seeping down from the ceiling hit the frozen puddles on the floor, each drop echoing loudly. If the local kids had managed to summon Savannah with their candles and Ouija boards, then Kate wished to release her.

The week she was killed, the media had swarmed into town like flies—bribing the residents of Blunt River for any tidbit of information about the dead girl. They were ecstatic when they found out about Julia's tragic death, feeding off her suicide for weeks; they knew how long it took for a person to drown, and what she had been wearing the night she jumped in the river. They found out who Kate and Savannah's best friends were, what kind of grades they got, and the fact that they walked past Henry Blackwood's house every day on their way to school. For the longest time Kate wanted them dead. She guessed it was easier to shoot the messengers than the murderer on death row.

A whispery kind of creepiness brushed against her skin as

she recalled that long-ago August night. The summer trees were silhouetted against the dying sky, and there was a poignant finality to the day. They'd left the car parked on the narrow logging road and walked into the woods together, sharing a single flashlight between them. The bugs were biting. After a few minutes of scratching, Savannah began to whine. She'd wanted to tag along so badly, but now she was bored and itchy.

The dank-smelling cabin hadn't been as decrepit as it was now—the roof was intact and the windows weren't all broken. Most of the kids were down by the lake, which was the cool new hangout that summer. The cabin was so yesterday. Good for Halloween scares and late-night bull sessions for the stoners who weren't part of the in-crowd, but not much else.

It was eight o'clock by the time Kate and Savannah got there, and the older kids wouldn't be showing up until after midnight to drink beer and smoke pot and talk trash. For now it was just Kate and her little sister—and the cute boy who'd been waiting for her to show up. He was surprised to see Savannah. "What's she doing here?" he asked, sounding miffed.

Kate tried to explain about their father, how he sometimes disappeared unpredictably, and how she couldn't just leave her sister home alone. How she'd broken all the rules to be with him tonight.

As the horizon faded from orange to purple, the cute boy persuaded her to come with him into a clearing in the woods, not far away from the cabin, where they could be alone. He had a dazzling smile. She told her little sister to wait in the cabin and promised they wouldn't be long.

"How long?"

"Just a few minutes."

"Why can't I hang out with you guys?"

"Because… I need to talk to him in private."

"What about?"

Kate smiled and ruffled Savannah's golden hair. "I'll be right over there, pipsqueak. See those trees? That's like… ten yards away. No biggie." *It was farther than that, but still. "Don't be scared. I'll be close by."*

"I'm not scared."

Sixteen years later, Kate stood in the exact spot where she'd abandoned her little sister. Just for a few minutes. Or maybe it was longer than that? Maybe it was ten minutes? Or fifteen? Or fifty? She couldn't remember. Her eyes filled with stinging tears.

She had lived with the consequences of that decision every day of her life—it hummed along the surface of her psyche, shimmering and alive, like a raw wire. She would have to lighten the load eventually. Now she fumbled in her coat pocket for Detective Dyson's business card. She took out her phone and dialed the number.

"Hello?"

"Hi, it's me. Kate Wolfe." She paused. "Do you still want to talk?"

Without hesitation, he said, "When can we meet?"

"I'm in Blunt River."

"Okay, I know a great place."

22

THEY MET IN ONE of the wood-paneled eateries across town. Kate took a seat in a back booth and ordered a cup of coffee. She watched as Detective Dyson drove up in a vintage white pickup truck and walked inside, making the old-fashioned bell jangle above the door. He spotted Kate and headed down the aisle, pausing to chat with some of the other diners along the way—clearly a popular guy. He removed his cowboy hat and smoothed the static out of his salt-and-pepper hair. He smelled like cigar smoke and wet wool. He peeled off his winter coat and said, "I haunt this place. But I am a quiet ghost."

She smiled. It was funny, even though she didn't get it.

He sat down opposite her and picked up the greasy menu. "They make a prize-winning grilled-cheese sandwich here, if you're interested," he told her. "They use gruyere and smoked bacon." He had walnut-brown eyes ringed by dark eyelashes. "You in?"

"No thanks, I'm good." She held up her cup of coffee.

He ordered a Coke and a grilled-cheese sandwich from the waitress, then turned his full attention on Kate. "Okay. This is how I see it. Henry Blackwood has maintained his innocence since day one. He passed a polygraph, and that ain't beanball. And now his niece, the state's star witness, has recanted her testimony. So if Blackwood was with her the whole time, then that begs the question—who killed Savannah Wolfe?"

Kate shook her head. "Nelly has issues. She could be lying or confused or deluded. My sister was buried in Blackwood's backyard. His fingerprints were on the shovel. They found his hairs tangled up in the rope."

"True."

"Besides, a jury saw all the evidence and convicted him."

"Not all of it." Detective Dyson's grilled sandwich arrived, and he wasted no time digging in.

"What do you mean—not all of it?"

"Put two lawyers in a room, they're gonna play games."

"Could you be more specific?"

"A couple of witness statements and other possible leads were never brought up in court. A red van was spotted in the neighborhood driving around suspiciously that day. Another witness reported seeing a young girl matching your sister's description get into a green pickup truck on Route 27, which connects to the logging road."

"So you think some random guy in a red van or a green pickup truck kidnapped my sister and buried her in Blackwood's backyard? Why? Who would do such a thing?"

Dyson paused to wipe his mouth on a paper napkin. "Bear with me. I'm just getting started."

"Look, I don't doubt for a second that Nelly is telling the truth about her uncle. I know a sexual abuse victim when I see

188

one. But that just reinforces his guilt in my mind, because it's not such a leap from child-molester to child-murderer."

"What would you say if I told you that everything you know about the case is wrong?"

"I'd say prove it to me."

"Okay," he said. "Let's set aside your sister for a moment. You've heard about the Hannah Lloyd case? That was a brutal crime. Some of the evidence pointed to her next-door neighbor, a convicted pedophile. We arrested him, but the DA couldn't prove it in court, and the trial ended in a hung jury. He went free. Then he offed himself, before the prosecutor could mount a new trial. A very convenient death."

Kate blinked. "Are you implying somebody killed him?"

He cleared his throat. "I think your sister and Hannah Lloyd met the same fate—same killer, similar *modus operandi*. Both died as the result of asphyxiation—suffocation or strangulation—and both had hair cut off. I believe the same psychopath was behind those two murders, as well as some of the other disappearances in the area."

She shook her head numbly. "Are you talking about Makayla Brayden? She was into drugs. She hitchhiked and came from a broken home—three factors that put her at risk of victimization by a stranger."

"Kate," he said softly. "I'm sorry, can I call you Kate?"

She nodded.

"Call me Palmer. Here's my theory. I'm sure it's tempting not to want to think about this, okay? He'll be dead in a few days. But if you're anything like me, you can't help but connect

189

the dots and realize things don't add up. That somebody else is behind everything that's happened in Blunt River County over the past two decades, including your sister's homicide."

A chill crept over her. He was asking her to fundamentally shift her entire way of thinking. For half her life, Kate had believed that Henry Blackwood had murdered her little sister. She shook her head. "If that's the case, then Henry Blackwood was set up. Is that what you're saying?"

The detective shrugged. "It's a distinct possibility."

"But that's crazy. It would mean whoever did this went to a great deal of trouble to make him look guilty. It would be wildly elaborate and hugely risky. What's your evidence?"

"We can go over the evidence later on. I've got boxes of the stuff at home. But there are other victims. Nine, to my knowledge." He wiped a daub of grease off his chin. "Look, I retired last year. And confidentially… can I confide in you, Kate?"

She gave a reluctant nod. "Sure."

"I have cancer. It was in remission, but now it's back."

"I'm sorry to hear that," she said sympathetically.

"Slow-growing Hodgkin's Lymphoma. Ten years ago, I was treated with chemo and radiation, my cancer went into remission, but there was a recurrence five years later. More treatment. I was in remission again. Now they tell me it's spreading. I've been told I'm therapy-resistant. So I applied for a clinical trial in New York for immunotherapy, but there's a long waiting list."

Kate didn't know what to say.

"Anyway, I found a clinic in Tijuana that specializes in

the same immunotherapy as the clinical trial. Hey, I know what you're thinking: medical tourism. But I've read up on it extensively. The therapy is non-toxic, harmless at worst. For me, it's a no-brainer."

Kate nodded, unprepared for this confession.

"Look, I've made my peace with it. You can only go through so many rounds of chemo and radiation before it knocks the piss out of you. But my bigger point is, it adds urgency to my mission. Not many people know about the recurrence, so please…"

"Of course. I won't tell a soul."

He waved a hand dismissively. "Anyway, back to what I was saying before. When Hannah's body was found in the woods, her hair had been shaved off, just like your sister. And both girls died as the result of having their air supply cut off, one way or another. This is why I believe the two cases are related."

Kate stared at Palmer. "You don't buy that Hannah was murdered by her neighbor?"

He squinted at her. "No. I think there's a bigger picture here."

Kate felt a heavy sadness dragging her down. "I've always wondered why Blackwood shaved Savannah's head."

"What's your best guess… being a psychiatrist and all?" he asked. "What does it signify?"

"That's just it, it doesn't make sense. Savannah was a little girl. Small for her age. I'd understand if he'd shaved the head of a grown woman, but a little kid…"

"What do you mean—grown woman?"

"To shave a woman's head is to shame her. To separate her from her femininity, her sexual power."

Palmer wagged a finger at her. "You're good. You went right to the heart of it. No bullshit. I like that."

"It's Psych 101."

"On the contrary. And I should know. I paid a lot of money for behavioral profiling back in the day. I'd like to get your take on some of the other missing girls, see if there are any other similarities between them and your sister's case, besides the ones I've drawn."

The bell jangled above the door again, and two middle-aged cops walked in. They waved at Palmer, and he waved back. He finished his sandwich and chased it down with the rest of his Coke. She listened to the ice chips clinking against his glass.

"My colleagues think I'm crazy," he confided. "But a long time ago, I noticed a connection, and I'm convinced there's a bigger story here. I want to prove those bench-warmers wrong."

Kate thought it sounded like bravado. "Do you have any kids, Palmer?"

He shook his head. "Just an ex-wife. The divorce rate for cops is pretty high. My wife used to complain because I worked all the time. She called me cold and distant, and that's funny, because I'm actually a warm and fuzzy guy. But I used to spend all my days hunting down killers, thieves, and rapists. That changes a person. We grew apart. I don't blame her. I couldn't stop obsessing over these cases, including your sister's." He grabbed another napkin from the dispenser and wiped his face. "Now I can't stop investigating, even though I'm retired. It's like the wheels won't stop turning."

"Were any other girls buried alive?" Kate asked, curious and resentful at the same time. She didn't want to believe it. She didn't want to be drawn into his obsession; and besides, what did that say about the court system and justice? What about Henry Blackwood? How could he possibly be innocent? After all this time? Kate knew all about copycat killers. She'd taken criminal psych courses in college.

"We don't know. Some of the girls are still missing. The rest were either strangled or suffocated before the bodies were staged."

"Staged?"

Palmer cleared his throat. "To look like accidents," he explained. "Like I said, we can go over the evidence…"

She touched her coffee cup. It was cold. "The way she died still haunts me," she confided. "Buried alive. People say upsetting things without meaning to… *I'm digging up dirt, six feet under, I clawed my way out…* a bunch of harmless clichés, right?" She shook her head. "It stops me cold."

He looked at her with compassion. Then he tapped his index finger on the table and said, "Would you be willing to check out some of these cold cases for me? See if you can spot any details that might correspond to your sister's case? Something you'd forgotten about?"

Kate groped for an excuse. She resisted it with every fiber of her being. She already knew who killed Savannah, knew it in her bones… and yet… could it be? She'd not known about Hannah Lloyd's hair being shaved off before. It wouldn't hurt to look at the other cases, at the very least.

"If I look at the files and come to the conclusion you're wrong about this… then I'm going to tell you. Point-blank. Because if you can't prove it to me, if you can't convince me he's a hundred per cent innocent, then I'm going to forget about it. Let him fry."

He nodded. "Maybe I'm wrong. On the other hand, perhaps we can solve this puzzle together?"

"Don't get too excited. I give a lot of weight to the jury's verdict."

"That's exactly what I need," he told her. "A pair of skeptical eyes."

23

BEFORE HEADING BACK TO Boston, Kate took a detour across town and visited the old neighborhood one last time. It was a cold and starry night. She parked in front of Henry Blackwood's Greek revival—it said *Dennison* on the mailbox now. A tall fence encircled the property and the long driveway led to an enclosed garage. The nearest neighbor was a couple of acres away, and the thick encroaching forest grew up around the house. Several blocks down the street, around the corner and up a hill, was her father's house. It gave her the chills.

She got out of her car and crossed the snowy front yard, trudged up the porch steps and knocked on the door. She rang the bell. No response. She cupped her hands over the glass and peered inside. She could make out a staircase and a hallway leading toward the back of the house. The rest was shadows and stillness.

On an impulse, she walked around the side of the house and felt a creeping sense of violation as she made her way across the wintery backyard. She'd only been here once before, many years ago, shortly after they arrested Henry Blackwood for murder. Sixteen-year-old Kate had crept through the woods and crossed a landmine of evidence flags in order to absorb Savannah's last few moments on earth and bury them deep within her heart for safekeeping.

Now here she was again. Looking for her sister's grave. So much time had passed, she couldn't find it in the snow. She remembered seeing a slight depression in the dirt where the backhoe had focused its energies. She remembered the old tire swing and the abandoned dog house, its rusty chain trailing across the grass. She recalled strands of yellow crime tape and a few wooden stakes—closer to the dog house than the garden. There. Beneath the sycamore tree.

Chilled to the bone, Kate went to stand on the periphery of her sister's unofficial gravesite. It felt more real to her than any cemetery plot. Savannah had pleaded for her life here. She'd taken her last breath here. This small section of earth was her true burial ground.

Kate could barely imagine the terror her sister must've felt that night. The shock of a young body being preyed upon by a muscular adult. Eyes open as the dirt surrounded her. And then… nothing.

Kate wondered if the people who now lived in the house had any idea what had happened. But of course it was all over the Internet. According to Kate's friend Heather, a succession of owners had fled the premises, spooked. Did Savannah's restless spirit haunt these grounds? Had the Dennisons realized too late they were living in a haunted house? Had they brought in a team of local ghost hunters to rid the place of Kate's little sister? Next time, the house would sell dirt cheap, Heather had assured her. And selling it again would be a chore. Too much history. Too many tenants. Too many rumors to deny.

Here was the bigger question: If by some incredible twist of fate everything she believed was wrong… would Savannah ever be able to rest in peace? Did she linger in this backyard, waiting for justice? What if Kate helped Palmer find the real killer? Would Savannah be able to move into the light?

Kate's mind grew hushed. All her prayers had been used up. Her emotions were threadbare. No thoughts or deeds would ever bring Savannah back to life.

Kate took one last look around. She would never come here again.

24

JAMES HAD A SURPRISE waiting for her at home. The dining room table was set, candles were lit, and a Duraflame flickered in the fireplace. Steam rose from Chinese take-out containers. "Ta-da," he said.

She beamed at him from the doorway. "Mary Chung's?"

"I heated it up myself." He pulled out a chair for her.

She slipped her arms around him. It was wonderful to be close to him again. To feel his breath on her face. It made everything better.

"How was the funeral?" he asked her.

"Heartbreaking."

"Sorry, babe," he said, kissing her forehead. He looked at her with concern. "You're feverish."

"Been a long day."

"Let's eat. Maybe you'll feel better."

"I'd rather fuck your brains out."

"Really?" He grinned. "That can be arranged."

She took him by the hand and led him into their bedroom, tugging off his sweater, unzipping her skirt, peeling off her pantyhose. Her heart beat at a furious pitch as she landed on the bed, and he climbed on top of her. He straddled her hips and kissed her.

Urgency and despair took over. She reached down and guided him in. *Please fuck the sorrow out of me, fuck me until I'm empty.* Her breathing grew labored as the animal part of her came alive and everything built and built inside of her, until she exploded in a cluster of confetti shivers. Afterwards she clung to him, exhausted and blank.

"Wow," he said, settling down beside her.

She cracked a smile. "You ain't so bad yourself."

"How are you holding up?"

"Okay," she said, wondering how much to tell him.

"You sure? Everything okay?"

"Fine," she lied, because a new emotion was stirring. Anger. She was furious at Detective Dyson for ambushing her, for suggesting that her worst fears—that her sister's killer was still out there—could be true. For supporting Nelly's story.

James smiled sadly at her. She realized she hadn't been thinking enough about him, how he was feeling. She'd just assumed he was as strong as ever, that he didn't need her concern.

"How about you?" she asked. "How was your day?"

"A crap sandwich, thanks for asking."

"Agatha?"

"She walked out on group again."

"What triggered it this time?"

"I completely lost my shit, Kate. We aren't supposed to do that, right? Isn't that in the Shrink Handbook or something? 'Never lose your shit?'"

"Verbatim. So what happened?"

"I might've sworn at her under my breath. I couldn't help myself. She pushes all my Mom buttons. I hate the fact that I'm only human. It annoys the hell out of me."

"You? Human? Hardly."

He laughed. "I feel better already. Back to you. What's going on beneath that Teflon exterior?"

She sagged a little. "I'm coping," she admitted.

He took her hand. "Where's the ring?"

She stared at her naked finger. "I didn't want my father thinking it was an engagement ring, so I took it off. Why open that can of worms?"

"You saw him today?"

"After the funeral. On a whim."

"How'd it go?"

"Fair to middling."

"Hm. I should meet this middling guy. We can dialogue."

She laughed. "No way am I ready for that."

"You never know. We could end up best buds."

"Yeah, right. Just like Vanessa and me."

"Mom loves you. She's an equal-opportunity narcissist."

Kate gazed out their bedroom windows. The full moon dusted the city in a soft glow. A chill wind whistled across the rooftop. James dragged the quilt up over their bodies, covering their nakedness, and held her close.

"Mm. Nice," she murmured. "Let's stay like this forever…"

"Okay."

"…underneath our guilt…"

"What?"

She stared at him. "What did I say?"

"Guilt." He grinned. "You said guilt. That was some Freudian slip."

"Quilt. I meant quilt."

"Your guilt will probably outlast this quilt, despite the high thread count."

"You're hysterical."

He smirked. "I know. It's exhausting being such a boundless source of mirth." He smoothed the hair off her face and kissed her gently. "Swear to me you're going to be okay, Kate."

"I'll be fine."

"Here you are, dealing with all this crap, and I'm cracking jokes." He squeezed her hand. "So that's it for the ring then?"

"No, silly. I love it. I'll be wearing it again tomorrow."

"Doesn't itch?"

"Not a bit," she lied. "Can I have my hand back now?"

"I think not."

"I think yes."

He released her and leaned up on one elbow. "So tell me everything."

She told him about the funeral. Then she said, "And I met this guy…"

The phone rang in the living room.

"Guy? What guy?"

She laughed. "It's not like that—he's older."

"How old? Ancient? Decrepit? Not young and handsome like me, right?"

"Nobody's handsome like you."

"Or young."

The phone rang impatiently.

James rolled his eyes and tumbled out of bed. "Sorry. You can only ignore my mother for so long before the talons come out. I'll keep it brief, and we'll talk over dinner, okay? I really want to hear about this ancient, creepy, ugly old guy you met."

"Okay." She nodded. "Say hello for me."

He gracefully stepped into his jeans and went charging into the living room. Kate heard him pick up the phone and say, "Hey, Mom."

She wasn't sure how much to tell him about her conversation with Detective Palmer Dyson. It felt as if she'd opened Pandora's box, and all the monsters of the world had come flying out, never to be put back again. She needed time to compose her thoughts. She would tell him tomorrow. Tonight, she would stay like this, safe and snug beneath her guilt.

25

MADDIE'S CONDITION HAD WORSENED over the weekend. Kate drove to the hospital early on Monday morning, knowing that a sudden downturn could precipitate a complete mental breakdown. She hurried through security and waited with growing impatience by the elevators.

Upstairs on the second floor, Yvette filled her in on Maddie's status as they approached Room 212. "She won't get out of bed. She refuses to join us for breakfast. Not even Tamara could persuade her."

Kate knocked on Maddie's door.

"Come in."

Sunlight weak as lemongrass tea filtered in through the windows. Lost in a tumult of blankets and pillows was Madeline Autumn Ward, age fourteen, possible differential diagnosis of schizoid personality disorder. She looked like a small blond smudge.

Kate dismissed the nurse's aide who had been watching the girl, and who seemed relieved to get a break, then studied Maddie's chart and said, "How are you feeling this morning?"

"My neck hurts."

"Where?"

She pointed.

Kate examined the girl's slender neck. "Would another pillow help?"

"Yes, but they won't give me one."

"Okay. I'll see what I can do," Kate promised.

Maddie sat up in bed. Her eyes were bloodshot. There were fresh-looking scratches on her arms—not a good sign. She gathered several plush toys around her, gifts from Tamara and Yvette, who often spent their own hard-earned cash in the hospital gift shop. Forbidden acts of compassion.

"I don't like her," Maddie said.

"Who? The nurse's aide? Susie?"

"She's been spying on me."

"It's called one-on-one. She's keeping an eye on you for your own safety."

"They're all spying on me."

"It's hospital policy."

"Why? Because I'm evil?"

"No, Maddie. Nobody thinks you're evil."

She began to cry softly. "Maybe I am."

"Whoever said you were evil?"

Maddie peered at Kate between her wet blond eyelashes.

"Does your stepfather tell you that?"

"No."

"Then why do you think you're evil?"

"I have bad thoughts sometimes."

"Like what?"

"Like I want to hurt myself."

"Okay. But why does that make you evil?"

Maddie blinked. "I don't have a sister. What's it like to have a sister?"

Confusion fell over Kate like a cloud. "It was nice," she answered truthfully. "I loved her very much."

"But she died."

"Yes."

"How come?"

A shiver passed through Kate, soft as a purr. "I can't talk about that now, Maddie. It's too sad for me."

"Why do people have to die?"

"I don't know. But it's a harsh fact of life."

"I don't want Mommy to die," the girl said softly.

"You love her very much, don't you?"

Maddie nodded. "Your mother drowned in the river, didn't she?"

Kate's stomach knotted up as she struggled to maintain her composure. "Who told you that?" When the girl didn't respond, she realized there was no sense in hiding the truth from her, so she took a deep breath and said, "My mother passed away when I was ten. Then my sister died six years later."

Tears sprang to Maddie's eyes. "That's sad."

"Yes, it is."

"Is it painful to drown?"

"I don't know. I've read different things about it."

"I heard that it really hurts at first… but then it feels natural, because there was water in the womb." Maddie hugged one of the furry toys to her chest, as if she were trying to merge with its softness. "I'm going to die soon," she whispered.

Kate drew back. "Why do you say that?"

"That was dumb," Maddie muttered.

"What was?"

"I shouldn't have said that about your mother."

"No, it's okay. I don't mind answering your questions."

"Oh God," she choked. "How stupid of me."

"You're just curious. Everybody's curious." As tears rolled down Maddie's cheeks, Kate handed her a box of tissues.

"I shouldn't have said that," Maddie blurted. "Stupid. Die. I'm going to die."

"What makes you think you're going to die?"

"Die. Die. What a stupid thing to say. What does it even mean? Die. Die. If you say a word over and over again, it loses all meaning, right? Die. I'm so stupid."

"You aren't stupid," Kate said soothingly. "Far from it."

"I am!" Maddie shrieked. "I'm stupid!"

Kate hesitated to make the comparison, then forged ahead. "Your mother calls herself stupid. Is that why you call yourself stupid? Does the voice inside your head sound like your mother? Is it your mother's voice? Or your stepfather's?"

The girl looked stricken. A person in the midst of a psychotic break had a tendency to view everything through a distorted lens. Reality lost all meaning and became perverted. They grew afraid. They felt disembodied. Maddie was on the verge of losing her grip on reality.

"Sometimes, we punish ourselves," Kate said quickly,

reaching out to stroke the girl's hand in a deliberate grounding motion. "We punish ourselves by internalizing other people's anger. For instance, if your stepfather calls you stupid, you might start to believe him. You might start calling *yourself* stupid."

Maddie tilted her head as if she were listening, but something had changed behind her eyes. "My head hurts," she complained. "I'm scared."

"I'm right here. I'm not going anywhere."

Suddenly the girl dug her nails into her scalp, drawing blood.

"No!" Kate tried to grab her hands, but Maddie struggled violently in her arms, screaming and flailing, kicking the blankets and plushies off the bed. Needing more leverage, Kate stood up and dropped the clipboard on the floor, and Maddie kicked her in the stomach. It happened so fast Kate didn't see it coming. She bent double. As she straightened, Maddie struck her across the face, arm whipping out like a snake. Kate stood frozen for a moment, stunned, then hit the call button for the nurses' station.

Seconds later, Tamara came running with a needle in her hand. Protocol was to offer the child a choice—needle or pill. But Maddie refused. She was too far gone.

Kate made the decision for her, and Tamara injected a sedative into Maddie's backside as the girl struggled. Years of experience and training had taught Kate that it would've been far worse—even ridiculous—to let Maddie's hysteria play itself out.

After Tamara had inspected Maddie's scalp and applied antibacterial ointment, she left them alone. Kate sat next to the bed, waiting for the medication to take effect. After a few minutes, Maddie's pupils became dilated and her heart rate eased. Kate's heart was still pounding.

"Sorry," the girl whispered from her nest of blankets.

"Don't worry about it. Comes with the territory."

"My head hurts," Maddie whispered.

"Do you have a headache?"

"No. It hurts from thinking too much."

"That's okay." Kate put away her stethoscope. "It's going to hurt."

"Why?"

"Because you're starting to feel. And feelings can hurt."

"Can't you make them stop?"

"Hurting? No. I don't want to make your feelings go away."

"Why not?"

"Because if you repress them, they'll only grow stronger," Kate explained. "Your feelings are an important part of you, and it's good to express them. Eventually, your feelings—good or bad—are going to help."

"But I thought you said it hurts?"

"Hurts and helps."

Maddie burrowed deeper into her blankets. "My uncle's going to die soon. I watched it on TV in the day room. The other kids were wondering... which would be quicker, lethal injection or the electric chair?"

"Did you ever meet him?" Kate asked.

"A few times. In prison. Mommy took me. She said I have his laugh. She doesn't like it when I laugh. So I try not to."

It suddenly dawned on Kate: the widow's peak; the pale freckled skin; the sea-green eyes. When Henry Blackwood wasn't wearing one of his baseball caps or that tattered black fedora, his hair was blond and military-short, with a distinctive widow's peak. If Penny Blackwood had gotten pregnant sixteen years ago, she would've had a baby nine months later. And that child today would be the same age as Maddie.

26

KATE HEADED FOR THE elevators, trying to pull herself together. It was quite a shock to realize she might be treating the daughter of the man who'd murdered her sister. She needed to talk to Ira about it.

An elevator arrived as Kate pressed the call button and out stepped Elizabeth McCormack, Nikki's mother.

"Dr. Wolfe?"

"Elizabeth," Kate said, startled. "Can I help you?"

"I can't eat. I can't sleep. I can't stop thinking about Nikki." A ripe smell came from her, as if she hadn't bathed for days. It was at odds with her expensive tailored coat, diamond earrings, and top-of-the-line knee-high leather boots. Her honey-blond hair spilled over her shoulders in greasy ribbons and her eyes were red from crying. "My mind won't stop racing. And I keep thinking—what if? What if we'd done something different? Would she still be alive?"

Kate's stomach seized. "Let's go to my office where we can have some privacy."

"My daughter came to you in a fragile state of mind," Elizabeth said. "Those pills you prescribed—psychotropic drugs—I just found out that they can sometimes do more harm than good. Did you know that?"

"I had her on the mildest dose of anti-anxiety medication."

"Some of her friends are telling me now that Nikki was very depressed. Why didn't you tell me?"

"You knew she was being treated for depression." Kate tried to keep her voice calm as Elizabeth's grew more agitated.

"No, I mean during the last couple of weeks, was she suicidal?"

"Nikki was doing very well in her therapy, but we had a long way to go."

Elizabeth stiffened. "How can you even say that? Doing well?"

"Elizabeth, please, let's go to my office."

"No." She angrily brushed her off. "I want answers. Why did she kill herself? We came home, and there she was, hanging from the ceiling. And I was standing there, looking at my daughter, and I didn't understand. It was as if the world had tilted upside down. But you're a doctor. You were supposed to warn us if she was suicidal," she cried. "How could you let this happen? How could you have missed all the signs?"

"I can assure you, Elizabeth, I didn't miss a thing."

"Oh! That's why my daughter is dead, right? Because you didn't miss a thing. You did absolutely nothing wrong."

"I'm not saying that, Elizabeth, please…"

"Stop calling me Elizabeth! Just stop." Suddenly she pushed Kate hard with both hands. Kate lost her balance, arms twirling, and landed on the floor with a graceless thud.

She sat there stunned, while Elizabeth clamped a gloved hand over her mouth and said, "Oh no."

"It's okay," Kate reassured her.

"I'm sorry. I don't know what got into me…"

A few of the hospital staff were gathered in the hallway. Somebody must've alerted James about the confrontation, because now he came charging toward them.

"Kate? Are you all right?" He helped her to her feet. "What happened? What's going on?"

"I'm fine. Just a little shaken." She looked over at Elizabeth. "This is Nikki's mother."

James spun to face Elizabeth McCormack. "Did you push her? Are you blaming her for this?"

"James, don't." Kate was mortified.

"No, this is ridiculous, Kate. They blame us when something bad happens, but they never hear the awful things their kids have to say about them."

"It doesn't matter," she said quickly. "She lost her daughter."

"Nikki's dead, and I want to know why!" Elizabeth was sobbing now.

"Kate did everything she possibly could," James said.

"James, stop. It's all right."

"No, it's not. It's called assault."

One of the elevators dinged open, and Elizabeth retreated into it and stared at them as the aluminum doors slid shut. James wrapped his arms protectively around Kate, and she let him hold her for a moment without resistance. She'd been struck twice in one day. That had to be a record.

He insisted on escorting her over to the nurses' station, where he made her sit down and found an abrasion on her elbow. The nurses came over and fussed with the Band-Aids and iodine.

"I'm okay," she told anyone who'd listen, but they all ignored her.

"Some of these people are the reason their precious offspring are here in the first place," James muttered.

"I wish you hadn't confronted her like that," Kate said.

"Why not? It's suddenly okay for her to assault you?"

"No. But have some compassion."

"Maybe I'm all compassioned out?" he snapped.

She rested a hand on his arm. "Listen, I'm sorry about the vacation…"

"No," he said, sounding distraught. "I've been such a dick about that. It's just that we were going to make sure you were far away from it all next week."

She nodded. For months they'd been planning what they were going to do on the night of Henry's execution. They were supposed to be luxuriating in some upscale Sedona resort, sampling Verde Valley wines and ignoring the news.

"And on top of everything else, I just heard that Mom slipped on some ice and broke her ankle."

"Oh no. When did this happen?"

"Half an hour ago. I have to drive to Massachusetts General and talk to her doctors. It's a really bad break—she's going to need surgery."

"Give her my love. I hope she's okay." She hugged him.

"And don't worry about next Wednesday. We'll spend the evening in bed and pretend we're in Sedona. We'll have our own wine-tasting party."

He smiled. "It's a date."

"Let me know how Vanessa is, okay?"

He gave her a kiss and walked away.

27

KATE KNOCKED ON IRA'S door.

"Come in," he said.

"Got a minute?"

"For you—anything." He dropped his paperwork. "Have a seat."

She closed the door behind her and muttered, "Where to begin."

"What's up?"

"Elizabeth McCormack just pushed me over."

"She pushed you?"

"In front of the elevators. Ten minutes ago."

"Are you all right?"

"Just a bruised ego."

"Excuse me a second." He picked up his phone and told his secretary to hold his calls. Then he said, "Okay. Sit. Talk."

She sat down and said, "She blamed me for Nikki's suicide."

"So basically—your worst nightmare."

She nodded. "It gets all those self-defeating gears grinding."

"Right, like this is all your fault. When we both know that's complete nonsense."

"A lot of things feel like my fault lately," Kate said.

"Such as?"

She rubbed her pounding temples. "It's complicated."

"I've got all day."

"No, you don't, but thanks anyway, Ira."

He heaved a sigh. "Kate. What's going on?"

"I met a man at Nikki's funeral… a retired detective who is trying to convince me that Henry Blackwood is innocent."

Ira frowned. "What?"

"I know. Sounds crazy, right?"

"The execution is only a few days away."

She nodded. "Wednesday night."

"It's a little late to be changing your mind, don't you think?"

"James said the same thing last night."

"Well, maybe he's right?"

Kate sighed. "People have been trying to convince me of Blackwood's innocence for years, so I guess it makes sense that things would escalate shortly before the execution."

"There you go," Ira said. "How's your new patient?"

"We're making progress. I think Maddie's stepfather may be abusing her."

"Sexually?"

"No evidence of that. But perhaps verbal and physical abuse."

"Have you confronted the patient about it?"

"So far she denies it."

He frowned. "Have you talked to the stepfather?"

"Not yet. The Wards aren't the easiest people to get a hold

of. They don't own cell phones apparently, just the landline, and half the time the answering machine doesn't pick up. But I'm worried about Nelly Ward. She comes across as a battered wife."

Ira took off his glasses and pinched the bridge of his nose. "Okay, couple of things. First, we need to step carefully. As you know, the hospital has specific requirements when it comes to child abuse."

"I'll document everything."

"Also, you need to meet the girl's stepfather as soon as possible."

"Okay."

"Once you've made an assessment, if you suspect there's abuse in the home, we'll get social services involved."

Kate nodded. Ursula O'Keefe was their go-to gal at the hospital. She would do a little sleuthing on her own—public records, police reports, domestic disputes. If it turned out to be true, then Ursula would contact the Department of Human Services, and they would obtain a court order to remove the child from the home. Maddie would be placed with a foster family. Some kids blossomed away from toxic family environments; others didn't fare as well. It was impossible to predict.

Kate frowned. "I'd like to take it slow, then."

He nodded. "That would be my advice."

"I want to make sure we do what's best for Maddie, given the alternatives."

"Agreed. Anything else?"

She hesitated, wondering if she should mention her

observation about Maddie's resemblance to Henry Blackwood. But it was only natural that Maddie would share some of her great-uncle's genes. Perhaps the resemblance only went as far as that.

"Keep me in the loop. And, Kate." Ira leaned forward. "Don't let yourself get trapped in any more conversations about Blackwood's innocence. Let justice take its course."

28

THAT NIGHT, JAMES WAS on the phone with his mother's doctors, discussing her treatment plan. Vanessa had undergone surgery and would be in a cast for several months. Instead of going back to work like he'd planned, James took the rest of the week off so that he could make arrangements for her recuperation and spend his days at Massachusetts General Hospital.

They went to bed late, and Kate wrapped her arms around James and held him close. "I love you," she whispered.

"I love you, too." He frowned. "They say trouble comes in threes."

"We're fine. Just take care of your mother. She needs you."

The following morning, Kate drove up to Wilamette to meet Maddie's stepfather. She got there in record time and parked in the driveway behind Nelly's navy blue Toyota Camry.

Nelly greeted her at the door with a disapproving scowl. In the clear morning light, her face looked slightly misshapen, as if she'd been someone's punching bag for years.

"Is your husband here?" Kate asked.

"No."

"When will he be back?"

"Tonight."

"It's important that I speak with him. Can I come in?"

"I guess."

The kitchen was a mess. Kitschy collectibles cluttered every surface.

"Coffee?" Nelly offered.

"Thanks."

Many of the ceramic pieces had been broken and glued back together, potential evidence of marital discord. Kate tried to feel some compassion for this woman. None of it was Nelly's fault. Her dysfunction was a survival mechanism, an outgrowth of her defensiveness—as was Kate's. But their respective tragedies had sent them rocketing in different directions.

What bothered Kate the most were Nelly's choices regarding her daughter. Surely her instinct would've been to protect Maddie from abuse, given her own experiences. There were plenty of organizations and shelters to choose from. If it was true that her husband had verbally abused her and Maddie, perhaps even physically, Nelly could've fought harder to protect her child.

"Where's your husband?" Kate asked.

"Pittsburgh," Nelly said, bringing the coffee over to the table. "There was a delay or something. He won't be home until later tonight."

Kate frowned. "But I thought you said he was home? Has he gone back to work already?"

"Whatever." Nelly brushed it off. She'd been caught in a lie but didn't bother explaining herself. "He won't be home until later tonight."

Kate let it go. "When are you coming to the hospital?"

"Soon," Nelly answered vaguely.

"Soon when?"

"I don't know." She puffed herself up with injured pride. "You have no right to look down your nose at me. You don't know anything about me."

"You're right," Kate said stiffly. "I don't. So enlighten me."

"I love that little girl. I have all her baby clothes. Every drawing she ever did. Every scrap of homework. Every report card. I know all her likes and dislikes. She won't eat a fleck of mayonnaise or ketchup. Just so you know."

Kate would have to sort out what was going on inside the Ward household if she hoped to help Maddie at all. At the same time, she didn't want to be unfair to these people. She was more than willing to listen to their side of the story before she made any moves that could potentially ruin their lives. But they were running out of time.

She decided to go for it. "Does your husband beat you?"

"Does he what?"

"Beat you?"

"No!"

Kate detected fear and evasiveness in Nelly's eyes, the slipperiness of deceit.

"Derrick wouldn't lay a hand on me."

"Look," Kate said with resignation, "it's important that you tell me the truth, because I'm going to have to make some decisions that will affect your entire family, and I need to hear your side of the story."

Nelly took a cigarette out of the pack on the table and rasped, "Are you asking me if my husband beats the living shit out of me? The answer is no. He's a good provider. A good father. Are you asking me does he hit Maddie? The answer is never. He wouldn't lay a hand on her. Maddie harms herself."

"So your husband doesn't beat you or Maddie?"

"I've had three." She lit her cigarette and inhaled deeply.

"Excuse me?"

"Three husbands." Nelly gave a snort of derision. "The first one beat me up pretty regular. Are you gonna arrest him? Good luck finding him."

"I didn't realize…"

"I had a difficult childhood. Some people never get over it. I thought that I could. Then I married that bastard. He seemed okay at first. He came across as charming. But as the months went by, it dawned on me what a bully he was. And I paid dearly for my mistake. So I divorced him and married my second husband. He was a charmer, too. Real nice guy. But guess what? Same damn thing. I swear, I must have the word 'victim' stamped on my forehead. *Doormat—step all over me*." She rubbed her brow and laughed. "Boy oh boy, he wasn't subtle at all. First it was a love punch. Then a wrestling match. And you figure—he's just goofing around, right? But then he hits you. And it becomes deadly serious. It ain't so funny anymore. And before you know it, you're in over your head."

"Did any of your husbands ever hurt Maddie?"

"The first one left when she was six months old. He didn't get a chance to hurt her, unless you count the times he punched me in the stomach when I was pregnant."

Kate winced. Those counted.

"My second husband wouldn't have nothing to do with Maddie. He barely acknowledged her existence. And now I've got this one here—Derrick. A good man with a good job. He loves her like a real daddy. But you know… turns out there are different kinds of bastards."

"What do you mean?"

Nelly ran her hands through her short dark hair. "Always with the criticism. Always with the harsh words. I thought it was my bad luck, you know? One lousy marriage after another. That's why I started collecting good-luck charms." She jangled the turquoise-and-silver bracelets on her wrists. "But now I suspect it's me. That I attract it somehow. Is there a victim gene? I wonder."

"So it's only harsh words? He never physically harms you?"

Nelly touched the mottled bruises on her neck. They had faded since Kate had first seen them. "Only when I piss him off." She had the laugh of a drunken librarian—there was a swaggering hush to it. "I do that sometimes," she admitted. "Piss him off."

"But you just said…"

"I *know* what I said."

"But it contradicts your statement…"

"My statement? Is this an interrogation? Am I under arrest?"

"No."

"I contradict myself a lot. Don't you?"

It was true. Most people contradicted themselves. But Kate kept her poker face on and didn't back down. "Then you admit he hits you?"

"It's not the same thing," Nelly explained. "My first two husbands beat the living crap out of me. Derrick gets pissed off occasionally. Once in a while, in the middle of a fight, he'll take a swipe at me. But only if I provoke him. He doesn't beat me as a rule. Mostly, he's super-critical, and that gets my mouth running. So I'll say something nasty. But look. It's a mutual thing with us—not me cowering in a corner and him stomping on my head, like it was before."

"Okay," Kate said. "And you swear he's never lost his temper with Maddie?"

"I'm telling you, he wouldn't raise a finger."

"I find that hard to believe, given Maddie's history of self-harm." Kate had seen it many times before—a child mimicking the behavior of her abuser and learning to hurt herself.

"Derrick's been good to her," Nelly said with an exhausted shake of her head. "It's hands-off when it comes to my child."

"But you finally admitted he hit you, after you swore he didn't."

"He loves Maddie. She doesn't piss him off the way I do."

"How often does he hit you?"

"I don't know. Couple times a year. Believe me, it's like a honeymoon compared to the other two."

Kate couldn't tell if she was lying or not. The whole problem was sorting out the falsehoods from the truth. Untangling the threads of a messy, contradictory life.

She braced herself for the next question—a tricky step. "Let me ask you something, and please don't be offended. It's protocol in situations like this. Did any of your husbands sexually abuse Maddie, to the best of your knowledge? Is it possible? Sometimes we deny the things that are the most painful for us to admit…"

"No! And I'm not in denial," Nelly barked, tamping out her cigarette with an exaggerated gesture. "I know what goes on inside my own home. Are we done?"

Kate stood her ground. "You haven't been to the hospital to visit Maddie. Could I ask why? I know she'd love to see you."

"I don't know," Nelly rasped. "Maybe I'm scared?"

"Of what?"

"What if she doesn't get better?"

"But your presence will help her get better," Kate reasoned.

"No, it won't."

"Why do you say that?"

"I worry…" Tears sprang to her eyes. "What if it's my bad luck that's doing this to her? I mean, what if it's contagious? My terrible luck. This time, I told myself to stay away…"

"But that's…" Kate bit her tongue.

"Ridiculous? Superstitious garbage? Is that what you were going to say?" Nelly grimaced as if she were in physical pain. "Just fix her. Please. I'm begging you. Fix my baby girl. That's all I want."

"I understand. But you have to come see her," Kate insisted.

"It reflects poorly on you if you don't. Please understand…
I'm trying to help you."

Nelly's face reddened. She sucked in a sob. "Okay."

"Do you promise?"

"Yes." There was panic in Nelly's voice.

"Thanks for the coffee." Kate stood up, then paused for a
moment. "One last thing. Who is Maddie's father?"

Nelly's eyes widened. "Does it matter?"

"I think so, yes."

She shook her head. "Who cares? He'll be dead tomorrow!"

Kate drew back. It felt like a punch to the gut. "Are you
talking about Henry Blackwood?"

Nelly shuddered. "Please go. Now."

Kate nodded, her worst fears confirmed. She put a hand
on Nelly's shoulder. The woman was trembling. "Please come
see Maddie."

"I promise."

29

KATE WENT HOME TO an empty condo. She sat on the edge of the bed and took off her ring. Her finger itched, and she rubbed the prickly skin. She closed her eyes and heard the sound of rope twisting. She saw her sister's face.

She took a shower and started dinner. While she was chopping vegetables, the doorbell rang. It was the UPS guy, carrying a large cardboard box.

The package was from Detective Dyson. She sliced through the packing tape and opened a box full of police files, thick heavy folders containing hundreds of photocopied pages.

At first, she tried to ignore them. She ate her dinner in front of the TV and watched the news, but it was all too depressing. She loaded up the dishwasher, started a pot of coffee brewing, lit a cigarette and sat on the living room floor. She opened the box and spread the files out before her, embarrassed by her morbid sense of curiosity.

There were nine victims between the ages of six and sixteen; mercifully Savannah's file was missing, but Kate mentally included her in the tally. Two of the girls had been murdered, four were missing, two were ruled as suicides, and one was an accident. The accidental death had occurred eighteen years ago in Blunt River; a six-year-old girl named Susie Gafford had fallen into an unmarked well on a neighbor's property. Kate wasn't sure why Palmer had included it, so she set it aside.

The second incident happened seventeen years ago, when a teenager named Emera Mason decided to thumb her way to a rock concert in Boston. She disappeared en route without a trace.

Sixteen years ago, Savannah Wolfe was brutally murdered.

Fourteen years ago, eight-year-old Vicky Koffman disappeared from a small community just north of Blunt River.

Twelve years ago, a preteen from Wilamette committed suicide by jumping off a cliff. The girl's cousin was arrested for manslaughter, but the case against him had fallen apart, and Lizbeth Howell's death was ruled a suicide.

Ten years ago, fourteen-year-old Hannah Lloyd went missing from her home. Six months later, her skeletal remains were found in The Balsams. Her head was shaved. Tucked into the folder were several gruesome crime-scene photos of the girl's remains. Kate couldn't tear her eyes away. Hannah Lloyd didn't look like a person anymore. The primary suspect was a pudgy, balding twenty-eight-year-old with an aura of sleaze about him. Also included were newspaper articles about the trial ending in a hung jury, and about his apparent suicide a few years later.

Eight years ago, another girl from the county went missing. Maggie Witt, age nine, was playing in a park when she wandered away from her friends, never to be seen again.

Six years ago, eleven-year-old Tabitha Davidowitz was killed in a freak accident, or perhaps it was a suicide. She either fell or jumped off an abandoned building in the old factory district and landed on top of a car. The girl couldn't have weighed more than sixty pounds, but she'd crushed the hood of the car and broken every bone in her body. The incident occurred in the middle of the night in an isolated part of town, and her remains hadn't been found until forty-eight hours later.

Finally, just last year, Makayla Brayden went missing after her best friend's birthday party. She was fifteen years old. There was a picture of the pretty teenager with the honest eyes and wide smile.

Kate had taken a few criminal psychology courses back in college and knew that most pedophiles had a predilection for a certain age, sex, and physical appearance. Except for gender, these victims were all over the map looks-wise—short, tall, thin, fat, different ages, complexions, hair and eye color. If by some chance Palmer Dyson was right, that the same offender had killed all nine girls, then it clearly wasn't the girls' looks that attracted him.

Her phone rang and she scooped it up without even checking the caller ID. "James?" she answered breathlessly.

"Palmer Dyson. Sorry to bother you. Is now a bad time?"

"No," she said, disappointed. "I got your package."

"So? What do you think?"

"So far, I don't see it," Kate said. "Four of the girls went missing, and three were suicides or accidents. Only Savannah's and Hannah Lloyd's deaths seem like they could be related."

"Okay, you asked for evidence. Let's look at the three girls whose bodies were found but whose deaths weren't thought to be the result of murder. Susie Gafford fell down a well, and it was ruled an accident. At the time, there was a dispute about the manner of death, but I believe she was killed *before* being thrown down the well. More significantly, some of her hair was missing. The medical examiner attributed the hair loss to it getting caught on the stone wall and pulled off on the way down. But I believe whoever killed her took a chunk of hair as a souvenir."

Kate rummaged through the pile of folders until she found Susie Gafford's. She studied the police photographs of the little girl's body, a lump forming in her throat. "I'm looking at the autopsy pictures now."

"Check out the left side, underneath her ear."

Kate nodded. "Hard to tell," she said.

"Let's go to the next one. Lizbeth Howell. She jumped off a cliff, and it was ruled a suicide," Palmer said. "Once again, there's evidence she was killed before her body hit the ground. Possible strangulation. Her hyoid bone was broken. While I was investigating the case, her mother mentioned that Lizbeth's hair was shorter than it had been before her death, and she just couldn't figure it out."

"Shorter?"

"Two inches off the bottom. But since there were no recent photos of the girl, it was put down to the mother's grief."

"And the last one?" Kate asked.

"Tabitha Davidowitz. Jumped or fell off a roof, ruled a

suicide. Once again, there was evidence of suffocation prior to the fall. Very difficult to prove, though. And it looks like she gave herself a haircut at some point before she went up to the roof. Just chopped chunks of it off, although we couldn't find any scissors or hair at the scene. She was a troubled kid, so again… the medical examiner had his opinion, and I had mine. There's a history of incompetence in the medical examiner's office. I'm talking decades of mistakes. But the medical examiner had the support of the chief, so guess whose opinion held sway?"

"What's his name?" Kate asked.

"Quade Pickler."

So the man who'd worked on Savannah's case still held the position. "And he disagreed with your findings?"

"He likes things neat and tidy. My theory's kind of messy. Quade's a political animal. Me, not so much."

"Does anybody else in the police department agree with you?"

"I have my allies. But like I said, I'm retired now. And with the opioid crisis and rising crime rate, the guys really have their hands full. No one has the time or the inclination to review the old cases."

"It's interesting," Kate hedged, "but it still seems like a stretch."

"I see a pattern. He cuts off their air, and he cuts off their hair."

A chill ran through her. "I really don't know," Kate said. "I need more time to digest this."

"Well, here's something else for you to chew on. Did you receive Blackwood's email yet? He sent it through his lawyer. I got one too."

She could feel the hairs rising on the back of her neck as she reached for her laptop and checked her emails. "I'm not going, Palmer. I already threw away my invitation from the DOC."

"This isn't about the execution, it's for the visitation beforehand. Sort of a farewell party."

"Why does he want me there?"

"He'd like to talk to you. A dying man's request."

Kate gazed at the night sky through the living-room windows. Beyond the city lights loomed a rich, cold darkness. "Will you be there?"

"Yes."

"How well do you know him?"

"Well, I've known Henry for years, since your sister's death of course. He wants to talk to you, Kate. I think he wants to make his peace with it."

She was repulsed by the thought.

"Blackwood's friends and relatives will be there, along with some other folks who've been involved in the case."

"What about Nelly?"

"No," Palmer said. "She doesn't want to have anything to do with him."

"Wise woman."

"Well, it's up to you," he said. "No pressure."

30

KATE CALLED JAMES TO discuss the pros and cons. In the end, she decided that it would be healing for her to confront Blackwood, after all these years. At first James tried to argue her out of it, but ultimately he agreed.

"How's your mom?" Kate said.

"There were complications. She has to go in for a second surgery."

"Oh God, that's upsetting."

"She's in good hands. She has the best orthopedist in New England. But I'm going to stay with her, okay? And I want you to do what you need to do, Kate. But remember, it's okay to change your mind."

The following evening, Kate arrived at the maximum-security prison around six o'clock. Located seventy-five miles north of Blunt River, the enormous complex of cement buildings was surrounded by a fortress of guard towers and razor wire. She found a spot in the vast parking lot and muttered, "I must be crazy."

Inside, it felt just as oppressive. She went through security, and was met on the other side by an armed guard who escorted her to the wing of the prison where the worst of the worst were housed. Gang members, murderers, violent offenders. The deeper they went into the bowels of the prison, the more she regretted her decision. Her knees had turned to jelly by the time they reached the death row unit, a grim concave of dank cells flanked by armed guards in bulletproof booths. Anxiety and tension were thick in the air. The guard radioed the control room and asked them to open the electronically bolted door. Ten steps in, the steel door slammed shut behind them with a resounding clang.

The thirty by forty-foot visitors' room was like a giant holding pen. Everything was painted white, even the steel-barred door that locked you inside with the prisoner—who would be housed in a separate unit, a Plexiglas cage built into the cement-block wall that looked like an animal display at the zoo. Behind the thick bulletproof glass was a six-by-six-foot enclosure with a single chair and a phone. On the visitors' side of the glass were several cheap plastic chairs and a wall phone for the guests to use.

The visitors' room was crowded with several dozen people. A line had formed at a banquet table in the corner. Kate was astonished that anyone could think of eating at a time like this.

"Kate?" Palmer emerged from the crowd. "Glad you could make it."

She was relieved to see him.

"How're you doing?" he asked.

"I'm nervous as hell. I almost chickened out."

"There's nothing to worry about. He'll be out shortly."

"What's up with the food?" she asked.

"Well, like I said, this is his farewell party. Most of these people are here to say goodbye. Can I get you something?"

"Any alcohol?"

He grinned. "Sorry."

"Then no thanks." Her stomach felt like a trash compactor for her emotions.

"Those two over there are his attorneys," Palmer explained. "That lady with the blue hair is his spiritual adviser. Those guys are from the Department of Corrections; they consider Blackwood a friend. Those three men are his cousins. And that group in back are from an anti-death-penalty organization, I forget which one. They're using him for political purposes—"

"I remember that guy," she interrupted, pointing out a man in his sixties with piercing blue eyes. "Isn't that the medical examiner?"

"Quade Pickler," Palmer muttered. "You know him?"

"I saw him at the morgue when my father went to identify Savannah's body."

Quade noticed them and nodded, and Palmer nodded back. The crowd stirred.

"Oh. Here he comes now," Palmer said, looking past Kate's shoulder.

Kate turned. An armed guard was escorting Blackwood into the enclosed Plexiglas cage. She was shocked; he no longer resembled the unfriendly neighbor with the troubled gaze and the military buzz cut who'd haunted her dreams. The fifty-five-year-old was older, leaner, tougher. He had collar-length silver hair and a jowly, unexpressive face. His arms and neck were covered in smeary prison tattoos. He wore an orange jumpsuit but wasn't handcuffed or otherwise restrained. He held a can of Diet Coke in one hand and a lit cigarette in the other. She couldn't detect any fear in his eyes as he sat down and smiled at his visitors. He waved at Palmer, but when he spotted Kate he looked away.

Blackwood's three cousins went over to talk to him first. There were hearty bursts of laughter and fist bumps against the bulletproof glass. Then it was Palmer's turn to talk to the prisoner. Ten minutes later, he stood up and signaled for Kate to come over.

She felt like the homecoming queen—all eyes were on her as she crossed the large, echoing room. She tried not to stumble as she sat in a chair, still warm from Palmer's body.

"I'll be right over there," Palmer said, "if you need me."

She nodded and picked up the phone.

Blackwood put down his Coke and held the receiver to his ear. "Hello," he said.

Old fears surfaced. Despite the protective barrier, she didn't feel safe.

"I appreciate you coming tonight, Dr. Wolfe," he said slowly, as if he were used to people misunderstanding him. "I wanted to tell you in person, ma'am. Here's the thing." He swallowed nervously. "I didn't kill your sister. I have no idea who did. But I swear to God, I'm innocent." He took a long drag of his cigarette, leaned back, and said, "If there's anything you'd like to ask me… now's your chance."

She swallowed the dry lump of revulsion in her throat and said, "I'm here because Detective Dyson persuaded me to come. He believes in your innocence, but I still have questions."

He nodded respectfully. "Go ahead."

"If you didn't kill my sister, then how did she end up in your backyard?"

"I've been wondering the same thing myself. I have no goddamn idea. Somebody must've framed me. God knows why. Doesn't make sense."

"Who would do such a thing?"

He looked at her blankly. "Whoever took those other girls."

So Palmer must've shared his theory with Blackwood. Palmer was clearly on the prisoner's side.

"Why didn't Nelly come forward sooner?" Kate asked. "Why did it take her sixteen years to come out with the truth?"

"I suppose her conscience finally got to her."

"What about your conscience?"

His eyes flared, and for a moment she felt his intense fury toward her, confirming her worst fears—here was a violent man, a dangerous man. But he swallowed back his indignation and kept his voice steady. "My conscience is clear when it comes to your sister," he said.

Kate realized something just then. It hardly mattered whether she believed him or not, because he'd worn a groove in her psyche. Henry Blackwood would always be the face of evil for her, no matter what the truth was.

He leaned forward. "Listen, Dr. Wolfe, what I did to Penny was wrong, and I've been punished for it. But they locked me up for a murder I didn't commit, and now they're going to execute me for it. Four hours from now, I'll be dead." He wiped the sweat off his face and swallowed hard. "My attorneys have presented the governor with some new evidence, including Penny's testimony, and I was hoping… well, it'd be extremely helpful to my cause if you'd ask the governor for a new trial. I'd sincerely appreciate it, ma'am. I swear to you," he said in a cotton-dry voice, "I didn't do those awful things to your sister."

To Kate's ears, these words sounded rehearsed. She stared at him. Her mind was full of nothing but the desire to escape.

"If I die tonight… in case the governor doesn't stay the execution… would you do me a favor? Will you tell Penny I love her? And Maddie, too?"

"Maddie?" Kate repeated dully.

He nodded. "I sure hope you can fix her."

"You know that I'm treating her?"

"The detective filled me in. I care about her an awful lot." It was the first time he'd seemed human to her. "She's a great kid. Smart, like her mama."

Kate didn't know what to say.

He leaned forward again. "That night, Penny and me were watching TV when it happened… swear to God. I was with Penny all evening long. I was helping her with her homework. We ordered a pizza. We were together the whole time. The police made her lie on the witness stand. But she's telling the truth now."

Kate almost believed him.

"I remember when you used to walk past my house on your way to school, and your sister would be talking a blue streak behind you. She sounded like a bird. She'd pick flowers from my yard. Why would I hurt somebody like that?"

Kate readjusted her grip on the phone. "I'll convey your message to Nelly. But I'll leave it up to her whether she wants to share it with Maddie or not."

"Okay. Thanks." He took a drag of his cigarette, and she envied him his pack of smokes. "Anyway. Listen. I'm pretty much resigned to my fate. Unless my attorneys can throw a Hail Mary pass or something… it's over for me."

Kate nodded. She was about to hang up when she hesitated. "Okay, look," she said thickly. "I'll call the governor and tell him I'm not convinced of your guilt. At least there should be a new trial."

He lowered his cigarette. "Thank you."

"Please don't thank me."

"No, no," he said emphatically. "*Bless you*, Dr. Wolfe. I appreciate this. It means so much to me."

She hung up and rose unsteadily to her feet, wondering if she was going to collapse. Her head was hammering as if she was underwater. Drowning.

31

KATE SPENT THE NEXT hour in a quiet corner of the death row visitors' room trying to reach the governor on her cell phone. Finally, one of his aides agreed to speak to her and took down her statement. He promised to let the governor know right away and reassured her of the importance of her call.

"Well, we've done everything we can," Palmer said.

The medical examiner Quade Pickler came over and introduced himself to Kate, and he and Palmer made small talk. When Quade turned his gaze on her, Kate felt the same chill she'd experienced sixteen years ago in the morgue. "I hear you called the governor's office?" he said with a wry smile.

She nodded slowly.

"Blackwood talks a good game but I've seen him lose appeal after appeal, trying to manipulate people into believing him. Sorry you were taken in, but I sincerely doubt the governor's going to change his mind." He turned to Palmer and said, "By the way, I saw your anti-death-penalty buddies out in force on the capitol steps today. An assorted crowd of mixed nuts and zealots."

"They aren't my buddies," Palmer said.

"Funny. Because it looks like you're working for the same side."

"Why? Because I don't like seeing an innocent man railroaded?"

"Oh come on. Don't you think it's time to hang it up, Palmer? Take up golf or something?"

"I'm just following my conscience."

Quade shook his head. "Well, I follow the evidence. Thousands of kids go missing in this country every damn year, and in a state like New Hampshire, over the span of twenty years, you'd expect to find quite a number of missing-persons cases. That's just the way it is. Especially when it involves teenagers and runaways, troubled kids on drugs or with psychological problems."

"Nelly's recantation is a pretty good argument for a new trial, don't you think?"

"Let me tell you something," Quade said. "My mother used to be afraid of public restrooms—she'd rather pee her pants than use a public toilet. Then one day, we were at the department store, and she had to pee real bad, so she caved and used the restroom. Two seconds later, she ran out screaming that there was a man in there, masturbating. The store called the cops, and guess what? There was nobody in there. My mother saw something that wasn't real; her phobia overcame reason. People lie all the time. That's just life.

"I hate to break the news to you, pal, but you're retired. You should probably call it a day. Chief tells me he still occasionally gets three AM calls from you." He laughed and turned to Kate.

"I think they've got a restraining order out on him by now. Well, I'm not sticking around for the main event. I just dropped by to make sure justice was done." He nodded and left.

"Wow. Real nice guy," Kate said sarcastically.

"Yeah," Palmer muttered. "He gives me sepsis."

The crowd was thinning out. Some of the visitors had already left. Should she go? She broke into a cold sweat. She couldn't believe what she was about to say. "Palmer? Is it too late to be a witness?"

He studied her carefully. "You've done your part, Kate. You can go now."

"But what if the governor has questions? I should be here, just in case."

"There's less than a fifty-fifty chance he'll stay the execution."

"I don't care," she said recklessly. "I want to stay."

"Are you sure?"

She nodded.

"Okay. Let's go talk to the warden."

Things happened quickly. Kate got special permission to be a witness—she was, after all, the victim's only representative. At 8:15 PM, the prisoner was escorted back to death row where, according to Palmer, he'd be allowed to walk the range and say goodbye to his fellow inmates. Then the warden and chaplain would begin preparations for the execution.

At 8:45 PM, everybody in the visitors' holding area was

frisked and shuttled over to the death house, a small brick building located a hundred yards away from the main prison. The group of twenty-four witnesses included relatives of the prisoner, state-selected representatives, members of the media, Blackwood's attorneys, law enforcement officials and the prosecuting attorney.

They entered a squat cement building, where they passed through a series of checkpoints and metal detectors before walking down a corridor toward the viewing room. Half the group was funneled into the main viewing room, while the other half was escorted into an overflow room.

Kate and Palmer ended up sitting next to each other inside the main viewing room. There were two rows of upholstered chairs, like a small multiplex theater, but instead of a movie screen, there was a large window into the death chamber. They had front row seats. The digital clock said 9:15 PM.

"The overflow room is for the media and prison officials," Palmer explained. "They'll watch the execution on closed-circuit TV, but we get to see it up close and personal."

The death chamber itself was a well-lit cement cell full of medical equipment and a gurney. There were two points of entry inside the chamber—a blue door to the left, and a red door to the right. The red door was closed, but the blue door was constantly in use as medical personnel kept shuffling in and out, testing the equipment and ticking off items on their clipboards.

"What's behind the red door?" Kate asked.

"A guard with a phone," Palmer said. "If the governor calls, then he'll inform the warden, and the whole thing will shut down."

At 9:30 PM, a man in scrubs came into the death chamber and drew the curtains closed so they couldn't see inside anymore.

"This is where they bring the prisoner into the chamber and get him settled in," Palmer explained. "Once he's secured, they'll open the curtains again."

At 9:45, the curtains were drawn back, and the tension in the viewing room became palpable. Blackwood lay on the gurney, secured at the wrists, shoulders, abdomen, and ankles with leather restraints. He was hooked up to a heart monitor, and there were two separate IV lines going into his arms.

The prisoner lay very still, gazing up at the ceiling. Kate wondered what he was thinking about. Escape? A last-minute reprieve? Heaven? Hell? He'd been a bad man who'd sexually assaulted his niece for years. He was scum. A bully and a pedophile. And yet, Kate couldn't help feeling sorry for him, just as she'd feel sorry for any human being who was about to be snuffed out before her very eyes. She didn't want to watch him die. She hoped the phone would ring. There should be a new trial, at the least. Maybe Palmer was right. Maybe she was about to witness a gross injustice.

A medical team entered the chamber and worked efficiently and swiftly, performing their assigned tasks. They glided back and forth in a choreographed fashion, and Blackwood seemed amused by all the fuss. One of the technicians draped a sheet over his lower body, while another technician listened to his heart through a stethoscope, and a third checked his pupils. The EKG machine began to blip. Then they left the chamber.

The whole thing felt hallucinatory. Kate could hear every cough and restless whisper from the other witnesses. Palmer kept glancing at his watch, the big hand sweeping around in a relentless countdown. Eight minutes to go. Eight minutes before the state took this man's life.

Unless the phone rang behind the red door.

An odd excitement filled the air as the warden and chaplain entered the death chamber. The chaplain spoke softly into the prisoner's ear, while the warden opened the red door and talked briefly to the guard.

Kate stiffened.

Last chance.

The warden closed the door and shook his head. No phone calls.

Palmer leaned over and whispered in her ear, "Notice those two IV lines? See how the tubes go from his arms all the way into that opening in the wall? That's because there's an anteroom behind the death chamber where the execution team is assembled. They'll be working the IV fluids and releasing the drugs. They're the ones who will actually kill him, which is why they'll remain anonymous."

Kate wondered if the execution team wore lab coats or business suits or guard uniforms? How many executioners were there? Were they doctors? Were they getting paid? How much? How many people had applied for the job?

She envisioned the lone guard sitting behind the red door,

waiting for the phone to ring. Did he periodically lift the receiver and listen to the dial tone to make sure it was working? Was he bored? Anxious? Had he let his wife know he'd be working late tonight? Had he told her why?

"What happens if the governor doesn't call?" she asked Palmer.

"Then they'll proceed as planned. At the warden's signal, the execution team will release the drugs. First comes the anesthetic—that should take effect in about thirty seconds. He may struggle a bit, but soon he'll close his eyes and relax into a deep sleep. Next, the saline solution will flush out the IV lines. Then a muscle relaxant will stop Blackwood's breathing. It works by paralyzing the diaphragm and lungs. That should take about three minutes. You won't see any reaction from him. Finally, they'll induce cardiac arrest. The whole thing should be over pretty quick. Five to eight minutes from start to finish."

Five to eight minutes.

It sounded like an eternity.

Henry Blackwood lifted his head and looked up at the assembled group in the viewing room. He nodded at his cousins, who waved. "We're praying for you, bro! Bless you, cuz!" He smiled at his attorneys, two well-dressed middle-aged men who nodded solemnly. He mouthed something to his spiritual adviser, the blue-haired lady who held up a hopeful fingers-crossed. Last, he smiled at Palmer and Kate. Palmer nodded. Kate didn't move. She could barely breathe.

At 9:56 PM, the warden announced that the execution would proceed as planned.

"Is there still time for the governor to call?" Kate asked Palmer.

"Right up until the paralyzing agent," Palmer explained. "But once that happens, it's too late."

Four minutes left.

Three.

Two.

One.

No phone call from the governor. No last-minute reprieve.

10 PM.

Blackwood's luck had run out.

The warden asked the prisoner if he had a final statement.

Blackwood nodded and addressed the crowd. "I've hurt a lot of people in my life, and I'm sorry for that. I apologize for the pain and sorrow I caused my mother when she was alive, bless her, and also my niece, Penny. The rest of my family, too, and all my friends who've stuck by me. Thanks, guys. I hope that someday you'll find it in your hearts to forgive me." He swallowed hard. "But I didn't kill Savannah Wolfe. That was not my doing. And I hope and pray that God will forgive my sins, and I pray He'll embrace me tonight and welcome me into His bosom." Blackwood let his head drop back onto the pillow. He turned to the warden and said, "I guess that's it."

The warden nodded. "Thank you, Henry."

For the first time since they'd brought him into the death chamber, the prisoner relaxed. He seemed to be relieved that it was over.

The chaplain whispered a few final words of comfort and

247

made the sign of the cross. The medical personnel took over, checking the lines, adjusting the equipment, and then the warden gave a signal to the executioners in the anteroom, and the injection of lethal dosages began.

Kate stared at the IV lines, hoping against hope that the governor would call—at least there should be a new trial to take account of Nelly's recantation. The seconds lumbered past.

Blackwood began to blink as the drugs flowed into his bloodstream and he struggled against the inevitable. He strained against his bonds, prison-hard muscles bulging in agony. Then, he collapsed against the gurney and grew perfectly still.

Five to eight minutes felt like an hour to Kate's racing heart. The silence was oppressive, like the vacuum of space pushing against her eardrums. It was bizarre—it reminded her of bad performance art, where everybody met their mark and recited their well-rehearsed lines, but the show itself was lifeless. There were no cries of protest, no shrieks or sobs. Just silence as they all sat watching a man die beyond a sheet of glass.

Finally, the EKG monitor flatlined, and the medical team pronounced Blackwood dead at 10:05 PM.

Five minutes was all it had taken.

A medical assistant snapped the curtains shut. The show was over.

Kate sat in dry-eyed shock. Palmer tapped her hand, and they all stood up and shuffled out of the room. She mindlessly followed the crowd into a conference room, where they signed a document attesting to the fact that they'd witnessed the execution. Then the prison guards whisked them outside, where they waited to board a prison shuttle van.

"Now what?" Kate asked Palmer, her shock like pins and needles prickling her consciousness.

"The prison officials are holding a press conference, if you're interested."

"No thanks."

"Me neither. That's enough government bureaucracy for one night. I'm heading home." He gave her a concerned look. "Are you okay? How're you doing?"

"I don't know."

"Well, I'm proud of you. You handled it like a pro."

They filed into the shuttle van, which drove them through the prison gates, past a rowdy crowd of anti-death-penalty protestors, and dropped them off in the middle of the vast parking lot. Palmer escorted her over to her car, where they stood beneath the starry sky for a moment, lost for words. The wintry air had a bite to it. "Call me tomorrow," he said. "We'll talk about it then."

"Okay." Kate's keys were in her hand, her car was right there, but she couldn't shake the feeling that she was lost.

"Drive carefully." He tipped his hat and strode away.

Kate got in her car and started the engine. She blasted the heat and watched Palmer locate his pickup truck among the rows of vehicles and drive away. Everybody else left as quickly as he did.

She switched on her phone and checked her messages. Two were from James. She took a couple of deep breaths and called him.

"Hello?" he answered.

"James, it's me."

"Hi, babe." He sounded happy to hear from her. "How did it go tonight?"

"First, how's Vanessa? How's she doing?"

"We're a little groggy, but the surgery went well."

"Good. That's a relief. Give her my love, okay?"

James muffled the phone, conveying her message, and then asked, "So what happened, Kate? Did you talk to him? What did he say?"

"He swears he didn't do it. He tried to convince me of his innocence. And I have to admit… James, I watched the execution."

"What? Why?" He sounded alarmed.

"I called the governor's office and asked them to stay the execution. I wanted them to at least consider Nelly's recantation."

"Jesus, where are you?"

"I'm at the prison. I'm about to head home."

"I can't believe you did that. Are you okay?"

"Yeah, I think so."

"Call me when you get back to Boston. And call me later on tonight if you can't sleep. Call me anytime, babe. I'm right here. You know that, don't you?"

PART II

32

RIBBONS OF SNOW BLEW across the highway as Kate drove home that night—no music, no radio, just dead silence. Back at the condo, she took a hot shower and had a light supper. The she poured herself a glass of wine, curled up on the sofa, and opened the box of police files. She spent the next couple of hours rifling through first-officer's reports, evidence submission slips, suspect interviews, and witness statements.

Kate poured herself another glass of wine and looked through Hannah Lloyd's file. There were dozens of photographs, but two of them stood out. One was a snapshot of the petite fourteen-year-old posing for her high school yearbook. She had a wide innocent face, long auburn hair, and a self-conscious smile. The second photograph showed irregular shapes jutting out of the forest floor. The top layer of dirt had been whisked away, exposing the partly mummified remains—part of a ribcage and two skeletal fingers clutching a bit of decayed fabric. Hannah Lloyd's shaved skull peeped out of the dirt. Was the killer taking souvenirs? Was this an act of aggression or a form of worship?

Kate leaned back and closed her eyes. She went back to the

balmy summer night she'd left her sister alone in the cabin, while she and the cute boy had wandered off. They settled on a patch of grass in a grove of evergreens and made out beneath the August moon. Overwhelmed by a surge of hormones, Kate didn't see or hear anything unusual that night—no vehicles coming up the logging road, no screams or shouts. All she heard was the boy's heavy breathing in her ear and the muffled beat of her own lustful heart.

But there had been a strange noise in the woods that night, deep and territorial. Five ominous hoots. *Hoo-hoo, hooooo, hoo-hoo.*

"It's a ghost," the boy teased, but Kate knew a great horned owl when she heard one. They were the largest nocturnal birds in New Hampshire, rust-colored with snow-white throats and tufted feathery horns. They had piercing yellow eyes, and their hoots came in series of fives. *Hoo-hoo, hooooo, hoo-hoo.*

The boy put his hand down Kate's pants and frantically unhooked her bra, and she vaguely recalled seeing splashes of light around the cabin in the distance, but she figured it was just her sister exploring, shining the flashlight around, because that's what Savannah did. She was the Curious George of little girls.

Kate wasn't completely irresponsible; at one point she tried to get up to go check on her sister, but the boy pulled her back down and kissed her all over, which made her swoon, until she was lying flat on the prickly ground, mesmerized by the things he was doing to her body.

"Wait," she hissed cautiously.

"What?"

"Do you hear that?"

Hoo-hoo, hooooo, hoo-hoo.

"Kiss me," he commanded.

She kissed him. She did whatever he wanted. She lost her virginity that night. She lost everything that night.

Now she sighed in defeat as she put the files back in the box. There was nothing she could tell Palmer he didn't already know. Her actions had been written up in the police report. She'd confessed everything to Detective Dunmeyer, down to the last lurid detail—the blood in her underpants, the stickiness between her legs, the boy's half-hearted attempts at consoling her afterwards—and worst of all, how she'd taken her sweet time getting dressed and going back to the cabin and finding it empty.

The phone rang. Kate picked up. "Hello?"

"Did I wake you?" It was Palmer Dyson.

"Can't sleep," she admitted groggily. "I was looking at those files you sent over."

"Yeah? What do you think?"

"I have my impressions, but nothing earth-shattering." A shiver made her draw her knees to her chest. "Do you want to hear them?"

"Nah. Let's talk tomorrow. I just took a couple of Ambiens."

"Actually, I could swing by your place first thing. What time's good for you?"

"I'm wide open."

"Really?" she teased. "You've got nothing penciled in?"

"I've got like zero social life."

"How's nine o'clock sound?"

"Sounds good. There's something I'd rather tell you in person anyway."

She frowned. "What?"

"Tomorrow," Palmer said, and hung up.

33

HANNAH LLOYD'S CRIME SCENE photos pushed their way into her dreams, and Kate woke up on Thursday morning in an absolute panic, clawing at the air. She sat up in bed with her temples pounding as the nightmare slowly receded. Something about skeletal fingers digging up fistfuls of spiders.

It was 5:00 AM, and James's side of the bed was empty. She missed him with a big sorry ache. She got up and opened the window and inhaled a chill blast of arctic air, and it shocked her lungs like a scoop of ice cream. She tried to shake off any lingering grief that should've ended with Blackwood's death and called Nelly at home, despite the early hour, but gave up after the tenth ring. The Wards must be avoiding the barrage of media calls, and who could blame them? Kate refused to answer her phone for the same reason—old friends calling to commiserate, reporters requesting interviews, bloggers trolling for click-bait. Savannah Wolfe was trending on Twitter. All she could do was wait it out, until the media winds blew over. How long that could take was anybody's guess.

She showered and got dressed, then grabbed her keys and headed for New Hampshire. Once she'd left the greater Boston area behind, the drive was relatively hassle-free, with very little traffic on the road. She passed dozens of New England villages nestled in snow-covered valleys, their lacy Christmas-card quality soothing her nerves.

Detective Dyson lived on the east side of Blunt River, at the end of a meandering country road. She parked in front of his tattered Queen Anne, took the shoveled walkway up to his rickety front porch, and knocked on the door.

They shook hands, and he seemed fully awake and brimming with energy. "Come on in. Watch your step. Gotta fix that."

The house was sunny and spacious, with old-fashioned drafty windows and gorgeous woodwork. The furniture was a blend of modern-discount and family heirlooms. Dozens of storage boxes were stacked around the living room, giving it a garage-sale feel. Every surface was covered with old police reports, dirty dishes, and textbooks on criminology. A standalone whiteboard in the corner was covered with names, dates, and timelines. There was a map of Blunt River County tacked to the wall, with colored pushpins indicating various abduction points.

"See what happens when your obsessions take over?" he joked. "They grow like kudzu. Grab a seat. Coffee?"

"Sure."

"Long trip?"

"Not bad."

"Be right back." He ducked into the kitchen.

Kate glanced around the living room, at the hardwood floor

and river-stone fireplace. A mahogany desk with an outdated PC and fax machine was bracketed by two glass-fronted bookcases crammed with leather-bound volumes. She took a seat in a plaid armchair facing a brown corduroy sleep-sofa.

"So," he said, returning with two steaming mugs on a tray. He handed her the milk and sugar and sat down on the sofa. "Let's talk."

She smiled uncertainly. "You said you had something to tell me?"

"First." He held up a finger. "What's your profile? What do you see in those files?"

She understood what he was looking for: a psychological cold reading. "My first impression? Well, we don't know anything about the fate of the four missing girls, so it's difficult to prognosticate."

"What about the others?"

"If you accept the theory that the suicides and accident were staged murders," Kate said, "and that the killer is obsessed with the victims' hair… then the next thing we need to do is look for commonalities between the victims. On face value their ages and physical characteristics are all over the map. But the two things they all have in common are their sex and general age range."

"Female children?"

"Yes. But I didn't see anything in the files to indicate they were raped, which tells me this isn't a sexual deviant. This is something different. A predator who's triggered by the hair of young females."

"Why? What's the psychological significance?"

"It's likely the result of childhood trauma."

"So he's acting out some sort of psychological ordeal from the past?"

"Possibly. Shaved heads and shorn hair are pregnant with meaning for him. The act of removing the hair is heavily symbolic."

"Symbolic of what?" Palmer asked.

"I don't know. Perhaps a form of punishment." It didn't escape Kate's notice that they were speaking as if she accepted the premise. "After World War II, the Allies shamed female Nazi collaborators by shaving their heads and parading them in front of a jeering crowd. It's a method of defeminizing. Or else he could be infantilizing his victims. By shaving their heads, they become like helpless infants. No longer a threat to his manhood."

"So he's scared of a bunch of girls? Is that what you're saying?"

Kate smiled. "There are other possibilities. For example, Buddhist monks and nuns will shave their heads as a purifying act before entering the order."

He nodded thoughtfully. "A renunciation of worldly pleasures."

"But I think it's much more personal than that. He may have witnessed something as a child—some traumatic event that disturbed him. His mother or some other powerful female figure could've come down with a debilitating disease that caused her to lose her hair, for instance. Or maybe she was mentally imbalanced and shaved it off in a fit of psychosis. Mental illness is a strong contender, since it's passed from one generation to the next. Whatever the reason, he's branding them. These girls are his. He puts his mark on them, and they become untouchables."

"Untouchables?"

"His alone. Forever."

Palmer leaned forward. "Okay, let's go with that. Let's say his mother lost her mind and that he inherited the condition. What's your prognosis?"

She shrugged. "These crimes are too methodical and well-organized to be the work of a delusional schizophrenic. He's in control of his impulses. And he isn't bipolar, because grandiosity would make him want to brag about his exploits. He'd be writing letters to the editor or taunting the police with his accomplishments. There are a couple of other possible disorders… but my best guess is sociopathy. Sociopaths can function normally in society. They can be clever and deceptive and highly manipulative. He doesn't care about the pain he's inflicted on others or the destruction and chaos he's left in his wake. He can't experience emotions the way most people do. So criminal behavior is easy for him."

"Which is why he hasn't raised any red flags yet."

She nodded. "Otherwise he would've been caught by now."

"Okay," Palmer said. "What are his weaknesses?"

"A penchant for young girls," Kate said. "A traumatic childhood. He's on the prowl. If what you say is true, then he's developed a pattern of abducting vulnerable children and

260

taking them someplace where he can cut their hair then dispose of their bodies, perhaps in the woods like Hannah Lloyd. Or else he stages suicides to see if he can get away with it. It's a thrill for him. I doubt he can stop voluntarily, which means he leads a secret life. He hides his true self from the world. And that's a great vulnerability."

Palmer cocked an eyebrow. "What's his motivation?"

"If these aren't lust kills, then it's all about power. He selects his victims carefully. He bides his time. There's nothing rushed about these crimes—the staging of Susie Gafford's, Lizbeth Howell's, and Tabitha Davidowitz's deaths shows that. Which means he's methodical and well organized. He knows what he's doing. He enjoys the hunt. He's devious. He likes to play games. But he's probably very afraid of getting caught. Bottom line, he hates to lose. That's his biggest weakness."

A slow smile spread across Palmer's face. "I want you to take a look at something for me." He rummaged through a pile of photographs on the coffee table. "Tell me if this gets to be too much." He handed her a glossy 8x11 of a young girl with a crescent-shaped bruise on her throat, and Kate recognized six-year-old Susie Gafford, the little girl who had fallen down a well. "See this bruise? That is what you call a compression injury." He pointed at the photograph. "It occurred antemortem, just before death. Any thoughts?"

Kate studied the photograph. Susie's eyes were closed. Her lips were blue and her neck was tilted at an angle. Her glossy hair was braided in pigtails and tied at the ends with satin ribbons. It was a horrifying sight, and yet Kate couldn't tear her eyes away. Susie had cuts and contusions on her body—no doubt from falling fifty feet down a stone well—but Kate could plainly see what the detective was talking about: a distinctive crescent-shaped mark on the victim's throat, about two inches long and half an inch wide. "Looks like a half-moon," she said. "A crescent. As if something was pressed against her skin."

"Exactly," he said.

There was something oddly familiar about the mark. Kate handed the photograph back and shuddered. Detective Dyson was leading her down a very dark path. "What does it mean?"

"I believe she was strangled with something soft, like a scarf or a blouse, placed over her throat lengthwise and gradually tightened. It was held that way with two hands, one hand pulling on either end. The hyoid bone was intact, meaning she wasn't strangled with a belt or a cord, or by a pair of hands. We didn't find any fingernail marks around the throat, which would indicate manual strangulation. Just this single compression injury, inflicted shortly before her heart stopped beating."

"So she was strangled to death?"

"It's called soft strangulation," he explained. "A piece of fabric, when used correctly, won't leave any telltale marks on the victim."

"But I'm confused. Why did the medical examiner rule it an accident?"

Palmer ran his finger around the rim of his coffee mug. "Quade and I were always butting heads. I objected to his ruling at the time. But soft strangulation doesn't leave any trace behind."

"Except the killer made a mistake, right?" she said. "Because there was something attached to the piece of material he strangled her with. Something that left this mark?"

"Right," Palmer said with a nod. "Perhaps a piece of jewelry; I'm thinking a pin or a brooch. He made a crucial error and didn't notice his mistake until it was too late. So he threw the body down the well in order to disguise the manner of death."

"But I don't understand. Why didn't the medical examiner see it?"

Palmer shrugged with resignation. "Her face wasn't congested or swollen, no petechial hemorrhages, no red dots or streaks in the eyes, no ligature marks, coupled with an intact hyoid bone… he concluded that she struck her throat during her tumble down the well. But you can't dismiss a compression injury. Especially when some of the blood settled into the back of the body—not much, but enough. Evidence the victim was lying on the ground when she died, not curled up inside the well. If Susie Gafford was his first kill, then the perp was bound to make a few mistakes."

Kate swallowed hard. They were talking about real events and real people. Real little girls. This discussion was no longer theoretical, and it scared her. She resisted. What if Palmer was wrong? What if the medical examiner was right? "I don't get it," she said. "Why aren't the police all over this?"

"You're talking about a skilled psychopath—you call him a sociopath, I say tomato. He probably has a good job—a teacher, minister, social worker—and this is his terrain—Blunt River County. He's comfortable here and can strike at any time or place of his choosing. Otherwise, he never would've gotten away with it."

"And the police don't see a connection?" she asked incredulously.

"First of all, there are four jurisdictions handling the nine cases, and each of these departments don't necessarily communicate with one another. They all have their own hotlines, with thousands of tips pouring in. You've got hundreds of witnesses and suspects to track down. It's easy for an investigator to get bogged down. Like I said, Quade and I strongly disagreed about a lot of things, but his word held a lot of sway. Still does."

"That's pathetic."

"Don't get me wrong. This is a great bunch of guys I'm talking about. They work their butts off. They want justice, same as me. But they've got a job to do and a board to clear, and things can get messy fast. There's a lot of infighting and there are budgetary considerations. Blunt River depends heavily on tourism, and the powers-that-be don't want any feathers ruffled unless the police are a hundred per cent sure of their facts." He shrugged. "So caution prevails. Shit happens."

"What about Quade Pickler?"

"What about him?"

"Don't you think it's weird? He just dismissed you outright?"

Palmer shook his head. "Like I said, he's not the sharpest knife in the drawer. He's as easily fooled as the rest of them."

"So you left it at that?"

"No, I didn't leave it at that. Given the age of the victims, I interviewed all known pedophiles in the area, family members, neighbors, teachers. It wasn't until years later that I learned…"

He looked at her. "There's something I have to tell you."

She nodded slowly.

"I already have a suspect in mind."

She drew back, unnerved by the revelation.

"He fits the profile I've built up of the killer: a loner in a position of authority. He's a professor at Wellington University, right here in Blunt River. And I think you know him."

Her heart skipped a beat.

"William Stigler," Palmer said.

Kate shook her head, confused.

"Professor William Stigler?" he repeated, then frowned. "You don't know him?"

"No, I've never heard of him." Kate felt suddenly angry. "Why didn't you tell me this sooner, Palmer? Why let me go on and on like that? I feel like such an idiot."

"No, no. Don't feel that way. I wanted your unbiased opinion. Everything you said makes perfect sense. It validates what I've been working on."

"You could've told me from the beginning and saved us both a lot of time."

"Are you *sure* you don't remember him?"

She shook her head angrily. "Why should I remember him?"

"He's a sociology professor in his late fifties. Over two decades ago, he did a residency at the asylum where your mother was confined. Like I said, I thought you knew. He was doing a postdoctoral thesis on family dynamics and mental illness. He asked for volunteers. Your mother was one of those volunteers. They grew… close."

"*What?*"

"Then you probably don't know about this either," he said bluntly. "But your mother and Stigler moved in together shortly after she was released from the hospital."

"Are you kidding me?"

He sat back. "Maybe it's time for me to stop."

She stared at him with ferocious intensity. "What the hell, Palmer?"

"You should talk to your father about this."

"I remember visiting her at the hospital," Kate said numbly. "She seemed so lost. When she finally came home six months later, she looked like a different person. She had this glow about her. We all figured she was better. But then, my parents started bickering again, and after a few weeks, she packed her bags and took off. Savannah and I had no idea where she'd gone, but Dad told us she went back to the asylum for more treatment."

"He never told you the truth?"

Kate shook her head. "I had no idea she was having an affair. What did you say his name was? Seegler?"

"William Stigler. I'm sorry, Kate."

"And you think he's a suspect?"

"He's my prime suspect."

"How do you know? What's your evidence?"

"It happened last year, during the Makayla Brayden investigation," Palmer explained. "Stigler approached us out of the blue and offered to help with the case, which is highly suspicious in my book." He leaned forward. "This is strictly confidential, Kate. You can't breathe a word of it to anyone."

"I'm a psychiatrist. I know how to keep a secret."

"Not even James," he warned.

She gave a grim nod.

He cleared his throat. "Stigler came to us uninvited, claiming he wanted to help. He did a few other things, too."

"Like what?"

"I can't get into that right now. You have to trust me."

Her temper flared. "Maybe I don't trust you anymore, Palmer? Maybe if you'd told me sooner—?"

"Kate," he interrupted, "the last thing I want to do is lose your trust."

Kate relented. She remembered visiting Julia at Godwin Valley Asylum, that bizarre Gothic fortress across town. A dumping ground for crazy people. She recalled her mother's pale dissociated countenance during those rare visits. Julia drifted through the halls like a ghost, looking straight through her frightened daughters. "I'm here for my nerves," she told them vaguely. "My nerves need rewiring."

Palmer steepled his hands together. "Any crime you're investigating, you develop a list of suspects. Mental patients, ex-cons, rapists, relatives, neighbors... whoever matches the profile. You gradually build your list, and one by one, you cross them off. My list is very short now. And Stigler's name is at the very top."

"Why haven't you arrested him?"

"For one thing I'm retired. I can't arrest anyone."

"But he's your prime suspect, right? Can't you get one of your pals down at the police station to arrest him?"

"My pals?" Palmer cracked a smile. "Believe it or not, Kate, I don't have that kind of influence."

"Okay, so last year, he offered to help you with the case. How does that make him a suspect?"

"You were right about the differences between the victims. They come in all sizes and shapes. But they do have another thing in common: they all come from broken homes. Divorce, domestic abuse, alcoholism, drugs. These weren't the happiest of families."

"So what's that got to do with Stigler?"

"He's a sociology professor. One of the classes he teaches is called 'Victimhood Among Children From Broken Homes.' Over the past couple of decades, he and his team of postdocs and research associates sent out thousands of questionnaires to at-risk families. His underlings weeded through the responses and conducted the initial interviews, but Stigler himself conducted select follow-up interviews. And guess which families he's interviewed personally?"

She took a stab. "All of them?"

"No. Seven out of nine of the cases I think are linked. Not your family, not Emera Mason's, but all the rest. I believe he selected them because they fit the criteria: troubled homes with abusive relationships or mental illness or alcohol and drug problems. He chose girls who were vulnerable to predation. What better way to find your next victim?"

She fell silent.

"Look," he told her gently. "I wouldn't blame you if you decided to stop. Sometimes the truth can get ugly."

She shook her head. "Don't you think I know that?"

"What I mean is… it's okay to quit."

She bit her lower lip. "After my sister died, I begged them not to cremate her. I didn't want her to end up in a box like our mother. My father agreed, so we picked out the casket together. I went to her room and found her favorite dress—it was lilac with an empire waist. I found her favorite doll, too. She'd given it a makeover—Magic Marker lipstick and a choppy punk haircut. I remember sitting there for the longest time with that ugly doll in my lap, sobbing."

Palmer nodded.

"Anyway, the doll's shoe fell off and rolled under the bed. And when I went to pick it up, I saw the biggest wad of bubblegum I've ever seen in my life—it must've weighed two pounds. Savannah would chew gum until it lost its flavor, and then stick it under her bed, where nobody could see. She must've stuck hundreds of pieces of gum there. I've never laughed so hard. That was my sister. She was the funniest kid in the world. She was my best friend. So when you tell me the truth can get ugly… it can also be beautiful."

A feathery silence landed between them. She stood up. "I have to go talk to my father."

He escorted her to the door. They paused on the threshold, while she dug her keys out of her bag. "Do you really think they're dead?" she asked. "The missing girls?"

He nodded.

"Every last one of them."

34

KATE DROVE ACROSS TOWN feeling nauseous and disoriented. Her father wasn't home. His Ford Ranger was gone from the driveway. She checked her watch: 10:30 AM. Being semi-retired, he had Tuesdays and Thursdays off. So where was he?

She decided to wait for him. He kept a spare key hidden under a flowerpot in the garden. She let herself in and started a fresh pot of coffee brewing. She took a seat at the round table in the kitchen and listened to the coffee maker as it gurgled, while morning sunlight spilled across the linoleum floor. The house had once been full of people. Now it was full of creaks and groans.

The washing machine in the basement was making a weird *chugga-chugga* noise, so she went downstairs to investigate. Cobwebs dangled from the ceiling and the water heater rumbled in a far corner. Bram's handyman tools were arranged by size and function on a large wooden pegboard: wrenches, hacksaws, band saws, hammers, screwdrivers. His workbench was cluttered with paint cans and plastic organizer caddies—nails, bolts, and screws segregated into little drawers. Duplicate keys dangled from hooks on a smaller pegboard—

the spare house keys, the garage-door opener, extra keys to his downtown doctor's office, the storage unit on Carriage Road, and finally, keys to the old farmhouse in Four Oaks, Maine, where Kate's grandparents used to live. Her father couldn't seem to part with the rundown farmstead.

The washing machine's balance-indicator light was blinking. She lifted the lid and struggled to free the twisted clothing inside the agitator basket, until the light blinked off. She dropped the lid and the clothes began to spin around again. No more *chugga-chugga*. No more banging and bumping, like angry ghosts.

She went upstairs and felt a nervous flutter in her stomach. The revelation that her mother had had an affair was still hitting her. And what if Palmer was right? Had Julia fallen in love with a serial killer? *Do we really know the people we love?*

She went into the living room and took a seat in the wingback chair, then powered up her iPad and googled Professor Stigler. His university profile popped up. He was handsome in a George Clooney sort of way, and had an impressive CV.

She heard a noise and jumped. She went over to the window, but didn't see her father's car. Where did he go on his days off and what did he do? She couldn't just ring him up and ask, because he didn't own a cell phone, the Luddite. He refused to buy into smartphones, let alone Facebook, Instagram, Twitter, or Skype. He only had the landline and an old-fashioned pager that was off-limits. The pager was for patients and emergencies only.

It wasn't difficult for Kate to understand why Julia had left him. His daily schedule was rigidly timed. Every clock in the house had to be accurate. He washed his hands methodically—typical for a doctor. He followed an elaborate grooming routine that couldn't be interrupted. He was controlling and didn't like to be challenged. Everything had to be perfectly aligned, perpendicular or parallel. His worldview required order and control.

When you lived with a doctor, you got used to the daily lectures on hand-washing and tooth-brushing. Kate had grown up without breaking a single bone. She'd never been seriously ill. Her father had managed to protect her from the hazards of everyday life, but what good were clean hands when your mother was dead? What good were straight As when your sister was gone?

Kate had seen pictures of Bram as a young boy, a skinny beanpole who towered over his classmates. Her mother once told her that Bram had grown up in a village full of rowdy farm boys who'd picked on him mercilessly, calling him Ichabod, Mantis, Lurch, and Chewbacca. No wonder he was so uncomfortable in his own skin. Grandpa Wolfe had been demanding and controlling of his son, although not of his grandchildren. The girls used to visit their grandparents' farm, and by then Gramps had been like a scary schoolmaster with a gooey center. All bark, no bite.

Kate drank her coffee and waited for her father's return, determined to confront him. She would bring up William Stigler and ask Bram why he'd lied about Julia going back to the asylum. She checked her watch and grew restless. She got up and wandered around the house, pausing in the living room to study the old gifts she and Savannah had given their father: smooth river stones painted orange and green; ceramic ashtrays they'd impressed with their fingertips; papier-mâché puppets that looked like mangled rats.

She circled the first floor, and finally entered his dark-paneled study—a forbidden place. She really shouldn't be in here, but her curiosity got the better of her. Maybe it was time to ignore his million little rules.

Sturdy oak bookshelves held her father's cherished medical textbooks, and the cracked-leather chair was older than Kate. A chrome light from the desk lamp fanned across his paperwork. Six steel cabinets bulged with decades' worth of medical files. Her father wasn't required to retain the medical records of all his patients, but he had a fear of malpractice suits. Once a patient's record was destroyed, it would be difficult—if not impossible—to mount a defense.

The urge to snoop became overwhelming.

She walked over to a file cabinet labeled A–F, opened the top drawer, and scanned the little plastic tabs, until her gaze landed on *Blackwood*.

Her heart skipped a beat. She pulled out Penny Blackwood's patient file from its hanging folder and rifled through the pages. She read her father's meticulous handwritten notes. Bram had been Penny's general physician from birth, right up until her senior year in high school. He'd stopped seeing her around the time Savannah was murdered.

Throughout the years, he'd carefully documented all of

Penny's illnesses and injuries. Starting at around age eleven, Penny began to complain about a lack of energy. She started having bad dreams and insomnia. In her early teens, she was treated for several yeast infections and vaginal soreness. There were unexplained bruises on her upper thighs and other possible signs of sexual abuse. What amazed Kate was her father's response to all these red flags. He dutifully recorded the details without drawing any conclusions or confronting the parents about the possibility of abuse in the home.

The front door was slammed open and shut by a determined hand. She heard footsteps in the living room. Dread settled in Kate's stomach. She wasn't fast enough. She froze with the file in her hands.

Her father appeared in the doorway. "Kate? What are you doing here?"

Her face flamed. She knew how wrong this looked. Her father was a private person, and it was such an invasion. But the medical file was splayed open in her hands—no sense denying it. "Penny Blackwood was a patient of yours?"

Bram snatched the file away from her. "You have no right. What're you doing here?"

Kate stood her ground. "*Vaginal soreness?* At age thirteen? Come on, Dad! You had to know what was going on. There was a pattern of possible abuse, and yet you ignored it."

He couldn't hide his fury and embarrassment. He jammed the file back in its sleeve, slammed the metal drawer shut and said, "You have no right to go rummaging through my stuff, Kate. What the hell were you thinking?"

"Didn't you see the abuse?" she pleaded, wanting him to defend himself. Maybe there was a reasonable explanation? Information she wasn't privy to?

"It was a complicated situation."

"Complicated? She was clearly being raped."

"I had my suspicions," Bram said, red-faced. "But if I'd lodged a formal complaint, then social services would've taken the child away permanently. I had to be sure about my facts. When I asked Penny about her symptoms, she denied anything was wrong. She refused to talk about it. Some girls mature early and start experimenting with their friends. I didn't know anything for sure."

"Yeast infections? The bruises on her upper thighs?"

"Don't you think I discussed those things with her mother, Kate? More than once? Several times, I separated Penny from her parents and asked her if everything was okay at home. But she insisted nothing was wrong. Her mother thought it might be the new laundry detergent or perhaps an allergy. Penny had sensitive skin. I'd treated her for contact dermatitis as a child. I also thought maybe she had a boyfriend and was covering for him. Her father seemed like a decent guy, not some animal who'd hurt his own daughter."

"That's because it wasn't her father," Kate practically shouted. "It was her uncle, Henry Blackwood."

Bram looked like she'd slapped him.

"He was molesting her. I just found out about it myself. But maybe if you'd done something about this years ago, maybe if you'd dug a little deeper instead of sweeping it

275

under the rug… then maybe…" She stopped herself. "I have to go."

"What exactly are you blaming me for?"

"Dad… I'm leaving."

He let her pass. She was afraid to touch him. She refused to look at him. She could feel the sorrow and fury emanating from his body in waves.

Out in the foyer, she stepped into her damp winter boots, grabbed her coat and gloves, and left without saying goodbye.

35

BACK IN THE CAR, a feeling of tightness engulfed Kate. Troubled families were never easy, she knew from her own experience. And Bram was right—a long time ago, things were different. Nobody wore bike helmets. People rarely fastened their seatbelts. Kids went out to play for hours and didn't get home until dinnertime. Her father had probably tried to do the right thing, just as Kate was struggling to do the right thing for Maddie Ward.

She drove around aimlessly, following the glistening river, going under an old railroad bridge before meandering into the wilderness south of town, where the long-abandoned mental institution was located. Ten minutes later, the woods gave way to a residential area of grid-like streets full of 1960s ranch houses painted pastel colors; her friend Jeanette Lamont had grown up in the mint-green one, and stinky Shannon Maguire grew up in the pale peach one. During the Christmas season, the colored lights gave these identical prefabs a magical glow.

She pulled into the abandoned parking lot of the Godwin Valley Asylum and killed the engine. The austere stone buildings had weathered a thousand storms, but the hospital had closed its doors for good in 1996, and everything had been left to rot. Now the weeds had taken over, dead brittle stalks pushing out of the snow.

Kate got out of her car and listened to the crazed chatter of the blackbirds that had overtaken the grounds. Twenty-two years ago, Julia Wolfe had been confined to this institution for six long months, and the girls had missed her terribly.

She trudged through the snow, stepping over a collapsed barbed-wire fence that wasn't much of a deterrent, and headed for the Female Convalescent Building, constructed in 1878. The looming stone edifice looked truly haunted, with its boarded-up windows and peeling gabled roof. She made it up the icy granite steps without falling on her ass, but the big front doors were padlocked shut. Fortunately for her, somebody had broken into the building through one of the first-floor windows, prying off the boards and pushing the broken glass inside, and then covering the whole thing with trashbags and duct tape.

She found a cement block to give her a boost. She peeled off the trashbags, clambered over the windowsill and dropped inelegantly to the floor. It was as cold as a tomb inside. She brushed the dust off her hands and assessed the grand, high-ceilinged lobby, the sound of her labored breathing echoing back at her. Every inch of wall was decorated with graffiti and the floor was littered with beer cans, cigarette butts and used condoms.

She remembered the precise moment her mother had lost her mind. Kate was doing her homework in the living room, when Julia plugged the vacuum into a wall socket and dragged it back and forth across the rug. Ten minutes later, she was still vacuuming the same spot. She seemed distraught and agitated, and Kate was afraid to ask why. Then Julia changed the nozzle on the hose and tackled a corner of the living room where the cobwebs grew like weeds. They had spiders in the house. Mice, too. You could hear them parading up and down inside the walls at night. You could hear them scampering along the rusty pipes, and if you pounded your fist on the wall, they'd stop for a while, but soon they'd be running around again. Her father used to put glue traps in the basement, but Julia couldn't stand the thought of a half-dead mouse squirming around in one of them, so she begged him to leave them alone, and as a consequence the mice had a lot of babies.

That day, Julia changed the brush for the nozzle attachment and scraped the nozzle against the hardwood floor, trying to suck up every last speck of dirt. The Hoover hummed industriously, while Julia cleaned the same spot over and over again. She wore a thin, almost translucent dress and seemed to be delicately outraged by something—deeply offended by the rug or the cobwebs or the mice or the house or Kate or perhaps her entire life. Her angry words crackled like frost: "I am so sick of this shit." She scraped the floor extra hard, repeating, "I'm so sick of this shit," until the plastic nozzle broke in half. Then she fetched a screwdriver from the basement, and came back upstairs to carve obscenities into the varnished wood: "fucking cunt." They were still there somewhere, hidden under the frayed rug.

Kate crossed the spacious lobby, letting old memories jab at her. The corners of the abandoned institution were dark and dingy. She passed the grand staircase and headed for the sunroom, where a few wheelchairs were overturned and the player piano was missing half its teeth. The nurses used to spend their time shooing unruly patients over to the board games. The stained-glass windows were shattered and the potted plants were dead.

Julia used to complain about the foul-tasting soup and the lumpy mattresses. She couldn't eat. She couldn't sleep. She would come shuffling down the hallway in her silk pajamas, barely able to say hello to her daughters, or hug them. Her medicated eyes were scarily vacant, as if she'd been abducted by aliens and replaced by a nothing-creature. Still, she was their beautiful mother—the most attractive woman on the ward. She floated in an aura of loveliness, while chaos swirled around her.

William Stigler.

Kate couldn't remember any handsome young men hovering around her mother—a smitten postdoc or bespectacled research assistant. Only the bulked-up orderlies who flew into action whenever violence erupted, and then hung back with their hands clasped, waiting for the next disruption.

She touched the tarnished VISITING HOURS sign and thought about her mother's psychiatrist, Dr. Jonas Holley, the eccentric old doctor who used to wear mismatched socks—sometimes green and brown, other times blue and red. Before each visit, she and Savannah would bet on what combination of colors he'd be wearing that day. Rumor had it he was colorblind. He had a bowl of Tootsie Pops in his office, and Savannah always chose the green ones.

Kate heard a noise and spun around. Something scuttled toward an ancient Christmas tree, trimmed in cobwebs. The gifts were gone, replaced by bird droppings. There were no answers here.

36

KATE SAT IN HER car and did an online search for Dr. Jonas Holley. He was retired now, but still lived in the area. She found his address and phone number online, and gave him a call. She explained her situation, and to her surprise he invited her to pay him a visit. He welcomed the company, he said.

Dr. Holley lived in a sky-blue Gothic with gingerbread trim on a residential street not far from the old asylum. She took the flagstone walkway up to the front door and used the heavy brass knocker. The door swung open almost immediately. Dr. Holley was frail and stooped, in his late seventies, wearing a faded maroon sweater, dark slacks, and polished Oxfords.

"Hello. I'm Kate," she said.

"*Bienvenue*, welcome. Come in, Kate. Quickly, please. My house doesn't like the cold." He ushered her inside.

"Thanks for agreeing to see me on such short notice," she said, following him down the knotty-pine-paneled hallway into a galley kitchen, where the Venetian blinds didn't hang straight.

"Have a seat. Would you like some tea?"

"No, thanks."

"Coffee? Water? No?"

She took off her coat and gloves and draped them over a wooden chair, then sat down at a breakfast nook cluttered with newspapers. "I'm surprised you remember my mother."

"Julia was unforgettable. One of a kind." Holley sat down opposite her and smiled.

"My father never mentioned William Stigler, so it came as quite a shock when I found out he and my mother had had an affair. I was hoping you could shed some light on it for me."

"First, I have a confession to make," Holley said. "I looked you up online a few minutes ago, just to make sure you are who you said you are. And I've got to say, Kate, your mother would've been very proud."

"Thank you." Kate smiled.

"But given your credentials, you understand my predicament, being a psychiatrist yourself. Doctor–patient confidentiality continues after death."

"But not for close relatives," she countered politely. "And not if you think your patient would've approved of such a disclosure."

He nodded. "And I have no reason to believe your mother would've objected to you finding out some things about her. However, there were a few… situations she would've wanted kept confidential, which I must respect."

"Whatever you can tell me, I'd be grateful."

Holley nodded slowly. "Julia came to us with several complaints upon admission. She was obviously suffering from depression and experiencing a sense of paranoia. She was having trouble sleeping. She'd been self-medicating at home—alcohol and marijuana. She was hearing voices and experiencing acute visual hallucinations. She was also convinced she'd contracted an STD, which turned out to be true."

"She had an STD?" Kate repeated.

"Which we treated with antibiotics."

Kate blinked. "Wait. So my father gave her an STD?"

"No. It wasn't him," Holley said gently. "Your parents weren't sleeping together at the time, according to Julia. She didn't want him to know about it. And due to the precarious nature of her depression, and also since your father wasn't at risk of contracting the disease, I complied with her request to keep it secret. The laws were different then. We didn't have to dot every *i* and cross every *t*."

Kate bristled with outrage on behalf of her father. "And this was *before* she met Stigler?"

Holley nodded.

"So who was the jerk who was banging my mom?"

Holley smiled indulgently and shrugged. "Julia was a free spirit. Her partner was from out of state. I've forgotten the name, but I doubt it would be helpful to you."

Kate was forced to rethink everything she knew about her parents. Mom slept around. Mom wasn't faithful. Bram had been the injured party all along.

"Her life was becoming increasingly chaotic," Dr. Holley continued. "She had poor impulse control and suicidal tendencies. She imagined 'shadow' people were following her around. She was convinced that some of her jewelry had been stolen. She believed her cat had been killed."

"Phoebe. Our long-haired Persian," Kate affirmed. "She was poisoned."

"No." Dr. Holley shook his head. "Julia believed that, but your father explained to us that the cat had been sick and most likely died of a virus."

Another myth shattered. The "poisoned cat" was one of those childhood legends that was deeply ingrained in Kate's psyche. She and Savannah used to wonder which of their neighbors had killed the cat. They both suspected Henry Blackwood.

"Her marital problems were more than sexual in nature," he continued. "Julia complained about your father's controlling and obsessive behavior. Bram didn't like it when she socialized without him or visited old friends. She felt it was impossible to live up to his exacting standards. Anyway, she presented with symptoms of psychotic depression, and I prescribed medication, along with regular counseling. We adjusted her meds, and after six months of gradual but steady improvement, we released her. Looking back, perhaps it was premature, but Julia seemed ready to resume her normal life. I had no idea she'd fallen in love during her stay at the asylum. I found out about it later on."

"So my mother never mentioned Stigler to you?"

"No. There were rumors, of course. But I make it a rule never to listen to idle gossip."

"What else can you tell me about him?"

"Professor Stigler? He was a postdoc at the time. A bright, ambitious young fellow, looking for test subjects for a study about the offspring of at-risk families. Julia volunteered."

"You didn't worry that it might interfere with her therapy?"

"On the contrary. I saw it as a useful adjunct."

"And you didn't realize they'd fallen in love?"

"They kept it hidden from everyone."

"But you said there were rumors?"

"You know how it is, Kate; nurses like to gossip. I always take it with a grain of salt. By the time I found out about the affair, your mother was dead, and Stigler had gone to work at the university. We bump into one another professionally, but he's much more of a political animal than me."

When Julia came home from the asylum, she had seemed to Kate like a changed woman. She couldn't stop smiling. Her skin glowed. Her eyes sparkled. But after a few weeks, the cracks in her marriage began to show, and then one day, Julia left. A few weeks later, she was dead.

Dr. Holley smiled sadly. "During her brief stay at Godwin Valley, I got to see a small slice of a rich and complicated life. Consider me one of seven blind men describing an elephant, while holding its tail. I couldn't tell you about the trunk, or the ears, or the tusks. Your mother's life was far grander than my summation of her illness. You understand?"

"Of course."

"I hope our talk was helpful."

"Thanks for your time." Kate got up to leave.

Dr. Holley walked her to the door. "I didn't tell you everything, but I told you enough."

She looked at him quizzically. "What do you mean?"

"Some things you're going to have to find out on your own, I'm afraid."

37

TWENTY MINUTES LATER, KATE pulled up in front of Nelly
Ward's mid-century modern house in Wilamette. No matter
how upset she was because of this morning's revelations, she
had to set all that aside. She'd had a message from Yvonne to
let her know that Maddie was acting out because Nelly once
again hadn't come to the hospital as she'd promised. She had
an obligation to the girl to visit the Wards and convince Nelly
to see her.

The neighborhood was quiet. Sunlight sparkled off the
icicles. Nelly's Toyota Camry was parked in the driveway. Kate
craved a cigarette. She rummaged in her bag and settled for a
Tic Tac.

She unbuckled her seatbelt and headed across the front
yard. Kate noticed a set of tire tracks belonging to a large
vehicle, a pickup truck or an offroader, arcing across the snow,
as if someone had left in a hurry. The windows were a lacework
of ice. The front door stood open. That was odd.

She glanced around the neighborhood. Snow was piling up
on the curbs. It was a typical suburban day, with most kids at
school and their parents at work. She climbed the porch steps

and wiped her boots on the welcome mat. "Hello?" she called through the open doorway. "Anybody home?"

No response.

She rang the bell. "Nelly? It's me, Kate Wolfe."

The hairs on the back of her neck stood up. She was tempted to call 911, but what if she was overreacting? Maybe the Wards were in the habit of leaving their front door open? Or maybe they'd had an argument, and Derrick had stormed off, and Nelly was downstairs doing laundry? She'd be furious if Kate called the police. *You have to stop making assumptions about my life!*

Kate decided to go inside, just for a second, to check it out. She held her phone in her hand, just in case. "Hello? Anyone home?" She glanced around the front hallway, at the haphazard collection of umbrellas and winter boots, a few empty QVC boxes, and the muddy welcome mat. "Nelly? It's Dr. Wolfe."

Still no response.

She headed down the hallway and peered cautiously into the living room, scanning the TV dinner trays and discount flatscreen.

"Hello?"

She thought she heard a noise and turned back into the hallway. There were several closed doors coming off it, and one of them had a child's handwritten sign taped to it, with big blocky letters warning, ENTER AT YOUR OWN RISK. Both cute and disturbing, *risk* being such a weighted word.

Kate knocked on the door. "Hello?" When there was no

answer, she pushed it open and entered a child's bedroom. Everything about it was too young for a fourteen-year-old: the walls were pink; the rug had a clown face on it; there were rainbow stickers on the bureau; there was a *Little Mermaid* hand puppet. On the wall Maddie's name was spelled out in construction-paper cutouts. M-A-D-D-I-E.

Kate crossed the toy-cluttered floor and stood in front of the bureau, on top of which stood a Hello Kitty jewelry box stuffed with silver crosses and rosary beads. On the floor at her feet were dozens of mutilated plushies, their fluffy ears torn off and tufts of fur missing. The four-poster bed was the scariest of all—there were four men's neckties tied to each post. She reached out to touch one, the twisted fabric stiff with sweat from little wrists and little ankles. Her heart leapt into her throat.

Kate fumbled with her phone and dialed Ira's number, desperately wanting his advice, but couldn't get any signal. She hurried out of the room and headed down the hallway toward the kitchen, hoping to get better reception. As she turned the corner, she slipped on something slick on the floor and landed flat on her back, the phone tumbling out of her hand. She hit her head and bit her tongue, warm blood pooling in her mouth.

She lay for a stunned instant, blinking up at the ceiling. That was odd. The kitchen ceiling was spattered with spaghetti sauce. She struggled to sit up, but her hands kept slipping in something. She finally wobbled to her feet and retrieved her phone, which had landed next to the kitchen island. She spotted an overturned box of Cheerios on the floor. There were smears of blood on the counters. There were bloody handprints on the fridge. Beyond the kitchen island was a widening pool of blood. She saw a skinny bruised arm and a curled hand, the fingers pale as petals.

Nelly lay dead in a pool of blood, her eyes open and unseeing. Her nose was broken. Some of her teeth were missing. There was a bloody hammer next to her head. She wore a bloodstained turquoise tank top and drainpipe jeans, and her bare feet were slick with blood. You could see where she'd tried to run away: crimson footprints zigzagged across the kitchen floor.

The room began to spin. Kate bolted out of the house and locked herself inside her car, where she dialed 911 with fumbling fingers. Panic took over. All she could see was Nelly's face.

38

DETECTIVE RAMSEY JOHNSON WAS a compact man with a deep voice and an assertive handshake. He asked Kate a bunch of questions, and she told him about the tire tracks in the snow, the open front door, and the restraints on Maddie's bed. He jotted it all down in a notebook full of cramped, indecipherable writing.

They stood talking inside the living room, while a team of officers trekked throughout the rest of the house, collecting evidence. The Wilamette PD had put out a BOLO for Derrick Ward's pickup truck. Paramedics had arrived and pronounced Nelly dead. They were waiting around for the medical examiner to show up before they transported the body to the morgue.

"We'll need your clothes for blood analysis," Detective Johnson told her.

Kate was taken aback. "Everything?"

"Coat. Boots. The works."

Adrenaline flooded Kate's veins as the shock receded. The back of her winter coat was covered in dried blood. So were the soles of her boots. She'd never wear her navy-blue skirt again. "Okay," she said reluctantly. "I have trainers and sweats in the car."

"Hold on. Santos?" The detective waved a female officer over. "We're ready for you now."

Officer Maria Santos was on the short side, with a barrel chest and a boyish face. She had a no-nonsense demeanor and got straight to the point. "Stand over there, please. Turn around. Hold it." She snapped pictures of Kate in her bloody outfit, then went to fetch the sweats and Nikes from the trunk of Kate's car. When she returned, Santos told Kate to change in the den. "Just don't touch anything."

The den was full of Derrick Ward's high school football trophies and overstuffed Naugahyde furniture. Officer Santos handed Kate a bunch of alcohol wipes to get rid of the remaining blood on her hands and held out a trashbag for Kate to deposit her stained clothing. Kate put on her sweats and trainers, while Santos twisted the bag shut and filled out a chain-of-custody form.

"Can I go now?" Kate asked with clammy anxiety.

"First, you have to walk us through what happened one more time."

They went over her movements on entering the house, while Detective Johnson drew diagrams and took copious notes, and Officer Santos snapped pictures of the living room, the hallway, and Maddie's bedroom. Kate pointed out where she'd fallen on the kitchen floor and was appalled to see the bloody snow angel she'd left behind.

"Can I go now?" she pleaded, trying not to look desperate.

The detective checked his notes. "We'll call you if we have any questions."

She thanked the female officer on the way out, but Officer Santos nodded indifferently, as if she'd already forgotten who Kate was.

Outside, the front yard was cordoned off with yellow crime-scene tape. Kate counted three or four officers spread out across the snow, documenting tire tracks and footprints, leaving little orange evidence flags in their wake. As she approached her car, the medical examiner's van drew up and Quade Pickler got out.

"Hello again," Pickler said, striding toward her, his breath fogging the air. "I heard you found the body?"

Kate nodded. "They already took my statement. I was just about to leave."

He tapped a cigarette out of the pack and offered her one. "Smoke?"

"Thanks." She took it, and he lit it for her, then he lit one for himself.

"These'll kill ya."

"Right." She didn't like him.

They stood together on the sidewalk, exhaling streams of smoke. Once you got past those judgmental eyes, Pickler was kind of handsome in a bland sort of way. In his late fifties, he had short, tousled gray hair that forked out in different directions, a square jaw, and a goatee. He had the same peppery smell as her dad. Old Spice.

"Why don't you believe Palmer Dyson?" she asked. "About Susie Gafford?"

He grinned. "You cut a wide path through the bullshit."

"Well? Aren't you concerned? What if you were wrong?"

Pickler stared steadily down at her, nostrils flaring. "You can't argue with the facts. I performed the autopsy myself. Victims of asphyxiation will often bite their tongues. They'll scratch their own necks and faces in an attempt to break free. They'll have defensive wounds on their hands and arms from fending off the perp. Even a little girl will put up the fight of her life, if you cut off her air supply. We didn't find any defensive wounds, no trace beneath the nails. She didn't scratch, bite or claw at an attacker."

He paused to inhale the nicotine deep into his lungs. "After she went missing, we scoured the area for miles. Eventually the dogs started barking at an abandoned well shaft—some of the boards covering it were broken in. Local and state police showed up, fire trucks, ambulances. We took turns trying to reach her but it was a tight space. We finally lowered a camera into the shaft, and you could see her little braids and her dinosaur-print shirt on the monitor. She was all twisted up at the bottom of the well. We were hoping for a happy ending. But some things aren't meant to be."

"What about that crescent-shaped bruise on her throat?"

"Impact injuries can produce contusions and lacerations to the skin. There were multiple projecting rocks and stones composing the walls of the shaft. Look," Pickler said, "I don't have anything against Dyson. Back in the day, he was good police. But his Achilles' heel is his stubborn streak. I could go through each and every case with you, but..." He dropped his cigarette in the snow and crushed it underfoot. "Anyway. He's retired now. He should be enjoying his life instead of pursuing bullshit theories. Have a good one, Doc." The medical examiner walked away towards the house.

Her phone buzzed and Kate checked the number. "James?"

"Just checking in. How are you?"

"Not good." She rubbed her forehead, trying to erase the image of all that blood. "I'm in New Hampshire," she managed to choke. "Something bad happened…"

"Kate? What is it?"

"Nelly Ward is dead. I practically tripped over the body."

"What?" James sounded panicked. "How did this happen?"

"I drove up here to see them, and the door was open, and I went inside, and…"

"Jesus," James hissed. "Are you okay?"

"No. I mean, I'm fine. Physically. But the police took all my clothes."

"What? Why?"

"Because I slipped in a pool of *blood*," she sobbed. "It got all over me." She took a few gasps. "It was awful, James. She was beaten with a hammer. There was blood all over the place."

"Okay. Listen. I'm coming home."

"Don't do that…" she said automatically.

"Where are you now?"

"In Wilamette. But the police said I could go."

"Are you okay to drive?"

"Yeah, sure." Her hands were trembling.

"I just have to make a few more arrangements, and then I'll be home."

"How's Vanessa?" she remembered to ask.

"Fine. We found a good physical therapist, and we're interviewing home care nurses… And, Kate?"

"Yes?"

"I love you."

"Love you too. See you soon." She hung up.

Forty minutes later, midway between Blunt River and Boston, she pulled into a rest area and called Palmer Dyson.

"I just heard," he said. "My buddy Ramsey filled me in. How're you holding up?"

"Not so great." She swallowed the burning lump in her throat. "I can't get the image out of my head. Poor Nelly."

"It'll fade over time. Trust me."

"The police think Derrick did it. They're looking for him now. They put out a statewide alert."

"I don't know about that."

"But the police said he left evidence behind."

"I don't think he did it, Kate."

"Seriously? But you should've seen Maddie's room. I found restraints on the bed—it was horrible. I think he's been abusing her, which is probably why she self-harms. It's classic projection…"

"No. Those restraints are for her own protection. Nelly told me about it years ago. If they don't restrain her at night, she climbs out of bed and hurts herself."

"Oh." Kate blinked. "But Nelly told me that Derrick hit her, and Maddie practically admitted that he hits her, too. And all I can think of is that Nelly must've confronted him about the abuse, and that's why he killed her."

"No, Kate. It's not like him."

She paused a frustrated beat. "The police sounded pretty confident."

"Then I need to find him before they do. He keeps a gun in his truck. They'll shoot first and ask questions later."

A pronounced silence settled in between them.

"Palmer," she said softly, "I don't think I'm built for this."

"But, Kate…"

"I'm sorry. But this is way too scary for me."

"I understand," he said hoarsely. "Listen, if you ever need anything…"

"Goodbye, Palmer. Good luck."

39

IT WAS LATE AFTERNOON by the time Kate got home to Cambridge. She felt stripped down, raw and emotional. She sat on the edge of her bed, kicked off her trainers, and studied the dried blood under her fingernails. She closed her eyes and said a little prayer. She wished Nelly hadn't had such a troubled life. She promised to make sure that Maddie would be okay.

But now she had a job to do. She took a long hot shower, got dressed, threw on her parka and last year's boots, scooped up her car keys and drove to the hospital.

The nurses greeted her with battle-hardened good cheer. "Hey, Doc. You missed all the excitement. Nothing but wall-to-wall drama queens this morning."

"Deep breaths, ladies. Any messages?"

Yvette handed her a stack of pink slips. "I'm afraid your favorite patient has cut herself again."

Kate shoved the pink slips into her coat pocket and headed for the Child Psych Unit. The common area was full of tweens and teens bickering over Boggle and backgammon and video games. They lined up twice a day for their meds, and most of them just wanted to go home.

Kate found Maddie self-isolating in her room. The nurses' aide was sitting cross-legged on the floor, writing her daily progress report on a tablet, while Maddie sat up in bed, hugging a brand new plushie—a pink poodle with floppy ears.

Kate told Claire to take a break, then pulled up a chair. "How are you feeling?"

The girl said nothing. Beyond the window the clouds parted, releasing a ray of sunshine that highlighted Maddie's face and golden eyelashes for a moment. Kate was struck once again by the eerie resemblance to Savannah—same pixie nose and whimsical blondness. There was a fresh set of bandages on Maddie's arm. The sun disappeared behind the clouds again.

"Where were you today?" Maddie asked, peering at her curiously.

"I went to see your parents." Kate didn't know how else to put it. "I'm afraid I've got bad news."

Maddie watched her expectantly.

"I'm afraid your mother's gone."

"Gone?" The girl blinked. "Gone where?"

Your mother is dead. Four simple words. And yet, all her years of training hadn't prepared her for this. Kate's own terrible losses hadn't prepared her for this. How did you tell a child her mother was dead? How did you soften the blow? The truth was, there would be no soft landings. Reality was blunt and merciless. Kate's own experience with death hadn't given her any advantage when it came to breaking the news to others. Death was the nightmare you simply didn't wake up from.

"She passed away this morning, Maddie."

The girl's eyes narrowed critically. "No she didn't."

"I'm so sorry." Kate waited for the information to sink in.

"I don't think I heard you right," Maddie said stubbornly.

"I know it's a lot to absorb. She passed away this morning."

The girl began to rock violently back and forth. "I don't believe you! It's a mistake. She can't be dead!"

"I'm sorry, Maddie." The only solace Kate could think of was that her grief would diminish over time—a lousy consolation prize.

"What happened?" she wailed. "How did Mommy die?"

"I'm afraid someone hurt her. The police are trying to figure out who's responsible."

The girl's distress ticked up a notch. "Somebody killed her?"

"Yes, Maddie. I'm so sorry."

"Where's my father?"

"They don't know."

"So he's not coming to get me?"

"No."

Fear flared in her eyes. "What are they going to do to him?"

"I don't know. They're figuring out the details now. That's why a police officer will be coming to the hospital tomorrow to talk to you."

"Talk to me about what?"

"Your mother and stepfather," Kate said. "They have a few questions about your home life. Do you think you can handle it? Because we can always postpone it for a few days." She'd protested to Detective Johnson when he'd told her he would be visiting, pointing out how unwell Maddie was, but there seemed to be no way to avoid the interview.

Maddie fell silent again. She wasn't rocking anymore. She clutched her pink poodle, stunned. Kate realized she was going into shock.

Kate gently pried the poodle from Maddie's arms and listened to her heartbeat. She examined her pupils and took a pulse. She found an extra blanket, draped it over the girl's trembling legs and made her drink some water. Finally, she asked, "Is there anything I can do to help? Would you like to talk about it?"

Maddie scooped up the poodle and resumed her anxious rocking. Then she started screaming.

Kate pressed the call bell for the nurses' station, and Yvette came running with the choice of needle or pills. Maddie choked down two pills with a cup of water, then resumed her out-of-control screaming. Eventually she settled into a kind of rhythmic sobbing.

Kate sat with her until the weeping subsided and the medicine took effect. Ten minutes later, the girl's pulse had resumed its natural rhythm, and she grew perfectly still.

Kate encouraged her to talk about everyday things in order to distract her. She touched the poodle's fluffy ears and asked, "Is this new?"

Maddie nodded. "Dr. Ira gave it to me."

"Dr. Lippencott?"

"He came to see me today. We talked about stuff."

"You did?"

"I like him a lot. Do you like him?"

"Very much."

"We're going to talk every day from now on, he says."

"You and Dr. Ira?"

Maddie nodded sleepily and closed her eyes, shutting out the world.

40

KATE BARGED INTO IRA'S office. He was seated behind his desk, going over some paperwork.

"Why didn't you tell me you were taking over Maddie's treatment?"

He looked up and gave a resigned sigh. "Have a seat, Kate."

"Why wasn't I consulted?"

"Sit," he commanded.

She sat down.

The office smelled of wood polish. His inbox was stacked two feet high. He put down his pen and folded his hands on the desktop. "Did you break the sad news to our patient?"

Kate nodded. "Just now." On the ride back to Boston, she'd informed Ira about Blackwood's execution and Nelly's murder, and they'd agreed she should be the one to tell Maddie.

"How'd she handle it?"

"She's resting now."

"Okay," Ira said. "I just got off the phone with the McCormacks' attorney. They've decided to file a lawsuit. Hopefully, it won't get very far. Risk Management's on the phone with them now, discussing the possibility of a settlement."

Kate pinched the bridge of her nose.

"Bottom line? I want you to take some time off. That's an order."

She winced. "So you're taking over Maddie's case?"

"Temporarily. Until things settle down. It's time to face facts, Kate. You're under an enormous amount of pressure right now, and that's precisely why we have vacation days and sick days. Understand?"

All Kate understood was that the hospital considered her a liability.

"How many vacation days have you accrued?" he asked.

"I don't know," she muttered. "Four or five."

"Days?"

"Weeks."

"Seriously?"

"They carry over."

"Sheesh. You're like a cyborg or something. Okay, you love to work, and that's admirable. But what are you saving them up for? I shouldn't have to twist your arm."

"We're in the middle of a crisis. I just told Maddie about her mother…"

"I have a question for you, Kate," Ira interrupted. "Can you be an objective therapist right now? First you witnessed the execution of the man who killed your sister. Then you stumble across a murder… It's too much." He threw up his hands. "Do you realize how bad this looks? Do you understand the position you've put us in?"

"I can still be objective about my patients, Ira," Kate insisted.

"Let's be real." He leaned forward. "You need to step away. Right now."

Kate felt herself growing incensed. "Step away from what? Since when are we supposed to step away from our patients in the middle of a crisis? I just told Maddie her mother was dead; she needs me right now—"

"Kate. You know exactly what I'm talking about."

She covered her face with her hands and drew a deep breath. "Have you lost faith in me, Ira? Because if you don't trust me anymore…"

He shook his head firmly. "I will never lose faith in you, Kate. I'm trying to help you."

She nodded glumly.

"Okay. I want you to take a couple of weeks off starting today. Not six months from now."

"What about my other patients?"

"I've asked Yvette to redistribute your appointments, and she just cleared your calendar. As of this moment, you're free."

"Free," she repeated dully.

"Come back to us refreshed and relaxed. I won't be assigning you any new cases until things have settled down. Let's start with two weeks and see where we are. We can always extend it to four if necessary."

"Four?" Kate said. "Am I being forced out, Ira? Tell me the truth."

He leaned forward and lowered his voice. "Just the opposite. I'm trying to keep you here."

"Really? Because it feels like I'm being kicked out."

"Let's just avoid stirring things up until we get this lawsuit sorted, okay? Rather than getting tangled up with another disturbed girl and her murdered mother." He softened his tone. "Look, sometimes we need our friends to remind us that we're only human." He smiled encouragingly at her. "It's not such a terrible thing, is it? A little R&R?"

"I guess not."

"Go home. We'll talk again in two weeks. See where we are."

41

KATE WENT HOME, UTTERLY exhausted. Ira was right. She was a self-admitted workaholic who didn't know how to relax. She'd gotten herself in too deep. She shouldn't have accepted Maddie Ward as a patient. Maybe this was a chance to regain control of her life.

She stood in front of the living-room windows and watched the dying sunlight glint in the icicles on the rooftops across the street. She craved a cigarette and needed a distraction. James would be home soon, the first time in three days. She suddenly realized how much she'd missed him. She found her mother's cookbook and decided to surprise James with a gourmet meal. Something French and Julia Child-ish.

That night, they made love.

James was gone early the next day, back to Massachusetts General. Kate wandered the condo restlessly until, at lunchtime, unable to bear the aimlessness any longer, she decided to drive to the hospital to pick up some files. She might as well catch up on some paperwork while she was on the bench.

As she was gathering what she needed, she noticed that the jar of peanuts was gone. She looked around the office, rummaged through her desk drawers, even checked the wastebasket. Nothing. The peanuts had vanished.

Kate, like most of her peers on the third floor, never locked her office door, since this wing of the hospital was restricted access only. She rubbed the gooseflesh off her arms and glanced around as if the peanuts might magically reappear. Her frustration turned to anger. She stepped out into the corridor and called, "Hey, guys? Has anybody been in my office recently?"

Heads popped out of doorways.

"Have you seen someone go into my office? Spence? Raj?"

Her colleagues shook their heads. "No, Kate. Sorry."

"What about Jerry?" she asked.

They shrugged. "Don't think so."

She thanked them and hurried down the hallway to Jerry's corner office.

"Did you take those peanuts out of my office?" she asked him heatedly.

"Peanuts? What peanuts?" His face was as round as an old-fashioned clock, with two small wet eyes.

"Come on, Jerry. Admit it."

"Admit what?"

"That jar of roasted peanuts. Very funny."

"Sorry." Jerry shrugged. "I don't know what you're talking about."

"A jar of peanuts showed up in my office one day, and now they're gone."

"Wow. Nuts? That's lame."

Kate went back to her office. She sat down at her desk, answered a few emails, and was about to turn on her email out-of-office and leave when she noticed her answering machine was blinking. She played back her messages. Three were work-related. One was from her father.

"Hello, Kate. You told me to call you sometime, and I just heard what happened. Bad news travels fast around here… I'd like to be the kind of father whose children can rely on him, not this person I've become… Anyway, I've taken the day off to run a few errands, but I'll be home for most of it. Give me a call if you'd like. Goodbye."

It was the warmest message she'd ever received from him. Maybe this was her chance. Kate scooped up her car keys, put on her parka, and left the hospital. If they were going to have a heart-to-heart about her mother, she wanted to do it in person.

An hour and a half later, she pulled into her father's empty driveway. The Ford Ranger was gone. Okay, he'd said he was going to run a few errands. Fine. She would wait as long as it took.

Dark clouds were accumulating on the horizon. She took the spare key from under the flowerpot in the garden and let herself in. The house was silent and museum-like. *What kind of errands?* she wondered. What did her father do in his spare time? Drive around aimlessly? Visit friends? Did he have any friends? Was he fucking his secretary—that white-haired old lady with seven grandchildren? A high percentage of physicians got hooked on drugs. Was he addicted to pharmaceuticals?

Did he pick up prostitutes? Gamble? Volunteer his time for good causes? Go to church? She had no idea. Her father was a mystery to her.

She went upstairs to her old room, which hadn't changed in over a decade. The shelves were crammed with books by Carl Jung, Jean Piaget, and Abraham Maslow. On the bureau were her old beauty products and garish makeup. On the walls were music posters: U2, Nirvana, Pink. The drafty old-fashioned windows overlooked the backyard. She used to watch the changing seasons from that painted rocker, while dreaming about becoming a famous psychiatrist and discovering the cure for her mother's madness.

Now she heard a noise and stepped out into the hallway. "Dad?"

Nothing but squirrels on the roof. Or mice in the walls.

She hadn't set foot inside her parents' room in decades. The maple door creaked on its hinges. The hardwood floor popped and snapped in all the familiar places. A few years ago, Bram had moved his belongings downstairs, but he'd left Julia's things intact, along with the four-poster bed with its scrolled walnut posts, the matching nightstands, the sturdy bureau, and the faded Persian rug. Kate sat down on the bed and listened to the springs squeak. She and Savannah used to climb all over their parents in the mornings, waking them up. Her father used to laugh a lot back then.

She got up and stood in front of the bureau and rummaged through the drawers, fingering her mother's lacy nightgowns and camisoles, her imitation Louis Vuitton handbag and her dark Ray-Bans. Julia's birth control pills had been abandoned mid-cycle. Everything smelled faintly of Dior Poison.

The closet was crammed with 1990s clothes. Kate found several labeled storage boxes tucked away behind the dresses and skirts and slid them out past a flotilla of high heels. She popped the lid off WINTER STUFF and examined the mothball-smelling clothes, scarves, and gloves. Tucked in between two cable-knit sweaters was Julia's jewelry box.

Kate grasped it with delight, and opened the lid. She scooped out a handful of bangles, beaded necklaces, and hoop earrings, looking for her mother's Man-in-the-Moon necklace, her favorite piece. Then she grew chilly with sweat, remembering the long silver chain with a smiling silver crescent pendant. A pendant about the size of the injury on Susie Gafford's throat.

In a panic, she dug her hands into the jewelry box, searching for the silver necklace, but couldn't find it anywhere. Dr. Holley had said her mother believed some of her jewelry had been stolen. Maybe Julia hadn't been so crazy, after all? Maybe whoever had stolen it had killed Susie Gafford? Maybe William Stigler…? But wait. Julia believed her jewelry had been taken *before* she'd gone to the asylum. *Before* she'd met Stigler. So it couldn't have been him. Kate shook her head. Or maybe the whole thing was ridiculous. There must've been a million silver crescent pendants sold in the nineties.

Kate dragged the rest of the storage boxes out of the closet, hoping to find the missing necklace. She opened a box labeled BABY STUFF and pawed through tiny baby clothes, rattles, and booties. Hard to believe she was ever that small. She found her favorite childhood sweater, a blue cardigan with an orange tiger patch sewn over the breast pocket, and shook it open. Out fell a stack of letters. She stared at her mother's meticulous handwriting. All the envelopes were addressed to Bram. She started reading.

Dear Bram,

How can I say this without sounding crazy? I'm being studied. Observed. As if I'm part of some huge experiment. Okay, that does sound crazy. I found a dead squirrel in the yard yesterday. What does it mean? And my doll, too, my favorite doll—I told you what happened, didn't I? I can't tell if some of these things I've been experiencing lately were done deliberately or not. Does this happen to other people? Or is it just me? I'm convinced somebody's been in our house, an intruder, and I know you don't believe me, but they must've broken in without leaving any proof behind. They must've taken that picture down off the living-room wall and put it on the dining-room table—don't you remember? The landscape with the barn? Am I crazy? And my favorite doll taken? Who would do such a thing? We need to do something. You have to believe me.

Julia

Dear Bram,

I know you want me to suffer. You must. That's the only explanation I can think of for your coldness, your remoteness, your barely disguised hostility toward me. Here I am in this awful place, because I came close to slitting my throat, and that scared the daylights out of me. I could've killed myself, and I've explored the many ways and possibilities... but I chose to seek professional help instead. Well, it was the best decision I

312

ever made. Dr. Holley is so understanding and sympathetic. The people here are wonderful. You wanted to punish me, I guess, and that's why I'm here. You punished me every day with your harsh criticisms. I can never do anything right. And even though my mental state isn't the best right now, I'm still stronger and healthier than I used to be, and I'm getting stronger every day, and soon I'll find the courage to leave you. There, I said it. I'm taking the girls with me, and you can't stop me. Maybe if you'd listened to me sooner.

Julia

Dear Bram,

I love you, I honestly do. But the question is—where did you go? Where is my loving husband? What caused you so much pain that you'd pull away from the only person in the world who loves you so much? Because I do, Bram, with all my heart. But I don't understand your behavior, and I can't live with it anymore. You make me feel bad about myself. I'm alive and emotional and I feel and I want. But I can't live within the walls you've constructed around yourself. It feels like a dungeon. Things have to change. We either face this together or we face it apart.

Julia

Kate devoured the rest of the letters. Some were filled with paranoid ramblings that supported Dr. Holley's memories of Julia's delusions: mysterious shadow figures following her around; the walls talking to her in "scratch language;" ordinary objects were in fact microphones. But other letters were sober and introspective. A few hinted at past love affairs, practically taunting Bram with her infidelity. Julia accused him of cutting her off from old friends and not letting her be herself. She'd given up so much to marry him—her freedom, her college education, her independence. She felt suffocated and unloved.

Julia's final letter to Bram bragged about her life with William Stigler—how supportive he was, what a good listener, how he didn't expect her to stay at home and take care of him. At last, here was a man who wanted her to be happy and fulfilled. How liberating! How exhilarating! She ended the letter by demanding a divorce. She wanted full custody of their daughters.

Kate pictured her father's impotence in the face of her mother's betrayal. She couldn't wait any longer. She needed answers now.

42

KATE DROVE ACROSS TOWN toward the sprawling university campus. She found a place to park and powered up her iPad, searching for more information on Professor William Stigler. Hundreds of articles and scientific papers popped up. She found his university profile again and checked out his lengthy CV. He'd attended Columbia University as an undergrad and received his PhD in Sociology from NYU. He'd come to Blunt River for his postdoctoral fellowship and had racked up an impressive number of private and government grants. He'd co-authored hundreds of articles. How could such a high-profile tenured professor be a serial killer? She studied his picture again. He was in his late fifties, around the same age as her father, and yet they were light-years apart. Stigler was swaggeringly handsome, with hipster eyeglasses, a fashionable tweed jacket, and a charming smile.

The Clarence Oberon Building was located a few blocks away from The Dude, a popular campus coffee shop. She stood outside the glass-and-steel structure and listened to the blustery wind. A massive storm was brewing, gray cumulous clouds towering ominously in the distance.

Inside, the vast open-concept lobby was sleek and modern, and the adjacent student lounge was crowded with young men in Sherpa hats and women in Patagonia jackets sipping mochaccinos and chai lattes. Tall windows and skylights soaked the place with a muted winter light. Kate signed in at the front desk and headed for the bank of elevators.

According to the directory, Stigler's office was on the fourth floor. Kate pressed the button and waited, feeling skittish. Palmer would be furious, but her curiosity was all-consuming. Anyway, Kate would be careful. She just wanted to catch a glimpse of the man who was Palmer's prime suspect.

She rode the elevator up to the fourth floor and stepped into a long corridor. Stigler's office was at the far end, past dozens of faculty offices and seminar rooms. She stopped about ten yards away and lingered in front of a bulletin board. Stigler's office appeared to be empty—she didn't detect any movement behind the etched glass.

A girl in a quilted parka hurried past, stopped in front of Stigler's door, and knocked. "Professor Stigler?" She tried the door but it was locked. She scribbled something on a piece of paper, folded it in half, slid it under the door and left.

As soon as she was gone, Kate ventured down the corridor for a closer look. She stood in front of Stigler's door, and studied the *New Yorker* cartoons taped to it. *How many sociologists does it take to screw in a lightbulb? One, but the lightbulb needs to sign a consent form.*

She felt a presence behind her.

"Hi. Can I help you?"

Kate nearly jumped out of her skin. "I was just reading the captions."

"Ice-breakers." William Stigler held a Starbucks in one hand and his keys in the other. He looked just like his photograph, with striking blue eyes and neatly trimmed hair going silver at the temples. He projected an aura of upbeat friendliness and openness—as if here was a teacher you could trust. No hint at the man Palmer claimed he was. "Can I help you?" he repeated.

Kate blushed. "I'm applying for a position in the psych department, and I'm interested in the work you did at Godwin Valley," she lied.

"In that case, come on in." Stigler balanced his drink as he unlocked the door and stepped aside. He gestured for her to go in first. "Sorry about the mess. I'm sure there are a couple of health code violations going on, but whatever." He flashed a rakish grin.

Kate hesitated on the threshold. Stigler's window offered a sweeping view of the winter-wonderland campus. Heaps of messy paperwork tumbled across his desk. She went inside, and it felt like walking into a buzz saw.

"Have a seat." Stigler let the door swing shut behind them and waved at the leather chair angled in front of his desk. He scooped up the note from the floor and dropped it onto his desk without looking at it.

She sat down and nervously crossed her legs.

"What can I do for you? Sorry—I didn't ask your name."

To her utter amazement, Kate said, "I think you knew my mother."

"Who's your mother?"

"Julia Wolfe."

There was a conspicuous pause, during which Professor Stigler sipped his coffee, then set the cup down and folded his hands on his desktop. "Ah. You must be Kate."

She nodded stiffly.

He studied her for a moment. "You know, I've always wondered if you'd ever get in touch. And here you are."

Kate could feel the heat creeping up her neck. "I had no idea you existed until yesterday," she said. "I just found out about your affair with my mother."

"Really?" He gave her a skeptical look. "Your father never mentioned me?"

"No." She shook her head. "Somebody else told me."

Stigler's jaw muscles tightened. "Let me guess. Palmer Dyson. That's why you're here, right? He sent you to spy on me."

Wow, that was dumb. She'd just blown everything in about two seconds. Palmer would be apoplectic. "No, he didn't send me," she insisted. "As a matter of fact, he warned me not to come."

"Right. Because I'm so dangerous." He laughed. "Right?"

She nodded reluctantly.

"Christ." Stigler's eyes grew cold. "After Makayla Brayden disappeared, I had the mistaken impression I could be of some use to the police, since I'd interviewed her family for one of my research projects. There was a history of alcoholism and domestic violence. But as soon as I came forward, it set off some kind of serial-killer radar in Dyson's head. He's been targeting me ever since, harassing the people I work for, violating my privacy, talking to colleagues, students, friends, neighbors. I swear to God, if it doesn't stop, I'll take legal action."

"Like I said, he didn't send me," Kate said firmly. "I came here of my own volition."

"Why?"

"I was curious."

"Let me explain something," he said, opening his top desk drawer.

Kate tensed, heart hammering. She had no idea what he was reaching for. She gripped the arms of her chair, ready to bolt.

Stigler held up a tin of Cavendish & Harvey Coffee Drops. "Want one? No?" He popped one into his mouth. "When Vicky Koffman disappeared, I was in Germany for a three-day conference," he said, sucking on the drop. "When Maggie Witt went missing, I was delivering a lecture at Boston University. The police have cleared me of any wrongdoing. Detective Dyson knows this, but he can't help himself. The guy needs a new hobby."

"Palmer knows this already?"

"Of course." Professor Stigler sighed. "Let me ask you something. Are you a perfectly normal human being? Because I'm not. I can't help what attracts me. I have a morbid curiosity. Dyson and I are actually very much alike. We're both obsessed with dysfunctional families and unsolved murder cases." He leaned forward. "You look like your mother, you know."

Kate gave a stunned nod.

"She created quite a stir at the hospital. She was gorgeous and charming. And she had a great sense of humor. She'd bum cigarettes from me, and we'd go hang out on the veranda. We got to talking. She was devastatingly intelligent. That laugh of hers… Mostly I listened, and after a while, she began to open up. Eventually, I had to eliminate her from the study because… well, our relationship progressed."

"You call that ethical? Falling in love with a patient?"

He shrugged. "Her marriage was already broken. Her relationship with your father was a farce. She was already going to leave him. Your father could be very controlling. Toward the end, she was even afraid of him."

Kate frowned. "What are you talking about?"

"Shortly before she came to us they had a fight and he struck her."

"No, that can't be right." Her mind felt foggy. "My father's never hit anyone in his life. He doesn't believe in corporal punishment."

Stigler shrugged. "Maybe it happened when you weren't there?"

Kate recalled her mother's increasingly bizarre behavior, her violent outbursts. But Bram had never responded in kind. Instead, he would take off in his car or go to his study, leaving Julia to lick her imagined wounds. Silence and retreat were her father's biggest weapons.

"She was determined to leave him," Stigler said. "What can I say? We fell in love. We were going to get married. She asked your father for a divorce, but he refused. Worst of all, he threatened to fight for full custody of you girls. I think that's what finally pushed her over the edge."

Kate flinched. "Wait a second. Are you blaming him for her suicide?"

Stigler sighed. "Look, I made peace with my losses a long time ago. I have no agenda in this discussion. I'm just laying it all out there. You can make up your own mind. I only know what your mother told me."

Kate recalled their beloved cat, Phoebe. It was Julia's cat, actually. A neighbor brought over a basket of kittens one day, and Julia had picked the runt of the litter. But Bram was very upset because he hadn't been consulted. The kitten was always underfoot. She peed on the rug and ignored the litter box. He would nudge Phoebe away with his foot and gripe about the high cost of cat food and vet bills. A few months later, Savannah shrieked when she found the dead cat in the yard, flies buzzing around the corpse.

"She was probably exaggerating," Kate protested. "She had a tendency to dramatize."

"But I believed her."

"How dare you blame him!"

"Look," Stigler said patiently, "you came to me, and I welcome the opportunity to share my side of the story. My truth. Isn't that what you tell your patients, Dr. Wolfe? Face the truth and know thyself?"

Kate felt lightheaded. "I should be going."

"I didn't mean to upset you."

Kate bolted out of the office and hurried down the corridor, her stomach roiling. She spotted a restroom and yanked the door open, but didn't quite make it into a stall. She threw up all over the checkered tiles.

43

KATE'S PHONE BATTERY WAS running low; she'd forgotten to charge it last night. She tried calling Palmer Dyson on his cell phone, but he wasn't picking up, so she left a brief message. "Hi, this is Kate. We need to talk. Give me a call as soon as you can." He'd be upset about her meeting with Professor Stigler, but she could live with the consequences.

She drove back across town toward her old neighborhood, and was relieved to find her father's Ford Ranger parked in his driveway. She got out of her car, hurried across the snowy yard, and banged on the door. After a few moments her father opened it.

"Kate? What are you doing here?" he asked.

"I got your message. We need to talk," she said, scraping her boots on the welcome mat.

"Come in. I was just putting some groceries away."

The house smelled of leather and rain. She sat at the kitchen table, while he started the coffee maker and put away the groceries. He reached the top shelves with ease and stacked items according to their expiration dates. Beneath the harsh fluorescent lights, the ravages of time were revealed on his face.

Kate stiffened her resolve. "Remember when Phoebe died?" she asked.

"The cat?"

"We thought she was poisoned."

"No, it was some sort of virus," Bram said.

"Really? Because I don't remember her being sick."

"Cats die all the time," he said irritably. "What's your point?"

"I think she was poisoned."

The coffee maker beeped, and the smell of fresh-brewed coffee filled the kitchen. "Where's this coming from?" he asked.

Kate decided to get straight to the point. "Did you ever hit Mom?"

He flinched involuntarily. "Hit her? No. Why? What's this about?"

"Did you hit her before she committed herself to Godwin Valley?"

He folded his arms across his chest. "I loved your mother. Why are you asking me these ridiculous questions? Where's this hostility coming from?"

"Dad." She jabbed the table with her finger. "We are going to have this conversation. It's a simple question. Did you hit Mom during an argument? Sometimes we lash out in anger. Nobody's perfect. Her behavior was becoming more erratic… maybe you lost your temper?"

"No, Kate." Her father shook his head. "It's not true."

"William Stigler told me that's exactly what happened."

"Who?" A pall came over him. "What did you just say?"

"I went to see him today."

His face fell. "You know about him and your mother, then?"

"Yes."

"Who told you?"

She stared at him in disbelief. "Are you serious? Did you think you could keep it from me forever?"

"I certainly hoped so."

"Why?"

"Because you wouldn't have understood."

"So you let me think she went back to the asylum?"

"It was just an infatuation," Bram insisted. "When your mother came home from the hospital, I was so relieved at first. I figured it was a fresh start. But then she told me she'd fallen in love with someone else, though I recognized it for what it was. She got crushes all the time. Your mother feared love. She feared commitment. She ran away from our marriage, but I knew that if I let her go, she'd be back. She always came back. So I called her bluff and told her to go. Told her, 'Move in with him, if that's what you want. Because God knows, feeling better about yourself is much more important than marriage and children.'" His eyes were fraught with pain. "I figured she'd come to her senses eventually, and the whole thing would blow over. Then after she died, I didn't think it mattered anymore. She was gone, and nothing was going to bring her back."

"She asked for a divorce?"

He gave a reluctant nod.

"And you threatened to withhold custody of Savannah and me?"

"No." He blinked a couple of times.

"But Professor Stigler said—"

"Well, he's lying!" Her father slammed his fist on the table. "That's nonsense, Kate. Complete and utter nonsense! First of all, your mother didn't commit herself voluntarily. I had to drive her over there myself. I could see she was losing her grip, and I was genuinely afraid for her. Her behavior was becoming dangerous. Don't you remember the morning she blew out the pilot light, turned on the gas, and was about to light her Zippo? She almost blew up the house, with you girls in it! I had to knock the lighter out of her hand. And she kept running away from home. I'd find her down by the river with her shoes soaked. She thought the coats and jackets were talking to her, and that there was an evil being living in the walls, talking to her in 'scratch language.' She was in an extremely fragile state of mind." Bram took a seat at the table and pressed his palms over his eyes. "Dr. Holley kept me informed about her progress, and I participated in some of her therapy sessions. I honestly thought she was getting better." He looked up at her. "I don't want to talk about this anymore. It's too painful."

The house was so still, Kate could hear all the clocks ticking at once, like cartoon bombs about to detonate. Her father got up and filled two mugs with coffee. He took a careful sip. His hands were trembling. He seemed so frail, despite his height, despite his righteous indignation. Kate suddenly pitied him. "Dad, I'm sorry if this upsets you... but you kept it hidden from me all these years, and that's not fair."

Bram nodded. "You're right. But please try to understand. I was always working. Twelve-, fourteen-hour shifts, six days a week, just trying to keep my practice afloat. You know how it is. You're buried under paperwork—insurance forms, lab results, clinical notes, federal regulations, taxes. I barely had time for my patients, let alone my own family. When Julia came home from the asylum, I was so relieved; she seemed like her old self again. The paranoia was gone and at first I made sure she took her meds and attended her weekly therapy sessions, but it didn't last long. It was as if our life together meant nothing to her."

"Did you threaten her with a custody battle?"

"I never threatened your mother. I rejected her request for full custody. I told her I'd fight it. She was becoming a danger to you girls again, and I couldn't allow that. She stopped taking her meds. She demanded her freedom, and so I gave it to her." He paused. "Are we done here?" he asked hoarsely, getting to his feet.

A strange, displaced energy wobbled between them, and she wondered if this was one of the factors that had driven her mother away—his tallness, his imposing physicality, his inability to hold a difficult conversation without becoming defensive and angry. His wounded pride.

"Yeah, Dad, we're done."

She got up and left.

44

BACK IN HER CAR, Kate cranked the heat and fiddled with the radio dial. Pop tunes. Anything to drown out what she was feeling.

A throbbing headache had lodged itself behind her eyes. Storm clouds were gathering in the distance, and the scrub pines swayed in the wind—dwarfish trees straight out of a Salvador Dali painting. Further up the road were the newer developments, too many FOR SALE signs popping up all over.

Her thoughts turned to Hannah Lloyd. On an impulse, she turned left instead of right and headed toward The Balsams, the thickly wooded area where Hannah's remains had been found ten years ago, just off Kirkwood Road.

Twenty minutes later, Kate parked by the side of the road, unbuckled her seatbelt, and got out. The last residence was half a mile back. She crossed the street and followed the signs to the trailhead. The old-growth forest was part of an extensive state park that stretched into neighboring townships, a shared treasure of woodlands and wetlands whose crown jewel was Mount Summation in Greenville, New Hampshire, attracting hikers, fishermen, and rock climbers from all over. The Balsams were unique, comprised of icicled northern hardwoods that loomed one hundred feet in the air—balsam firs, red spruce, old-growth oaks—and a lower canopy of hickory, dogwood, and scrub pine.

She listened to the crunch of old snow under her boots as she headed a little ways into the woods and realized the cabin wasn't far from where she stood. The rocky trails eventually led to Parsons Road on the other side of town. "Her" side of town. It hit her hard. There was a direct route from Hannah Lloyd's dumpsite to the cabin from which Savannah had disappeared.

It had always been a mystery to her how the killer had managed to snatch her sister away without Kate or any other witnesses spotting a vehicle on Parsons Road. The answer was obvious to her now. Savannah had been led out of the woods in the opposite direction, along one of these trails, probably with a gun pressed to her back or a knife at her throat.

It began to snow, gentle white flakes fluttering down from the sky. Kate wrapped her scarf tighter around her neck and shivered as the wind picked up, goosebumps rising on her flesh. *Okay, time to go.* A trek through the woods would have to wait.

She was about to leave when she spotted something fluttering through the woods about a dozen yards away. A ghostly swirl. A vortex of motion. *What was that?*

She blinked and it was gone. Probably an optical illusion. She could feel a migraine coming on, constricting her blood vessels. She shook her head and saw flashes of color darting through the trees—cardinals, seeking shelter from the storm.

Kate scanned the forest again, and there it was—further

away this time, a small figure drifting through the woods on an easterly trajectory. She squinted hard. Was it a deer? A dog? Sensory overload? Visual exhaustion? Stress could do that to a person. Too much cortisol released into the bloodstream, combined with a subliminal desire to see something that wasn't there, and your subconscious would fill in the gaps. An ethereal child walking through enchanted woods. "Enthrallment" was a psychological term used to describe a subset of joy. It was a state of intense rapture that occurred when you experienced something that significantly elevated your mood. Kate was feeling that now. She didn't know why.

The snap of a twig.

"Savannah?" she shouted.

A flash of movement.

Where did it go?

Get a grip. You're losing it.

She just had to know what it was. Snow crunched underfoot as she ventured further into the woods. The forest was eerily beautiful. The wind was a siren song. Majestic trees swayed, their boughs creaking like rocking chairs. A flock of birds burst out of the canopy, screeching hauntingly. The snow fell around her like the world's largest snow globe. She followed the trail deeper, avoiding fallen branches, protruding rocks, sudden ruts. She would have to step carefully if she didn't want to break her neck.

She reached a point where two trails overlapped, and directly in front of her was a six-foot embankment. Once she'd reached the top, she paused to look around. Nailed to several nearby birch trees were round plastic disks about the size of an orange. These colored disks, secured to every tenth tree or so along the trail, indicated which type of activity was permitted by the state park. Green disks were for mountain-biking, red disks were for horseback riding, and orange disks were for hiking. Unmarked trails were privately owned and not meant for public use. As a safety precaution, all the colored tags were numbered so that, if you ever got lost, Search & Rescue would be able to pinpoint your location.

Kate wondered if Savannah had seen these disks sixteen years ago, as she was marched through the dark woods— crickets in the underbrush, a summer breeze rustling through her hair, a man's heavy footsteps behind her, his gruff threats prodding her on.

Kate climbed back down the embankment and stepped over a fallen log. She continued along the hiking trail, until it dropped down into a washout. There were icy patches hidden under the snow. *Here*, she thought. This was the place where she'd seen the ghostly little girl. As expected, there were no tracks in the snow, animal or human.

Snowflakes caught on her eyelashes, and she blinked them away. The afternoon air was as cold as steel. Beyond an old stone wall, the hiking trail split off into two tracks.

Hoo-hoo, hoo-hoo-hoo.

She spun around.

A small voice carried on the wind. *"Kate?"*

She spotted something at the top of a rocky eroded hillside about twenty yards away. It stood relatively still, like a tornado hovering in the distance. She tried to blink it away, but a little girl stared back at her. Not a girl. A blur. The suggestion of a girl.

"Savannah?"

Her head throbbed. *This is crazy. You're acting crazy.* Adult onset schizophrenia could happen at any time—but especially in your twenties and early thirties. Was she having a breakdown?

The figure dissolved in a gust of wind.

Kate shook her head. There had to be an explanation. Pine branches swaying in the wind. The wind kicking up snow. Her growing migraine.

You're losing your freaking mind.

She headed toward the snow-swept hill and began to climb. It was steeper than it looked and she worked up quite a sweat as she ascended, her breath clouds lacing the air before her. At the top, there was nothing there.

The howling wind stung her face. Time to go. The Balsams were known for absorbing stray hikers every couple of years, especially those stupid enough to go exploring during a snowstorm. The trees creaked in the wind. *Mom lost her bearings around the same age as me. Maybe this is how it starts?*

Kate began to make her way down the hillside, but after a couple of minutes, she came to a sharp drop-off she hadn't seen from above and had to start over. The trick was finding a gradual descent without any hidden ledges along the way. At the mid-point, rocks gave way to ice, and she slipped and fell, soaking her gloves and parka. She picked herself up, brushed herself off, and continued her slippery descent.

Kate made it to the bottom and headed back to Kirkwood Road—or at least in the direction she thought it was—but then the hiking trail turned into a series of washouts, and she no longer recognized where she was. She doubled back, but the storm had grown in its ferocity. She could barely see five feet in front of her.

It took another couple of minutes to realize she was lost. The temperature had plummeted. She picked a direction, but the trail was so eroded that she was forced to double back again. Soon she couldn't find any of the colored disks on the trees marking an official trail. She must've wandered off the public trail onto private property.

Her head was beginning to throb. She'd left her backpack in the car. She took off her gloves and dug her hands into her pockets, looking for an Aleve. She found one lint-covered pill and swallowed it dry, then took a moment to gaze at the towering treetops. There were no colored disks anywhere to be seen. She edged down a moderate-sized hill and came to another fork in the trail. Which way? Left or right?

Neither, she decided. She began retracing her steps, but now the snow was coming down even harder, making progress difficult. She tried to bully her way through the icy wind but couldn't see three feet in front of her. Her legs were growing numb. She stomped her boots to keep the blood circulating and refused to panic. Panic only made things worse. Panic got you killed. The driving snow was devouring her footsteps behind her.

Kate craned her neck, searching for any colored tags, but all she saw was snow and trees. Her head was pounding. Her ears were ringing. Her vision began to blur. She took out her phone and stared at it. Despite the dire circumstances, she couldn't bring herself to dial 911 yet—not just yet. The potential for humiliation was too great, far worse than being lost. The police, Search & Rescue, a call for volunteers. Her embarrassing adventure would end up on the nightly news. *Dr. Kate Wolfe got lost in The Balsams today during white-out conditions. What she was doing in such a remote location during a blizzard is anyone's guess. Thirty-two-year-old Kate—a child psychiatrist and the sister of murder victim Savannah Wolfe—had no backpack, no compass, no water, and no explanation. Sources suggest she was chasing the ghost of her dead sister. News at eleven.*

The snow fell around her silently. This blizzard would smother her slowly, inch by terrifying inch. Death by soft suffocation.

Kate glanced at her watch. 4:15 PM. She didn't have much time left. In forty-five minutes the sun would begin to set. Unless the Aleve took effect soon, her migraine would cripple her with debilitating pain that could last for hours.

Snow. Trees.

I'm so fucking lost.

45

KATE TOOK OUT HER phone but there was hardly any charge left. She thought about calling James, but then she couldn't deal with the blowback. He would be worried sick about her. He might even be angry. *What do you mean you're lost in the woods? How the hell did that happen? Didn't you see the weather report? What were you thinking, Kate?* Besides, all he could do was call Search & Rescue, and she could do that herself.

But Search & Rescue wouldn't be able to locate her if she was on a private trail. She squinted around at the trees. Still no colored disks anywhere. Maybe she should call her father? But he'd probably come down equally hard on her, and she couldn't face his criticism. She needed someone steady and non-judgmental, somebody who'd "get" why she was there in the first place. Kate didn't want to have to explain herself. So she called Palmer Dyson.

"Hello?"

"Hi, it's me. Kate. I did something really dumb."

"What's wrong?"

"I'm lost in The Balsams," she said, trying to keep the tremolo out of her voice.

"How did that happen?"

"Listen, my phone's about to die. I forgot to recharge it."

"Okay, calm down, I know the area," Palmer said. "Describe where you are."

"I have no idea. I'm all turned around, and it's snowing pretty hard."

"Where did you park?"

"Kirkland Road, next to the trailhead. I've been wandering in the woods for about half an hour."

"How far into the woods—your best guesstimate?"

"I don't know. Maybe two miles."

"Do you see any colored disks on the trees?"

"No. I've been looking. I'm on a private trail."

"Okay. Keep walking and describe it for me. What do you see?"

She trudged along the trail, fighting her own exhaustion. "Snow. Trees."

"Not helpful, Kate."

"Underbrush… rocks, a few boulders. I don't know what I'm looking for," she admitted miserably.

"All right. Listen. If you keep walking, you're bound to come across a stone foundation or an old well, something along those lines."

"All right." She came to a fork in the trail. "Oh. I'm at a fork."

"Good. Pick a direction and keep walking."

"Okay. I'm going left."

"See any of those disks?"

"No."

"Keep going. Anything yet?"

"Not yet."

"Okay. Turn around and try the other fork."

She did.

"Anything yet?"

She spotted an orange disk nailed to an ash tree. "Yes! Found one. It's orange."

"Great. You're on a hiking trail. Can you read the number for me?"

"Two zero something."

"Can't make it out?"

"Hold on…" She reached up to wipe off the snow.

"Kate?"

"Just a second." Her cell phone sputtered with static. "Palmer?"

For a moment, there was nothing but silence.

"*Palmer?*"

He came back. "Kate?"

"Thank God. You were fading out for a second."

"What does the number say?"

"Two zero nine."

"Okay. Hold on."

"My phone's dying," she said plaintively.

"Stay calm. I'm looking at the map now," he said. "Two zero nine. Got it. I know exactly where you are. I own a cabin not too far from there. It's closer than where you left your car on Kirkland Road. That okay?"

"Yes. What should I do?"

"Stay on the trail for a couple of minutes, until you come to another intersection of hiking trails. Let me know when you reach it."

"Okay."

"Take your time."

After several laborious minutes, Kate said, "Okay. I'm at the intersection."

"Read the number on the nearest disk."

She did.

"Okay, good. I want you to take the left fork and stay on this trail until you come to another fork, where you'll take a right. Be careful here. If you get on the wrong trail at this point, you'll end up on a two and a half mile loop. We need to avoid that if possible."

"Okay," she said, struggling to stay focused.

"After about ten minutes or so, you'll come to the foundations of an old homestead and a rusty pump nearby. I want you to draw a line from the foundations to the pump. You're going to follow this imaginary line out of the woods. Understand? Are you getting all this?"

"Yes," she said above the howling wind.

"Okay. I want you to follow this imaginary line until you come to a gravel road, which will be aligned in a south–north direction. You're going to cross the road and take the trailhead back into the woods. From that point on, you've got maybe forty yards to go before you'll reach my cabin. Got it?"

"Okay," she shouted above the wind. "Got it."

"Pace yourself. Stay focused. I'll meet you there in twenty minutes."

Her phone began to beep as the charge ran out.

"At some point you'll come across a stream, but it will be frozen—"

"Palmer? Palmer?"

The line went dead.

She felt an adrenaline spike as she pocketed her phone. With the wind in front of her, she powered her way through the flurries. The day was dying. Hypothermia was a real threat. Her face was rubbed raw from the wind-chill. Her legs were numb— it was like walking on stilts. She couldn't afford to mess up. *Right at the fork—stone foundations—cross the road—back on the trailhead…*

She trudged through the deepening drifts, sweating and swearing, before she spotted the crumbling foundations dusted with snow. She located the rusty pump and drew a mental line from the foundation toward it, then aimed herself in that direction. With great trepidation, she stepped off the trail. Her boots descended into hidden holes and ravines full of rocks. She focused on the whiteness beyond the trees—a dead space that could only mean one thing. A clearing. A road.

It seemed to take her forever, but she finally managed to burst out of the woods onto an old logging road. She cheered with relief, her breath clouds billowing eastward. Almost there.

She jogged across the road and found the trailhead back into the woods. After a dozen yards or so, she came upon a stream. It was frozen over. She tested the solid block of ice and made it to the other side without incident. Then the last bit of daylight blinkered out. Flurries pummeled her from all sides. She took out her keys and used her halogen penlight to guide her way, keeping her head down.

Five minutes later, she spotted a pair of headlights cutting through the darkness. As she drew closer she saw a cabin, then Palmer waiting for her. He aimed a heavy-duty flashlight in her eyes, blinding her momentarily before swinging it away.

"Kate?" he shouted through the wailing wind.

She laughed so hard, she nearly choked, and ran toward him.

46

PALMER HELD THE CABIN door open, and they stomped the snow off their boots. He hung his overcoat on a hook in the front hallway, and Kate hung her parka up next to it. She kicked off her boots and followed him sock-footed into the kitchen.

"Grab a seat," he said, starting a pot of coffee.

She sat down at a square table made of rough planks and massaged her sore arches. The snow was tapering off. Dean Martin was crooning from the sound system in the living room, an old-fashioned boozy love song. She tried to calm down, but she couldn't stop shivering.

"I'm not going to lecture you," he said, "but that was—"

"Dumb. I know," she completed the thought. "By the way, that qualifies as a lecture."

He smiled. "You need dry socks. Be right back." He disappeared upstairs.

Kate examined her feet. Her toes were swollen and painful to the touch, but she could still wiggle them, and they'd stopped throbbing. Her left calf cramped, and she massaged it until the muscles softened. Her nerves were on edge. She would have to tell him about William Stigler.

Soon Palmer was back with a pair of clean white athletic socks, and she asked him where the bathroom was. He pointed down the hallway. Inside the white-tiled bathroom, Kate peeled off her wet socks and put on the new ones. She studied her face in the mirror. Her cheeks were red and her lips were cracked. She took a deep breath. She could've died out there. She washed her face with warm water and ran her fingers through her hair.

Back in the kitchen, Palmer poured them two coffees, added generous helpings of milk and sugar, and Kate gulped hers down, savoring every last drop.

"I went to see Stigler today," she confessed.

His entire demeanor changed. "Kate, no."

"I just wanted to catch a glimpse of him, that's all. But we ended up talking."

He shook his head. "I never should've told you about him."

"He said he was in Germany when Vicky Koffman went missing, and in Boston when Maggie Witt disappeared, so the police have ruled him out as a suspect. He said you know this."

"Kate, listen to me. The man is an exceptional liar. Vicky Koffman disappeared eight hours before Stigler's flight to Germany. And Maggie Witt's mother thought she was at a friend's house, but she never made it there—there was some confusion about the timeline. So there was a window of opportunity of about five hours when he could've abducted her before heading off to Boston. And yet you believed him."

She nodded slowly. "He came across as charming and reasonable…"

"Stigler fits the profile. He's divorced, no kids. He has a

house by the lake with plenty of acreage, so he's fairly distant from his neighbors—he'd need access to an isolated location where he can indulge his fantasies. His job puts him in touch with his victims. He's manipulative, deceptive, and highly intelligent. He's tenured and beyond reproach. It's a great disguise." Palmer pinched the bridge of his nose. "There's something else we need to discuss."

Kate braced herself, ignoring the twinge in her stomach.

"I think your mother was murdered and that her suicide was staged, just like Susie Gafford's accident."

Kate balked. She shook her head. "No. She killed herself the same way Virginia Woolf did—by filling her pockets with rocks and walking into the river. She loved reading Virginia Woolf."

"Yes, which is something Stigler would have known. The rocks became part of the staging. He and your mother were living together at the time, and their relationship wasn't good. Neighbors complained about the noise, loud arguments coming from the apartment in the days prior to the event."

"Wait," Kate sputtered. "Are you saying that the professor I met today killed my mother and made it look like a suicide? Because he reminded me of every college professor I've ever had. Arrogant, maybe, but nothing out of the ordinary. He came across as fairly warm and caring—my mother would've responded to that. She craved attention. My father can be so cold."

"But you know even better than I do, psychopaths can fake empathy. Stigler had an alibi for most of the day your mother died, but not all of it. There's a two-hour gap, and that's plenty

343

of time to kill someone, trust me. Besides, I didn't agree with the pathologist's time of death, which could've given him another couple of hours. There's plenty of room for doubt. I just haven't been able to prove it yet. But your mother was cremated. We can't exhume the body and do another autopsy."

Outside the wind rattled against the windowpanes with an erratic beat, like a child's fists. *Let me in. I'm cold. I'm hungry.*

"Your mother was a strong swimmer, right?" Palmer said. It was true—Julia used to brag about the swimming trophies she'd won back in high school. She was fearless in the water. "It takes four or five minutes for a person to drown," he continued, "and that's a long time to be struggling for air. Even if you wanted to kill yourself, your natural instinct to survive would kick in after thirty seconds or so, no matter what your original intentions were. Now, the medical examiner argued that even if her will to survive *had* kicked in, the powerful currents combined with the rocks in her pockets would've exhausted her. He ruled that the wounds on her body were a result of the current pulling her under and smashing her against the boulders."

Kate took a breath, feeling sick.

"But you've got a person who's emotionally distraught," Palmer went on, oblivious to her distress. "There's proof she'd been drinking. What if your mother and Stigler had an argument that night? What if he followed her down to the river in his own vehicle? What if they continued to argue, and he took advantage of her intoxicated state and killed her? What if he struck her over the head, filled her pockets with rocks and pushed her into the river?"

She felt a tremor in her bones, like the wake of a passing boat.

"Quade and I disagreed about a lot of things, and this was one of them. He used your mother's history of mental illness and the quantity of alcohol in her system as corroborative evidence. There was no suicide note, but she'd threatened to kill herself in the past. And the fact that her lungs were full of water proved she was alive when she jumped in the river, according to him. The rocks in her pockets pointed to a conscious decision to end her life. Case closed. However, I still believe it was a homicide staged to look like a suicide."

She stared at him, glassy-eyed. "You're suggesting Stigler killed my mother *and* my sister?"

Palmer took a sip of coffee. "I used to follow him on my off-duty hours. I even brought him in for questioning once, but he threatened to sue the department, so I was ordered to back off. I'm retired now. I live off my pension. I don't have much of a budget, but I can do whatever I please."

"But the medical examiner came to a different conclusion?"

"It wouldn't be the first time one of us disagreed with Pickler."

"So the other detectives had concerns about him?"

"The few of us who were vocal about it are either dead or retired." He shrugged.

"But you don't have any evidence. It's all circumstantial."

"It's a difficult case to prove."

She shook her head skeptically. "What tipped you off to the connection between the victims and Stigler in the first place?"

"Vicky Koffman's mother first mentioned the study to me. I soon found out that six other families were involved, and some interesting details emerged. Maggie Witt's mother mentioned that during the interview process, Stigler would brush the hair out of Maggie's eyes. Same with some of the other girls. I looked into Stigler's background and discovered that he came from an abusive home. His father was a drunk who used to beat him and his brothers and mother, then abandoned the family when Stigler was seven. His mother was a drug addict and occasional hair stylist. As a small child, Stigler would play on the floor of the beauty salon where she worked."

Kate nodded slowly. "That's interesting, but still…"

"Trust me, there's enough red flags. He's gotten away with it for so long now, he's convinced that everybody else is either too stupid or too blind to see it. As long as he doesn't take any risks, he can keep on killing. In the meantime, he puts on a friendly face and pretends to be a normal, decent human being. But deep down, he knows what he is. And he's proud of it."

"Let me talk to him again."

"Absolutely not. I don't want you going anywhere near the guy. Not while he thinks he's impervious."

"So what can I do?" Kate asked.

"Sit tight." Palmer scowled at her. "This man is dangerous. By showing up at his office today, you've piqued his interest. You might have made yourself a target."

Kate nodded nervously. Palmer was right. If by some chance Stigler had murdered Kate's mother and little sister, then he would have no compunction about killing her.

"Promise me one thing," Palmer said. "No more adventures. Be careful. Watch your back. Keep your doors locked. And call me if anything unusual happens."

"Unusual?"

"Hang-ups. Anonymous gifts. Unsigned letters. Damage to your property."

"Are you serious?"

"Wait here a sec." He got up and left the kitchen. She could hear him in the living room, opening drawers. He came back and handed her a canister of pepper spray. "Keep this handy."

"Pepper spray?"

"For self-defense. Just in case."

"Great," she said sarcastically. "You really think he'll come after me?"

"He may try to intimidate you but he won't do anything rash. Not now. He knows I'm watching him. Besides, you're too high-profile. He doesn't want to get caught. Psychopaths hate to lose."

"You're really creeping me out, Palmer."

"Nobody's going to hurt you, Kate. Not on my watch." He stood up and put on his coat. "Listen, it's getting late. Why don't you stay the night? I'll swing by in the morning and take you to your car."

She glanced at her watch. It was getting late.

He handed her the cabin keys. "Help yourself to whatever's in the fridge. The clean linens are in the closet upstairs. The landline works, if you need to call anyone, and I've got a spare phone charger so you can juice yours up."

"I don't want to impose."

He smiled. "No trouble. I'm beat myself. I'm heading home."

"Okay. I'll take you up on it."

"Good."

She walked him to the door. "Thanks for rescuing me today," she said.

"Any time."

She drew the chain-lock behind him.

47

KATE POURED HERSELF A cup of coffee and called James.

"Jesus, where've you been?" he asked. "I've been trying to reach you for hours. I've been worried sick."

"My phone died and I've only just been able to recharge it," she explained. "I'm so sorry, babe."

"I called your father when you didn't come home. He said you'd left his house hours ago. Where'd you go, Kate?"

"I got lost in the woods. The Balsams. I took you hiking there once, remember? Anyway, I had this crazy idea… and I was following a trail, when all of a sudden I thought I saw Savannah. And before I knew it, I was lost."

"Oh, Kate," he said with sympathy.

"By the time I realized I was in trouble, it was snowing really badly. And I could feel another migraine coming on. My phone battery was dying, so I called Palmer…"

"Palmer?"

"Detective Dyson."

"Oh."

"…because he knows the area really well, and he was able to walk me through it."

"Where are you now?"

"In a cabin. Palmer's cabin."

"He has a cabin?"

"Yes. He's letting me stay the night and says he'll come and pick me up in the morning and take me back to my car. I feel like such an idiot for getting lost."

"I'm just glad you're okay," James said. Then, almost as an afterthought, "How'd you reach him if your phone was dead?"

"I had a few minutes left," she explained. "I would've called you instead, but it would've taken you hours to get here, and then you'd have had to call Search & Rescue anyway, and I couldn't face the humiliation."

"Don't get me wrong. I'm glad he rescued you. I'm fucking relieved. But this has to stop."

Kate shook her head. "What does?"

"I found the police files, Kate."

"You went through my stuff?"

"You left them all over the living room. How could I not see them? And how sick are those pictures? This isn't you, Kate. It's that detective guy. I can't believe he sent you those disgusting things."

"He didn't send them, James. I asked for them."

"Seriously? Why?"

"Because there's a possibility that Blackwood didn't kill Savannah."

James sighed loudly. "Didn't we unpack this already? If the guy was innocent… if there was any proof of his innocence at all, the governor would've stayed the execution."

"Not necessarily."

"Look, I'm sorry I went through your stuff, okay? I shouldn't have done that. But, Kate… do you think this is healthy? What's the end game? I mean, let's say Dyson is right. Let's assume there's a serial killer out there. What are you going to do—play Nancy Drew?"

Kate buried her face in her hands. She wanted to tell James about Stigler, but she couldn't betray Palmer again. "You make it sound like a bad thing, that I want to know definitively who killed my sister."

"We know who killed your sister."

"But I'm beginning to think maybe Blackwood was telling the truth."

"Then let the police handle it."

"But that's the whole problem," she protested. "The police aren't handling it."

"Maybe because it's not true?" James practically shouted. "Maybe it's bullshit? Maybe Dyson wants to play the hero? You said the medical examiner didn't agree with him, right? I mean, if this is for real, shouldn't the police and the media be all over this?"

"Don't you think I've wondered the same thing myself?"

"Come on, Kate. Whatever you think you're doing, it's dangerous. Not only does it freak me out that this guy is pulling you into his orbit, but you've been hallucinating again."

She felt a sudden disconnect, as if a plug had been pulled. "That's because of the migraines. We talked about this…"

"Kate, just send those files back. End it."

She closed her eyes. "I'm exhausted. Can we talk in the morning?"

"Yeah, sure."

"I'll see you tomorrow, okay?" She hung up.

48

THE UPSTAIRS BEDROOM CONTAINED a lot of books. Kate changed the sheets on the bed and perused the oak bookshelves. There were biographies of FBI agents and serial killers, textbooks on forensic psychiatry and criminalistics, maps and travel guides to New Hampshire, and plenty of true-crime nonfiction. It also looked as if Palmer had collected all the published works of William Stigler, PhD. There were dozens of scientific journals with his name highlighted in the contents, research papers with titles such as "The Impact of Family Dysfunction on Adult Psychopathology."

Kate took a few of the journals back to bed with her, and as she was settling in, she noticed a stack of books on Palmer's bedside table. She picked up an old hardback with Dr. Holley's name on the cover, entitled *Grandiose Times at Godwin Valley: A Psychiatrist's Life in an Asylum*. The chapters were named Patient A, Patient B, Patient C, and so on. "Patient J" was highlighted in yellow, and the corresponding page was folded down in the corner. Kate propped the book in her lap and started to read.

Patient J had grown up in a sleepy New Hampshire town, where she was raised by a distant mother and a fawning father who'd molested her at an early age. This caused "J" to become a sexually dysfunctional adult who slept with dozens of men, before finally settling down and marrying a stable breadwinner in good standing within the community. However, one year after the wedding, she cheated on her husband. There were many infidelities after that, and the marriage began to fall apart.

Patient J came to the asylum showing symptoms of a psychotic depression. During her analysis with Dr. Holley, they were able to get to the root of her trauma (an abusive father) and expose her habit of treating every man she met as a potential father-substitute. The author went on to discuss various aspects of her treatment, including medication and drug interactions, as well as talk therapy, which gradually assisted her return to a more rational state of mind.

"As we delved deeper into her background and it was revealed how her father's abuse had shaped her life, Patient J trusted me enough to confide that one of her children was the product of an affair. I recognized immediately that her guilt over this sad reality had triggered her psychosis. Worse, her husband had no idea the child wasn't his. Patient J's infidelity and its consequences had a profound effect on her psyche, and we spent our time at the asylum trying to repair the damage. Her choice was simple: either confess her secret to her husband, or learn to live with it. She decided, for the child's sake, to keep it hidden."

Kate's heart began to thunder in her chest as years of confusion fell away. Savannah didn't look like anybody on Bram's side of the family. The Wolfes were tall, pale-skinned, dark-haired, and blue- or brown-eyed, whereas Savannah was a tiny thing with golden hair, mermaid-green eyes, freckles, and a widow's peak, which contributed to her mischievous appearance.

Kate herself mostly took after their mother's side of the family, but she'd also inherited some of Bram's physical attributes: his left-handedness; the ability to curl her tongue; a crooked pinkie finger; his straight nose. Savannah didn't have any of these traits. Of the two of them, Savannah was the genetic anomaly.

Another thing. When Bram took the girls to visit Julia's grave, they always brought a trashbag to clear away old bouquets of roses from the headstone. Who had left them there? Their presence was never explained.

Kate recalled how beautiful Julia was. Men would stare at her everywhere she went—the grocery store, the gas station, strolling along Main Street. Her mother not only welcomed the attention, she craved it. She would often stop to flirt with complete strangers, which embarrassed Kate. And her parents used to throw parties when she was very young, full of drunken adults dancing to The Bangles and U2, until Bram grew tired of Julia's flirtatious behavior and put an end to them.

From the second she met Maddie Ward, Kate had been struck by the resemblance to her sister. Had Julia slept with Henry Blackwood? Was it possible? What did it mean?

If Henry Blackwood was Savannah's father, did Bram know about it? Or had Julia managed to keep it hidden from him? Did William Stigler know? Was he jealous? Had he killed Kate's mother in a fit of jealousy and rage? And then, six years later, buried Savannah alive in Blackwood's backyard as vicious payback? Could anyone be so depraved? Was Professor William Stigler capable of such madness?

49

THE PALEST LIGHT. DAWN. Dripping icicles. Kate woke up in a strange room and almost panicked before realizing where she was. It was 6 AM. She put the journals and Holley's book away, took a shower, got dressed, and went downstairs, where she made a pot of coffee and waited for Palmer to arrive.

Brilliant sunshine was pouring into the kitchen through the old-fashioned windows. It was going to be a beautiful day. Fifteen minutes later, there was a knock at the door.

Palmer's hair was peppered with silver and his eyes were bloodshot. There were deep worry lines on his face she hadn't noticed before. "Morning," he said with a smile. "How'd you sleep?"

"Like the dead."

"You ready?"

She picked up her bag and handed him the cabin keys.

As they drove to Kirkland Road, Kate confessed, "I think I'm seeing things."

Palmer cocked his head. "Would you like to talk about it?"

"I watched my mother go crazy. One day, I came home from school, and she was hacking away at our hedges with a band saw." She shrugged. "You grow up believing that this person you love will always be there for you. But then one day, she looks at you with cold eyes, and you realize she's a complete stranger. And you may never get her back."

"I'm sorry you had to deal with that," Palmer said.

"Sometimes it feels like *I'm* going crazy." Kate pinched the bridge of her nose. "I've been seeing my dead sister lately. I know it's just a symptom of my migraines—they cause visual hallucinations sometimes, when combined with stress. But that's how I got lost yesterday. I was chasing a ghost through the woods."

"You've been seeing your sister?"

Kate nodded. "James blames you."

Palmer frowned. "Why?"

"He saw the files you sent me. He thinks it's unhealthy. He told me to let the police handle it." She sighed heavily. "But don't worry. He doesn't know about Stigler."

"Thanks for keeping it confidential. I appreciate that."

She gave Palmer a plaintive look. "But I need to see this through. Or I'll always be afraid."

"What are you afraid of?" he asked.

"That I killed my sister by leaving her alone in that cabin." Tears sprang to her eyes. She nodded slowly. "Everybody tells me it wasn't my fault. They've been saying it for years. But it's a lie. Because it *was* my fault. I took her there. I should've paid more attention. I should've never left her alone."

"Do you think she would blame you?"

Kate blinked. "Savannah?"

"Do you think she would want you to live in fear forever?"

"No. She never blamed anyone for anything."

"But deep down, you don't believe that yet. And until you can square it with yourself, you'll always have this fear."

"So you're saying I should put the blame where it belongs."

Palmer nodded. "Stigler."

Kate tried to regain her composure. "Okay, look. If there's one thing I understand, it's mental illness. If you think Stigler is a psychopathic killer, I can help you catch him. I did a two-year residency at McLean Hospital, where I worked with violent juvenile psychotics. I have the training and the experience."

Palmer released a soft exhalation that wasn't quite a breath. "It'll have to wait I'm afraid. I'm going away for a while."

"What for? When?"

"Remember I told you about the medical clinic in Mexico? I'm flying down to Tijuana today. Eight therapy sessions over the course of two weeks." He glanced over at her. "The Mexican doctors have shared some impressive statistics with me."

Kate had read about foreign clinics that preyed on vulnerable cancer patients. "Are you sure the procedure is viable?"

"Believe me, I wouldn't be going through with it if I thought it was a scam. This place is legit, with a good rate of remission. Don't worry about me. Okay?"

"Okay," she said, not wanting to undermine the hope in his eyes. "Just get well. Focus on your health." Then another thought occurred to her. "What about Stigler?" she asked. "You told me he wouldn't come after me—but what if he finds out you're gone?"

"Nobody knows I'm leaving the country except for you, my ex-wife, and a couple of buddies down at the station. Stigler thinks I have eyes all over the place." Palmer dug his hand into his pocket and took out a small blue flashdrive, still keeping his eyes on the road. "Hold onto this for me, okay?"

Kate stared at the flashdrive in her hand. "What is it?"

"It's got everything on it, all my years of research. It connects all the dots. Just in case."

"In case what?"

"Just in case anything happens to me."

She shuddered. "Please don't say that."

"If it does, I want you to give this to Cody Dunmeyer, my old partner, now Chief Dunmeyer. He'll know what to do with it. But I'll be back in two weeks, ready to nail this guy. I've been thinking a lot about how to proceed, and I've got a plan. I can't share it with you yet, but trust me… you're going to be okay."

She gave a reluctant nod.

They pulled up behind Kate's car and Palmer put the vehicle in park, then turned in his seat, his expression serious.

"I should give you my emergency contacts," he said.

Kate handed him her phone, staring out of the passenger window at the woods while he programmed in the information. Strange to think how sinister they'd seemed the night before. Eventually Palmer returned her phone, grinning apologetically.

"Sorry. Modern tech can take me some time."

Kate grinned back, but it was forced. She hadn't realized until right that instant just how much he'd changed her life. And now he was abandoning her.

50

BEFORE HEADING HOME, KATE took a detour across town and
visited Dr. Holley, who seemed surprised to see her. "What
brings you to my neck of the woods?"

"It's about Patient J."

He nodded thoughtfully. "Ah. So you found my book. *Entrez
vous.*"

He led her into the sunny living room, where "Norwegian
Wood" by the Beatles was playing softly in the background.
She took a seat on the beige sectional sofa and said, "I know
Savannah was only my half-sister. She didn't look like anyone on
our father's side of the family. But I have the Wolfe nose, among
other genetic traits." She paused. "Henry Blackwood's daughter
Maddie looks quite like Savannah did around that age."

Holley shrugged. "I wouldn't know about that."

"My mother never told you who Savannah's father was?"

"No. I'm sorry."

"And my father doesn't know anything about it?"

"Not to my knowledge. However, it's possible he may have
read my book and figured it out. I have no way of knowing."
He smiled sympathetically.

Kate sighed with frustration. "You told me you could never betray my mother's confidences, and yet you spilled all her dirty secrets in your book."

He shook his head. "No. Patient J is a composite of several women I treated. Patients A through Z are all composites: I changed their names, ages, and physical appearances in order to protect their privacy."

"You didn't disguise her enough, obviously."

"It got a pass from the legal department." He heaved a sigh. "Anyway, the book is out of print. It sold maybe five thousand copies."

Kate touched her feverish forehead with her fingers. Just like that, her sister was her half-sister. Her mother had betrayed them. Her father was a cuckold. Everything felt dangerous. It was like walking across a rotten floor—at any second she could go crashing through.

"Should I tell my father?"

"I wouldn't do that," Dr. Holley advised. "He raised you girls alone, and Savannah was his daughter, whatever the biology. It would be wrong to take that away from him."

She thumbed tears out of her eyes. "You're right. It would kill him."

The old psychiatrist stroked his chin. "You know, when my wife gave birth to our daughter, I fell instantly in love with her. I couldn't believe that tiny little being was mine. She won my heart. As a parent, you never get over that feeling. You think your arms will always be able to protect her."

She looked at him intently. "Would you tell me who the father was, even if you knew?"

"No. But my conscience is clear. Your mother took that secret to the grave."

51

KATE FOUND A PARKING space, retrieved her ring from the glove compartment and slipped it on. She tucked the pepper spray Palmer had given her into her coat pocket and tried not to slip on the icy cobblestones as she made her way toward the building.

She rode the elevator to the eighth floor and fumbled with her keys. Her stomach was in free-fall as she unlocked the door. "James?" she called out.

He met her in the hallway in his wool coat and boots. He kissed her hello.

"Sorry I worried you yesterday," she said.

"No, the important thing is you're okay."

"Can we talk?"

"I was just leaving. I have to consult with Mom's doctors again. They're worried about blood clots now. And she's reporting numbness and tingling."

"Oh God. How can I help?"

"Come by later on and see her. That'll cheer her up."

"Absolutely."

"Look, Kate." James took her hand. "I want you to be

happy, not scared and stressed out, and I think digging into your sister's murder is bad for you. But I support whatever you think is best. I just don't know how to deal with it sometimes."

Kate squeezed his hand. "We'll talk later, when your mother's feeling better."

He gave her a long hug and left.

Hours later, and bone-tired, she nibbled on a salad and changed for bed. She'd driven to Massachusetts General to visit Vanessa, and back again—alone. James, concerned about deep vein thrombosis, had opted to stay with his mother, while Kate had come home and worked her way through a mass of paperwork. Now she traced her fingers over the small scars on her upper thighs and forearms—little teardrop dimples, tiny nicks in an otherwise smooth surface. She recalled the stab of the thumb tacks, and the accompanying numbness. Cutting herself was like walking into a much clearer reality. She studied the jagged suicide scars on her wrists, the hesitation cuts. She remembered the crackle and snap of pain as the razor sank into her flesh. She had survived all this—she could survive whatever was coming.

Kate woke up in the middle of the night with a start. She glanced at her clock. 3:00 AM. It was windy outside, the bulk of winter hunkering against the panes. An unfathomable loneliness crawled underneath her skin.

She picked up her phone from the bedside table and saw that she had a voicemail from Palmer Dyson. "Greetings from sunny Tijuana. Lousy flight. Crappy airplane food. How are you doing? Call me when you get this. The operation's tomorrow."

She had no idea what time it was down in Mexico. She called him and got through to his voicemail. "Hey, it's Kate. Sunny Tijuana sounds pretty good right about now—it's like five below here, I think. Anyway, good luck tomorrow. Call me after the operation." She hung up and closed her eyes.

It seemed like only seconds later that the phone rang in her ear.

It was Ira. "Sorry to wake you," he said.

She sat up in bed and peered out the window. The rising sun was hidden behind a few scraggly electric-pink clouds.

"No problem," she said groggily. "What's up?"

"Maddie Ward has been cleared for release. She'll be in foster care later today. I thought you should know."

"What's the rush?"

"Her insurance plan was twelve days max. So it was either this, or go the residential route. And you know how I feel about that."

"Right," she agreed. Throwing a teenage girl who cut herself into an institution full of violent juvenile offenders was not an option.

"Anyway, Ursula found a terrific foster family willing to take in a child with Maddie's history of instability. No small feat. They have an excellent track record. We had to act quickly."

"You had no choice, right?"

"We got lucky. Anyway. Maddie's been asking about you.

Her foster family is picking her up at ten, and I was wondering if you'd like to swing by this morning and say goodbye. A purely non-professional visit."

"I'll be there at nine o'clock."

"Good."

It was a beautiful day out, the sky an azure blue. The drive into Boston was a breeze. The Children's Psych Unit was bustling with clowns—volunteers in greasepaint who handed out balloons and scared some of the younger kids. The teenagers rolled their eyes at the magic tricks but always asked the nurses when the clowns would be back.

Kate found Maddie huddled in her room, lost in thought. She wore a pink T-shirt, blue sweatpants, and a brand-new pair of Nikes; the nurses must've passed the collection plate around again. Kate reminded herself to chip in. Maddie's bags were all packed, and her pink quilted coat was folded up beside her. She was ready to go—physically at least.

"Good morning," Kate said.

Maddie smiled brightly. "You're back! I wondered where you'd gone."

Kate pulled up a chair. "How are you feeling today?"

"Okay, I guess. The police came to visit me on Friday. They asked me all sorts of questions." Maddie unzipped her backpack and took out a battered photo album with a white embossed cover that said MEMORIES on the front in sequins. She opened the album and smoothed her hands across the transparent sleeves. "They brought it from home. They thought it might help me remember stuff." She showed Kate Maddie as a baby, Maddie as a toddler, Derrick and Nelly Ward as newlyweds. She turned a page. "That's me when I was six."

Kate studied the photograph. Maddie and Savannah could've been twins.

"And look. Here's Uncle Henry and Mommy."

Henry Blackwood wrapped a possessive arm around skinny fifteen-year-old Penny. The teenager seemed both proud and cowed. Without his baseball cap, Blackwood's blond buzz cut with its distinctive widow's peak was on full display. He had striking green eyes, just like Savannah and Maddie. In Kate's memory, that baseball cap had always shaded his eyes, hidden his golden hair. But in the picture, Kate could plainly see where Savannah and Maddie had gotten their looks—from their father.

"I had a dream last night," Maddie confessed, stuffing the photo album into her backpack. "Mom was driving me to school, when all of a sudden we went into the ocean, and the car started filling up with water, and we nearly drowned."

"Wow. Sounds scary."

"I woke up before it ended though."

"What do you think it means?"

She shrugged. "I nearly drowned in the bathtub a bunch of times. Same as my dream."

Kate blinked. "I'm sorry—what do you mean?"

"In the bathtub. Mommy sometimes held my head underwater until I almost drowned, but she let me go before

I died. Once it was snowing, and we were coming home from the supermarket…"

"Is this another dream?"

"No. It really happened. We came home, and I was helping her bring the groceries in from the car, when I slipped on some ice and a bunch of eggs broke. She said that I disgusted her. She called me stupid. My stomach hurt so bad, because I knew what was coming. She had that look in her eyes."

"What look?"

"Daddy told me not to worry. Said it would blow over, but it never did. He didn't get it, because he was hardly ever at home."

"What happened when she got that look in her eyes, Maddie?"

"She would fill the tub with water and make it so I couldn't get away. Then she'd hold my head underwater, until it felt like I was going to die. But then, she'd let me go at the very last second."

Kate hadn't suspected Nelly Ward, although it made sense. The abused often became the abuser. "Are you saying your mother tried to drown you? More than once?"

"Lots of times," Maddie admitted softly.

"Did you tell the police this?"

She shook her head. "They didn't ask."

"Did you tell Dr. Ira?"

"Not yet."

"And your stepfather knows? He knows your mother tried to drown you?"

Maddie shook her head again. "No. He doesn't know anything."

"But you said he pushed you once, remember?"

"He doesn't know about Mommy. He wouldn't hurt me. He loves me."

"Did she do anything else? Hurt you in any other way?"

She nodded solemnly. "I don't feel so hot."

"But your stepfather doesn't hurt you, right? Only your mother did?"

"He'd kill her if he found out, Mommy said. She told me not to tell a soul."

It struck Kate hard.

Maddie rested her hands on her stomach. "I don't feel good."

"Thanks for telling me this, Maddie. It took a lot of courage."

The girl began to tremble. "When am I going to see my dad?"

"The police are still looking for him."

"Can I see him when they find him?"

"I don't know what the procedure is, but I'll look into it."

Maddie nodded, apparently satisfied.

"I want you to understand one thing. You're going to be okay."

Maddie peered skeptically up at Kate. "How do you know that?"

Kate decided to level with her. She would tell the girl the truth, even though it meant she'd be effectively removing any chance of treating Maddie as a patient again. But the girl was in good hands with Ira.

"How do I know?" Kate rolled up her sleeves. "I used to cut myself, too. And I'm okay."

Maddie stared at the old scars. "What did you use?"

"Tacks. Pins. Razor blades. Scissors. Anything I could find."

"Did you hear voices?"

"No." Kate rolled down her sleeves.

Maddie sat up straighter.

"That voice in your head? It's not the devil, or a monster, or anything like that. The voice comes from your subconscious. It's a coping mechanism. When someone in your life, even somebody you care about, starts treating you badly, it creates an echo chamber inside your head. None of it is true, and once you understand where the voice is coming from, it's much easier to ignore. And once you ignore it, it fades away."

Maddie nodded thoughtfully. "Am I ever going to see you again?"

"I'm sure I'll see you around. You'll be continuing therapy with Dr. Ira on an outpatient basis."

A slow smile spread across Maddie's face. She reached into her backpack and took out a brand-new cell phone. "Look what Ursula gave me. It's from my foster family. They all have one. Cool, huh?"

"Awesome."

"Look. My weather app says more snow." She showed Kate the screen. "Can we trade numbers?"

"Good idea," Kate said, and they took turns inputting their contact information.

"Hey. Can we take a selfie?" Maddie asked excitedly.

"Love to."

They posed. "Smile!" Click.

"I'll text it to you," Maddie said. Kate's phone buzzed, and they looked at the picture together—both of them smiling.

There was a knock on the door, and Ursula O'Keefe, the hospital social worker, poked her head inside.

"Sorry. Did I interrupt?"

"No, we were just saying goodbye," Kate said.

"All packed?" Ursula asked, and Maddie grabbed her coat and backpack and hopped off the bed.

Maddie flung herself into Kate's arms. "See you soon." She clung.

Kate gently broke the embrace. "Just remember. It's only echoes."

Maddie smiled bravely. "Echoes."

"Well, young lady. Time to meet your new foster family," Ursula said. "I hear they have a dog named Winnie the Poodle…"

Maddie giggled, and Kate watched them walk away together.

52

KATE COULDN'T WAIT TO share the harrowing news of Nelly's actions with Ira—this was exactly the breakthrough they'd been hoping for—but he was in a meeting and couldn't be interrupted. She felt conflicting emotions as she headed down the corridor toward her office. Nelly had suffered all her life, and she'd forced her daughter to suffer the same fate. It was tragic. But that was what abuse did to you—it tainted everything you touched. At least now Maddie had the chance to lead a normal life.

Kate paused in front of the plate-glass windows overlooking the hospital courtyard. Across the way was the multi-story parking garage, and down below she could see three small figures in the glassed-in passageway—Maddie and her foster parents heading into level one. Maddie was chatting happily with the foster mom as they disappeared into the garage—a good sign. Children sensed danger. Like animals, they knew whom not to trust.

Kate's ring finger began to itch. She scratched the inflamed skin as she entered her office, where she took a seat at her desk and checked her text messages.

She could feel another headache coming on and reached into her bag for an Aleve, rummaging through the pockets. Instead of a bottle of pills, her fingers closed around the flashdrive Palmer had given her for safekeeping.

She sat with it in her palm. She glanced at the clock. She allowed a few seconds to pass before she inserted it into a USB port and double-clicked.

The drive held ten folders: *1_STIGLER_J. Wolfe*, *2_STIGLER_Gafford*, *3_STIGLER_Mason*, *4_STIGLER_S. Wolfe*, *5_STIGLER_Koffman*, *6_STIGLER_Howell*, *7_STIGLER_Lloyd*, *8_STIGLER_Witt*, *9_STIGLER_Davidowitz*, *10_STIGLER_Brayden*.

Kate sat for a suffocating moment with her finger poised on the mouse. Then she opened *1_STIGLER_J. Wolfe*, to reveal three Word docs and a PDF. She opened the document named *Case Summary*. In his two-page summary Palmer made the case for homicide by quoting from the medical examiner's report:

> From Quade Pickler's autopsy report: "Water in the lungs and stomach indicates death by drowning, as does hemorrhaging in the sinuses and trachea. Victim was alive when she was immersed. Evidence of the victim coming into contact with rocks while being carried by the current: antemortem bruising to the thorax and abdomen, broken phalanges (two on right hand, one on left—see diagram), lacerations to the forearms, and a single blunt force trauma to the right side of the cranium, resulting in a depressed fracture. Body was retrieved 48 hours postmortem."

Palmer's own observations were typed underneath:

Lacerations to the arms and hands could've been caused by a struggle with her attacker. Blunt force trauma to the head could've occurred before the unconscious victim was pushed into the water, with rocks added to the pockets to make it look like a suicide. Alcohol levels in her system could've further reduced her ability to defend herself. Unconscious-but-alive would explain the presence of water in the lungs. She had several broken fingers, which could've been the direct result of trying to protect herself from an attacker wielding the blunt object that caused the head injury and perhaps rendered her unconscious. Cranial trauma: A powerful blow to the right side of the skull is indicative that the perpetrator was left-handed. William Stigler is left-handed. The fracture pattern indicates a sharp, angular tool such as a tire iron, rather than a river boulder (suspiciously no tire iron was found in either vehicle at the scene—my guess is that it's at the bottom of the river). Conclusion: Potential homicide staged to look like a suicide.

However, homicidal drowning is almost impossible to prove. There was a rainstorm that night, which eradicated the victim's footprints from her car, so it is unsurprising that no sign of a struggle was found. No suicide note was ever recovered. Witness interviews indicate that the victim and primary suspect (Stigler) had been arguing with escalating intensity. The suspect had no solid alibi for a portion of the time the victim allegedly committed suicide. I also disagree with the medical examiner's time of death. Victim could've been killed an hour earlier than estimated. This case should be reopened, in my opinion.

Kate opened the document labeled *Witness Statements*. Inside were dozens of interview transcripts, most of them along similar lines.

Tricia Landreau (neighbor): I heard a commotion next door and opened my window, and they [Stigler and Wolfe] were having one of their knock-down-drag-outs again. Yelling and screaming and swearing… He was jealous and she kept threatening to leave him. Then I heard the crash of breaking glass and a loud scream from a woman. I was about to call 911 when it suddenly stopped. I only hoped she wasn't dead. But I saw her the next day and she seemed okay, except for a few bruises, so I figured I should mind my own business.

Nicholas Valentino (neighbor): Oh yeah, they fought all the time. My wife was especially concerned, but I figured it was none of our business. They were at each other's throats twenty-four/seven. The police responded once or twice that I know of, but they didn't arrest anyone. I think it's because he's a doctor and she was in the loony bin, and also because she refused to press charges. When we heard about the suicide, we weren't all that surprised.

Kate devoured the rest of the witness statements, before

opening the third Word document, *Police Report*. Then she opened the PDF. Fear crawled inside her as she clicked through color photographs of her mother's abandoned car, the eroding riverbank, and Julia's dead body. There she was, sprawled across the weedy shoreline, limbs twisted into unnatural positions, face coated in mud, clothes clinging to her like wet dishrags, open eyes dazzled by death.

With shaky fingers, Kate clicked out of the folder and stared at the nine other folders stored on the USB. She warned herself not to go any further, but her finger double-clicked on *4_STIGLER_S. Wolfe*.

Inside were three Word docs, the same as Julia's: *Case Summary*, *Witness Statements*, and *Police Report*. The PDF was labeled *Autopsy Photographs*. Without hesitation, she opened the file and was bludgeoned by a series of heartbreaking pictures. There was Savannah with her eyes closed and her head shaved, bald as a baby chick. Her pink T-shirt and white shorts were dirt-stained. Her lucky sneakers were missing. The soles of her feet were dusk-blue. Her fingernails were impacted with dirt. There were red scratches on her arms, like lipstick samples. Her tiny body barely took up half the autopsy table. Her face was as calm as a bowl of rosewater.

Revulsion spread through Kate. The raw truth was hard to take. But it was somehow more healing than Savannah's open coffin had been. The undertakers had applied thick coats of foundation to Savannah's skin, and Kate never got over the sight of her sister's ill-fitting blond wig and those penciled-in eyebrows. She preferred this—the truth. Here was brutal honesty. Here was how Death had taken her.

Dark thoughts spread like blood branching through water. She clicked out of Savannah's folder without opening the rest of the documents. She'd seen enough.

Kate ejected the USB and sat in a state of agony. Everything seemed to be crowding in on her. She felt a creeping terror along with growing nausea. Had William Stigler buried her sister alive in order to both punish and frame Henry Blackwood for getting Julia pregnant? It was vicious payback. *Here's your biological daughter, and guess what? You're going to spend the rest of your life rotting on death row.* Blackwood's fingerprints were on the shovel. The police found his hairs tangled up in the rope. Stigler must've stalked Henry and gained access to the property prior to the murder. He must've known where Blackwood kept the shovel and rope. Perhaps he'd gained Blackwood's confidence and had been invited into his house. The crime took cunning and careful planning. In one Machiavellian masterstroke, Stigler had inflicted great pain on not just one, but two of his rivals for Julia's affection: Henry Blackwood and Bram Wolfe.

She tucked the USB drive back into her bag and took out her phone. Her father would be at his Sunday surgery. She decided to call him at his downtown office.

"Dr. Wolfe," he answered with bland professionalism.

"Hi, Dad. It's me."

"Hello, Kate."

"Look, I'm sorry about what happened."

"That's okay. We were both a little emotional," he said.

"I love you. You know that, right?"

His voice ticked up a notch. "I love you, too, Kate."

"Something's come up. Do you have a minute?"

"I'm a little busy right now—"

"I wouldn't interrupt if it wasn't important."

He paused. "All right. I have fifteen minutes before my next appointment."

"I was just wondering… what if Mom didn't commit suicide? What if she was murdered, and it was made to *look* like a suicide?"

"Kate, this is getting out of hand…"

"I have her autopsy report right here. She had a head wound that could've been made by a tire iron, according to a detective. She had what could have been defensive wounds to her arms and hands; it's possible she was hit on the head and then pushed into the river. Witnesses claim that she and Stigler were fighting a lot, enough to call the police, and he didn't have a solid alibi for that night. There's evidence to indicate—"

"What are you saying? Are you suggesting that William Stigler killed Julia?"

"Detective Dyson thinks so. He believes it was staged to look like suicide."

He hung up.

"Dad? Dad?" Kate tried to get him back, but the line was busy.

She sat, stunned. What had she done?

53

KATE TRIED REACHING HER father again, to no avail. She gathered up her belongings and left the hospital. Boston's winding streets and left turns were difficult to navigate at the best of times, let alone the dead of winter when the roads were full of potholes and icy patches. She drove through the angular streets past office complexes, strip malls, and gleaming contemporary buildings, afraid Bram might've done something stupid, like gone off half-cocked to confront Professor Stigler at the university. She could almost picture him barging into the professor's office and looming over his desk, hurling accusations, maybe threatening physical violence. What if he lost it completely—that hair-trigger temper of his? The campus police would haul him off in handcuffs.

And it would be all her fault.

At every stop light, she dialed her father's office number and listened to the busy signal. Finally, his secretary picked up and told Kate that he'd cancelled all his appointments and stormed out of the office without a word of explanation, leaving the phone off the hook. Kate thanked her and hung up.

By the time she reached her father's house on Three Hills

Road, Kate had worn herself out with worry. His car wasn't in the driveway, so she headed back to town and parked a few blocks away from the university. She crossed the snowy campus to the Clarence Oberon Building, where she took an elevator to the fourth floor, only to find that Stigler's office was dark and his door locked.

She found the Sociology Department main office at the other end of the corridor and stood in front of the administrative assistant's desk, tapping her nails anxiously on the wood. The middle-aged woman seemed mildly annoyed to be interrupted. "Can I help you?"

"I'm looking for Professor Stigler."

"He had an early class then went home for the day. Would you like to leave him a message?"

"Actually," Kate confessed, "I was looking for my father, Bram Wolfe. I think he might have come to see the professor."

"Oh!" the woman exclaimed. "You must be Kate. I've heard so much about you. Dr. Wolfe has been our family physician for years. He's taking care of my grandkids now, can you believe that?"

Kate nodded. "So he was here?"

"About an hour ago. I sent him over to the lake house."

"Lake house?"

"He said it was urgent, so I gave him Professor Stigler's home address." She searched her computer database. "623 Lakeview Drive."

Kate thanked the woman and left. She drove north of town, where the million-dollar homes hugged the lake. She passed renovated neo-Gothic bungalows and stately mansions where some of the wealthiest residents of Blunt River lived: university faculty members, small businessmen, and local politicians.

623 Lakeview Drive was located at the end of a private road, separated from its nearest neighbors by a tall cedar fence and thick pine woods. She parked next to her father's Ford Ranger, then got out and stood for a nervous moment. There were no other vehicles parked in the driveway and no garage. She wondered where Stigler's car was. Where was her father?

The wind picked up, howling through the pines. Stigler lived in a lacy Victorian wedding cake of a house with Baroque-style turrets and a wraparound porch. Down by the lake, a wooden dock stretched out over the ice. The view was wild and desolate.

She was heading toward the house, boots crunching over gravel, when something caught her eye: a set of drag marks in the gravel, two slender grooves made by a pair of heels, accompanied by a trail of blood drops.

Kate froze. Someone had been dragged out of the house, down the porch steps, and across the driveway. The blood drops stopped where Stigler usually parked his car—she could see tire impressions in the gravel, deep wells made by something rugged, perhaps an off-roader or an SUV.

Kate took out her phone and dialed 911.

"911, what's your emergency?" the operator answered.

Her mind went blank.

"911, what's your emergency?"

"I think my father's dead," Kate blurted out.

54

TWENTY MINUTES LATER, KATE stood shivering on the wraparound porch, where Chief Dunmeyer had told her to wait. It was freezing, maybe thirty degrees. *My father must be dead.* According to the police, no bodies had been found inside the house, but there was blood in the upstairs bathroom and the shower curtain had been torn off its rings.

She could figure the rest out for herself: her father had come over to confront Stigler, and Stigler had killed him. Then Stigler had dragged the body out of the house, dumped it in the back of his car—a BMW X5 SUV, according to the police— and sped away. Her father was dead. Simple deduction.

Her fingers and toes were growing numb. She moved around in aimless circles to keep the blood circulating. She peered through one of the windows, cupping her hands over the glass.

She called Palmer, but he wasn't picking up. He was probably in the middle of the operation, or maybe post-op by now. Heavily drugged in the recovery room. She left a voicemail. "Hi, it's Kate. I hope the operation went well." She paused. "I really need to talk to you. Something's happened. When you're feeling better… please give me a call."

Her eyes teared up. She tried to reach James, but it went directly to voicemail. She wanted to leave a message, but the words wouldn't form. She hung up.

A crowd of onlookers had gathered on the sidewalk in front of the house. Kate didn't feel like waiting on the porch anymore. She walked around to the backyard, where she lit a cigarette and watched the police dogs—there were two of them now sniffing around the trees.

A middle-aged man in a gray suit came out of the house and introduced himself as Detective Lucas. Kate told him everything she knew—about the flashdrive, and Julia's autopsy report, and how she'd tried calling her father back but he'd already left his office.

"Detective Dyson gave you a flashdrive?" Detective Lucas asked. "Can I see it?"

Kate held it out. "He told me to give it to the chief."

"I'll take it to him."

"No, he gave me explicit instructions." She tucked it away in her bag.

"Wait here." Lucas left.

She noticed a helicopter circling in the distance. A news chopper. *Great*, she thought angrily. The TV networks would dig into their archives and the Wolfe family tragedy would be splashed all over the media again. A police officer was leading a Labrador Retriever around by its leash, and the dog was sniffing around the base of a tree.

Chief Dunmeyer came out of the back door and met her at the bottom of the steps. He was fit and trim with a silver mustache and goatee—he hadn't aged much in sixteen years. He wore dark slacks, a pinstripe shirt, and a red silk tie beneath the *de rigueur* BRPD parka.

"Do you have any idea what happened to my father?"

"We put out a statewide BOLO for Stigler's SUV. We'll find them. Detective Lucas said you had something for me?"

She unzipped her bag and took out the flashdrive. "Palmer said you'd know what to do with it. I haven't been able to reach him yet, but I'm sure he'd understand why I'm giving it to you now."

Dunmeyer frowned. "What's on it?"

"His research on nine missing and murdered girls, as well as my mother's suicide. He believes that Stigler's responsible for all of them. He said it connects all the dots."

Dunmeyer nodded. "Palmer and I were partners for a long time. I trust the guy with my life. But his theories never quite added up for me. I told him time and again—present me with some new evidence, something solid, and we'll follow up."

Kate nodded. "But you'll look into it now?"

"We'll look into everything now." He glanced around and lowered his voice. "You've got to understand, Dr. Wolfe... half of these cases aren't in our jurisdiction. Three occurred in other townships, two were suicides, and one was an accident. Kids go missing all the time. They run away. They do drugs and mess up their lives. Quade Pickler is highly respected, he's been with us for thirty-five years, and I had to bow to his judgment on those autopsies."

The news chopper swooped down low overhead.

"They're going to rip my life apart again, aren't they?" Kate said.

Dunmeyer looked at her sympathetically. "I'm afraid so. No way to avoid it."

"Do you think my father's dead?"

"I can't say either way until Forensics gets here, but for my money, there isn't enough blood in the house to infer that someone died there. But I don't want to raise your hopes. Circumstantial evidence points to a homicidal attack, with your father as the likely victim, since it's Stigler's vehicle that's missing. We're going to run tests on the blood, fast-track the DNA. In the meantime, we're doing everything we can to find them."

"Will you catch him?"

Dunmeyer nodded. "They don't usually get very far nowadays. Now if you don't mind, I'd like one of our detectives to escort you back to the station for a more detailed statement. Also, we can help you with media contact or any other questions you may have."

"Thanks."

The barking dogs caught his attention. "Excuse me, I'll be right back," he said, tipping his hat and walking across the backyard.

All of a sudden Kate couldn't handle the thought of sitting in the police station. She quickly walked back to her car, started the engine and pulled out cautiously between two police cruisers. Her phone buzzed with a text message. It was from Palmer. *I'll be starting the treatment tomorrow, Kate. Wish me luck.*

She'd never felt so alone.

55

KATE TOOK THE PREDICTABLE cross-hatching of streets toward her father's house, hardly aware of what she was doing. She spotted an old-fashioned clothesline in a front yard; it made her think about the rope Nikki had used to hang herself with. How had Nikki learned to tie a slipknot?

Her heart was banging in her chest by the time she pulled into her father's driveway. She let herself in and stood in the front hallway for a moment, chilled by the silence. She felt so ripped apart inside, she wanted to scream. Was her father really dead?

She went upstairs to her parents' bedroom and tore the place apart, searching for any links to the past. She dragged the storage boxes out of her mother's closet and upended them on the floor. She felt like an archeologist digging through the wreckage of her family history, searching for evidence—still not sure what she was looking for.

She found another batch of her mother's letters, all of them addressed to Bram, and read them quickly. Julia swung between grandiosity and depression, happiness and misery. "You can barely rub two words together in my presence. And yet, when you finally talk to me, you always say the wrong thing. A word of advice: stop crowding me, Bram. People need space to fall in love, and they need space to remain in love."

There were wild accusations and crazy denunciations. Julia wanted her freedom and she wanted her family. She wanted to fling her life away, and she wanted Bram to forgive her. She wanted an abortion and she wanted more children. Kate overturned the sequined jewelry box, searching for the silver necklace with its crescent-shaped pendant, but only found her mother's Zippo lighter—compact with a retro paisley pattern. Julia used to claim that her mentholated cigarettes helped to ease her headaches. Maybe Kate should give it a shot. She put the Zippo in her bag and dug through her mother's old steamer trunk, sorting through piles of linens, tennis rackets, and knick-knacks.

She found Julia's high school yearbook and thumbed through the pages. Julia Knight was one of those girls you just knew was going places. She was gorgeous, athletic, and whip-smart. She was a member of the Honor Society, Girls' Leadership, the chorus, the photo club, the pep squad, and captain of the swim team. She'd been voted Most Popular, and her yearbook quote was from *Love Story*: "Love means never having to say you're sorry."

Instead of bedtime stories, Julia used to regale her young daughters with tales of her wild, irresponsible youth. She drank and drove. She got stoned and played musical chairs. She jumped off the highest cliff into Moody Lake and had her pick of boys. It had taken Kate years to process how inappropriate her mother's behavior was, to be sharing these stories with her impressionable children, but you couldn't stay mad at Julia for very long. There was a tragic depth to her that made you want to protect her.

At the bottom of the trunk, Kate found a battered shoebox stuffed with snapshots spanning decades of Julia's life: birthday parties, high school graduation, college years, her wedding day. Bram and Julia on their honeymoon. The early years of their marriage. Dinner parties. Sunbathing in the backyard. Her first pregnancy. Her second pregnancy.

There were quite a few pictures of drunken cocktail parties from the late eighties and early nineties. The women wore bold-colored dresses with shoulder pads and big hair. The men sported rock-star haircuts and *Miami Vice* tans. Her mother looked radiant in slinky dresses and stiletto heels, the belle of the ball. Men flocked around her, while Bram was always lurking somewhere on the sideline. He didn't dance, but Julia couldn't stop dancing. She seemed much too excitable to be married to a man like Kate's dad.

Kate recognized some of the men in the pictures: a younger Quade Pickler sporting a mullet; handsome Cody Dunmeyer; Mr. Mason, father of Emera, the girl who had gone missing on the way to a concert. Wait. Her heart began to race. She scrabbled through the pictures. There was Tabitha Davidowitz's father dancing with Julia. Julia's head was thrown back, exposing her pale throat—you could almost hear her laughing.

Kate couldn't believe it. She began searching frantically

through the box of photographs, looking for more of the victims' fathers, but most faces she couldn't make out. The snapshots were overexposed or underexposed, or the picture-taker had been too drunk to hold the camera steady and the image was blurry.

In one picture, Bram and Julia were arguing in a dark corner of a dance club, surrounded by distracted friends. Julia's lipstick was smeared, and her eyes were blurred with tears. Bram's fists were balled tightly in anger. Whoever had killed Julia was left-handed. Kate's father was left-handed.

Kate's heart ached dully as she scooped up the last picture from the bottom of the box, taken at the asylum. Julia's face was pale and drawn. She'd lost a lot of weight. Yet there was an ethereal beauty about her, a tender grace untouched by the situation. "The monster's wife" was scrawled across the photograph in Julia's handwriting.

Kate tried to shake off her suspicions. Yes, her father could be socially awkward, jealous, and possessive. But so were a lot of people. He was an admitted obsessive-compulsive. He sometimes disappeared for hours at a time. He was uncommunicative and narcissistic, but he'd never hurt Julia, no matter what she did to him. Not in a million years. He was no monster.

He's lonely. He's isolated. He doesn't have a clue how to bond with other human beings.

She went downstairs, where she opened all the curtains and let the afternoon sunshine into the stuffy house. She stood in the middle of the living room trying to locate the exact spot on the floor where her mother had carved those forbidden words into the varnished wood. She inched the heavy armchair to one side, moved the coffee table over about a foot, peeled back the braided rug, and there it was. "Fucking cunt." So raw and ugly. It chilled her to the bone. A rolling wave of fear crested and broke. Psychopaths were very good liars. They were highly intelligent and deceptive. They could fool the people closest to them. They were known to fool their own psychiatrists— Kenneth Bianchi, the Hillside Strangler, Ted Bundy.

Kate had to know. She walked into her father's study and started rifling through the old steel file cabinets. She became aware of her crazy heartbeat as she tore through his archived patient files, looking for Makayla Brayden, Tabitha Davidowitz, Susie Gafford, Lizbeth Howell, Vicky Koffman, Hannah Lloyd, Emera Mason, Maggie Witt.

Nothing. Maybe he'd hidden them away?

Terrible, unwanted thoughts crowded into her feverish brain. What if the police were wrong? What if *Stigler* was dead? What if her father had attacked him with a knife, then dragged the body outside and driven away in Stigler's SUV? What if he'd staged the entire scene to throw the police off his trail and staged his own death? Perhaps he'd staged Savannah's death to frame Blackwood, staged Susie Gafford's accident and her mother's suicide?

All the signs were there. Bram organized his days with precision. He was a person of habit. He was methodical, detail-oriented, deliberate, cautious—you could set your watch by him. He was always disappearing; he was secretive and brooding. He was a physician, and therefore spent a lot of time around children and their families. He could've used his position in the community to lure his victims. He was well-respected, having held the same job for decades.

Kate chipped away at layers of denial with a delicate stubbornness. What if her father had followed Julia down to the river that night? What if he'd begged her to come home with him, but she refused? What if he'd lashed out in a rage, striking her with a tire iron and then staged her death to look like a suicide? What if this event had triggered something deeply sick inside him, something that had been festering for years but which he'd managed to suppress? What if it gave him free rein to finally be himself? To kill?

Did he know about Savannah?

She knelt down in front of the bookcase and traced her fingers over the spines of her father's paperbacks and hardcovers, searching for *Grandiose Times at Godwin Valley* by Dr. Jonas Holley. And there it was. Bottom shelf.

She slid out the dusty book, and it fell open at "Patient J." Somebody had flagged passages in orange highlighter. *"As we delved deeper into her background and it was revealed how her father's abuse had shaped her life, Patient J finally trusted me enough to reveal that one of her children was the product of an affair."*

So he knew.

But was he capable of such brutality? Such ugliness? Such inhumanity? Was he truly a monster?

Stunned and bewildered, Kate sat behind Bram's desk and opened the wooden drawers, rifling through his bank statements, business licenses, insurance premiums, and tax returns. Proof, she needed proof. At the back of a drawer was a manila folder labeled FOUR OAKS, MAINE. The deed to her grandparents' farm was inside.

He'd need access to an isolated location where he can indulge his fantasies.

The barnyard used to smell of silage, and the milking parlor housed the restless cows, who mooed and stomped their hooves and raised their tails, releasing arcing streams of urine, which made Savannah giggle.

Kate went down to the basement to fetch the keys to her grandparents' farm. This was crazy. This was dumb. But nothing was going to stand in her way.

56

KATE FOUND A LOCAL news station on her car radio. "Multiple law enforcement agencies have joined the search for Professor William Stigler, who is wanted for questioning in the disappearance of Dr. Bram Wolfe, also from Blunt River. Police have put out a BOLO for the missing vehicle, a black BMW X5 SUV. It is unknown at this time what exactly happened inside the professor's house on Lakeview Drive, but our sources indicate foul play. Dr. Wolfe's daughter, Savannah, was murdered sixteen years ago—the man convicted of the crime was executed last week..."

Someone in a charcoal-gray Jeep Renegade was following her. It freaked her out a little, because the windshield was tinted and she couldn't make out the driver's face. He dogged her for a couple of miles before she lost him in heavy traffic outside Sanford. Maybe it was nothing. She told herself to calm down. Classic paranoia, believing someone was following you. Next she'd be hearing voices.

In the distance, she could see the mountains with their snow-powdered peaks. She turned up the radio.

"Authorities are scouring the nearby woods with cadaver

dogs and a Forensics team is using ground-penetrating radar in the backyard of the property to identify any abnormalities in the soil that might point to a clandestine gravesite…"

Kate shot forward in her seat. *Gravesite?*

"Police officers have been seen taking dozens of evidence boxes out of Professor Stigler's home… sources tell us… police have found photographs going back several decades… a pattern of missing and murdered girls in and around the area… we've just learned that some of these children and their families participated in research projects run by Professor Stigler…"

Kate's head spun. If they found human remains on Stigler's property, that would mean Palmer had been right all along. And if Stigler was a serial killer, then Kate's father was most likely dead.

But why would he bury victims in his own backyard?

What if Stigler had been set up to take the fall, just like Henry Blackwood? What if the real killer buried one or more bodies on Stigler's property to implicate him? Whose blood was really inside the lake house? What if Stigler was dead and her father was alive? What if he'd only made it look like the opposite was true? What if Bram had staged his own death?

By the time she'd reached the village of Four Oaks, Maine, an hour later, it was beginning to snow. The downtown area consisted of a post office, a grocery store, three churches, and a feed store. Her grandparents' farm was way out in the boonies, nestled in a landscape of ice forests and frozen lakes. She recognized the battered mailbox and pulled over.

Dead grape arbors lined the entranceway to Wolfe's Dairy. The old sign was falling down. She let the engine idle. It was obvious nobody had been out here in quite some time. She couldn't detect any tire tracks in the snow, just virginal drifts where a driveway should be. There was a back entrance, but you had to take a series of dirt roads to get there.

She tried calling Chief Dunmeyer via the police station, but he wasn't taking any phone calls. She left a message with the desk sergeant and hung up. There was very little traffic out this way. Snowflakes swirled down from the sky with gentle, sinuous movements. She got out of her car, zipped up her parka, and headed for the farm through the knee-deep drifts. By the time she'd reached the broken picket fence, she was drenched in sweat.

The farmhouse sat on twenty abandoned acres, surrounded by dilapidated outbuildings. The snowy yard was etched with deer prints, like her grandmother's pie crust poked with a fork. This used to be a working dairy. Now everything was buried under the merciless Maine winter.

A sudden flurry of snow hit her, and Kate ran for cover up the old porch steps. A rusty cowbell hung by a length of rope from the doorknob. She crossed the sagging porch boards and fished the keys out of her pocket. The cowbell jangled as the front door popped open.

An eerie chill surrounded her as she stood in the front hall, waiting for her eyes to adjust to the dim light. A bad odor filled her nostrils, and she spotted a dead squirrel in the hallway. She turned a corner into the living room, where the moth-eaten furniture, once upholstered in soft blues and ginghams, was covered with mold and dust. The kitchen smelled of decay. Various creatures had left their fetid aroma behind. She tested the faucets, but no water came out. She opened the cupboards and found her grandmother's pie plates and Mother Goose cookie cutters blooming with rust.

The dining room was separated from the rest of the house by an arthritic pocket door Kate could barely shove open. She stood clapping the dust off her hands and listening to it echo off the walls. She remembered dinners with Gran and Gramps, their stories about farting cows and charismatic men who could make it rain for a price. She went upstairs, recalling the thrill of staying up late at night with Savannah, playing word games in the dark and listening to the newborn calves mewling in the barn. Now every corner contained dead insects stuck in cobwebs. The floors were slanted and the doorways were crooked. She could hear the blustery wind outside. The weather was becoming increasingly rough.

There were no signs of foul play. No serial-killer souvenirs, clothing or jewelry lying around. No scalps. No chainsaws. Her father wasn't a serial killer. She'd been wrong. Palmer was right. Case closed.

She went downstairs and wandered through the back of the house—the mud room, rodent-infested pantry, her grandfather's study. She poked through the dusty books and papers on Gramps' desk and found an old class photo of her father and his schoolmates. Bram Wolfe had to have been the tallest ten-year-old in Four Oaks Elementary. He stood in the back row, hunching his shoulders like a fairytale goose trying to fit in with the ducklings. He'd grown up in a village full of rowdy farm boys who wanted to be hockey stars. No doubt they had wanted to knock him down a few pegs.

Kate felt an excruciating sadness. Her father had lived a life of self-imposed isolation. He was a difficult person to love—but that didn't make him a monster. He'd loved Julia with all his heart. He loved his daughters, too. His only sin was marrying a woman who couldn't be faithful.

Gray shafts of light filtered in through the dusty windows. She put the picture down and turned to leave. Then she saw it. A jar of Planters Roasted Peanuts perched on top of her grandfather's bookcase, covered in a light sheen of dust. Her heart began to race.

The cowbell jangled on the front door.

Kate spun around.

Someone was inside the house.

57

A SHADOW TREMBLED ON the wall, moving swiftly toward her. A tall figure, the shape of the head unnatural. A ski-mask?

Dad?

She tried to run, but he tackled her and they went tumbling to the carpet, kicking up huge plumes of dust. She screamed, but he clamped his hand over her mouth. She bit down hard on a leather glove, and he jerked away, allowing her to scramble free. Kate took off running for the front door. She bolted down the porch steps into the knee-deep snow. He was fast on her heels, and soon overtook her. Now they were facing each other, breathing hard, the snow obscuring her vision. He stood between her and the driveway. Between her and freedom.

Dad?

She reacted with pure animal terror, waves of fear galvanizing her. She took out the pepper spray, aimed it at his expressionless eyes, and pressed the nozzle, but nothing happened. She shook the canister and tried again. Nothing.

Oh my god, oh my god, oh my god.

She dropped the can in the snow and tried to run past him, but he barred her way, as if they were playing a game of cat and mouse. She took off in the opposite direction, heading for the barn. The barn had pitchforks, tools she could use as a weapon. She plowed through the snow and looked back over her shoulder. He was bounding after her.

The world became a blur.

Fear pounded into her.

She reached the barn door, grasped the rusty handle and jerked it open. She ducked inside, her eyes adjusting to the gloom. The weathered interior was like an enormous shipwreck, full of rotten beams held together by rusty nails. The wind was howling eerily through the rafters. She streaked past tractor parts and old tires stacked on top of milk crates, heading for the back. She found a rusty machete hanging on the wall, right where her grandfather had left it, and grabbed it. She spun around.

He was barreling toward her.

"Dad! Don't!" she screamed.

He tackled her around the middle and they landed on the rotten boards. She ate a mouthful of dust as she shrieked, "Dad, it's me! Kate!"

He knocked the machete out of her hand.

"Stop!"

The dry winter air crackled with static. His full weight was on her. Fear took over completely. She screamed until there was nothing left but raw rags of breath. With her last ounce of strength, she reached for the ski mask and yanked it off his head.

Palmer Dyson was staring down at her.

He wrapped a muscular arm around her neck, and Kate's world guttered out.

58

KATE CRACKED AN EYE open. Her body felt battered and sore all over, as if she'd been lying on top of a shattered mirror. Her vision was blurry. She had a pounding headache. How long had she been out? A minute? A day?

She struggled to sit forward, but her body refused to cooperate. It felt as if she weighed a ton. There was duct tape wrapped around her wrists, legs, and ankles. She was buckled into the back seat of a Jeep—the Jeep Renegade that had followed her, she realized—and Palmer Dyson was behind the wheel.

"Hello, Kate."

She stared at him in disbelief.

"How are you feeling?"

She struggled to free herself, but the tape dug into her flesh and brought tears to her eyes. "I thought you were in Mexico?" she gasped with stunned incomprehension.

"Relax. Everything's going to be okay."

Her adrenaline spiked as she tried to figure out what was happening. They were driving through the wilderness. Where were they? All she could see were woods. She panicked. "Where are you taking me? What's going on?"

"You're in shock. You need to calm down."

Everything outside of her window grew misty around the edges as the Renegade rumbled over cracked asphalt and sleet streaked against the glass. The road was free of traffic, but even if another vehicle had driven past, the Jeep's tinted windows provided protection from prying eyes. No hope against the automated door locks. She leaned forward, muscles trembling with effort, but a wave of nausea forced her back against the seat.

"Don't fight it," Palmer said. "It'll be easier if you don't fight it."

She stared at him. "Where are you taking me?"

"Somewhere safe."

"Safe from what? Why am I tied up? What the hell is going on?"

"I was thinking about the various ways I could handle this," he said in a confessional tone. "But then I thought… honesty is the best policy."

Oh my god, oh my god, oh my god.

The spindles clicked softly. The tumblers fell into place. All the doors swung open at once. She saw it with crystal clarity—Palmer Dyson's limitless deception.

She reared like a horse twisting in its bridle, screaming and thrashing as the duct tape bit into her flesh. He observed her coldly, analytically. Zero emotion. Not a flicker.

She stopped struggling and swallowed her outrage. "This isn't you," she insisted. "You're a good person, Palmer. Stop the car and let me go. I promise I won't tell a soul."

"Sorry, Kate."

Dumb. How dumb to have trusted him. She felt a pure shining hatred for this man, the same raw fury she'd seen in some of her chemically restrained patients—the impotent rage of the captive. "You're *sick*," she spat.

"You have no idea," he said.

Her mind went blank. She screamed and twisted in her seat, flailing and thrashing again, wearing herself out completely, until a brutal hopelessness threaded through her veins. She collapsed, panting with exhaustion, like an insect trapped in a web.

"Face it, Kate. You put yourself into this position. I told you not to be naïve."

A stillness closed around her. "Are you going to kill me?"

He smiled at her in the rearview mirror. "Why would I do that? I feel a bond between us."

"A *bond?*" she sneered.

"I know you feel it, too."

All she felt was a humming, deafening terror.

"I consider us close. Yes, I do. I hope to explain it all to you someday soon. We can play shrink and patient, how about that? You can psychoanalyze me, and I can tell you how and why I did it. And then you'll have your answers and I'll have mine."

Another rolling wave of fear crested and broke inside of her. She twisted and pulled on the duct tape, but it only made things worse.

"Calm down," he said, watching her.

She caught her breath and contemplated her next move. She would have to talk him out of whatever he was thinking. In a hostage situation, you were supposed to develop a rapport with your captor. Use their name a lot. Appeal to their ego. She would have to be smart if she wanted to survive.

If Kate couldn't use force, then she'd have to use stealth. She needed something sharp, something to cut through the duct tape binding her wrists. She looked around, but there was nothing in the back seat. She clasped her hands nervously together and noticed James's ring. She felt the setting with her fingertips.

"They won't find the bodies until the spring," Palmer said softly, and Kate glanced up. "A hiker or a hunter will stumble across the SUV on an old logging road. Stigler blew his brains out. He left a suicide note—I dictated it myself. Your father was his last victim. Stabbed twenty-two times. As a psychiatrist, I think you can appreciate the symbolism."

"What symbolism?"

"Think about it."

Twenty-two times. Her mother had died twenty-two years ago. She stared blindly ahead, trying not to lose it completely as she angled the ring into the duct tape and began to saw back and forth with tiny motions. She kept her hands in her lap, out of sight.

"Anyone who is the least bit curious might get it. But I doubt the local police will be that astute. Regardless, Stigler will go down in history as one of the greats. He'll be right up there with BTK and Ted Bundy."

"You sound envious," Kate said.

"Nah. I'd rather be a hero. You gave Dunmeyer the flashdrive, right?"

She nodded. She felt a glaze of sweat break out on her face.

"They'll be honoring me posthumously. It's all been arranged. I died undergoing an unproven treatment. A Mexican official will be sending my ashes stateside soon, along with the death certificate. You'd be amazed at the things people will do for a buck."

Her anger flared. "Do you even have cancer? Or was that a lie, too?"

"It's in remission. Going on ten years."

"So you aren't dying?"

Palmer shrugged. "Not today."

She took a sharp breath. The sleet was tapering off. The sun peeked out behind the clouds as the road began to climb. They were heading into the mountains, and the view was surreal. Remote as a postcard.

She had to stay focused. She sliced into the tape with tiny precise movements—the tear was half an inch deep now. She had to keep him distracted. "You said you wanted to explain it all to me someday. Tell me now, Palmer."

He stared at her. "You'll have to work harder than that, Kate."

"Come on. Psychiatrists are like priests. You want to confess. You're dying to tell me about it. I'm the only person in the world who knows what you've done, that you spent decades setting up this elaborate game, and for what? So you could disappear and pretend it never happened? Be a dead hero? Doesn't that bother you? It must feel like you just won at the Olympics, only you can't even brag about it."

Palmer shook his head. "Don't play me, Kate."

"I'm not playing you. You have your sick pride, and you're the hero of your own story. So tell me why you did it. Natural psychopath? What catastrophic event in your childhood triggered all this carnage?"

"That's not a worthy question."

"Suit yourself."

He shrugged. "Why did I do it? Because nobody stopped me."

"That's a lie. There's a deeper reason."

"Are you trying to shrink me? Because it isn't working."

"I want to know why you did it. I want to know why I'm going to die. Come on. Talk about your most fascinating subject—you."

He grinned. "Ya got me."

"How did it start?" She moved the ring back and forth—there was a one-inch-long cut in the tape now. Gradually, very gradually, she could feel it loosening. "I really want to know. What's the reason?"

"Does there have to be a reason?"

"There's always a reason."

He scowled. "You think you're pretty self-aware. But I know you so much better than you know yourself. You haven't done a very good job of self-discovery, Kate. You have a lot of work to do."

"What are you talking about?" she said.

"Oh come on. I led you here. To this time and place."

"You led me?"

"Like a mouse in a maze. It was so predictable."

She thought for a moment. "You mean Dr. Holley's book? Patient J?"

"I intended to get you to notice it at some point, but when you got lost and I invited you to stay at the cabin, it was too good an opportunity to pass up. I left it right where you'd find it. And the next morning, you handed me your phone to put in my emergency contact details, remember? Never give your phone to anyone. They're surprisingly easy to hack. I downloaded a couple of apps, and I've been tracking you ever since. Reading your texts, listening to your conversations. Tracking your GPS."

Kate sawed harder at the duct tape.

"Those peanuts in your office? I bribed one of the cleaning crew. I thought it was a pretty good joke. Your patients are nuts. I enjoy my little misdirections. Did you notice all the other things that've gone missing over the years? Reading glasses, undergarments…"

"Why?"

"Whim."

She stared at him with revulsion and imagined her father's body wrapped in a plastic shower curtain. She pictured Stigler slumped over the wheel, his skull like a burst water balloon.

"I enjoy watching you try to figure things out, Kate. You keep looking for answers when they're right in front of you." He grinned. "I left a trail of breadcrumbs. You nibbled them up."

A thick fog cushioned her brain. *Don't stop what you're doing. Stay focused.* "So you led me every step of the way? How did you know I was going to look at the flashdrive? How did you know I'd tell my father about Stigler killing my mother?"

He sighed with impatience. "Come on, Kate. I knew you wouldn't be able to resist the flashdrive, and when you inevitably checked it out, I knew there was a high probability you'd tell your father about it. I had other plans in place in case you didn't tell Bram about Stigler, but these things have a way of working themselves out."

A trickle of sweat curled down her forehead. "*You* left the peanuts at my grandparents' farmhouse?"

"A few weeks ago."

"Why? What was the fucking point?"

"When we talked about the killer's motivation, you said it was all about power and control, and that's true. But it's also fun to confuse people. It amuses me. I know everything there is to know about the people of Blunt River. I like to mess with their heads. I've been to your grandparents' farmhouse a handful of times. I was wondering when you'd venture out that way, but I had no idea you'd go there thinking your father was a serial killer." He laughed. "I liked it when you called me 'Dad.'"

She stared at him in disbelief.

"I wanted to tear you down, bit by bit," he said. "You once bragged that you could handle it—that you worked at McLean Hospital, remember? Trust me. You aren't prepared for this."

Her hands were covered in sweat. She momentarily lost her grip.

"I've known you longer than you realize."

"What are you talking about?" she breathed. "We only met properly a week ago."

"I've known you since you were a baby. I'd sneak into your parents' house late at night and watch you play in your crib. They kept the spare key under a flowerpot, imagine that? People are dumb. Sometimes I'd watch Julia sleep. She clung to her side of the mattress and got as far away from your father as possible. I stole little things—jewelry, books, letters. I killed her cat. She was already losing her grip. I like to think I helped."

Kate realized he was talking about the moon-shaped pendant. "So you stole my mother's necklace and strangled Susie Gafford with it?"

"Like I said, that was a rookie mistake."

She could feel her thoughts spinning out of control. *Stay focused.*

"I've been over every inch of that house. I know where your mother kept her birth control pills. I know where your father stashed his porn. I know where you kept your razor blades, Kate. I saw the wad of bubblegum under your sister's bed long before you did. I know more about your family than you do. I know everything there is to know about you."

Kate stared at him.

"This is what you're dealing with. This is who I am." He looked at her with dead eyes. "Cue the applause."

"Why?" she asked breathlessly.

"Why not?" he said defiantly.

Kate's eyes burned as she resumed her desperate task. The tear was two inches long, and the duct tape beginning to loosen around her sweaty wrists. *He had watched her sleep. He took her things.* "This is all about my mother, isn't that right? It's why you framed Henry Blackwood and William Stigler. Because they slept with her. That's why you killed my father."

Palmer shrugged. "You're the psychiatrist. You tell me."

"You hated that she slept with other men. You were obsessed with her."

"I loved her," he confessed. "And she betrayed me."

"How? Tell me what happened."

"We went to school together. I've known her since she was a skinny, ugly little thing. She was supposed to be mine. But she threw it all away."

"So you killed her?"

"No, no, no. You're missing the whole point. I didn't kill her. Stigler did. He was drunk, he was jealous, and she provoked him. She was very good at that. He followed her down to the river and killed her, and then he covered it up. It only took me twenty-two years to get even with the son of a bitch."

She stared at him. "So this was all about revenge?"

"Why does that confuse you?"

She scissored through the duct tape with frantic little motions. Almost there.

"Your mother had a rare kind of beauty, a special quality... but she threw it all away. She treated herself like dirt. Half the men in town were crazy about her. I was fourteen when she took pity on me. We slept together a couple times before she dumped me. She was fickle that way. She ended up marrying your father, God knows why. You'd think being a doctor was better than being a rock star. Anyway. He took what was mine. So I took what was his—his daughter, his peace of mind. People should pay for their actions."

She felt a sharp pang as she spotted a road sign—they were in Piscataquis County, heading north. Twisting through the mountains. The road was narrow and curving. It had stopped snowing, and she could see down into the valley, a vast expanse of old-growth forests and lakes.

"So you killed Savannah to get even with my father—and with Blackwood, once you realized he was her biological father, even if he clearly never did?"

"Yes."

"What about the other girls?" Kate asked. "How did you choose them?"

"I convinced Stigler's research associate to give me the names of the study subjects. It was easy. He was a drug addict, so I blackmailed him."

"Once you had the names, there must've been hundreds of girls to choose from, right?"

"In every instance, I had to wait for the opportunity to present itself."

"Meaning… you had to wait until it was safe to abduct them?"

"And the timing had to sync up with Stigler's out-of-town trips."

Kate nodded. "In order to bury the bodies on his property without anyone noticing? And that's where the police are going to find the four missing girls—in his backyard?"

"Asphyxiated. Heads shaved."

"Why would you shave some of the victims' heads, and not others?" she asked. "You told me Susie Gafford and the two suicides only had small pieces of hair cut off."

"I can control myself when necessary, so long as I get a little of what I need. It would have been pretty dumb to go to the trouble of staging suicides only to attract attention with matching buzz cuts."

"And you built this case over years… How did you know you could pull it off?"

"I've developed a knack for predicting behavior."

"In my profession, they call that grandiosity."

"It's a small town, Kate. Small minds. After years of observation you know how people will act. On the other hand, sometimes you can predict the behavior of a complete stranger. All you have to do is find out their daily habits—a few days' stakeout will often suffice. What time she leaves the house in the morning, how hastily she departs, how icy her porch steps are. Especially after you've hosed them down. Sorry about your mother-in-law. That was unfortunate."

Kate struggled to grasp what he was saying.

"James was becoming an annoyance," Palmer explained. "But easy to predict that he'd abandon you in favor of mommy dearest. On the other hand, I *didn't* predict you'd drive up to your grandfather's house today. I just ran with it.

And you thinking Bram might be the killer was a wildcard."

Kate sagged. She had a sudden heartbreaking vision of Nikki hanging in her parents' house. "Did you kill Nikki McCormack?"

"How else was I supposed to get your attention, Kate? You ignored all my letters. I had to orchestrate our meeting at the funeral somehow."

"And you've been following me around for years?" she said. "Why not just kill me?" Her voice was shrill, but Palmer didn't respond. Kate choked back a sob. "Did you kill Nelly, too?"

"No. But there's no mystery about who did: Derrick Ward's a brutal man."

"Who are *you* to speak of brutal men?"

"I wasn't always this way. I was an obedient child. But your mother changed me. I loved her, and she mocked me for it. There were hundreds of girls in Stigler's study—why did I choose only nine? Julia had a thing for Eddie Gafford. She flirted with Emera Mason's father. I could go on."

"So everything goes back to my mother?" Kate exclaimed. "It's her fault?"

Palmer shrugged. "None of us is innocent."

"She never did anything to you."

"She shamed me."

Kate tried to keep her voice even. "I don't believe she made you who you are. Something happened, something that made you turn a corner. So what was it, Palmer? What allowed the pre-existing psychopathy to bloom?"

Palmer raised an eyebrow. "You want a convenient story?

413

Fine. My father was a beat cop in Manchester. Same shift for years, noon to midnight. Everybody knew him, and they relied on him to keep the neighborhood safe. But at home he was a mean bastard, who beat up me and my mom. He left us when I was six, and after that, Mom fell apart. Looking back, there was always something beneath the surface, but Dad kept it in check with his fists. Once he was gone she became paranoid, she smoked and drank and watched TV for hours. She went for long walks and came back with grass clinging to her ankles. I suspected she went down to the train tracks, that she was thinking of throwing herself in front of the train.

"Gradually she became more unhinged." Palmer smiled crookedly at Kate in the rearview mirror. "You'd have recognized the signs. She became like Julia. The house was filthy. One day I found her kneeling on the kitchen floor, picking up grains of spilled oatmeal, sobbing. Another time she became convinced her face was lopsided. She spent hours staring at herself in the mirror. That's when she started buying dolls from Goodwill. She said their faces were perfect. Soon our house was full of them. At first they scared the daylights out of me—they never moved, they never spoke. But I grew to like them for that very reason.

"Every day after school, I'd come home and Mom would be playing with her dolls. She painted their faces and cut their hair. One day, she attacked me with a pair of scissors. She stabbed me sixteen times—luckily she didn't hit anything vital. Then she sat on my chest and cut off my hair, even my eyebrows. She claimed that I brought lice into the house, and

414

they were eating her brains out. After that they put her away, but the doctors never made her right. Treatment back then was brutal—hydrotherapy, lobotomy, meds that gave her the shakes. She died in an asylum." He shrugged. "That's the end of my story."

They were traveling in the foothills along the western slope of a mountain. Tight and winding curves. Sharp drop-offs on either side of the road.

"Once you enter the darkness," he said, "the darkness enters you."

A trickle of sweat curled down Kate's cheek.

"A dead person smells almost sweet," he went on, "like rotting fruit. Once you carry a dead person in your arms, she's always with you."

Kate's heart fluttered. She sawed at the tape. *Almost there. Keep going.*

"You're a psychiatrist. What do you think I suffer from? Persecutory delusions? Narcissistic personality disorder? Or just plain old ordinary psychopathy?"

She paused, breathing hard. "You want the truth?"

He shrugged. "Give it your best shot."

"I think you're sick and tired of playing games. You want to show the world who you really are and what you've accomplished. You want to brag a little."

His face twitched. "I've done all the bragging I care to."

She softened her tone. "You're damaged, and maybe you can't be cured. But you can change. You can stop any time you want."

"Kate." Palmer laughed. "That's so transparent."

"Talk to me. I'm not going anywhere."

He let the silence stretch.

"You know what you are. But I'm sensing you want to change that." She was lying—he would never change. She was stalling for time. Her fingers were busy. She could feel pins and needles in her hands as she worked the ring back and forth in a sawing motion. "You must be tired of playing games with people who don't realize what you've done. But in a world where everyone else is stupid, doesn't it get boring?"

"That's why you're here. I'm not done with you yet." He raised an eyebrow. "And isn't that the real question? What I'm going to do with you?"

She nodded slowly.

"So? Spit it out, Kate. Quit beating around the bush."

She swallowed hard. "What are you going to do to me?"

He smiled broadly. "I don't know yet. That's the beauty of it. But you belong to me now."

She had no emotions left to bargain with. She felt her resistance melting, like flesh melting off bone.

Then in one swift motion, she ripped the duct tape off her wrists, unbuckled her seatbelt, reached forward, and grabbed Palmer by the neck. She squeezed tight. His hands left the wheel and he slammed on the brakes. He lost control of the vehicle.

There was the smell of burning rubber as they slewed across the road and plunged down an embankment, dropping through the snowy woods, bumping over ditches and overgrown trails until they hit a stand of trees.

The collision was explosive. Glass shattered. Kate flew forward into the front seat as the airbags burst open like rotten watermelons. She felt her face colliding with plastic and trapped air, and then... nothing.

59

KATE HEARD A SOFT ticking sound and opened her eyes, only vaguely aware of where she was. She saw the world through a fuzzy lens. Fear burned through her. The Jeep had collided with a huge evergreen tree, now bent at an angle, the bark stripped off and the trunk split. The vehicle was upright but leaning at a steep angle. The front end was crumpled, and the windshield had shattered.

Steam. Smoke. She stirred in her seat, and pieces of glass shifted off her lap. Shattered glass fell out of her hair. A chilly breeze blew across her face. The driver's side door was flung open, and Palmer was gone. She looked outside into the whiteness and couldn't find him anywhere.

She tried to open her door, but of course it was locked. She started to pull herself into the front of the car to get out of the driver's door, but her legs and ankles were still bound together. The glove compartment had popped open, flinging its contents into the back seat. Kate rummaged through the debris—road maps, spare change, sunglasses, a greasy red bandana. She wrapped the bandana around her hand for protection, selected the biggest piece of glass she could find, and then used it to cut the duct tape off her legs and ankles. Moments later she was free.

Kate crawled across the front seat and propelled herself through the open driver's door. She dropped onto the ground and landed on unsteady legs in the knee-deep snow, where she struggled for balance and surveyed the scene. They had plunged thirty feet down the side of the mountain before slamming into the tree. Steam wafted from the mangled Jeep; the impact had ripped the metal apart like gossamer. One of the rear doors was torn off its hinges and the hubcaps were missing. Gasoline leaked from the undercarriage, and the smell filled the air. The trunk had sprung open, leaving a debris field in the snow—suitcases, jumper cables, an ice scraper, bags of road salt, a spare tire, a snow shovel.

Kate heard a low groan and turned. Palmer was lying face down in the snow about fifteen feet away. He wasn't moving. Clots of blood had frozen on his skin and in his hair. One of his arms was twisted behind him, perhaps broken. She tensed, ready to run. She would have to climb back up the mountainside at a fairly steep angle, unless she could find a switchback trail through the dense cedars and firs.

"Kate." Palmer raised his head, blood trickling down his face. "Help me." There was blood on his teeth.

She felt a surge of disgust. She picked up the heavy snow shovel and stood her ground, watching for any sudden movements.

"My arm… I think it's broken," he muttered.

Kate adjusted her grip on the shovel and wondered if she

could outrun him. Even with a broken arm he might be too fast. He'd caught her before. She glanced up the mountainside. Should she risk it?

He used his good arm to wipe the blood off his face, then drew a painful breath. "I was never going to hurt you."

She shook her head, nausea building. "Just… don't move."

"I was never going to hurt you, Kate. That wasn't part of the plan. We had something, didn't we? Didn't you feel it?"

"Fuck you. I have no idea what you're talking about," she hissed. Her temples throbbed. All she could hear was the pounding of her own heart. "You killed my family. And for what? For jealousy and revenge. You're a pathetic little man."

He had a dead stare, like a shark. She could read her immediate future in that cold, calculating gaze. "I swear to God, I was never going to hurt you."

She stared at him with revulsion. She didn't care. She had watched her entire world melt to zero before her eyes. "Do you really think you can manipulate me? Look at you." She took a step backward. "I'm leaving. I don't know if I'll make it, but the odds are looking better for me than for you right now."

"You can't just walk away. That isn't who you are."

She glanced up the mountainside and spotted a cairn, a pile of stones hikers used for marking trails. There were drainage channels trailing down the mountainside—maybe the trek back up wouldn't be as daunting as it had first appeared.

"Kate?"

She looked down at him.

"Don't kid yourself," he said. "You're never going to forget you left me here to freeze to death."

Syrupy waves of nausea rolled over Kate as she turned her back on him and headed for the tree line. It took all of her strength to stagger through the snow. She plowed forward, leg muscles cramping as she dug in with pounding strides.

She had only gone ten yards when she tripped over something half-buried in the snow. The shovel flew out of her hands. An old leather briefcase, thrown from the Jeep, was sticking out of the snow. Kate pulled it free.

The interior was like a salesman's display case, with blue velvet compartments lined with small glass vials, each one tucked into its own velvet pocket. Some of the vials had scattered across the snow. She picked them up. Inside each vial was a hair sample, twined at one end—blond, brunette, redhead, raven. Each vial was carefully labeled with a name and date. She sank to her knees and gathered them all in her lap—*Susie Gafford, Emera Mason, Vicky Koffman, Lizbeth Howell, Hannah Lloyd, Maggie Witt, Tabitha Davidowitz, Makayla Brayden.* There were other names she didn't recognize.

Kate searched the snow for Savannah's vial. Where was her sister? She tore through the briefcase—there were so many vials! She poked her fingers into velvet pockets, pulling out the remnants of other girls... until she found it. *Savannah Wolfe.*

She collapsed in the snow, limp as a ragdoll, dazed, staring at her sister's golden hair inside the glass vial. Her breath plumed before her.

"Kate?"

She looked up.

Palmer Dyson was towering over her.

She tried to scramble away, too late. She had no strength left. Her feet were blocks of ice. She sobbed as she groped for the shovel, an inch or two beyond her grasp.

"Do you really want to know what my plan is for you, Kate?"

60

PALMER GRABBED KATE BY the hair and lifted her up off the ground with both hands. *His arm* isn't *broken after all—it was just another game.*

She clawed at him blindly, and he punched her in the face. Her jaw cracked as her head jerked backwards, a squib of crimson jetting across the snow. The pain was so intense, she couldn't catch her breath.

He cupped her face and showed her the blood on his fingers. "Stop fighting me. I don't want to kill you." He slammed her up against a tree, and she felt herself lose consciousness for a second. He shook her until she revived, then pinned her against the tree one-armed. She practically choked on the warm blood pooling in her mouth.

He observed her carefully. "Sooner or later, we'll all be dead. It's so boring. Death is pedestrian."

She spat blood, seeing light trails, and kicked out at him, but it was hopeless.

"I've killed more people than you know." His tone was confiding. "Okay... so maybe I can't be cured. Maybe I can't change, Kate. Maybe it's time for *you* to change." He grabbed her by the throat and squeezed, applying expert pressure with his thumbs until her windpipe closed and she couldn't breathe. He drew so close, she could feel his heartbeat right next to hers—the banging muscle tissue, heart valves squeezing open and shut, lungs expanding and collapsing. She experienced a pure shining hatred as she struggled in his arms, but he only squeezed her tighter.

"You can't win. You know that."

He released her, and she collapsed to her knees. He grabbed her by the hair and dragged her toward the wreckage of the Jeep, smoke wafting up from the mangled mess. She twisted around, scratching and clawing at his hands, but Palmer seemed oblivious as he pulled her over to where a coil of rope lay in the snow and picked it up. Kate spotted a tire-pressure gauge a few feet away, a pencil-thin metal rod. She grabbed for it, but he hauled her upright and started looping the rope around her wrists. She screamed and tried to fight him off, struggling fiercely, but he was too strong. "It'll be much easier if you don't fight," he said angrily.

"No!" She punched him in the face, and James's ring sliced into his cheek.

He touched his cheek and felt the gash. Before he could grab her again she tackled him, and the two of them went rolling down the snowy incline. Kate scooped the tire gauge out of the snow and plunged the metal rod into Palmer's neck, but it only penetrated about half an inch, not deep enough to do much damage. It just made him angry. He yanked it out and flung it away, then pinned her to the ground.

"Don't move," he said, softly. "I'm going to see you through this, kid. That's a promise."

"See me through what?" she asked in the smallest of voices.

"Every. Last. Thing."

She felt a kind of transcendent numbness. "What are you going to do to me?"

"You'll see. It won't make any sense to you now. But the bigger picture will become clear later on."

"What bigger picture?"

"You're going to be all right," he promised, wiping the blood off his face. "I'm going to take you someplace safe."

She struggled to keep breathing through her terror. "And do what?"

"Shh." He smoothed the hair off her face. "Don't worry. You'll be well fed and taken care of. You're my Julia now."

A welcome rush of adrenaline flooded her veins. She screamed, her voice echoing off the mountainside. Maybe somebody out there would hear her?

He clamped a hand over her mouth. "I want to tell you about your sister," he told her. "She taught me about humility. That night, she cried at first, but then she looked at me clear-eyed. She gave in, understood there was a greater will at work, that I couldn't be defeated. It gave me pause, because I knew what I was going to do, you see. But it was all planned. There was no stopping it. She gave me the gift of acceptance. And that's the only thing I want from you, Kate. Acceptance."

She heard a thumping sound and realized it was her wildly beating heart. She thought of Savannah in this man's hands.

He picked up the rope again, but before he could bind her hands together, she reached up and screwed her thumbs into his dead eyes. He cried out in pain and stumbled backwards, fighting the pitch of the slope. Kate leapt up and looked around for a weapon. Anything. She picked up a broken branch and flung it at him. It landed a heavy blow to his chest, and he groaned. He glared at her.

She picked up another branch and charged forward, swinging it hard at his face, the impact reverberating through her arms and chest. She could hear the bones of his nose crack as he dropped to his knees, dazed, eyes going in and out of focus. There was blood pouring out of a deep gash in his forehead. Now she had a shot.

Kate ran for the shovel a few yards away, a mad fury driving her. She grabbed it and went storming back to him, found her footing in the snow and braced herself. A monstrous energy came over her as she swung the shovel high overhead and brought it down hard on top of Palmer's skull.

She heard a hollow sound as the impact knocked him forward, flat on his face in the snow. She watched with a total lack of emotion as he took a ragged breath and tried to crawl away on his hands and knees, pathetically inching his way down the incline toward the wreckage of the Jeep. Drops of blood splattering the snow. He stumbled to his feet and started veering right, as if he had no idea where he was. She'd injured him. Something wasn't working in his brain.

She followed cautiously as he tried to regain to his bearings, stumbling and falling, then crawling the rest of the way toward the Jeep. He touched a dented door panel with bloody fingers. He looked around a confused instant, and then locked eyes with her.

She stood motionless, gripping the shovel. A horrifying feeling punched her in the gut as he got to his knees, reached out, and sputtered, "Kate." Then he reeled backward and dropped like a dead weight, landing flat on his back, arms outstretched, gasoline dripping and pooling over his body.

A dull ache spread outward from her chest as she waited for him to wake up. He didn't stir for the longest time.

"You're lying," she hissed. "You aren't dead."

She inched a little closer, ready to swing the shovel again. She felt a sick desire for his complete destruction.

Still, he didn't move. Blood ran from his wounds, branching inkily into whiteness. She didn't trust it. He'd lied to her before. He was probably lying now.

Very carefully, Kate crouched down next to the body. Was that him breathing? Had his eyelids flickered?

She waited. Gripping the shovel. Blinking the sweat out of her eyes.

What if he woke up and grabbed her? What if he made her his Julia? A Julia he could control?

She moved back, safely out of range.

He didn't make a sound.

She glanced over her shoulder at the mountainside. A formation of wild geese winged by overhead. It was freezing cold. She would have to aim for the cairn and climb up the mountainside to safety. She spotted a bottled water in the snow, scooped it up and drank thirstily. Now was her chance. She looked around for her bag. There, over by the jumper cables. She rummaged around for her phone and tried calling 911 but she couldn't get a signal. She noticed scarlet ribbons running down the front of her parka. She was covered in blood. She didn't care. She found a first-aid kit and a couple of protein bars and shoved them in her bag. She picked up a flashlight, tested it, and tucked it in her pocket. She found her mother's Zippo lighter at the bottom of her bag, lit it, and studied the flickering flame.

The first thing she would do when she got back home— she'd ask James to marry her. Then she'd help Maddie Ward become a normal teenage girl. She would make peace with herself.

A low groan.

Kate turned around. *Oh God.*

Palmer was stirring.

She pocketed the lighter and raised the shovel again.

He propped himself up and stared at her wild-eyed. He tried standing up.

"No," she said loudly.

He stumbled to his knees. "Don't!" she screamed. But he ignored her, and stood up to his full height.

"People pay for their actions," he said.

The air reeked of gasoline—his jacket was soaked in it. Fear galvanized her. She took out the old Zippo and held it up threateningly. "Stay where you are! Don't come any closer."

He ignored her and took a step forward, while she took

a staggering step back. With complete clarity she realized he wasn't going to stop. And she'd run far enough. She lit the Zippo and threw it at him.

There was a loud whoosh, and his jacket went up in flames. A sulfurous smell filled her nostrils as she turned and ran, scrambling up the slope and crouching behind a boulder. It was a moment before she could bring herself to look back, to watch him thrashing around blindly, fueling the fire with more oxygen and collapsing next to the Jeep. He flung out his arms, his left hand hitting the leaking fuel tank, and there was a brief lull before the Jeep exploded—a sound so loud, it volleyed off the mountain in a thunderous roar as a fireball rose. Kate hugged the boulder as the shockwave rolled through her body, muscle and bone. Clods of dirt fell around her, and she shielded her head with her hands.

She waited what seemed like an eternity before she took a peek. The Jeep Renegade had flipped on its side and some of the nearby trees were on fire. Thick plumes of smoke rose from the wreckage in a steady roar. She spotted something black on the ground, flames lapping at the burnt and twisted limbs. He was dead. It was over.

She sank down into a snowdrift out of sheer exhaustion. She wondered how long it would take to freeze to death. The temptation to close her eyes was great. *It would be so nice to fall asleep...*

A strong wind stirred through the treetops, carrying the smoke in the opposite direction. She worried he might come crawling out of the ashes toward her. She felt her emotions unraveling. She inhaled the crisp bitter air and drew her coat collar tighter as a flock of birds passed by overhead, rushing toward the sky.

At first, she thought she was imagining the figure in the smoke. Then she realized she was looking at a girl, a girl wearing a summer dress the color of skim milk—the palest of curdled blues.

"Savannah?"

The girl walked out of the whiteness and stood before Kate. Her green eyes sparkled, and her hair fell around her shoulders in an exaggerated halo.

Kate's head was spinning. Her skull throbbed. Grief and guilt threaded through her heart. It was time to say goodbye.

Knock knock.

Who's there?

Savannah.

Savannah who?

See? You've forgotten me already.

Kate smiled. The air smelled chaotic, of balsam and dead flowers. "I'll never forget you, little sister." She looked around. Savannah was gone.

She wiped her tears away and made for the cairn on the side of the mountain, climbing the rugged trail past ancient evergreens, conifers, and Douglas firs. She would climb out of these woods.

EPILOGUE

Six months later

KATE PLUGGED IN HER cam and clipped an ascender to the line, heat steaming off her skin as she groped her way up the rock face. The last leg of the journey was always the hardest. She reached into her chalk bag, clapped some loose powder on her palms, and gripped the rock before adjusting her position. Her arms shook with strain as her toes sought refuge in the smallest indents, and her fingertips pressed into cracks the width of a dime.

She reached the top of the six-hundred-foot cliff and pulled herself up over the edge, breathing hard with exertion. She stood on the precipice and turned toward the morning sun, catching the light on her face and shoulders. August in Seattle. To the west was Puget Sound. To the east were the Cascade Mountains, snow-capped peaks jutting above the tree line. Down below, spread across the foothills for hundreds of miles in all directions, were the wilderness trails. A long morning hike had brought them to this crustal block after a steep drive along a wooded road. She took her bottled water out of her backpack and drank greedily, then wiped her mouth with her hand. There was a sultry, leathery smell to her sweat. It had been a tough climb, but well worth the effort.

Six months ago, Kate had crawled out of the Maine woods in the dead of winter with nothing worse than a mild case of dehydration and a couple of bruised ribs. Only her psyche had been battered and broken.

Palmer Dyson had left two deep purple thumbprints on her windpipe. She'd watched them gradually fade away, going from cobalt to green to yellow in a matter of days, until there was nothing left. Healing took time—she reminded herself of that every day.

The depth of her fear had woven itself into her nightmares, which smelled of wet adrenaline, of the burning urge to flee and hot dry breaths. Nightmares could be cured through therapy, but the payload of fear lingered. You couldn't turn it on and off like a light switch. You couldn't medicate it away. You had to coax it out into the open, then try to reason with it and convince it not to take up so much space in your life. Recovery was slow. But her life was gradually taking back its natural rhythm.

Kate was back in therapy, and Ira was helping her deal with her losses. She missed her father terribly. She felt guilty for ever suspecting him. He'd tried his best. At first a question nagged at Kate: Julia could've had any man she wanted, but she'd chosen Bram Wolfe. Why? Julia was beautiful and vivacious. Men flocked to her. But the more she thought about her father, and about her mother's final days, Kate grew to realize that what Julia had loved about Bram was his essential decency. He'd managed to keep her grounded for a while.

Palmer Dyson had left a trail of death behind him. There were thirty-eight hair samples in the briefcase, and he was linked to disappearances as far away as Oregon. The Blunt River PD was cooperating with jurisdictions from at least six states. There was speculation Palmer went on holiday murder sprees, killing all over the country to get his fix. Cold cases were being reopened, and the media dubbed him the Shaved Head Killer. For Kate, it revealed Palmer's lies, the way he had tried to blame her mother for his twisted nature. He had murdered many girls without even the slightest connection to Julia Wolfe or his desire for revenge against William Stigler. He had just loved to kill.

She struggled with the fact that she'd killed another human being. It was as if Palmer had crawled into her head and taken up residence. No charges had been brought against her; the police, the DA's office, the media, and the public had all concluded that it was a case of self-defense. Some hailed her as a hero, but Kate couldn't help thinking—once you entered the darkness, the darkness entered you.

Derrick Ward had been charged with Nelly's murder. He claimed that one of their frequent arguments about his wife's treatment of Maddie had gotten out of hand, when he had returned home to discover that Nelly had left her daughter in Boston. He admitted that he had been drinking heavily, and that it wasn't the first time he had laid hands on Nelly. Maddie

Ward would never be going home, but her foster placement was working well, and she remained under Ira's care. While she was no longer Kate's patient, she needed friends, and Kate was happy to fill those shoes.

James clambered over the edge of the cliff and joined her. "Phew. Where were all the fucking handholds? Talk about a hairy climb."

"Nah," she bragged. "Piece of cake."

"Yeah right, Lara Croft." He brushed the dirt off his hands and grinned at her. "I definitely need some new material, huh?"

She smiled at him. "You think?"

"I'm still hilarious, though, aren't I?"

"My boyfriend is badass."

"I'm badassical." He grinned. He locked his arms around her waist and wove his fingers together at her tailbone. They were standing on a large sandstone overhang that dropped off precipitously over a breathtaking view. The air was thick with the heady scent of western pine.

"It's pretty, huh?" she said.

"Beautiful." He'd been doing a lot of crunches and dead lifts at the gym, burying his anxiety in physical activity. Athletic, tanned, handsome, as cocky as ever, James suffered in secret, she knew. He pretended to be strong for her.

There was a picture she kept in her desk drawer at work, something from Dr. Holley's archives: an old Polaroid of Palmer Dyson's mother taken fifty years ago at an asylum in Manchester. She looked like a cornered rat. She'd been admitted in the midst of a nervous breakdown, having just attacked her son with a pair of scissors. Luckily, none of his vital organs or major arteries had been hit. Otherwise, Palmer Dyson wouldn't have survived to become one of the most notorious serial killers in modern history. Every day when Kate looked at that photograph, she couldn't help wondering—how the hell did you miss his heart, you stupid woman?

She wanted to throw the Polaroid away, because it made her feel sorry for him—just a little. It kept her from hating him as completely as she wanted to. It spoke to her of inherited traits, monstrous parenting, nature versus nurture. As a child psychiatrist, she couldn't help but feel a little empathy for the victim. Mrs. Dyson's face revealed that the leap from sanity to insanity was separated by the thinnest of membranes.

Anyway. It was time.

Kate unzipped her backpack and took out the gifts Nikki McCormack had given her six months ago—a barnacled pair of 1950s eyeglasses, a tortoiseshell comb, a corroded compass, and last but not least, a skirt weight from the twenties.

She said a few words, then tossed them over the side, and they both watched as Nikki's gifts disappeared into a landscape of eroded sandstone and basalt, a bleeding watercolor of burnt siennas, terracottas, and yellow ochers. They landed without a sound.

James was watching her closely, looking for signs of trouble. "You okay?"

Kate panicked for a moment. What could she say? No? I'll never be okay again?

She blurted out, "Will you marry me?"

He didn't respond immediately. Instead, she waited for several awkward seconds before he emitted a surprised hoot of laughter. "Whoa. Did you just ask me to marry you?"

Her eyes filled with tears. "I thought it was time."

"You amaze me," he said.

She smiled so hard, her cheeks hurt.

"I'll marry you on one condition: I want my ring back. Then I'm going to ask you properly, like a *prop-pah* British gentleman, and slip that ring on your finger, and see if it stays put. I want to see what happens when it's an actual engagement ring."

"That is so manipulative of you," she said with a laugh.

"I can't help it. I have a scientific curiosity about your finger."

"Really? Guess which finger I'm holding up now?"

He smoothed his hand down her cheek and cupped it lovingly. "My girlfriend is gorgeous."

That night in bed, he held onto her and refused to let go.

The world felt fragile, full of lacy edges you could drop off of. She wanted closure. To put an end to these agonizing road trips down memory freaking lane. She had managed to slay the monster, but he'd transformed her into a killer. She was changed forever.

3:00 AM. Kate lay in bed and gazed out the hotel window at downtown Seattle. Tomorrow was the last day of their vacation. They'd be heading back to Boston to resume their lives. Only now there would be a wedding to plan. Funny how the world kept spinning.

She lay awake, waiting for dawn. Her breathing and James's sounded perfectly synchronous. He'd fallen asleep on his stomach, with his left arm tucked under his pillow so that, in the morning, he'd complain about the tingling sensation in his fingers. Like always. People were nothing if not predictable.

She closed her eyes and saw it again. The twisted burnt body. She could soak her eyes in bleach and it would never go away.

She woke up with a gasp. She hadn't even been aware of dropping off.

James caught her. He always caught her. "Hey, sweetie. You okay?"

"Scary dream." She rolled closer to him.

He gathered her to him with tenderness, and they gazed at the city lights. Once in a while, the earth tipped over, and the truth got really ugly. But it could also set you free. The world revealed its colors. And it was shining brightly on the other side.

ACKNOWLEDGEMENTS

SPECIAL THANKS TO:

Titan Books for this bright, new beginning.

My extraordinary agent, Jill Marr, for her exhilarating honesty, wisdom and passion. Thanks, Jill, for getting the best out of me.

My editor at Titan, Miranda Jewess, for her keen eye and meticulous insights.

My Rights Manager, Andrea Cavallaro, for her mad skills.

The exceptional Sandra Dijkstra, and the great team at Sandra Dijkstra Literary Agency, including book-whisperer Derek McFadden.

The essential team at Titan Books, including Sam Matthews, Katharine Carroll, Lydia Gittins, and Joanna Harwood.

Doris Jackson, for helping me untangle my past.

Christopher Leland and Peter LaSalle for inspiring me at a critical time in my life.

My father, who taught me how to see the world. I miss you, Dad.

My family for surviving and thriving.

My brother, Carter. Thank you, Super-8 collaborator, you nudged me over the finish line.

My gifted husband, Doug. High hopes on my windowsill. I met you and I lost my will.

ABOUT THE AUTHOR

ALICE BLANCHARD won the Katherine Anne Porter Prize for Fiction for her book of stories, *The Stuntman's Daughter*. Her first novel, *Darkness Peering*, was named one of the *New York Times Book Review*'s Notable Books. Her second novel, *The Breathtaker*, was an official selection of the NBC *Today* Book Club. Alice has received a PEN Syndicated Fiction Award, a New Letters Literary Award, and a Centrum Artists in Residence Fellowship.

A BABY'S BONES
REBECCA ALEXANDER

Archaeologist Sage Westfield has been called in to excavate a sixteenth-century well, and expects to find little more than soil and the odd piece of pottery. But the disturbing discovery of the bones of a woman and newborn baby make it clear that she has stumbled onto an historical crime scene, one that is interwoven with an unsettling local legend of witchcraft and unrequited love. Yet there is more to the case than a four-hundred-year-old mystery. The owners of a nearby cottage are convinced that it is haunted, and the local vicar is being plagued with abusive phone calls. Then a tragic death makes it all too clear that a modern murderer is at work…

PRAISE FOR THE AUTHOR

"Finely observed, beautifully written"
Daily Mail

"Marks Alexander as an author to watch"
The Independent on Sunday

"A wonderfully and uniquely inspired novel"
Historical Novel Society

THE BLOOD STRAND
CHRIS OULD

Having left the Faroes as a child, Jan Reyna is now a British police detective, and the islands are foreign to him. But he is drawn back when his estranged father is found unconscious with a shotgun by his side and someone else's blood at the scene. Then a man's body is washed up on an isolated beach. Is Reyna's father responsible?

Looking for answers, Reyna falls in with local detective Hjalti Hentze. But as the stakes get higher and Reyna learns more about his family and the truth behind his mother's flight from the Faroes, he must decide whether to stay, or to forsake the strange, windswept islands for good.

"A winner. For fans of Henning Mankell"
Booklist

"A tense crime thriller woven around
a captivating family mystery"
Paul Finch, bestselling author of *Stalkers*

TITANBOOKS.COM

TWO LOST BOYS
L.F. ROBERTSON

Janet Moodie has spent years as a death row appeals attorney. Overworked and recently widowed, she's had her fill of hopeless cases, and is determined that this will be her last. Her client is Marion 'Andy' Hardy, convicted along with his brother Emory of the rape and murder of two women. But Emory received a life sentence while Andy got the death penalty, labeled the ringleader despite his low IQ and Emory's dominant personality.

Convinced that Andy's previous lawyers missed mitigating evidence that would have kept him off death row, Janet investigates Andy's past. She discovers a sordid and damaged upbringing, a series of errors on the part of his previous counsel, and most worrying of all, the possibility that there is far more to the murders than was first thought. Andy may be guilty, but does he deserve to die?

"This is a must-read"
Kate Moretti, *New York Times* bestseller

"Suspense at its finest"
Gayle Lynds, *New York Times* bestseller

"Grips from the first page"
Andrew Cartmel, author of *The Vinyl Detective*

TITANBOOKS.COM

AFTER THE ECLIPSE
FRAN DORRICOTT

Two solar eclipses. Two missing girls. Sixteen years ago a little girl was abducted during the darkness of a solar eclipse while her older sister Cassie was supposed to be watching her. She was never seen again. When a local girl goes missing just before the next big eclipse, Cassie – who has returned to her home town to care for her ailing grandmother – suspects the disappearance is connected to her sister: that whoever took Olive is still out there. But she needs to find a way to prove it, and time is running out.

COMING MARCH 2019

For more fantastic fiction, author events, exclusive
excerpts, competitions, limited editions and more

VISIT OUR WEBSITE
titanbooks.com

LIKE US ON FACEBOOK
facebook.com/titanbooks

FOLLOW US ON TWITTER
@TitanBooks

EMAIL US
readerfeedback@titanemail.com